From *In a Wild Wood*

Brogan looked at Matalia, his innards twisted with anxiety. When she had been inside the cottage boundaries she had been completely inacessible to him. That sense of helplessness enraged him . . .

Brogan shuddered. He pulled his sword from its scabbard and swung it in the air, fighting the demons in his mind. He parried and thrust, practicing war maneuvers, releasing his fear in the only way he knew. Again and again, until he was dripping with sweat, and then he turned on branches and bushes around him, mowing them to the ground with a vengeance.

Matalia breathed quickly, thrilling at the sight of his thoroughly male form bulging with power and strength as he swung his sword, releasing his frustration and anger. The stance of his body was phenomenal, awe-inspiring, and incredibly sensual. Matalia felt weak, her body trembling with desire. She did not want to live at the cottage. Despite her misgivings, her fears, and her anxieties, she knew that she wanted to be with Brogan. An emotion blossomed deep inside of her. She wanted him. She wanted his strength and his passion, for her own wild spirit ached with unfulfilled needs.

Also in the *Wild* Series
by Sasha Lord

Under a Wild Sky

IN A
WILD WOOD

SASHA LORD

A SIGNET BOOK

SIGNET
Published by New American Library, a division of
Penguin Group (USA) Inc., 375 Hudson Street,
New York, New York 10014, U.S.A.
Penguin Books Ltd, 80 Strand,
London WC2R 0RL, England
Penguin Books Australia Ltd, 250 Camberwell Road,
Camberwell, Victoria 3124, Australia
Penguin Books Canada Ltd, 10 Alcorn Avenue,
Toronto, Ontario, Canada M4V 3B2
Penguin Books (NZ), cnr Airborne and Rosedale Roads,
Albany, Auckland 1310, New Zealand

Penguin Books Ltd, Registered Offices:
80 Strand, London WC2R 0RL, England

First published by Signet, an imprint of New American Library,
a division of Penguin Group (USA) Inc.

First Printing, August 2004
10 9 8 7 6 5 4 3

I would like to dedicate this book to my boys. Family is always the most important thing in life, yet we often put work and chores ahead of the very people who make living worthwhile. I love you, J-Team. I promise that you two will always come first.

Acknowledgments

Just as a family is important at home, a smooth, effective, and caring team is important at work. Crystal, you make everything possible. Jennifer McCord, Bob Mecoy, and Ellen Edwards, you are the best!

Prologue

The squall of infants reverberated in the massive chamber, but the cacophony was far preferable to the screams of moments before. Hours had stretched into days as the Countess labored in agony, screaming, panting, sweating, crying. Inside the chamber a wizened midwife spoke soothingly to the young woman as she dabbed the droplets of blood staining her thighs.

"Easy now, you've done it. They are a fine pair of boys, as fine a pair as any has a right to be. The Earl will be right proud, he will, but you've got to rest now." The old woman finished her ministrations just as the chamber door flew open. In strode a massive man, his brows drawn into slashing marks. The midwife quickly pulled a sheet over the Countess and stepped respectfully away from the bedside. The Earl approached the bed and stared down at the pale woman dispassionately.

"Did she give me a son?" he asked of no one in particular. The Countess fluttered her eyes open and smiled tremulously. No answering expression encouraged her, and the brief illumination fluttered away.

The midwife shuffled forward. "Oh yes, my lord! Not one, but two, did she give you!" The old woman nodded and clapped her hands. She motioned behind her at the handmaidens who were carefully bathing the squalling babes. The Earl was momentarily surprised, his eyebrows lifting a trifle before descending in anger once again.

"Good. Then remove the Countess before the sun sets next eve." A brief flash of pain spread a jagged crack over his countenance before he masked it with disdain. "I do not want her adulterous heart anywhere near Kirkcaldy!"

The Countess clenched her eyes, missing the spasm of emotion on the Earl's face. Whatever color had remained upon her cheeks drained away. Looking up, eyes dulled with pain, she asked him, "Have I not been forgiven then, my lord?"

"Never," he replied, his voice hard and brittle.

"You accuse me of something I have not done, husband. We wed in love and spent two years in bliss. Why would you doubt me now?"

"Do not pretend to be innocent!" he shouted at her. "I saw him wearing the ring I gave you! The ring I gave you as a symbol of my love!"

The Countess shook her head, her gaze pleading. "I told you before. You misinterpreted—"

"Whatever emotion I once had for you is gone," the Earl interrupted. "I care naught whether you live or die. I do not ever want to see you again. As the Earl of the Kirkcaldy, I forbid you to ever walk upon my lands. The trees around the perimeter of my property will be burned as a symbol of my intention to keep people like you out. Go away and never come back!"

Abandoning her bedside, he turned toward the twins and forced a smile of welcome. "Bring forth my eldest, my heir," he demanded. The handmaidens looked quickly toward the midwife, and the Earl followed their gaze. He was aware of a sudden agitation among those in the chamber, and his flinty eyes swept the room. The maids trembled and looked down. Finally the midwife stepped forward.

"We know not which was the first, my lord, for

while the Countess lay bleeding, we placed the babes in the bassinet.'Tis uncertain which was first, and they look like exact replicas of each other, my lord."

"How can you not know which is the heir!" he thundered, causing the infants to scream louder. " 'Twill be your death!"

"Nay!" whispered the Countess. "Blame not the midwife, for had I not been so weak, she would have tied a ribbon upon the finger of the first son.'Tis my fault. Blame me . . . as you have blamed me for so much already."

The Earl's rage vibrated from his shoulders. The delicate sunlight that lit the room suddenly winked out as the sun sank below the horizon as if it, too, feared his fury. The midwife lifted one of the infants, holding it out to him. He ignored the proffered one and stalked over to the bassinet where he stared down at the other crying child.

The baby's face was scrunched fiercely over tightly closed eyes. One hand broke free of the blankets and waved in the air, striking the Earl's massive chest. The Earl's anger subsided momentarily and he looked at his son with wonder. Distantly, he noticed that the other infant had ceased crying, but his attention was focused solely on the one in front of him.

He reached out a large hand, a hand that was easily the size of the infant's head, and touched his son for the first time. The baby's eyes sprang open, and a matching angry steel gray gazed out, though the infant's eyes were hazy and unfocused. In awe, the Earl stood still for several moments, amazed at the echoing noise produced by the tiny body. Then the lack of cries from the other infant caught his attention, and he turned around in sudden fear.

His gaze swung quickly around the chamber, finally alighting upon the bed. The pale Countess lay propped up, her hair a tangled, fetching mess around her shoulders. At her breast, the other son suckled, his calm, cloudy gray eyes locked with hers. A wave of longing swept over the Earl, and he involuntarily stepped closer. He reached out to the pair, wanting to be a part of their combined beauty. She and the babe . . . his love and their child . . . a Madonna. Suddenly confused, he checked his stride and stared at them. At his movement, the Countess looked up, her face tear-stained with a mixture of joy and pain.

"After I am gone, how will you choose the heir?" She glanced down and smiled lovingly at the child in her arms.

The Earl turned away and stood with his back to the room, trying to gather his emotions. In a harsh voice he answered, "I cannot choose randomly, for 'twould be a great sin to place the wrong one forward. I will let them decide."

The Countess gasped. "No! To leave the succession unclear is to invite strife and rivalry between brothers. Pick one and let it be known," she begged.

His anger resurging, the Earl spun back around. "You argue with me yet again! Is there no end to your lack of wifely virtues? I said, I will let the boys decide. You keep that one, and I will keep the other. Instill whatever morals you can into the babe, and I will teach the other what I believe he should know. I will teach him to be strong, to despise the weaker sex, and to set the legacy of Kirkcaldy above all else."

"You cannot separate them!" the Countess wailed as she leaned forward. The child at her breast was displaced, and he suddenly cried, joining his brother in mutual discontent.

The Earl's fury blinded him, and he shouted at her, "We will see who raises the stronger man! Whichever son first amasses a fortune, produces an obedient, docile, and trustworthy wife, and conceives a child shall inherit it all!"

Part I

The Meeting

Chapter 1

The third blow to his head finally defeated him. He swung his broadsword with failing accuracy as his brother's minions assaulted him with deadly intent. His awesome power faltered, and he stumbled. Bright lights sparkled at the edge of his vision, then blossomed into spearing rays of brutal strength. He collapsed upon one knee as the world spun around him, opening his mouth to gasp air just as a blow to his solar plexus sucked the remaining breath from his lungs. He heard the snap and snarl of his Irish wolfhound hovering over his suddenly prone body until a sharp thud caused the dog to land crosswise over his face.

With a final burst of stubbornness, Brogan O'Bannon shoved at the massive weight and pulled himself onto all fours. The effort was useless, for another punch to his kidneys dropped him back to the ground. As Brogan crumpled, his head crashed against a rock and the shards of light abruptly turned black.

The dream came to him then, the dream that had followed him from country to country as he traveled to gain wealth and renown. The dream had first found him when he was a small boy, trapped in the dank caverns of his homeland after he and his twin brother had become lost. Each had been forbidden to play in the caves, each had been forbidden to play with each other, yet they had done both time and time again. They had romped together for many summers, sneaking out of their respective homes and meeting in secret.

But one night their relationship had changed. The brotherly camaraderie had shifted as the reality of their conflict became undeniable. His twin had dared him to enter the bear caves, knowing that Brogan feared the dark. Once he was deep inside, the blackness and the beasts it cloaked had overwhelmed him, and he had crouched in terror for hours until the dream had rescued him.

It had come to him in the dark, a soft blessing of hope during his childhood panic, and had remained with him as a guiding message throughout his adulthood. Brogan welcomed the familiar comfort, relaxing into the enveloping fog.

She walked toward him, her face lost in the mists, her hair trailing behind her. She wore a gown of damp, gossamer silk that stuck briefly to her legs with each step forward. Shadows surrounded her, leaping and darting through the heavy clouds. A faint howl swept through the grove. Suddenly she leaned down and stroked his face and the warmth of her touch filled his soul.

There was never more to the dream, yet it went on for an eternity. The warmth, the mists, the silk . . . She stood near him and stroked him, and he felt more at peace in those sleeping moments than ever in his waking ones. In the dream he smiled at her faceless visage, his mouth awkward in the unfamiliar expression, and instinctively knew that she smiled back. He no longer tried to capture her as he woke, for long ago he had realized that seizing her meant losing her to the mists for months. He simply lay still and felt her soft fingers.

When the dream found him, he could forget for a

moment about his quest, forget the constant anger that
surrounded him, forget his unending fight against the
other half of his soul, his twin brother. When dreaming, he did not have to accumulate wealth, nor did he
have to prove his worth, for his dream woman understood him and accepted him. She filled him with im-
measurable peace. She brought him light to brighten
the darkness, and Brogan let himself drift into her
arms.

A shaft of pain burst through his consciousness,
and he jerked his eyes open. Pandemonium raged
around him. Hundreds of wolves seemed to swarm
over his outstretched legs and around his bound
body. Brogan tried to shake his head clear of the fog,
but the action made him dizzy and the wolves appeared to double. Growls, snarls and multitudes of
fierce, wild sounds roared over and around him, mix-
ing with human screams. He ducked to defend himself against the wild dogs, yet found that his arms
were tied behind his back around a solid Scottish Ash
tree. He yanked with his considerable strength, but
could not snap the sinew that held him. He was
propped up in a seated position and discovered that
he could not rise despite his struggles. A clank of
steel against steel caused him to look up, and he saw
one of the men that had set upon him earlier engaged
in battle with a young woman. In surprise, Brogan
stilled and stared at her.

She wore a thick skirt of blue wool that fit closely
to her body until it flared around her hips below a
hammered girdle. Her hair was blacker than the darkest cave and curled in furious ringlets down past her
waist. She leaped at the man she fought with terrifying
focus, her sword flashing in the meager twilight. Brogan closed his eyes, then opened them to view her
incredulously. She struck the man, then deliberately

ran her sword through his side. As she pulled the steel free, the wolves pounced upon him and began to shred his flesh.

The man screamed, flailing against the wolves. He stumbled to his horse, and kicking out at the beasts, dragged himself across the saddle. He hauled himself upright and looked angrily at Brogan.

"You are warned! Leave Scotland!" he screeched as he clutched his bleeding side. A sudden flurry of hoof beats announced the rapid departure of the remaining attackers, and the injured man swung his horse around and galloped after them.

The woman glared at their retreating backs as she waved her sword in the air. "Cowards!" she screamed after them. "Think you afore poaching on this land again!" she yelled over Brogan's shoulder, facing toward him for the first time.

Brogan gasped at the gleaming turquoise of her eyes. The color was so fantastic, he could not believe it belonged to a woman of flesh and blood. A shiver of disquiet raced up his spine as he wondered if she was of the faerie people.

Matalia stared in surprise at the man trussed to the tree. She swung her sword up, placed the point at his throat, and looked fiercely into his eyes, daring him to cry for mercy. A wisp of twilight mist snaked between them, then was swept away.

Brogan sat still, his heart caught in the morass of her eyes. He felt the tip of the sword press into his neck, yet it was not in his nature to feel fear. He noted the fine beads of perspiration that dotted her forehead and watched in swift arousal as one drop curled down her temple and into the hollow between her breasts. He felt his thudding heart send blood rushing to his loins. Instantly hardening, he lifted his eyes back to her face.

Matalia trembled slightly. Her hand on her sword

wavered and the blade nicked the man's throat. A small rivulet of blood traced a path down his neck. Shocked, she realized that his eyes were upon her breasts and he was ignoring the cut to his skin.

"Have you no fear, trespasser? I hold a blade above your vein of life. Should I press down upon it, you will bleed to death in moments," she mocked him, her voice low and husky.

Brogan felt desire swamp him at the sound. His perusal sank lower, caressing her hips. She shifted her weight, and a fold of wool became trapped momentarily between her thighs. Brogan's eyes burned into the vee and a groan slipped past his lips.

"Ach, mi lass, untie me and I will give you liquid more precious than mi blood."

Matalia stepped back as if scalded. She glared at him, her exquisite eyes snapping in fury, although Brogan detected a flicker of uncertainty in the turquoise depths.

"You are a fool to taunt me so when you are at my mercy. I will not have you speak to me so dishonorably." She raised her sword yet again and made to step forward. Brogan's gaze bored into hers so powerfully, she froze. His eyes were stone gray, humorless and hard. Twilight mists rose again and poured through the trees, enfolding him, matching the color of his eyes. A trail of blood ran down his head and merged with the red upon his neck. Muscles rippled in his arms and chest, visible even through the layers of clothing. With a start, Matalia realized that he was pulling at his bonds, attempting to break free. Curiously detached, she tilted her head to see if he would succeed.

As she watched him, her gaze crept slowly down his body, to the bulge between his legs that pulsed and grew as she watched it. Startled anew, she looked swiftly up into his eyes.

"Come, little maiden. I'll appease your curiosity and teach you things your husband will never learn much less share with you. Come hither, and cut my ties." His voice was seductive and masculine. The controlled stillness of his body was like a coiled snake and Matalia felt a whisper of desire slither through her. She looked around at the creeping mist and darkening forest. Brogan watched her thoughts flit over her countenance and he tensed with anticipation.

Suddenly a howl burst out of the woods beside them and Brogan leaped, every muscle straining as he desperately sought to escape. "Quick!" he shouted. "Afore the wolves descend upon us again. They will smell the blood and attack us as the dusk moves in!"

Another howl bounced across the clearing, and then three wolves stepped into the fading light. Horror-struck, Brogan waited for them to leap upon the superb woman. A fierce growl came from his throat as he struggled mightily to break free. The wolves circled the woman, pulling their lips back in a hungry snarl. They snapped at her gown, grabbing it and pulling her toward the trees.

Then, when Matalia jerked her dress from their jaws, they lay in a semicircle around her, facing Brogan. Realization came to him. The hundreds of wolves he had seen earlier were actually only these three wild canines that flocked around the faerie maiden as if under her spell. He looked around quickly, remembering his own beast, and saw the wolfhound on his side, breathing deeply but still unconscious. He glanced back at the maiden and saw that she was approaching him cautiously.

"Can you not free yourself, man?" she queried softly. She leaned over slightly to look around him, and Brogan saw the wool gape away from her breasts. A fine barrier of silk encased her body, underneath, barring his view. He felt his head move forward as if by longing alone he could taste her flesh. She jerked back, abruptly aware of his gaze. "I asked you a question," she said sharply. "Can you not break those bonds?"

"Lass, if I could, I would have done so a thousand times over by now and put my arms to better use than cradling this tree trunk behind my back. Take pity, love, and free me." Brogan tried to keep his voice light and unthreatening, despite the turgid pain developing in his lap. He inched his hips forward to ease the strain, but stilled as the woman's eyes swept down to observe his movements.

With deep, unfathomable eyes, Matalia tossed her sword away and kneeled down next to him. She reached out to touch his cheek. "I find that I am interested in how you feel, trespasser." She pulled back, surprised at the sudden wariness in the man's eyes. "I am interested . . ." Her voice trailed off as she touched the first button on Brogan's shirt. Mist drifted in and out of the clearing, as swift as a deer in flight.

"Release me now, faerie maiden," he whispered as she unbuttoned his shirt. "Do as I say, little lass, for I can be a tender lover or a terrible foe."

Matalia stopped, considering. "What mean you, lover or foe?"

Brogan smiled seductively. "Undo my bonds. I can make you feel as if the heavens have opened and the stars are colliding in the sky. But I must have my hands to slide over your precious skin, to reach inside your private heart."

She jerked back, frightened both by his words and her response to them. She felt heat warming her thighs and blinked quickly. "You should not say those things to me," she murmured.

"Why not?"

She shook her head, not sure how to answer. She

slowly backed away, calling her wolves to her side. "You should not say those things," she said again with more conviction.

Brogan snarled in frustration. "Come back here!" he commanded. "Untie me! Those men will come back and murder me. Set me free to defend myself!"

"I think not. The thieves are gone."

"They are not thieves. They are men sent by my brother to prevent my return to—" he said, but she was already disappearing back into the forest. He shouted at her again, infuriated that she would leave him so helpless, but she did not look back. He yanked on his bonds, then flung his head back and screamed his rage. Fifteen years of struggle! Fifteen years! And now this small, black-haired girl thwarted him with her stubbornness!

Matalia entered the castle slowly, lost in thought. She did not know what to do about the stranger tethered to the Ash tree, despite thinking about it all the way home. Something about him frightened her, but also intrigued her. No one she had ever known had stared her down before, had spoken back to her before. She was Princess Kalial's eldest daughter, the sixteen-year-old heir to her mother's forest kingdom. Her father was Laird Ronin McTaver, leader of the McTaver clan. With such powerful parents, no one had dared to be anything but supremely respectful toward her.

As soon as she crossed the great hall, Princess Kalial and Merkle, the Princess's adviser, approached her. "Duncan just sent word that you refused his offer, Matalia," her mother said. "Why? Why would you refuse him? You have known him since childhood. You are close friends."

Matalia frowned, irritated that she had to discuss her future once again. "I told you, I do not want to marry just anyone."

"But, Matalia, you have to choose someone soon."

"Why?" she cried, although she knew her mother's response by heart. "Why must I marry?"

"You need grounding. You need someone to lean on. You need someone to help guide you."

"I will not wed without love!" she shouted, stamping her foot.

Kalial frowned back. "And I would never ask you to. But you and Duncan have grown up together. You are fond of each other. He is a good man."

"Is that what you feel for Father? Is that why you married him? Because he is a good man? "

"Of course," Kalial replied, confused. "I love him *and* respect him."

Matalia spun away, unable to express herself. She raced from the hall, sobbing with youthful frustration.

Kalial turned to Merkle. "What did I say?" she asked.

Merkle shook his head sadly. "She is just a young girl trying to become a woman. Perhaps you should not push her into any particular path."

"But if I don't," Kalial argued, "she will become lost! She is so impulsive, so wayward. She needs to raise her own family so she can learn responsibility and maturity."

Merkle looked up the stairway to where Matalia had fled. "I think you should trust her. She will find her own way."

Kalial nodded sadly. "I just want what is best for her."

Matalia gripped her sword and lunged at the shadows, fighting her imagined opponents fiercely. Colleen stood silently, letting her mistress vent her anger. When Matalia finally grew tired, Colleen cleared her throat.

"Another argument with your mother?" she asked astutely.

"Yes." Matalia sighed. "Why doesn't she understand that I want to find the same sort of bond that she has with Father? I want to feel special, feel treasured, feel . . . different."

"Duncan is a good man, and he is your friend. You could do worse."

"I want to do better," Matalia hissed, her anger rising again. "I want to feel excited!" She slanted a look at Colleen, debating, then strolled nonchalantly to the window. "I met someone today."

"Oh?" Colleen asked.

"Someone who interested me."

"Who?"

"Just a simple traveler . . ."

Colleen looked at her suspiciously. "Are you thinking about your *idea* again?"

"Yes!" breathed Matalia as she turned around. "I want to experience what lovers do. I want to know what makes my mother and father smile. I think I have a right to know what happens between a man and a woman before I consent to marry. How do I know if I will like it?"

"I should never have told you about those things."

"But you did, and I am curious. Besides, I have to bring him some food. I will be back shortly. You won't tell, will you, Colleen?"

"What do you mean? Why do you have to bring him food?"

"He is tied to a tree in the forest. I can do whatever I want with him and he cannot refuse me!"

"You go too far, Matalia! I can understand your desire to experiment, but you cannot hold a man captive!"

"Why not? Do you think it would be safe to let him go, and *then* do it?"

"No! You are far too beautiful. No man should be trusted. I have told you that before."

"Then this is the perfect solution. He waits in the forest, and I have him completely under my control."

Colleen sighed. "Just be careful," she said with resignation. "And remember, men have a curious way of turning the tables on you."

Chapter 2

She looked at him, her eyes gleaming in the descending darkness. He watched her silently, only his eyes showing the blazing emotion he held in check. She leaned down and lifted some dried meat to his lips, and he took it, hating her but hungry nonetheless. Her heavy hair swung freely, and he swallowed, fighting the instant attraction she aroused.

"I told you the thieves would not return," she said as she stood up.

"I told you to release me," he countered.

She walked behind him. "My name is Matalia." She stood just out of his sight. "Who are you?"

Brogan tried to turn to face her fully, but he could not move any farther. Even though he had bedded women from France, England, India and Arabia, something about her faerie quality intrigued him more than any other woman. She was more than lovely. She was fascinating.

He heard rustling, sticks breaking and then the sound of a flint being struck. The fine crackle of kindling and the sudden warmth told him Matalia's activities. He waited, his blood hot, and he breathed deeply, trying to smother his sexual thoughts. He needed to get free, and only she could release him. "I am a wanderer," he finally answered.

"A wanderer?"

"I have no home." He leaned back against the Ash tree and stared out sightlessly, infusing more meaning into the words than Matalia would understand.

When the fire glowed behind his head and cast orange reflections into the night, Brogan heard Matalia circle back to his front. In utter shock he beheld her standing there half-naked, her woolen gown discarded. She inched slowly forward, the pleading look in her eyes vying with her determination.

"You see, I find I am curious about something. Here you are at my mercy. You are a simple traveler and will soon be gone. But while you can go from adventure to adventure, I have few opportunities to explore unknown feelings. My body longs to learn the secrets between a man and a woman. You, here as you are, have been given to me by the forest, like a gift." The silk of her undergarments brushed his hips as she sank down to look into his eyes. " 'Tis only one night." She slid her hand into the exposed area on his chest. "And I wish to take this night before I have no more chances."

Brogan twitched, and his eyes blazed. "You are crazy! No woman accosts a bound man! What kind of woodland faerie are you to take advantage of a warrior? Release me first, and I will take you gladly."

"But, sir, surely you do not think me so unwise in the ways of men that I would trust you not to hurt me?" She looked down and touched his shaft through his clothes, causing it to convulse against her fingers.

"I would control myself," Brogan gritted through his teeth, faintly aware that he might not be able to live up to his word. The slide of silk against his bare chest and the rasp of Matalia's breath upon his neck were driving him wild. His anger at his body's responses fueled his energy, and he struggled anew against his bonds.

Matalia bit her lip as she watched the man, and she

prayed the sinew would hold. She pushed her hair out of her face, not realizing that it swung around and tantalized his cheek. Brogan twisted his head out of the way, but in his effort to avoid the satin of her hair, he bumped his mouth into her scantily clad breast. Matalia gasped and shrank back.

He waited, watched her struggle with her fears, then lean toward him, granting him access. Unable to deny himself, Brogan reached out with his tongue and flicked a thrusting nipple. The fabric instantly became transparent, and Brogan saw the dusky peak bloom in the reflected firelight.

A tiny mew of pleasure escaped Matalia's lips, and her eyes darkened to aquamarine. She sank into his lap, allowing the silk to billow around her, producing a flush of sweet and arousing scent that wafted to his nostrils. He groaned in response and leaned his head down to suckle her exposed neck. She pressed against him as she pushed the edges of his shirt farther apart, then leaned back to look at his tanned chest. Brogan jerked forward, forgetting for one moment that he was bound as he tried to grab her to bring her back. As the bonds strained, a wave of anger swept over him, and he glared at Matalia's sensual face.

Ignoring his furious gaze, she scooted back and began to untie his breeches.

"Stop, woman! If you seek a stud to teach you the ways between man and woman, go to the village and hire one, but leave me be!" His thunderous voice carried throughout the forest, but there was no one to hear. Matalia responded by pulling the laces farther apart and looking at him with one eyebrow lifted.

"I do not see how you can stop me, trespasser. Besides, you will get exactly what you seek, except you will do it under my direction. You fuss too much. Really, sir! You should relax and enjoy." Matalia dropped her gaze, slightly discomfited by the steel of his look. She pulled his breeches down with some difficulty and then stared at his shaft thrusting upwards. She bit her lip and wrinkled her brow, unsure how to proceed.

Brogan emanated waves of fury. To be raped by a tiny woman as he was trussed to a tree! He had fought Vikings, conquered kings! He had mastered the seas and dominated the mountains on many continents! Even now his ship was unloading his fortune, forming a long caravan to transport the bounty through the Scottish Lowlands toward his birthplace, where he intended to return, triumphant. Men quaked at the call of his name on a battlefield. No one dared to impose their will upon him, yet this girl dared that and more. She meant not only to immobilize him physically—she meant to take his manhood!

He felt blood seep from wounds on his wrists as he clenched his fists. He desperately tried to block the passion filling his loins, attempted to will his shaft to shrivel. But the member had other thoughts, and it reared up, engorged and ready, seeking independently to find a slick, wet haven between the promise of her white thighs.

Matalia reached forward and placed a finger upon the tip. A burst of agony erupted from Brogan's throat, and he thrashed, trying to avoid her simple touch. Shocked, Matalia watched him, her hand hovering over his rod, until he settled again. She shifted forward, raised her shift and sat down upon his lap with her knees on either side of his hips, then slipped down with his cock jutting between her legs. Brogan fought to remain still while his tumescence jerked and pulsed, unhappy that it had missed the entrance it sought.

Matalia wiggled slightly, pressing her pleasure spot against the side of his shaft. She gasped slightly and her gaze flew up to meet his. She moved experimentally and felt another trickle of pleasure. She glanced down and lifted her shift to view his organ. She moved again, trying to see how they fit together while Brogan took short, shallow breaths in an attempt to maintain his control.

She leaned onto his chest, tilting her pelvis, and the wet cavern slipped teasingly over his member. Brogan gave in and pushed his hips forward, trying to help Matalia in her struggles. However, in her innocence, she shifted away, accidentally inhibiting his penetration. With a fierce growl, Brogan reached with his teeth and gripped the strap of her shift, pulling her closer. She resisted, suddenly frightened of his fury. She blushed at her ineptitude and leaped up, ripping her shift as she gained her feet.

"Oh!" she cried as the silk shredded in his mouth and bared her to the waist. "What am I doing wrong?" She crossed her arms in front of her chest, cringing from the anger and passion blazing from Brogan's eyes. He spat out the cloth and glowered at her, hating himself for reacting to the sight of her gorgeous, thrusting breasts. "Perhaps I must be lying down," she mumbled, slanting a cautious look at him.

The image of her lying in the leaves with the firelight dancing over her flesh made him shake. The indignity of his position vied with the overwhelming hunger he had for her. She approached him again, letting her arms drop, and tried to angle her body over his in a prone position. The brush of her nipples against his nearly sent him over the edge. Despite his disgust with himself, he adjusted his angle to better suit her position, thrusting his hips up to connect with her thighs. He groaned as the heat between her legs swept over him. She looked up, distressed, and Brogan was able to stare directly into her fantastic eyes.

This close, he could see tiny flecks of dark blue and gold surrounded by deep turquoise, framed by lush, spiky black lashes. Spots of color burst upon her cheeks at his intense perusal, and she dipped her head, sending her curls tumbling upon his bare chest. She writhed to and fro, seeking a connection between them but failing. Brogan felt his jaw strain as he clenched his teeth tightly. Shame warred with passion as his mind tried to pull away from her, but his body shifted itself underneath her.

When Matalia relaxed against him, her brow knit in confusion, Brogan used the opportunity to slide his shaft into the wet nitch guarding her passage. With a surge, he pushed forward, ready to feel the sweet cocoon enfold his cock in slippery splendor. But just as he lifted into her, she abruptly scrambled off and stomped her foot in vexation.

"Bah!" she exclaimed. "This doesn't work!" Brogan looked at her standing above him and panted with the frustration of barely missed satisfaction. His gray eyes narrowed and he trembled so hard, the tree shook. He opened his mouth to speak, to tell her what to do, then closed it with a snap. Feeling his heart beating erratically, he forced himself to look away from the fetching sight of her in front of him. He smiled grimly, aware that he would have scoffed if anyone had suggested he would be in such a predicament.

"You are laughing at me," she shouted at him, her own breath coming in tiny pants. Frustration made her bold. She leaned down and placed her nose level with his. "I will figure it out, never you fear, even if I have to keep you until it works."

A horrible suspicion entered Brogan's mind, and he watched her angry eyes warily. " 'Twould be very ill advised of you to detain me, lass. I am en route to meet my bride, and surely you would not want her to wonder at my delay? She would send scouts out to search for me, and should they find you, they would string you up for the forest beasts. Obviously your

body is incapable of completing the act," he spat out,
"so leave now while my anger is short-lived."

Matalia looked at him with fury that soon dissolved
into disdain. "I do not fear you and your alleged bride.
I am Matalia, daughter of Princess Kalial and Laird
McTaver, and I shall have what I want from you
whether you will it or nay." She spun around and
picked up her gown, jerking it on. "You can sleep out
here tonight and think upon your obstinance. Until I
learn what this . . . this feeling inside me means and
how to fulfill this craving I have, you will remain my
prisoner." She glared down at him, fully clothed while
he sat helpless, his chest gleaming with sweat and his
cock still pointing straight up, pulsing with unfulfilled
need. With a final humph, she stalked away, disappearing into the woods. Brogan looked at the three
wolves that had watched the entire proceedings. One
by one they, too, stood up and walked into the trees
after their mistress. Only the crackling fire and the
sleeping wolfhound kept him company in the deepen-
ing night.

When morning came, Brogan's mood was more foul
than a rancid carcass. His eyes were gritty from lack
of sleep and his arms alternately tingled with pain or
trembled with cold. His helplessness rankled him the
most, and he dwelt angrily upon the lass who had left
him trussed overnight. Someone singing a lilting song
interrupted his thoughts, and he froze, trying to locate
the source. Sudden hope flared, and he shouted for
assistance.

"Ho there! Lady! Please come hither and help a
poor traveler." He scrambled to cover himself as best
he could, but knew that his bare chest would startle
any maid who happened to be passing. Thankfully he
had managed to shift his breeches over his hips, but
the laces remained loose and part of his manhood was

still visible. He listened intently as the song petered to a stop and a pair of women's voices rose in hushed conversation. Try as he could, he could not make out their words, but he was encouraged to hear their steps approach.

"Young maids, I beseech you. I am fair frozen to death and am in need of a caring hand." He stopped and listened to see if the women would answer. He could feel their eyes upon him and he tried to look as unthreatening as possible with downcast eyes and relaxed shoulders. Yet, unbeknownst to him, his aura of coiled power made a mockery of his submissive stance.

"See, he is as I told you, tied to a tree and none the wiser," he heard the unmistakable husky voice whisper to her companion. With a jerk, he glared into the forest toward two human shadows.

"He looks awfully angry, Lady Matalia," a new voice whispered back. Her tones were older and rougher, sounding more like a peasant's.

"Well, I suppose he is a bit annoyed, but what could I do? It was not like he would stay still overnight and wait for me to bring you, now would he?"

"No . . ." the peasant replied, "but I am not sure he is a good choice, m'lady."

"What better!" Matalia exclaimed. "He is handsome in a brutish sort of way. He is a wandering trespasser, unknown to all. And best of all, he is unable to do anything I do not wish!" Matalia sighed heavily at the woman's continued look of doubt. "Come, Colleen, do not fash out now. I want to do this, and surely no better opportunity will present itself." With that declaration, Matalia McTaver stepped into the clearing.

If Brogan had thought her beautiful the night before, he was stunned this morning. Her riotous curls tumbled down her back with two purple combs hold-

ing the bulk of it from her face. Her nose was thin and
sculpted, and her mouth was succulent. The bottom lip
pouted and curved, formed in such a way that every
time she spoke, the flesh became subtly moist. Her
figure was encased in thin, white linen, showing hints
of dark, forbidden places within the folds. She walked
toward him slowly yet confidently, trailed by the
three wolves.

A sudden growl beside him made Brogan start. His
wolfhound, now fully recovered, rose to his feet and
snarled a warning at the approaching party. Matalia
froze, her eyes wide with surprise. The wolfhound's
head came to her shoulder and his body outweighed
her two times over. With challenging steps forward,
the wolfhound bore down upon the woman.

In a flurry of movement, the wolves behind her
sprang forward, their snaps and snarls filling the air.
In shock, both Matalia and Brogan watched as the
opposing beasts circled each other, hair raised and lips
drawn. With a slinking dart, one of the wolves slipped
forward to bite the wolfhound's hind leg, but the enormous dog whipped around and snapped, his huge jaws
grazing the smaller wolf. In retaliation, the wolf
snarled more ferociously, and specks of foam dripped
from his canines.

Distantly, Matalia heard the man tied to the tree
call out, but she was hypnotized by the battle in front
of her. She walked forward, unconscious of her behavior, placing herself within the ring formed by her
wolves. She stared into the eyes of the furious wolfhound. He lunged at her, his teeth aiming for her face
and throat when he was pummeled from the side by
two wolves, knocking him off balance. He spun
around, ready to tear the beasts apart, when a sharp
command from his master made him hesitate. He
swung his glazed eyes back to the woman. Then, with
a last warning growl, he backed away and stood protectively next to the man.

"You fool! Are you daft to enter into a dogfight?" Brogan shouted at her. "Or are you an imbecile? Have you no sense that my dog would have torn you to pieces within seconds?" He glared at Matalia, his angry words finally penetrating her fog. She shook her head slightly and blinked. The odd trance that sometimes overtook her drifted away, and she took a deep breath. Her hands shook and it required a moment for her to focus clearly. Recovering slowly, she motioned her wolves forward. They slunk with raised hackles, staring at the wolfhound with yellow-eyed suspicion, then milled several feet behind her as if contained within a glass cage.

She then drifted forward and sang softly, the same lilting refrain that Brogan had heard earlier. The hair on the back of his neck lifted as a hazy glow suffused her, and the wolves sat down and joined her song. The music she sang made him drowsy and a sense of peace swept over him. In surprise, he looked up to find her in front of him, reaching out toward his wolfhound. He opened his mouth to warn her that the punishing jaws would bite through her fragile wrist, but to his utter amazement, she placed her fingers upon the dog's head and stroked it. As if spellbound, the wolfhound suddenly dropped his fierce stance and licked her arm.

She leaned her head forward and brushed her cheek against the bristly hair of the wolfhound's muzzle. She closed her eyes, her song slowed, lengthened, then ended in a soft sigh. Finally opening her eyes once again, she turned to Brogan and spoke. "What do you call this marvelous creature?" she asked. Dumbfounded, Brogan could only stare at her and the dog.

Narrowing her eyes, Matalia repeated her question. Because Brogan had never thought to call him anything other than Dog, he remained silent, trying to figure out how the ferocious beast had become tamed in scant seconds. "I see that your obstinacy has not changed." In astonishment, Brogan watched the woman's eyes darken with anger as she turned her back on him and spoke to the peasant who remained hidden at the forest edge.

"You see? He has few redeeming qualities. He is rude, aggressive, bulky . . . and . . . and all sorts of other things, yet he appears to be built well enough to serve my purpose."

"I don't know, m'lady. I'm thinking that you ought to let this one go and wait for one that is, well, *smaller,*" she answered.

"Colleen, you and the other servants are always talking about how good a big man is. Surely you do not want me to experience someone inferior?"

Brogan looked between the two, astounded. He tipped his head back and closed his eyes, certain that he must have fallen asleep and was dreaming this ridiculous conversation. His eyes sprang open as he heard Matalia continue doubtfully, "Although I am not sure he *works,* you know, for he could not function well last night."

"Really?" questioned the peasant as she stepped closer, keeping a wary eye on the watchful wolfhound. She maintained a distance when the dog started to growl. "Would it not rise?" she asked. Brogan's steel-gray eyes flicked dangerously as he glowered at the red-haired woman. She grinned in reply and winked. "Ah, I think it might work if we give it a bit o' incentive."

"I tried."

"What did you do? Command it, m'lady?" When Matalia looked at her with an arched eyebrow, the peasant sighed. "You canna command a man, m'lady, for they don't work well under those conditions. You have to nudge it a bit, touch it and so forth to make it ready, all the while talking sweet things that make the fellow's pride swell along with his cock."

Brogan looked back and forth between the two as Matalia kneeled next to him and looked at him consideringly. She reached a finger forward and poked at his nether regions. In fury, Brogan kicked out and sent Matalia sprawling.

"Ouch," she murmured in a hurt tone. A series of howls behind her made the wolfhound spring up, but Matalia looked at her wolves and they instantly quieted. After a moment, the wolfhound sniffed and lay back down.

"Ach, m'lady. You no understand the thick of it. You need to be soft. Shall I show you?" Colleen questioned while looking at Brogan hopefully. He shot her a glare of such fury, she took a full step backward. "Mayhap not. Well, we ought to move him to the cottage then, for it might be hard to keep him tied to the tree."

"How do we move him?" Matalia queried, glancing at Brogan's thick arms.

"Knock him senseless first, then drag him behind your horse." Colleen smirked at Brogan's horrified expression. "It'll be the safest method." Brogan barely saw Matalia nod before pain burst from his temple, and for only the second time in his life he slumped down, unconscious.

Chapter 3

Matalia gazed around the small cottage room and down at her prize with satisfaction. The man lay sprawled upon the bed, tied spread-eagled. His breeches and shirt had been removed and no sheet covered his masculine body. Matalia sat upon the bed on a level with his hips and let her eyes rove freely. She had done it! She had collected a male specimen and would be able to indulge her curious urgings. Next time her mother hinted at what she was missing by avoiding marriage she would be able to answer her with authority. She could experience sexuality, but still maintain her unwedded state.

As one observing the scene, it would be impossible to decipher Matalia's thoughts, for she sat quietly beside the naked and slumbering man, dressed in her white linen, with purple combs restraining her hair. Her face was soft and gentle, and she appeared hesitant and shy.

Brogan drifted in his daze, the sense of urgency that drove his waking moments missing temporarily. He let his mind wander, nay, asked his mind to wander, seeking the mists of his familiar dream. He reached for her, seeking her, calling out for her, until finally he saw her in the distance. She walked toward him, enveloped in wet silk, as always. But today she had curves, a rounded softness to her shape that he had never

seen before. An arch of a breast, a jut of a hip . . .
Brogan watched her walk in the mists and waited for
her comforting touch, feeling for the first time a desire
to stroke her in return.

Endless touching. Eternal stroking. Blissful connection. The mists cloaked them from view as they reveled in their new relationship. Brogan smiled again,
painfully, unsure how to make his lips work, and
waited for her returning smile.

A light touch on his body brought him to instant,
angry consciousness, and his dream vanished. Brogan
gathered his muscles and tried to spring forward, only
to find himself bound yet again. His eyes snapped
open, and he glared with terrible fury at the girl sitting
beside him.

"Damn you to hell!" he spat at her, feeling her light
touch upon his male nipples.

Matalia started, surprised from her musing by his
abrupt waking. She arched her brow at his angry
words in a now-familiar gesture.

"Tut-tut," she mocked. " 'Tis not a pleasant riser,
is he?" Matalia pulled her hand back and stared at
him thoughtfully. "Are you hungry?" she asked.

Brogan felt a pang in his gut at the mention of
food but kept stubbornly silent. Matalia shrugged and
moved off the bed. Brogan felt the bed rock with her
action and suddenly became aware of his surround-
ings. He was in a one-room cottage, upon a large bed
occupying the right corner. A banked fire glowed in
the hearth. A single chair stood in front of the fire
next to a small table laden with bread, cheese and
fruit. A flask of wine stood on the floor next to the
table due to the lack of space available on it. Thick
curtains covered the windows, but Brogan could hear
the rustle of leaves outside. He swung his head toward
the woman and rested his flat gray gaze upon her in
an unnerving stare.

Matalia shifted away and picked up a peach. While biting with her teeth, she used her free hand to wrap her riotous curls into a long twist and then let it go. This she did several times while she ate the peach, her turquoise eyes meeting his gray ones with careful challenge.

"I understand," she finally said as she tossed the peach pit into the fire, "that you are uncomfortable with this arrangement. I am frankly curious why you would not be willing to give something you so clearly want to take." She stopped fiddling with her hair and lifted her hands in a gesture of confusion.

Brogan broke eye contact by closing his in frustration. How could this be happening to him? How could he, a great fighter, a wealthy and soon-to-be very powerful man, be trapped in a small cottage with an exquisite virgin who desired his sexual services at the price of his pride? He growled an inarticulate response, then scanned her figure with forced disinterest.

"Some things are not enticing enough," he finally muttered, wishing to humble her haughty arrogance. He was unprepared for her instant anger.

Another peach, a true delicacy of only the very rich, was flung at his chest, breaking open and splattering him with juice. With supreme control, Brogan did not flinch or show any indication that he had noticed her flair of temper.

"You seek to shame me for your lack of ability," she railed at him, stomping back to the bed to glare down at him. "I will have it known that I asked around and was told that if it does not happen between a man and a woman, it is the man's fault!"

Brogan stared at the wall, forcing himself not to look at her full lips and flushed cheeks. He shrugged as well as he could in a prone position. "If you say so," he murmured. He turned his mind to unpleasant thoughts, ignoring the outraged shriek above him and the flood of words coming from her dusky lips. He thought ahead, thought of the meeting with his father in two weeks' time. He thought of his twin, his nemesis, his rival, and knew he would be there as well. He thought of his mother, last seen over fifteen years ago when he was stripped from her side at age fourteen, and wondered if she still lived.

The sudden silence in the cottage caught his attention, and he glanced up at Matalia. She was staring down at him with concern, her brilliant eyes temporarily mesmerizing him.

"What are you thinking?" she asked.

Brogan glared at her. "There is no force on this earth that would induce me to talk to you, Lady Matalia. You made a grave mistake when you decided to use me as your experimental male."

"Really?" Matalia countered. "Because you find me so unattractive?" she added sarcastically.

"That is part of the reason, yes," he lied coldly.

Matalia narrowed her eyes. She leaned over and ran her finger through the peach juice glistening on his chest. Then she placed her finger in her mouth and sucked on it while staring at him through her lashes. Brogan remained perfectly still, his immense willpower struggling to act unaffected by her childish attempts at seduction.

"You really are boorish, you know," Matalia complained. "It is not so much that I ask of you. A simple evening is all."

"You want me to fuck you," Brogan returned harshly, causing Matalia to flinch.

"No, I want to—to—" She trailed off, unsure how to phrase her request.

"I know what you want," he finished for her, "and I am not willing to give it."

"Well, then, I shall have to make you!" With that pronouncement Matalia stomped out of the room, slamming the cottage door behind her. Brogan was once again left alone, tied and helpless, his fury raging. He twisted and turned, bloodying his wrists and ankles, until he fell back, drenched in sweat.

Matalia raced home, her elation soaring. Her wolves scampered around her skirts as she ran, encouraging her rapid pace. As she neared the castle, she slowed to a walk and gasped in air, trying to quiet her breathing. "I did it," she whispered to her four-legged companions. "I did it! I have a captive to experiment with. I caught a man that no one knows so I can learn the secrets of marriage without having to make a formal commitment. I won't be told how to live my life as if I were a child. I can make my own decisions. I can seek out"—here she drew in a deep breath as she climbed over a log—"my own experiences. There is no reason why I should not be able to explore such sexual aspects simply because I have not found a man I wish to marry. I will do what I want and none the wiser!" She patted the head of the nearest wolf, and he licked her wrist.

Reaching the drawbridge, Matalia skipped over the moat and into the large courtyard. Colleen spied her and hustled over, leaving the remaining wash for the other women. They glared at her and shook their heads, grumbling among themselves.

Matalia grasped the servant's hand eagerly and pulled her up the stairs to the great hall. "He is awake," she said happily.

"Be he angry?" Colleen questioned with concern.

"Not in the least," Matalia replied. "He is anxious for my return."

"Did ye already do it then, m'lady?"

Matalia looked at her friend with a raised eyebrow and a suggestive tilt to her head. Colleen stared at her, wrinkling her nose in concentration. "I think not," she finally pronounced, causing Matalia to pout.

"How can you be so certain?" she asked.

"Because you don' have that certain air about ye yet."

Matalia rolled her eyes and swung her arms wide to include the entire hall. "Can you tell me, just by looking, who in this room has and who has not?"

"Pretty close," Colleen replied, pointing several people out and nodding or shaking her head at each. Then she looked up at Matalia and giggled. Matalia, who had been concentrating carefully on each person, looked at the laughing servant with affront.

" 'Tis unkind to tease me," she murmured as she walked away. Colleen simply grinned and followed her. They soon reached Matalia's room, where a dress was laid out upon the bed, complete with a delicate chain girdle and a jeweled headpiece. Matalia groaned.

"We must have guests," she grumbled.

"Yes, the son of The McDougal has come to call."

"Bah! When will they understand that I want nothing to do with him and his fawning ways! I made my opinion clear."

"I daresay your parents will disagree with you, Lady Matalia. They may think you are a spoiled child who needs to learn her duty."

"You have been listening to my mother," Matalia accused.

"How could I not when she speaks of nothing else these months past?"

"Just get me my bath and leave me be. I will dine with them tonight, but later . . . later you and I must go to the cottage."

"Fair enough, m'lady. Your bath is already waiting in the closet."

Matalia smiled at her friend in gratitude. The eldest child, and separated from her younger siblings by many years, she had befriended Colleen when they were both little girls. Although they were of different classes, their devotion to each other as best friends had never faltered. Aspects of Matalia's life intrigued and bemused Colleen, whereas parts of Colleen's life fascinated and bedeviled Matalia. Ever willing to share with each other, Matalia spent many an exciting night with Colleen's father, mother and siblings, and Colleen had frequently been invited to the castle.

Colleen had slept with the smithy's son many months ago, and since then the girls had frequently discussed many aspects of intimacy. Colleen had described the experience glowingly, and Matalia had determined that she, too, should try it. Lately however, Colleen had become nervous with Matalia's interest in sexual activities. Regretting her earlier frankness, Colleen had tried to remind Matalia that she was expected to remain a virgin until her wedding day, but Matalia had ignored her completely. She wanted to experiment. It was her "grand idea."

Oblivious to Colleen's concerns, Matalia hugged her friend briefly, then removed her outer garments and stepped into her tub wearing her linen chemise. Matalia was careful to scrub behind her ears, under her arms, and between her toes. "I cannot believe he finds nothing about me attractive," she grumbled to herself. "Men are always exclaiming about my eyes or my hair." She leaned over and dunked her curly locks into the water and lathered them in lavender-scented soap. "He cannot truly find me that unacceptable . . . can he?" she asked the wolf that sat closest to her. He was gray with a band of black around his neck. He had pale blue eyes, which made him appear blind to many who saw him. Matalia, however, knew that his vision was perfect and that in the moonlight, he saw better than the others.

"Do you really think he does not want me?" The wolf opened his mouth and panted. With a shrug, Matalia rinsed her hair and picked up a jar containing a mixture of oil, thyme, wheat, aloe and citrus juice. She poured a small amount into her palm and rubbed it into her hair. The ointment helped her hair stay untangled and kept it feeling soft and silky. Her mother had made it for her when she was only five years old, when she had absolutely refused to have anyone brush her hair due to the pain it caused. No more enormous knots formed at night, and Matalia used the gloss religiously to keep it that way.

Stepping out of the tub, Matalia dried off, then sat in front of her window and carefully combed her curls until they were a rippling mass. A bell chimed in the distance, and Matalia sighed. Another of her wolves, this one red with a black undercoat, woofed softly at her, rubbing his body against her legs. Matalia absently pushed him away, unaware of the dusting of reddish black hairs he left upon her linen shift. She twisted in her stool and stared at the bed where her clothes had been laid out. She grimaced. Then with another sigh, she walked over to the dress.

Careful not to snag the delicate material, she pulled the dress over her head and pushed her limbs through the armholes. She had to wriggle a bit to force the material to slide over her slightly damp underclothes. The gown was a pale sea green with green and black embroidered designs upon the numerous seams and along the hem. She pulled her hair out from the neckline and allowed it to drape down the back of the dress while she affixed the girdle over her hips. Then she placed the headpiece on her brow, letting the jeweled amulet drape at the center of her forehead. The stone was emerald, and it brought a green glow to her changing eyes.

As she opened her door, the three wolves leaped up and raced after her, anxious for the dinner that awaited them below. Matalia walked slowly, making the canines circle and return for her, one of them whining slightly as he nudged her forward.

"I am not nearly so eager for the supper table as you, my friend," she whispered as they began to descend the curved stone steps. "But the sooner it is done, the sooner I can return to my project at the cottage." She smiled in the dim light.

"I pray that your smile is for me," Duncan McDougal said as he stepped forward from his position against the wall. The low growls from Matalia's wolves kept him from approaching any closer.

" 'Tis most certainly not, Duncan! Why are you here?"

"To pay court to you, my dear."

"Bah! I have made myself more than clear. Your presence only confuses my mother into thinking there is a chance of our union."

"Is there not?"

"I thought that the slop I poured in your lap made you quite aware of my feelings the last time you visited!" Matalia exclaimed.

"So it did, darling, spoiled Matalia. It most certainly did. Peace, please. I come on business with your father and use you only as an excuse." Matalia looked at him warily. "Come. Let me take your arm and let us dine as friends."

Matalia looked him up and down, assessing the truth of his statement. Duncan was a handsome young man, clever and strong, from a good family. Matalia understood that he was considered an excellent matrimonial prospect, which was the only reason she had turned her back on his friendship in the past year. Duncan himself had been amused by her sudden coolness after years of comfortable companionship and was well aware of her reasons.

"Very well," she finally demurred. "I will sup with you." Duncan chuckled and approached her only after she waved her hand toward her wolves to cease their protective stance.

They descended the stairs together, entering the hall as the food was being served. Several other guests already sat around the table. Ronin McTaver glanced up at her tardy appearance with a hint of disapproval. Saying nothing, however, he motioned for her to sit at his right and for Duncan to sit on his left. His wife and beloved, Kalial, sat at the other end of the table, watching Matalia's behavior with a shake of her head.

"The power of the Highlands may well shift in the near future," Duncan was saying.

"So I hear. Have you no word on the succession?" Laird McTaver asked.

"Nay. I have only some rumors."

"Then we must pay heed to rumors, for 'tis better than naught."

"I hear that one of the brothers has made his claim," Duncan answered.

"And the other? Is he still missing?"

"Aye. Brogan O'Bannon has not been heard of in years. Many think that he is dead."

"Then there will be no struggle for the title," McTaver replied, slightly surprised.

"The Earl is withholding his decision until the end of the year, waiting to see if Brogan returns."

"This entire mess is foolish," McTaver grumbled. "The Earl may have been a great warrior on the battlefield and a brilliant strategist, but he is unwise in his family affairs. I have never met a more miserable man."

"Miserable perhaps, but powerful nonetheless. The son who succeeds him will control much of Scotland."

Ronin nodded. "But what else have you to say? I know, despite what my wife desires, that you did not come all this way merely to partake of my daughter's hospitality."

Matalia glanced up, glaring at the two men and tossing her hair back from her shoulders. She reached for her wine goblet and sipped, bored with their conversation.

Duncan winked at her. "I would cross a thousand oceans just for your daughter's smile."

McTaver chuckled. "Well, since that expression has not lately graced her countenance, I advise you to purchase a hardy vessel!"

"Father!" Matalia interjected.

The two men laughed at her disgruntled face and then proceeded with their discussion. "I do have one other piece of information that may be important. I heard that the middle daughter of Gavin Soothebury is about to be married, but the engagement is to be kept secret."

"Who would ask for her?" questioned McTaver, his full attention caught.

"She is broad hipped, mild mannered, from good stock, unassuming to the eye. . . ."

"God's breath! The way you talk of marriage. 'Tis like going to the market!" exclaimed Matalia. "And you wonder why I will have naught to do with the arrangement?"

"Matalia, do not curse in front of guests," warned her father. Matalia rolled her eyes and stuck out her tongue, eliciting a sharp reprimand from the other end of the table.

Duncan leaned forward. "I'll not wish you on any man, my friend, and should you get shackled, I will pray for your poor husband's survival." Leaning back, Duncan grinned as Matalia flushed pink with embarrassment.

"My appetite has fled," she murmured, rising.

"You will finish your trencher," commanded the Laird, "and stay seated until your mother rises."

Sinking back into her seat, Matalia cast her eyes down and pouted.

"I apologize for teasing you, Matalia," Duncan said. "Forgive me, and please stay." As Matalia settled her expression, he continued. "I know that you will find the right match someday, but 'twill be a merry chase. We meant only that the Soothebury girl is completely your opposite. Docile and biddable, she desires marriage and longs for children, but she is unlikely to get many offers. Can you say the same for yourself?"

"Heavens no!"

"Soothebury's girl needs a quiet, mild-mannered husband, whereas you need a strong, uncompromising one," Duncan concluded.

"I do not need any kind of husband," Matalia responded angrily as her father rubbed his forehead in frustration for the third time that day. She looked back at her food, but her appetite had indeed left her, and rebelliousness welled inside her heart. She thought of the man in the cottage and sniffed. *If they only knew,* she thought to herself, *they would never speak about marriage to me again!*

She picked at her food, glancing up periodically, wishing that her mother would finish quickly and release her from the prison of good manners. At last, Kalial rose and the other ladies began to disburse. At a short nod from her father, Matalia left the table, and the men continued to discuss the succession of the powerful O'Bannon Highland earl.

Matalia scampered gracefully up the stairs, then sneaked down the servant passageway to where Colleen was waiting.

"What took you so long?" Colleen demanded. "I was certain you had lost your courage!"

"Of course not," Matalia said haughtily. " 'Tis just that my mother thought Duncan McDougal worthy of seven dishes! I would that he had thrown up after the third."

Colleen laughed. "Come then, we must get moving.

What are you wearing, m'lady? You canna wear that in the marsh."

"I do not have time to change. Let us depart before someone sees us in the passageway." Colleen shook her head but obediently followed her out to the one-person bridge that spanned the moat. The bridge had been built to protect the castle as well as provide ease for the servants. It allowed only one person abreast and could not support the weight of a horse. As such, it permitted the servants to come and go without lowering the drawbridge after dark, but could not be utilized by an invading army. Laird McTaver was a master tactician regarding armaments and defense, ever since his family had been murdered in his own castle many years ago, before Matalia was born and before he had met and married Kalial. Since then, he had implemented many protective measures.

Matalia and Colleen were interested in using the bridge to escape the castle. Throwing a woolen coat over Matalia's silken dress, Colleen shuffled across the bridge and then motioned for Matalia to follow. As one of the wolves started across after her, Matalia stopped him with a low command, knowing that the beasts' presence would alert the sentries to her departure.

Holding hands, the girls walked down the road toward the village until they rounded a curve; then they struck out into the woods toward the hunter's cottage. Matalia felt her fingers tremble slightly. She giggled nervously and Colleen looked back, shushing her.

This is the night, Matalia thought, *the night I will learn what it feels to be with a man!*

Chapter 4

At last they reached the cottage. The big Irish wolf-hound lay alert but calm on the porch. Matalia rubbed his cheek. "You are a good beast, though I have never seen your like before. You watch over your master well."

Within the cottage, Brogan was past anger and now simply seethed with the desire for vengeance. The hours in the dark had given him time to plan, and so he had developed and studied many ideas, rejecting some and accepting others, thinking of ways to take advantage of any opportunity. He fixated upon the door, hearing the swish of skirts approaching and the low, husky murmur of Matalia talking to his wolf-hound as he forced his muscles to relax into a semblance of mellow welcome.

When Matalia carefully opened the door, she peeked in and saw the handsome Brogan sprawled with seeming nonchalance upon the bed, his gray eyes twinkling and the corner of his mouth turned up in a small, wry smile. Colleen pushed next to her and looked over at Brogan as well. She shook her head in suspicion.

"Lady Matalia, I still think this is the wrong way to do it."

Brogan glared at her, his relaxed face swiftly changing into fierce fury. " 'Tis not your choice then, is it?

What is done is done, and releasing me now will change naught. The fair maiden ought to at least get what she captured me for."

Colleen continued to shake her head, but Matalia pushed the door wider and stepped inside. She was uncharacteristically silent, and both Brogan and Colleen looked at her with interest.

"Think you to change your mind, m'lady?" questioned Colleen hopefully.

Matalia took off her peasant cloak and carefully placed it across the back of a chair. Brogan noticed immediately that her hands were shaking and her face was pale. The soft sea-green silk of her dress highlighted her turquoise eyes, making them seem huge in her white face.

"No," she finally whispered, "I'll not change my mind." Then, her voice getting stronger, she gestured to Brogan. "But you will have to help me . . . organize this."

Brogan began shaking his head immediately. "I will not, not with her here."

With a flash of returning spunk, Matalia retorted, "You have no choice! You are bound upon the bed and can only do as I demand." She tilted her head at a haughty angle, but ruined the effect by nibbling her lower lip with nervousness.

Softly, with a thread of masculine supremacy, Brogan answered her. "Believe me, fair maiden, you will need my compliance. I have had time to think, and I have decided to assist you in your pursuit of knowledge. But it is a process for two, and she"—he jerked his head toward the scowling Colleen—"would only distract us."

Matalia turned and looked at her friend. She raised her hands in question.

"Well," conceded Colleen, " 'Tis true that I might inhibit the activities. But you must promise to be safe. I do not trust this one. Not one bit. I ask once more, will you not let me find you a farmer's son instead?"

Matalia laughed quietly. "And what do you think I have found?"

"He is no farmer, that I know," answered her friend.

"What are you?" questioned Matalia, looking back at Brogan.

Forcing an easy smile, Brogan replied smoothly. "A traveler. No more, no less."

Matalia shrugged and turned back to Colleen. "It does not matter. He is who I have, and I will do what I intend. After tonight, there will be no more talk of marrying me to whomever they think might suit."

"Ach, 'tis not as if your parents would force you into a marriage you have no desire for."

"They persist in discussing it. I am tired of the conversation and I seek to end it forever. Besides, we have already talked about this. I lack carnal knowledge and thus cannot debate whether I want marriage or no. This way I can tell them that I am not missing anything by avoiding marriage."

"Perhaps you will come to a different conclusion," murmured Brogan. "But all this talk delays your experiment. Send your friend away . . . stoke the fire . . . undress and come to me."

Matalia froze at the commands, her fists clenching. She debated, wanting to do as he demanded but not wanting to follow orders. She sauntered over to his bedside and stared down at his bound form. She then deliberately checked his bonds. She saw the telltale flicker of tension in his cheek, even though he tried to act unaffected by her blatant reminder of who was in charge.

Brogan felt his stomach knot at her look, and the boiling anger he was masking almost erupted. With supreme self-control he met her eyes and shook his ties. "Tight enough for you?" he challenged softly.

Matalia raised an eyebrow but turned away without answering. She walked up to Colleen and whispered to her, "Perhaps it would be easier on me if you were not around to see everything. I am a bit nervous, but he is well and truly trussed and cannot do anything I do not wish him to do."

Colleen peered over at the bed, and glared at Brogan, who promptly glared back. With a huff, Colleen moved toward the door. "Very well, but be careful. And remember, men need encouragement to perform correctly. You cannot just order him about."

Matalia grinned. "Do not worry so. Once assured of his compliance, I will take my dagger off and place it on the mantel so as not to intimidate him."

Brogan felt his heart race at the information that a blade was nearby. His gaze raced swiftly over her clothed form, searching for a bulge that would indicate where she kept the weapon. Seeing nothing but silken skirts, he closed his eyes and breathed deeply, bidding himself to remain patient. He opened his eyes again as he heard the door close after Colleen. Suddenly alone with Matalia, knowing her mission, Brogan felt an unexpected surge of excitement. Whether it was for the possibility of escape, or for the knowledge that she was soon to mount him, he could not decide.

Matalia moved over to the fire and placed two logs upon it, crossing them slightly to allow for the free flow of air. She stared at it for a moment, making sure the flames welcomed the new food. Finally, knowing she could delay no longer, she turned and stood at the foot of the bed. She was breathing rapidly, and she tried to act calm, but failed completely. Her eyes were dark with fear and nervousness, and her body shivered.

Brogan silently watched emotions flit over her face. The emerald amulet dangling upon her forehead wavered and drew his gaze from her face to her hair. It swung loose behind her back as virgins wore it, and it appeared to have recently been washed, for the heavy curls looked soft and shiny. The black embroidery on her dress was dull compared to the sheen of her locks in the fire's glow.

Matalia let her gaze drift over Brogan's form, alternately fascinated and frightened by the shape and size of him. She bit her lip again, wondering if Colleen had been right after all, and she should abandon her plan. Involuntarily, she took a step backward and raised a fist to her mouth. She nibbled gently on her thumbnail until Brogan finally broke the silence.

"Let me not think you have suddenly become frightened, little faerie." His gray eyes looked like dark smoke, and Matalia quivered. She said nothing in reply, but took a breath and reached behind her to undo the pounded girdle from her hips. The tinkling of the chain sounded loud, accented only by the crackling of the fire.

Matalia felt her feelings skip and jump. She wanted to do this, she did, but now that the moment was at hand she was not sure how to proceed. Last night, she had been unable to do much more than climb around atop him. She looked up through her lashes and wondered whether he would help her this time. She had no idea how sensual she appeared, her blue-green eyes slanting over toward him through a screen of black lashes and her rounded hips unencumbered by a metallic belt. She began plucking at her ties, loosing them with trembling fingers.

Brogan was faintly surprised by her evident nervousness. He had expected her to act as brash as her plan, to disrobe in moments and mount him immediately. He was ready for her assault, not this slow, virginal hesitation. He glared up at the ceiling, pushing thoughts of pleasure from his mind, and attempted to focus on his revenge. He would do this thing for her, but not in a way she expected. There would be no surrender on his part. He would control her, whether she knew it or not. He would make her cry with wanting, humble her with the force of her capitulation to his power.

With that reminder, Brogan looked back at Matalia. She was staring at him, at a loss. Her ties were loose and her silken dress hung like a robe around her body.

"I will need to undress completely," she stated, more to herself than to him, and Brogan nodded briefly in response. He clenched his teeth, bracing himself for the revelation of her exquisite body once again. *Control*, he told himself. *Control*.

Matalia looked down at the floor, then up again in determination. "Yes," she said aloud, making Brogan wonder what question she answered, for the wealth of emotion in the simple word was clearly not in response to whether or not to remove her dress.

She shrugged and twisted, trying to slide out of the silk, but her curves hindered her progress. Brogan felt his lids grow heavy with desire, but he fought the feeling, trying to remain detached. As her body finally escaped the clinging seafoam, Brogan's cock pulsed, anxious to touch the mermaid revealed in the flickering flames. His arm muscles twitched, and he involuntarily tried to reach for her before finding himself caught by the rope bindings. A flash of renewed anger swept his mind, but his body ignored him, eager for Matalia to find the courage to approach the bed.

Matalia drew another deep breath. She felt slightly awkward standing at the foot of the bed, naked but for her light chemise. She climbed up on the bed between Brogan's spread legs and pulled the chemise out from under her knees so that it formed a pool of linen around her waist and thighs. She felt a wave of exhilaration race through her and licked her lips, making them moist. She looked up at Brogan once again, shocked to find his expression shuttered and fierce.

"I would like to get atop it," Matalia murmured hesitantly, worried that her approach would fail once again.

With effort, Brogan looked over her form, noting finally where a ripple in the fabric indicated a strapped dagger. "I am at your disposal, fair maiden, but grant me one request."

Matalia's eyes narrowed and she leaned back. "I'll not set you free," she said crossly, but Brogan simply stared up at her, then dropped his eyes to her clothed breasts.

"I would have the pleasure of seeing you . . . completely." Matalia twitched in surprise, then glanced around the room as if looking for observers.

"There is none to see you but me, a wandering traveler whom you will never meet again. Why not allow me this small favor?" Brogan's voice was deep and powerful, and Matalia found herself lifting her shift almost immediately. She felt the caress of Brogan's gaze over her bare skin as he devoured her form, inch by inch, while she pulled the cloth over her hips, up her waist, and over her breasts with a firm tug. Even as the linen still covered her head, she felt Brogan's gaze sweep her skin, causing it to flush with heat.

Finally, Matalia was free of the cloth, and she dropped it to the floor next to the bed. She remained sitting on her knees, staring at the tied Brogan as if asking him for the next instruction. When none was forthcoming, she leaned forward and lay full length upon him. Both of them gasped at the unexpected sensation of flesh against flesh, Matalia because she had never felt a man's muscled length before, and Brogan because he had felt all too many women before, but knew that her skin was more like satin than any he could remember.

Matalia breathed deeply through her nose, inhaling the scent of his maleness, and nuzzled his neck. She brushed her lips against his skin, then shifted to angle them over his mouth.

With a jerk, Brogan bucked her off, toppling her so that she landed flush against his side. "No," he growled at her, glaring into her surprised turquoise eyes.

"No what?" she questioned as she leaned up on her elbow to look down at him.

"Do not use your mouth upon mine."

Matalia looked at him with confusion. "But should we not kiss first?"

"No," repeated Brogan with a shudder. Matalia looked at him bemusedly, then licked her lips and brought her fingers to her mouth, rubbing them.

"I thought—"

"I said no," Brogan repeated, this time softer, "but if you move over here, I would taste a bit of you." He dropped his gaze from her moist mouth to her breasts pressed against him. When Matalia did not respond, he dropped his voice lower and urged her to sit up and lean over him.

Relenting, Matalia shifted, straddled his chest and leaned down, placing her nipple near his mouth. He flicked his tongue out, brushing the sensitive peak, feeling an ache in his groin at the way Matalia gasped and quivered at the simple touch. He did it again, this time capturing the nipple between his tongue and upper teeth, and sucked briefly before she jerked away. Matalia stared down at him, her face flushed. Her nipples were both so hard they hurt, and she rubbed them in confusion.

Brogan watched her motions, feeling his cock begin to strain upwards. He thought briefly of trying to prevent his arousal, then instantly argued against himself. Such a fight would be useless, and it would go against his plan. Instead, he let his blood rush from his heart, down to his groin and center there, swelling his genitals to three times their quiescent size. His gray eyes darkened further and, despite his hands being bound over his head, he exuded strength and male power that swept over Matalia, making her light-headed.

"Come here," he commanded in a low tone, his

voice rippling with sexual intensity. Matalia felt the force in his voice, and she obediently leaned over him once more. Again he captured her nipple and sucked on it with a short, strong pull, then rasped it with his teeth before laving it with a supple tongue. Matalia let out a small sound, not quite a gasp and not quite a moan, and bowed her head in submission. The action made her abundant hair drip from her shoulders to spill over his chest, and Brogan paused to fully appreciate the new sensation. He lifted his chest slightly, and her hair slid and whispered over his skin, making him want to clutch it in his hands and rub himself fiercely with its softness.

"Straddle my hips lower," he said harshly.

Matalia sat up and shifted backward, pushing the moons of her bottom against his thrusting shaft. She twisted around and looked down at it, but had to tilt her pelvis forward to better view his manhood behind her. The action pressed her clitoris against Brogan's hard stomach and she cried out in shock at the sensation. Brogan, too, groaned aloud, feeling the moisture of her entrance as she experimentally rocked again.

"Good God, what have I done to deserve this?" he groaned, unsure if it was a blessing or a curse to be forced into sexual activity with Lady Matalia. He pulled at his bonds, wanting more than ever to loosen his hands so he could push her deep into the mattress and fuck her, but the rope continued to hold and Matalia wriggled and rocked upon him, her brilliant eyes temporarily closed as she reveled in the new sensations.

"Go lower," he growled again, interrupting her concentration, so she shifted down farther.

She gazed at him with unfocused eyes, waiting for his command. She felt as if she were drifting free, that the feelings were almost unreal, while the press of his cock against her back was both insistent and demanding.

"What now?" she whispered.

"Lift up and over it," he replied, "and spread your lips so I can enter you." Matalia tilted her head. She lifted one leg up and placed it against his hip, then did the same with the other, but his cock leaped and slid in front of her instead of inside her. Brogan groaned, more than frustrated. Tears sprang into Matalia's eyes, and she made to move off when Brogan noted her intention.

"You had best not dare! Hold it in your hand and use the other hand to open yourself. Believe me, if you leave me now, you will never know the pleasure you are seeking." His snarled warning made Matalia pause, and she lifted frightened eyes to his. He was surprised to see her desperation, so he softened his tone and nudged her with his hips. "Come on, sweetling, try again. I need you now. Do not leave me again."

Matalia took a trembling breath. God, how she wanted this! She looked at Brogan's gray eyes and nodded. She braced her hands against his chest, curling her fingers into his muscles, feeling her nails scrape through his hair. Brogan looked back at her and smiled his half smile.

"You are not a quitter, Lady Matalia. Come on. Try again. I'll guide you."

Matalia nodded and slowly ran her hands down his ribs, feeling his muscles twitch and jump under her caress. She dropped her fingers even lower and finally wrapped them around the base of his manhood, encircling its thick width with her fingertips. They could not meet and Matalia's eyes widened.

"Perhaps it cannot . . ."

"It can," he answered firmly. "Now rub it around slowly, keeping your hips steady. . . . There, that's right." A deep groan slipped out of his throat as he felt the head of his penis slither back and forth over her opening.

Matalia rubbed it as he had instructed, finding her clitoris again and rubbing his head over her nubbin. Brogan sucked in a breath at the incredible pleasure she elicited. His sensitive tip rolled over her hard clit, then slipped into warm wetness, and then was pulled back over the nub. He felt a surge sweep his groin, but he battled it back, making his body obey.

Matalia rubbed faster, oblivious to Brogan's struggle, and started to pant. A swirl of sensations raced through her body, showering sparks in her blood that made her tingle. Her mouth opened and she began to slump forward, her climax fast approaching.

Brogan watched her, mesmerized by her slack, pleasure-filled face. Her thick lashes flickered and danced over her cheeks, and her nipples softened as all of her attention became focused on her nether region. A small squirt of come escaped his cock, moistening her thighs, and Matalia paused for a moment to feel the substance, her eyes widening.

"God help me," he murmured. "Come here. Crawl up here." Matalia did as he instructed, her moistened thighs sliding over his sweaty skin, her clitoris throbbing, her insides clenching, wanting something more. "Higher . . ." he whispered, urging her to climb over his chest. "Now, turn around. . . ." he commanded in an urgent voice. Matalia trembled at the idea of exposing herself to him so intimately, but feeling safe, she twisted about and came face-to-face with his throbbing, glistening rod.

She stared at it, fascinated by the veins and ripples, and reached a hand out to stroke it. She felt Brogan nip her thigh, and thinking he was encouraging her, she wrapped her fingers around his cock again and rubbed it. She felt his teeth once again on her soft inner skin, causing the tingling in her body to spread. She felt him breathe into her nether curls, and she began to turn but was halted by his swift denial. Then the sensation was gone, and she could focus once more upon the manly part in front of her. She drew her nails lightly down the length of it, seeing another pearl of come bead the tip. She felt his body move and shift under her, so she writhed against him, enjoying the feel of their paired, sweaty bodies.

Then, suddenly, she was shoved to the side, her body dumped upon the bedsheet, her hair tangling around her face. With a cry of surprise, she felt Brogan's hands wrap around her waist and fling her around until she was prone upon her back with his huge form towering over hers. He held her knife in his hand, and the cut ends of his bonds swung freely. She tried to lift her hands to shove at him, but the weight of her desire made her slow and languid. Instead of pushing against his shoulder, she lightly gripped it, kneading the slippery muscles like a kitten.

Brogan roughly spread her legs and settled his hips between hers. "Now," he grumbled, "*this* is how it works!" He lifted his hips and then plunged down, hard, sinking fully into her in one, thick, pulsing stroke.

Chapter 5

Matalia screamed, both from abrupt pain and sudden shock, her erotic haze swiftly departing in the face of his primitive lust. She felt his immense form stretching and tearing her and she began to struggle in earnest. But Brogan ignored her flailing, and instead, gripped her wrists and held them down.

"There is no way in hell I am not going to get every drop of your virginity. You asked for this, and by God, I will give it to you!" He reared up and pulled out of her, dragging his cock out of her warmth until the tip almost left her, then he plunged it back in, hitting into her so hard her breasts bounced and she was shoved an inch closer to the headboard. Momentarily distracted, Brogan bent his head again to her nipples, biting them and sucking them until the tips puckered in glistening splendor.

"Fuck, you are gorgeous," he rumbled, sliding into his Scottish burr as he buried his head in the valley between her breasts, "and ya deserve to be fucked until ya canna move for a month!"

Shock sizzled through Matalia at his words, and she found her hands gripping his, their fingers intertwined as he pulled out and slammed inside her again. This time the pain was lessened, as she felt an unfamiliar warmth suddenly flood her insides, making his rough passage smooth and slick.

She gasped, flicking her eyes over his hard visage as he pounded her again, shoving her another inch forward such that he had to push after her. Irritated at her movement, even though he was the one who caused it, he released one hand and wrapped it around her waist, encircling her and holding her tight against him. Using just his lower body, he began pumping her, hard and fast, not caring where she was in pleasure. He simply wanted to reach the pinnacle that beckoned. He pumped and pounded, his thick cock sliding easily in and out of her heat while Matalia squirmed and wriggled, her body tensing and flexing with sensations.

She was no longer fighting, although Brogan held her as if she were. She was trying to move with him, trying desperately to join him in his journey to a place she did not know existed. She felt the stretch of his cock inside her, hurting just a bit with each stroke, yet feeling incredible. She wrapped her legs around him, then gasped because he could enter that much deeper. An unearthly moan of pleasure escaped her throat, and she tightened her legs, reveling in the feelings. It was not pain . . . it was fulfillment, surrender, submission. "This once," she murmured, not knowing she said it aloud, not hearing his reply.

Suddenly, swiftly, unexpectedly, the sensation came to her. The flood overwhelmed her, the darkness enveloped her, and she was soaring into the sky. She still felt him pounding, but her body was detached from her soul and she felt as if she were looking down upon their entwined bodies, watching their naked limbs crawl over each other in uninhibited glory. She spun and floated, while lightning tendrils shot out of her center and snaked through her mind and then out to her fingertips. She drifted farther; then she heard a shout of triumph and felt him swell and contract within her. The sensation grounded her instantly, and she slammed back into her body in time to feel him ejaculating into her, his body jerking with spasm after spasm, his fingers gripping hers so tightly she could no longer feel them, his body so heavy as it collapsed upon her she could barely breathe.

Then he rocked his head back and took a deep breath, pressing only his hips into hers, driving her so deep into the mattress she was sure she would fall through. He blinked twice, let out a primal groan, and then swung his gaze back to her.

Gray and turquoise met in a clash like a stormy sky over a seething ocean. Matalia forgot about his heavy weight, and Brogan felt his cock rush full of blood again. "Damn!" he growled, and he rode her again, this time slow and steady, staring into her brilliant eyes until hers closed in a ripple of tiny climaxes, and he poured another shot into her dampness.

Afterwards they lay, side by side, both exhausted. Brogan opened his mouth and closed it over her pink nipple, sucking it slowly, softly, while tangling his hands in her wealth of hair. Matalia closed her eyes at the sensation, her body completely sated, her soul open and free.

Neither of them heard the sound of approaching feet, nor did either of them hear the warning growl of the wolfhound. They were unaware of the search for Matalia going on outside their cottage. Instead, they lay in a close embrace, forgetting the circumstances of their meeting and simply reveling in the lassitude they felt after such exquisite ecstasy. They were found just like that, her leg over his waist, his mouth around her nipple, when the troop of McTaver warriors, Merkle the wise man, Duncan McDougal, and Ronin McTaver flung open the cottage door.

Ronin stood in shock, his entire frame frozen in horror. He gazed with complete incomprehension at his daughter entwined in the arms of a stranger. Lifting his broadsword, he held it out in front of him, as if the blade could slice through the image of his naked daughter and return her to her bedroom, clothed and untouched. His roar of rage ripped through the tiny room, finally shocking the two inhabitants into frantic action.

Brogan leaped up, grabbing the dagger he had taken from Matalia's leg in his right hand and shoving her naked body off the bed and onto the floor away from the warriors. Matalia yelped in surprise, but she scrambled to her feet almost immediately, forgetting her state of undress until she saw the eyes of her father's men start to rove over her flesh. Gasping in dismay, she sank back down, using the bed as a shield while she searched frantically for her clothing.

Brogan, on the other hand, cared naught for his naked state, and he quickly reached for a chair and gripped it, feet outward, as a shield against the swords in front of him. He, too, was a warrior, and he had no intention of dying, despite the overwhelming odds against him. The silence in the room was deafening. Brogan stood in a fighting stance, his dagger in one hand and the chair in the other, while Ronin McTaver and his men stood in the doorway, their broadswords raised. No one moved forward. They eyed each other, all unsure how to proceed, until Duncan's voice echoed in the chamber.

"I take it this means that we will not be wed?" he questioned dryly. Brogan noted the McDougal plaid and a new wave of unease swept over him.

" 'Tis not what you think," he started, only to be stopped by the snarl on Laird McTaver's lips.

"Do you know who that lass is?" he thundered.

Brogan O'Bannon searched his memory, quickly sorting the information he had gathered and finally settling upon the inescapable fact that the girl who had captured and subsequently seduced him must be this man's daughter. Furthermore, it appeared she had been engaged to The McDougal. At a loss to say anything else, he blurted out the only thing that he knew was true. "She was willing, m'Laird. There was no force. Not only willing, but she requested the pleasure."

Merkle walked forward, staring at Brogan intently. He turned to Ronin, nodding his head. McTaver's face darkened as he noted the ropes around the bedposts and the bloodstains upon the coverlet.

Brogan, following his gaze, seethed. Never would he admit to being tied down. Let the older man think what he would, thought Brogan, but he would be damned if he would tell of his forced sexual performance!

Matalia shivered in the corner, pulling her silken dress over her head without the benefit of underclothes since they were on the other side of the bed, near her father. She tied the strings loosely, not realizing that her breasts, still swollen with lovemaking, filled the silk in a tempting array.

She took a breath and stepped forward. " 'Tis true, Father. This man is nothing. He did no harm to me."

"Nothing!" thundered McTaver as all male eyes swung toward her. "Nothing! He despoiled you and you say he is nothing!"

Matalia cringed at her father's wrath. This was definitely not what she had expected as a reaction to her exploration. Trying to restore calm, she implored her father, "Can you not see that I was only taking Mother's advice? She said I did not understand the benefits of marriage, so I undertook an experiment to see what she was talking about."

McTaver opened his mouth in stunned amazement, then shut it with finality. He lowered his sword and jerked his head at his clansmen, who lowered theirs as well. Matalia was surprised as well as relieved.

"Thank heavens you seem to understand, Father.

You made me apprehensive for a moment," she said, a tremor in her voice. "This traveler is on his way to marry his bride, and I have learned what I needed to know. I understand what Mother is talking about now."

"Your mother never meant for this to happen. You have deliberately misinterpreted her concern for your future. This . . . this is terrible, Matalia."

Silence filled the cottage once again, and Matalia looked around nervously. Brogan had not dropped his stance, and he was eyeing both Duncan McDougal and Ronin McTaver with wary distrust.

"You look very familiar," mentioned Duncan with a casual shrug. "In fact, you look much like the old Earl of Kirkcaldy."

Brogan narrowed his eyes, the gray color darkening with rage.

Duncan stepped back and sheathed his sword. "It would seem that I was mistaken about what kind of husband the Soothebury girl would attract. I believe we have solved two mysteries, Laird McTaver."

Ronin McTaver looked Brogan over with a critical eye. The smell of sex still permeated the room, not just the smell of a man's release, but that of a woman's as well. He glanced at his daughter's face and saw the glow of satisfaction suffusing her cheeks even though her eyes appeared troubled. He looked over at Merkle and then back to Brogan.

Sensing the father's thoughts, Brogan's anger flared, his muscles twitching and pulsing in barely contained rage.

Abruptly, Ronin McTaver called for one of the men to fetch his wife. "Get dressed," he told Brogan roughly, and then to Matalia, "and fix your hair before your mother arrives. I will let you collect yourselves." Then he waved the men outside, followed them, and shut the door.

Brogan lowered the chair and looked over at Matalia. "How dare you do this to me!" he whispered at her furiously.

"Do what?" she whispered back, confused. "You are not in trouble. I am the one who will have to bear my mother's wrath. You will be let free, just as you wished."

"Are you daft? Do you not see what they intend?" he replied, incredulous.

"Intend?" Matalia repeated with a shake of her head.

"God's blood! You are the worst thing to happen to my life, and believe me, that is saying much!" He strode over to the fireplace where his clothes had been neatly folded and yanked them on. "The only thing I demand of you is to say nothing of how we came to this impasse. I will do what I must, but never, *never* tell anyone how you tied me to the bed."

"Why?" Matalia questioned.

"Why? God's breath!" he swore again. "Just promise me that, m'lady, and I will give you whatever freedom you desire."

Matalia looked at him with confusion, but was halted from questioning him by a hard knock upon the cottage door. Brogan took a deep breath and then walked forward and opened the portal. Kalial McTaver stood there, her golden eyes troubled.

"Daughter?" she whispered and swept into the room with Merkle at her side. "Are you hurt? Are you injured?" Kalial's eyes flicked over Brogan O'Bannon and then returned to her daughter. When there was no reply, she shook her head and sat in a chair in front of the fire as Merkle guarded the door. Brogan bowed to her and moved to the mantel. Matalia glared at all of them and huffed.

Finally, Kalial asked her most pressing question. "Why, Matalia? Why this man?"

Matalia looked at her mother in rebellious disobedience. "I am tired of being pressured," she said spitefully. "I want to make my own rules and not be dictated to by you and Father! I want to do what I want, when I want!"

Kalial looked up at her with sad eyes. "You think this will get you freedom?" she asked softly.

"I do not need to marry now," countered Matalia. "There is no argument you can give me about what I am missing and how it will give me grounding." Matalia looked at her mother triumphantly.

"Oh, daughter. I did not mean only the physical side of marriage, but the emotional peace it grants. I hope you have chosen wisely. But fate is fate, is it not, Merkle?" she said, glancing at the forest man. "Matalia, you have sealed yours. Instead of avoiding marriage, you have now assured it."

"You can not frighten me, Mother. There is no way you would marry me to a simple traveler. This man is unknown. A drifter. You would not force me to marry against my will, and you could not have me marry a nobody."

Brogan looked away, his heart pounding. Fifteen years! Fifteen years of gathering wealth and renown. Fifteen years of planning the perfect family, the perfect wife. Fifteen years of struggle and strife, almost over, almost complete. Only days away from his docile bride awaiting him in Soothebury. Days away from completing the tasks set to him by his father.

His angry gaze clashed with Kalial's calm golden one, then turned to view the innocence in Matalia's brilliant orbs. He noticed with detachment that Matalia's turquoise eyes were an unusual mixture of Ronin McTaver's striking blue and Kalial's gold, dusted with a sprinkling of green. He ran his fingers through his hair, weighing his options, analyzing the possibilities and finally settling upon the only answer.

The answer everyone but Matalia had already figured out.

"But, darling," purred Kalial, "this man is no traveler. He is the son of the great Earl of Kirkcaldy, and you *will* marry him, for by joining your body with his, you have made your decision."

Chapter 6

Matalia was hoarse from screaming. Her voice sounded scratchy, and she had to strain even to whisper. Her face was pale with bright red splotches on her cheeks and her lips were tinted blue from the bruising she had given them by biting on them in her frustration at her predicament.

Colleen was sitting quietly in the corner, her face drawn and sorrowful. The room itself was in shambles, for long ago Matalia had flung every movable object from end to end of the chamber while kicking and shoving the more immovable objects. She still wore the sea-green silk dress, but the fabric was twisted and wrinkled from the gnashing of her hands upon the delicate threads. Even the three wolves lay silently, their paws over their noses.

Matalia finally flung herself onto the bed and wept. Colleen stared at her miserably. There was nothing more she could say. The Laird and Lady McTaver had commanded a marriage, and none in Scotland would either disagree or disobey the dictate. None but Matalia had even dared voice an objection. Brogan O'Bannon, for all his snarled disgust, had conceded and accepted the resolution. He would marry Matalia McTaver, he had said, his voice dripping with scorn, but it would be on the condition that she bear him a child with due haste and travel immediately to his father's estate so that she may convalesce in his father's manse. He then stated that he would grant her a return to her familial lands after the birth of the child, and even if all had heard his muttered oath, it was generally considered a fair arrangement.

Except for Matalia. For all her planning, she was now about to be bound in matrimony to a virtual stranger, dragged from her home, and treated like a breeding mare. Matalia could not contain her devastation, her desolation. She had implored her mother to intervene, but been rebuffed gently and firmly. She had pleaded with Duncan to speak sense to her parents, but he had only shaken his head and shrugged. It was for the best, he had told her, his mouth grim. She had even turned to Merkle.

"You of all people should not bow to these rules!" she shouted at him.

Merkle shook his head sadly. "You are part of both the wild and the civilized worlds. You have the spirit of your magical ancestors but the soul of modern times. You are one of the few who has the power to alter your path based upon your decisions. Remember that, Matalia. You do have control over your destiny, and your choices over the next year will determine your happiness."

"How can you say I have control when I am being forced into marriage? How could my mother make me marry against my will?"

"You chose him," he answered calmly. "Your mother has only acceded to your decision. She would have preferred someone else."

Matalia had shaken her head, disgusted. And thus she had fled to her room where she now lay sobbing upon her coverlet, exhausted and depressed.

Brogan, on the other hand, was working hard to turn the situation to his advantage. He had spent over a decade building his own fortune, and through that struggle he had learned to twist any situation to his favor. Inside he seethed. Matalia's childish game had nearly disrupted the tide of power in Scotland, yet his mind continued to function, to plan. He penned a note to Gavin Soothebury apologizing for the change of plans and included a substantial gift to soothe the anger the man was sure to experience at the loss of a husband for his homely daughter. In it he explained with gritted teeth that he had stopped at the McTaver castle for an eve, become instantly enamored of Matalia McTaver, and had opted to wed her immediately. Such was the story all had decided upon. Love at first sight. Brogan shuddered at the fallacy. The only redeeming part of the entire escapade, he thought, was that he now had the power to make the fair Matalia suffer dearly for her intrusion into his life!

In their master bedroom, Kalial questioned her husband. "Think you that we are doing the right thing? She is so upset. . . ."

"She should be upset. She was caught in the arms of a man not wed to her! She should feel the shame and bear the consequences."

"Oh really, Ronin," Kalial replied dryly. "As if men do not indulge their desires before wedlock! As if we did not, either!"

" 'Tis different," grumbled Ronin.

"How?"

"She is my daughter."

Kalial sat back and looked at her husband with glowing eyes. "Because she is your daughter, do you not want the best for her?"

Ronin turned away from the window and faced his wife. "I do think this is the best. You did not see them as I did, their bodies wrapped around each other. I saw a look of peace upon Matalia's face that I have not seen since she was twelve years old and she found her wolf pups. I think that this man is strong enough for her, which is why she was attracted to him."

"I doubt she will relent," replied Kalial. "She says she does not want marriage because she has found none to match you."

"Perhaps," answered Ronin with a sigh. "But time will tell. She is like any daughter, thinking that her father is the only good man. This is for the best. She needs to leave to learn what she really wants from her life. I believe that Brogan has the strength to do well with her. I give him my admiration. Only a man with a powerful character would come back to challenge Xanthier O'Bannon for the inheritance."

"Why does he need to fight for his title?"

"The Earl cast a curse upon his own family due to the alleged unfaithfulness of his Countess. Two people who had once been in love became bitter enemies, and the twin boys were caught in the middle. 'Tis a tragedy. No one knows much about Brogan, for he left Scotland at a young age, but Xanthier is well-known. He is a brave fighter, ofttimes vicious in his methods, but well respected. 'Tis said that he would do anything to win the ascendancy. He has reached the Earl's estate and has with him his own bride." Ronin turned toward Kalial. "You should be grateful that Matalia did not come across Xanthier. His single-minded intention to win Kirkcaldy would make him a very poor husband."

"Do you think Brogan will be any different?"

Brogan approached Matalia's door and braced himself. He took a deep breath and knocked loudly, expecting further screams. Instead, a subdued Colleen opened the door, and upon seeing who was at the portal, she ushered him inside and slipped out, closing the door behind her. Brogan took in the room's disarray. He finally located Matalia curled up on the bed, her tears drying upon her face, watching him warily.

He saw the womanly curves encased in rumpled silk and flashed briefly upon the memory of how soft her flesh had been. Despite his anger at the situation, he felt a stir in his groin at the thought of having her at his will. What an ironic change of fate. She had tried to control him to suit her wayward desires. Now he had complete control over every aspect of her life. She was going to be his wife, his property, his chattel. His nose flared as he involuntarily drank in her scent, which permeated her chamber.

Annoyed at his own reaction to her, he spoke much more harshly than he had intended. "Are you finished with your antics, then?" he snapped, dragging his eyes away from her, scanning the room for the source of the low growls. Locating the three wolves sulking in the shadows, he eyed them cautiously and placed his hand upon his sword.

"Aughhh!" Matalia replied, her voice so raw she could not articulate her words. She clambered up, not realizing that her skirt rode high on her thighs before it fell back down to her ankles as she stood up, defiance in every line of her body.

Brogan schooled his expression into one of boredom. "I will take that as assent. I have no more time to waste. I advise you to change now for travel, for we are to go downstairs to the hall and speak our vows. Then we leave immediately for Kirkcaldy."

"No," Matalia whispered, but the weight of her rebellion was fading and hopelessness was finding its way to her heart.

Taking pity upon her, Brogan stepped forward and placed a warm, powerful hand upon her shoulder. "Stop fighting, little faerie. Learn a lesson I learned long ago. In many matters, 'tis best to endure what you must and fight only for what you can win.

Today . . . today is not the day to fight. The forces of too many are against you. I made a promise to your parents and I will adhere to it, if you do your part. Just give me a child, act the part of wife for one year, and then I will return you to this home where you will truly have the freedom you seek. Think on it, Lady Matalia. You will be the wife of a powerful but absent man. No one, not even your father, will be able to dictate to you."

Matalia looked up at his handsome face, her cheeks flushing at his nearness. She turned her head away, not liking her body's response, but unable to forget that only hours ago she had lain beneath him, screaming in pleasure. She shivered as a flicker of feeling tingled between her thighs, and she abruptly pulled away from Brogan's comforting hand.

Narrowing his eyes in distrust, Brogan watched her move away toward her wolves, which rose immediately at her approach. She glanced over her shoulder, then turned toward him fully. "I have no choice?" she whispered through her strained vocal cords.

Brogan shook his head.

"I have never left this land," she murmured, her confusion evident. "I have been only in Castle Roseneath or Loch Nidean. . . ."

"You can only take what will fit upon your mount."

Matalia's eyes widened. " 'Tis not fair!" she replied fiercely, albeit hoarsely. "What about Colleen? You would not have made such a request of Lady Soothebury!"

"No," answered Brogan with no attempt to justify his response. "Have the rest of your things packed. Even now my caravan is heading to Kirkcaldy. I will send word for them to wait for your belongings before crossing the hills. However, you and I must travel much faster. You will have to do with the bare essentials."

"I need clothing, and brushes, and dishes, and sheets . . . Colleen . . ." Her voice trailed off at Brogan's leering grin.

"For what you must do as my wife, you need barely anything at all. Except perhaps the sheets." He ducked as Matalia flung a shoe at his head and then strode quickly to her side and gripped her around the waist, towering over her.

"Seek not to enrage me further," he growled with menace. "I have had enough of you! Get your things together and be downstairs in ten minutes or whether you're dressed or not, I will come get you and tie you over my saddle!"

Matalia was frozen, her body squeezed against his, her hair tangled in his hands so she could not even lower her head. She had no choice but to stare up at his face, noting the shadow of growth upon his jaw, seeing the bloom of a bruise upon his cheek. She lifted a hand to touch it curiously, but was instantly shoved away as Brogan released her in haste.

"I said no kissing," he hissed, and Matalia looked at him in surprise. Wisely, she decided to remain silent. Finally dropping her eyes against his angry glare, she watched his boots as he spun around and exited the room. "Remember, ten minutes."

Matalia descended the stairs dressed in a black velvet traveling habit. Her eyes were massive in her tiny face, and her full lower lip glistened slightly. Her midnight curls were drawn back into two braids on either side of her head, and intermixed within each braid were cords of gold. She wore black leather gloves and carried a riding crop. Her three wolves circled around her skirts, their heads ducking low as they scanned the great hall, searching for the source of their mistress's disquiet.

Brogan watched her descent, faintly surprised that

she had come down of her own accord. His mood was foul. He heartily disliked the sidelong glances cast his way by the family members who assumed he had unfairly seduced Matalia. His honor rankled at their belief that he had taken advantage of a maiden, so he glowered in silent challenge at any who dared to face him directly. Seeing Matalia sweep down the stairs in her unaffected beauty only infuriated him more.

Matalia's legs were trembling. She had no doubt that Brogan would do exactly as he threatened and drag her screaming down the steps if she did not come. She looked around, searching for him, and easily located his penetrating gaze in the crowd that included her parents, her siblings, and the men of Roseneath. *He never smiles,* she thought to herself as she observed his angry look. Forcing such an expression to her own face, she turned her lips up at the corners and took the last stairs with bold bravado. Her younger sisters raced up to her, talking rapidly and tugging on her gown.

"Is it true, Matalia?" Nathina whispered loudly. "Are you marrying that big man over there?"

"He is awfully scary!" cried Mackenzie. "Are you sure you want to go away with him?"

Matalia looked down, suddenly contrite. She smiled bravely. "Of course, Bobbins. He is a fine man. Am I not lucky to have such a handsome husband?"

Nathina and Mackenzie looked doubtfully over at Brogan. Kalial shooed them from the chamber, casting a grateful look at Matalia. Waving good-bye to her sisters, Matalia walked in a cloud of velvet up to the scowling Brogan and lightly gripped his elbow. She leaned into him, pressing her breasts suggestively against his arm, causing Ronin McTaver to rise from his seat in anger.

Kalial reached over and caught her husband's arm, keeping him from approaching the young pair, her eyes casting a warning. She looked over at her eldest daughter, frowning at her choice of black velvet as a wedding gown. Matalia, seeing the effect she had caused, rubbed against Brogan once more before stalking toward the door. She looked over her shoulder, fluttering her long lashes over her brilliant eyes, and smiled seductively at Brogan.

"I am ready," she murmured huskily, then ducked out the door and proceeded to the church.

The hall fell silent as her skirts swept outside. Ronin glowered at Brogan, who glared back. The other men in the hall shuffled uncomfortably, the image of Matalia's sexual look making several of them stir. The women, on the other hand, suddenly began whispering among themselves, the pitch of their gossipy voices high and strident.

Brogan cursed her under his breath. After fifteen years of planning, he was completely disgusted at how so many of his plans were crumbling around him. First his alliance with Soothebury was ruined. Now, any allegiance he might have garnered from the McTavers or the McDougals was shattered, despite the marriage tie they were about to make. Brogan ran a hand through his hair, and briefly closed his eyes in frustration. And it appeared that Matalia had changed tactics. Instead of fighting her family, she had decided to flaunt her union with him. With a wry grin, Brogan admitted to himself that she had more courage than many a man he had fought on the battlefield.

In sudden decision, Brogan turned abruptly and followed Matalia, not waiting to see if the others would follow. Outside, the dawn was striking the horizon, its tendrils of orange and pink snaking across the clouds in a riotous display. The air was heavy with gray twilight, and little birds chirped continuously. Ahead, Brogan saw the sway of Matalia's black-clad hips approaching the church. The shadows of her wolves rippled around her.

Inside the church, Matalia took a deep breath. She looked around at the leaded-glass panes, seeing the sunrise colors reflected in shards across the stone floor. She shivered, knowing that God watched her irreverence and was displeased with her. With failing courage, she stepped forward and knelt at the altar.

How has this come to pass? she wondered silently. *How has my life suddenly become the opposite of my desires? Trapped in marriage to a domineering man when all I wanted was a small life experience?* Brogan would never have been her choice. He was far too authoritarian, far too dictatorial, far too overwhelming.

Feeling someone's presence, she glanced up as Brogan knelt at her side. They looked at each other, their thoughts mirrored in each other's eyes. Brogan sought freedom, too. Freedom from the contest that had guided his every step since childhood. He sought the title of Earl of Kirkcaldy. He needed to win it away from his own brother by virtue of his strength and amassed fortune, via his wit and cunning. Seeing Matalia's rebellious albeit alluring eyes, his heart sank. She was nothing he sought in a wife, nothing his father wanted. She was far too beautiful, far too willful, and far too unpredictable.

They stared at each other, both desperate to halt this wedding, but neither able to alter the forces arrayed against them. And so the priest found them, kneeling together, side by side, both dressed in black, surrounded by sparks of yellow, orange and red as the sun rose over the church spires and cascaded over their touching bodies.

Only Ronin, Kalial, Duncan and Merkle were present for the ceremony, which was mercifully quick. In moments, Brogan had slipped a carved copper band from his little finger and pushed it onto Matalia's middle finger. Matalia looked at the Celtic symbols in surprise.

"My mother's," was Brogan's only response to her unasked question. At the conclusion of the vows, Brogan lifted Matalia's hand from her lap and brushed his lips over her knuckles. The marriage was sealed.

Matalia trembled harder, feeling her legs begin to give way. She felt her heart thud, and the blood drained from her face. She swayed, stunned and shocked at the abrupt turn of events. Suddenly, she felt Brogan's arm grasp her firmly about the waist, and he led her from the church and out to a pair of steeds.

Leaning down, he whispered, "Stay strong, faerie."

Still, not knowing what to say or how to respond, Matalia let Brogan lift her onto a dark bay mare. He tightened the horse's girth and checked the saddlebags. Then he mounted his own charcoal stallion in the post-dawn silence. The early birds squawked tenuously before falling quiet.

Matalia looked around at her family, then lifted her eyes to the castle she had known as her home since birth. In one of the upper windows, she saw Nathina and Mackenzie waving to her frantically, and she thought mournfully that she would not see them for a very long time.

Her mother and father were staring at her with trepidation, and she knew they were debating whether they had done right by her. In a rare show of compassion, Matalia smiled at her parents, trying to indicate forgiveness and, perhaps, a trace of happiness, on this dreary morning. Then she turned her mare toward her new husband and nodded at him.

Brogan watched the flood of emotions ripple over Matalia's face. The sudden softness she displayed made her beautifully sculpted features seem ethereal in the first rays of sunrise. He sucked in his breath and felt a wave of possessiveness sweep his soul. *Mine. All mine.* He had an image of her sitting in the first room of his father's castle, a child in her lap, staring up at him with just such an expression. He breathed out, snorting in repugnance of his fantasy. He had no desire for a real family. He wanted only a wife to breed sons and otherwise leave him alone. With that thought, he turned away, dug his heels into his stallion, and set out over the moat, peripherally aware that Matalia's mare followed close behind.

Chapter 7

For several hours they traveled in silence. The colorful sunrise gave way to a gray dawn, and then to a bright, sun-filled morning. The birds, initially hesitant, broke into full song and the air echoed with their lovely voices. Behind the horses ran the three wolves, and next to them, the massive wolfhound. The Irish dog growled whenever the wolves sidled too close, and the wolves lifted their lips in silent but fearsome retort. Brogan rode with his broadsword across his thigh, and he noticed that Matalia had placed her light sword in a scabbard attached to her saddle.

Matalia scowled at Brogan's back as morning shifted into afternoon and he showed no intention of resting for the midday meal. She shifted uncomfortably in her black dress, which had been chosen to make a statement and not necessarily for traveling comfort. Her head ached from the weight of her braids and her stomach growled. She felt hot and sticky and tired. Furthermore, her inner thighs ached, and she felt intensely aware of the movement of the horse beneath her rump. The constant sway was achingly suggestive.

Matalia bit her lip and scowled deeper. She was uncomfortably aware that their bout of sexual intercourse had far exceeded her expectations. She was not pleased that thoughts raced through her mind about how she had felt when he had suddenly cut his bonds and loomed over her, taking control and completing the act so forcefully. She clenched the reins reflexively when she thought of how his hands had gripped her wrists and how his male scent had all but paralyzed her ability to fight him. There was no way, she thought to herself as she looked away from his broad back, no way she would succumb to him again. He may have thought she would accept him simply because she had sought him out initially, that she was wanton because of her initial desire. Matalia humphed, causing Brogan to glance back at her briefly. She would not accept him again, she vowed silently, tilting her head defiantly.

Brogan watched her flare of waywardness, and he frowned, wondering at its cause. He slowed his stallion slightly, letting her mare come abreast of him, and he looked Matalia over carefully.

"What are you plotting?" he questioned suspiciously.

Matalia looked away haughtily, flipping one of her braids into his face. "My thoughts are none of your concern," she replied, then gasped as Brogan gripped the offending braid and wrapped it around his fist. "Let go!" she shrieked, dropping one of her reins as she pulled uselessly at his fingers.

Brogan reached forward and grasped the loose rein, then used his weight to instruct his stallion to stop firm. He pulled against the braid, dragging Matalia's head up to his face.

"Your thoughts," he snarled, "belong to me. *You* belong to me. If you thought your parents controlled your life, you will think I *am* your life."

"You fool!" snapped Matalia, glaring up into his smoky eyes. "I will never bend to your bidding. The best you can hope for is that I am already breeding, for if I am not, you will get no other chances. I intend to do what I want, with whom I want." She tugged at her braid, tears springing to her eyes as Brogan tightened his hold in response. "In fact, I have heard you have a rather handsome brother—"

Brogan leaped off his steed, dragging the hapless Matalia with him by her hair, ignoring her screams of fury and pain. He flung her to the ground, finally releasing her braid, only to grip the folds of her velvet dress as she scrambled to her knees. She twisted away from him, attempting to gain her feet and thus her horse, when Brogan jerked her dress, toppling her easily. She turned, furious, and kicked him, pummeling his chest forcefully with her petite boots.

Brogan was pushed back, a grunt of pain escaping his tight lips, but he held her dress and pulled her back flush against his chest. Matalia twisted again and swung her arm out, chopping against his neck. Enraged at her continued struggles, Brogan wrapped one massive arm around her middle and reached out for the offending arm that was spinning toward him for another blow. He bent it around, holding her wrist up to the small of her back.

Matalia gasped with sharp pain, freezing for a second to catch her breath. Brogan took immediate advantage of the hiatus and shoved her facedown into the grass, almost underneath the hooves of the horses. A sharp whinny caught his attention, and he rolled quickly, just avoiding a kick from the frightened bay mare. Matalia tried to rise, but Brogan shifted back, grabbing her legs and pulling them toward himself, letting the heavy velvet ride up on her thighs. He reached higher, releasing her ankles to grip her legs, and he cast his weight half upon her to hold her still. Releasing her with one hand, he shoved the rest of her skirts up, baring her underclothing.

Tearing and ripping, he divested her of her linens and exposed her bare cheeks to his view as she bucked, trying to get away from him. The horses neighed again, accompanied by the sharp barking of the Irish wolfhound and the snarling growls of the wolves. Brogan braced a heavy hand upon the back of Matalia's neck, holding her firmly onto the ground, while he rotated his torso to avoid the stamp of his stallion's hooves.

Using his free hand, he yanked her thighs apart. Matalia felt the brush of a horse's tail over her exposed cheek and she cringed, sure that she was about to be trampled. A surge of heat swept her nether regions as she felt the fire of Brogan's hand between her legs and she had time only to drag in a desperately needed breath before he speared into her, his manhood swollen and thick.

Next to her face she saw one of the horses stumble as its front hoof landed with a thud onto the muscle of Brogan's arm. She felt his sudden tensing, but instead of leaving her, he pushed in harder and placed his body completely over hers, protectively. He shifted his angle, pulling out a few inches, then surged back in, quickly, again and again. Matalia could not move, her struggles completely quelled as Brogan took her from behind in a primitive declaration of ownership.

Within seconds he pulsed and poured into her, shoving his hips onto her, making sure that every drop if his essence filled her womb. He shouted aloud and grabbed her braids, digging his fingers into the base of the confined hair where he could still touch her. The horses suddenly bolted forward, leaping over their forms as they headed for a stand of trees.

Matalia felt Brogan ripping at her hair, untangling the golden cords until her tresses were completely unbound. He then pulled out of her and flipped her over, holding her down once again by her hair. She stared up at him, her eyes wide with fright, panting. Brogan, too, was breathing heavily. He leaned down and bit her neck, sucking hard until a bright red mark bloomed upon her skin.

A spasm of desire swept her body at the intimate gesture, but Matalia fought it, frantic to combat her feelings. She arched off the ground, whereupon Brogan slipped a hand under her hips, holding them off the dirt as his cock reared up again. He glared into Matalia's eyes, silently daring her to struggle anew, and slid inside her again.

This time the passage was slick, moistened with his juices, and he felt warmth enfold him. Matalia gasped, feeling her insides involuntarily clutch at him, a tiny spasm ripple inside her. She twitched her hips away, but he drove after her, unrelenting, and began a slow, rhythmic pounding as his stormy eyes bored into hers. He drove again and again, this time with incredible control, amazing purpose, until he saw Matalia's eyes start to flutter, her skin start to flush, her breathing become more erratic.

She bent her neck, exposing her vulnerable skin, and Brogan leaned down again, licking the red mark, stroking it gently with his lips and then traveling up to her ear. He breathed onto her, and she quivered at the plethora of sensations he evoked until she felt her heart begin to pound.

She bit her lip, trying to withhold her cries, but Brogan rubbed his rough cheek against her soft one and she heard his whisper. "Let go . . . let go, Matalia," and she did. She moaned with her release in rapidly escalating sounds, and she dug her fingers into the earth, desperately trying not to grip his shoulders. Her legs shook and she discovered afterwards that they were curled around his thighs, trapping him in her cocoon of wet ecstasy.

Brogan stared down at her flushed face, watching her fight her feelings, flooded with immense satisfaction when she could no longer contain them, experiencing his own climax with powerful fervor. He pressed down upon her, letting both of them linger in the throes of pleasure for infinite eons. Tingling . . . floating . . . experiencing pure rapture.

Brogan recovered first. He pushed up, untangled Matalia's legs from his and stood, staring down at her with scorn. He casually laced up his breeches while his eyes insolently swept her half-naked figure.

"Never deny me," he said with soft menace, "and do not defy me again. And I strongly advise you do not spend much time near my brother." Then he turned from her and walked away, acting as if he were strolling in a courtyard.

Matalia scrambled up, shoving her skirts down and trying to salvage her underclothes. She felt weak and shaky from the aftermath of lovemaking and confused and frightened by the absolute power he had been able to so easily exert over her body and mind.

She stumbled in place, almost falling to her knees. Her wolves were standing, crouched, their hackles raised, held at bay by the Irish wolfhound that guarded them. Matalia stared at the beasts, further confused that her fierce creatures could be cowed by a single dog. She took a step forward, but tripped upon the torn hem of her skirt and fell down. With a sob she looked up, only to see Brogan calmly munching on some bread, watching her.

Matalia cast her eyes down, submissive, whereupon Brogan walked forward, leading her mare. He lifted her up and placed her once again in the saddle.

"Shall we continue, then?" he questioned coldly. He remounted his stallion. Looking over at her tear-streaked, pale face, he felt a flash of remorse, which he quickly stifled. It was crucial she learn who her master was before they reached Kirkcaldy. Her spoiled behavior could not be tolerated. She was his now, and he was determined to make her know it before the journey was through, for once they reached Kirkcaldy the most important phase of his life would begin.

That evening they camped in a small, secluded meadow adjacent to a little stream. They were well away from the road so their campfire was completely hidden. Even so, Brogan built it low and smokeless, then left her to find food. Matalia yearned to ask why he was being so careful, but she had said nothing since their afternoon interaction and had determined that she would not break the silence that yawned between them.

She felt very different, as if the person she had been yesterday was no longer the person she now was. One sunrise had changed her entire destiny, one man had toppled her world. She leaned against a tree, her legs curled up underneath her dress, and stroked the head of her nearest wolf. A fine connection linked her and the beasts, a connection that was unspecified but enduring. Matalia welcomed their presence now, feeling comforted, but she was intrigued by the Irish wolfhound.

The big dog was almost her height, though his body was wiry and thin. Her wolves were smaller, only slightly bigger than a normal farm dog, but their weight was significantly more substantial. Despite their heavy musculature, they were still young and untrained. The wolfhound, on the other hand, was incredibly obedient to his master's will. A flick of the hand, a nod of the chin, and the big dog would bound off and catch a rabbit or search around the bend for unfriendly travelers. Matalia stroked her wolf's head, murmuring softly.

In the woods, Brogan stared into the darkness, feeling a familiar connection. He lifted his lip, snarling into the night. "Xanthier . . ." he growled. Although no answer came out of the forest, he felt his twin. Despite their animosity, they were linked. Their mutual time in their mother's womb had melded them, and though they fought against each other, they knew each other better than any other. They instinctively knew what was happening with the other even when they did not wish it. Brogan shook his head roughly. "You thought I would not return, but here I am," he said into the silent night. "I will win this contest, brother, and I will see you admit defeat!"

Brogan gripped a tree, feeling the rough bark dig into his palm. The love-hate relationship between him and his twin throbbed in his soul, tearing at him as it had since the day of their birth. He bowed his head, immersed in the emotions. Soon he would confront Xanthier and prove his worth to their father. He trembled with the repressed feelings, the power of his anger and determination spreading from his thudding heart to his fingertips.

When Matalia's soft voice reached him, he looked up and took a deep breath. She was speaking quietly to her wolves in a singsong cadence. The tone was soothing, and Brogan slowly released his grip on the tree and stood straight. As he peered through the darkness where the campfire flickered, he could see her shadowed presence. He walked forward, drawn by her peaceful aura.

He reentered the clearing, watching her from across the small fire. He was struck by how perfect she was, how incredibly alluring even when tousled and dirty. Her hair hung heavily around her heart-shaped face, twisting and curling into hundreds of black ringlets. It was shorter in front, making the ringlets bounce upon her brows and over her temples, framing her eyes, nose and lips. He dropped his gaze, watching the steady rise and fall of her breasts as she breathed. The top two buttons were missing and there was a small tear in her collar from their earlier tussle in the meadow. He saw the sheen of her flesh through the rip and his eyes narrowed.

Matalia glanced up, feeling his gaze, and lifted her chin at the sudden gleam in his eyes. She pursed her lips, unaware of how the pucker stirred him, and raised an eyebrow. Brogan continued his perusal, dropping his gaze to her waist and then lifting it to her face once again. They stared across the fire, Brogan debating silently, Matalia desperately trying not to look intimidated.

He should not have this effect on me, she thought to herself. *I should not be tempted by him after what he did today. . . .* She blinked, trying to break their eye contact, but Brogan kept her captured and his breathing rate increased. He felt his rod stir, then waken, and he started to rub his fingers against the cloth of his breeches. Matalia bit back a soft sound, appalled at herself, but unable to escape his magnetism.

Brogan lifted a hand and waved it with a brisk motion. "Take it off," he commanded, voice low and rumbling.

Matalia felt her head shaking, denying him on instinct, while at the same time her fingers clutched at her buttons. Brogan said no more, he simply stared at her, his smoky eyes pale silver in the moonlight. Slowly, despising herself for her surrender, Matalia unfastened first one button, then another of her dress, and felt the whisper of cool air dance against her bare skin. Her lower lip trembled and she licked it nervously.

"More . . ." he whispered to her across the campfire, and Matalia unbuttoned the dress further, down to her waist, and the lapels sagged open and exposed her to his sight.

His gaze swept over the light pink of her nipples.

He noted that her chemise was discarded, probably torn and useless, left behind some rock along the road. His nostrils flared as he saw the breeze skate over her skin, tightening the nubs into firm, suckable points.

"All of it," he said hoarsely, fighting his impatience by gripping his thighs until the whites of his knuckles showed. Matalia slowly pushed the sleeves down, exposing her soft shoulders, revealing a single bruise on her upper arm where Brogan had held her before. He stared at it, and at the red mark upon her neck, and felt a quickening in his gut. A wild filly, tamed with a firm hand, made to respect her master's law, *made to want her master's touch.*

Matalia shivered, feeling her will slipping away under his look, feeling his control sapping her strength. She stood slowly, then pushed the dress down, feeling it catch on the swell of her hips before she could drop it to the ground in a pool of rich midnight velvet. In one quick movement, Brogan stepped over the fire to push her down onto her back upon her discarded dress. Matalia tensed, expecting violence, but his touch was gentle. He positioned her beneath him, then lightly ran his fingers over her cheek and down her neck, trailing over her mark. He then let his fingers sweep over her shoulders, delicate but strong, and over her upper arms.

"Does this hurt?" he questioned gruffly, stroking the bruise on her flesh. Matalia shook her head, dazed at the sweetness of his touch, watching his hard face relax into sensuality. His gaze briefly flicked to her eyes, assessing the truth of her response, before returning to watch his fingers as they continued their leisurely exploration.

He shifted to her breasts, forgoing roundabout foreplay and instantly settling his fingertips over her pink nipples. Matalia moaned high in her throat and felt her body twitch upwards. Brogan's lips lifted in a small smile, and he circled the nipples again, watching them fold into tiny creases as they hardened. He leaned down and blew on them, and Matalia rocked her head back and forth, completely pliant to his desires.

He bent his head and licked them, forcing himself not to suck on them, teasing himself, taunting himself. He blew again, and Matalia groaned aloud and lifted her breasts up, pushing them into his lips. Brogan backed away slowly, longing to accommodate her unspoken request, but stubbornly denying them both. Instead, he dropped his head and licked her navel, grinning at her sudden squirming. He blew on her skin there, too, and ripples of sensation spread from her belly, down to her inner thighs, which fell open, vulnerable and welcoming.

Brogan smelled her, breathing deeply through his nose, and lay his cheek upon her smooth stomach. Matalia's hands crept up, tangling in his hair, and she let herself touch his nape and upper shoulders with featherlight strokes of her nails. He rolled his shoulders, liking the feel of her touch, then sat up and stared at her entire body.

He gazed at her hungrily, eyes sweeping every curve of her flesh, and his heart beat erratically. Incredible, he thought. Beyond exquisite.

He opened her thighs further, then ran his fingers through her private hair, delighting in the thick, black curls that matched her hair. He was faintly surprised that the thatch was full but small, forming a dainty covering over her inner secrets. He spread her lips open and gazed down, exploring her folds with his eyes. He brushed his thumb over her clitoris, but was forced to place a heavy hand on her belly to keep her still when she twitched in reaction. He lifted his thumb to his mouth, sucking upon it, and Matalia's mouth opened as she watched his action. He then dropped his hand back down, rubbing the now-wet pad of his thumb over her again. Matalia gasped aloud, opening her thighs further, begging mutely for him to continue.

He stroked her, first with one thumb, then with two, while his fingers held her pelvis still, twirling his thumbs over each other in a never-ending wave of sensation, causing Matalia to pant quickly, her mouth open, her eyes squeezed shut. Brogan lifted his eyes and observed her face, feeling desire almost overwhelm him at the image of her sexual abandon. Shifting slightly, he twisted one of his hands so that his fingers could reach inside of her. Still rubbing her with his thumb, he sank two fingers inside, his eyes widening with masculine satisfaction at the wet heat enfolding him.

He stroked her with his fingers, still rubbing her clitoris, slowly, deliberately, forcing her to climb swiftly. She reached down and gripped his thick wrist, holding it, pulling it away from her, but Brogan persisted, ignoring her weak efforts and demanded she accept the sensations, submit to the vibrations racking her core. Then, just as she felt her body clench down, he removed his abrasive thumb and replaced it with his tongue, kissing her, licking her, sucking on her as his fingers pounded into her. Matalia gripped his shoulders and lifted her knees, her head twisting frantically, her throat exploding with sound. She climaxed, sweet and long, feeling the rasp of his tongue and the ribby sensation of his knuckles lift her and carry her until she collapsed into complete lassitude.

He finally pulled his fingers out of her and stared at her body. He rubbed his hands rapidly over her flushed skin, touching every part of her quickly, forcefully, possessively, into her slack mouth, even slipping between her ass cheeks, over her tingling toes. He reared up and gripped his cock, placed it inside her glistening opening and pushed it home with a sudden, violent surge. Matalia felt her body jerk, pounded by his weight, but she had no energy to react, no ability to respond. She lay quiescent under his attack, letting him spend his force upon her body. Letting him use her as his sexual vessel. Letting him do whatever he desired to her.

He pounded his hips into hers, feeling her soft skin melt under his assault, seeing her brilliant eyes fade into peaceful gems as she let him take her. He felt the folds of her inner sanctum swell and he shouted aloud, needing to feel her wanting him. Matalia shivered, quivered, her thighs sore, her passage raw, yet the tide of ecstasy she was beginning to know approached, teased, flaunted, then swept over them both, flooding them with an ocean of orgasms.

Chapter 8

Afterwards, Brogan collapsed next to her and pulled her deep into his arms. She was his, he thought with satisfaction. Perhaps by a circuitous route, but she was his and he rather liked this part of it.

In the morning, they awoke to the tinkling of the small stream racing beside them. Matalia smiled up at Brogan and was rewarded with a tiny lift of one side of his mouth in return. Giggling with delight, Matalia was not offended when Brogan pushed her off of him and rose to dress. When he was done, he reached a hand down to her and lifted her up, flush against his clad form. He leaned down and nuzzled her hair.

"Never braid it again," he murmured, and Matalia nodded immediately in acceptance. "I like it flowing freely." He pulled away and trailed a finger down her cheek. Then he winked and pushed her away. "We are less than a day's ride from the Kirkcaldy border, and only a few days from the castle. Perhaps you should bathe as best you can in the bend of the stream."

Matalia raised an eyebrow and smiled again. " 'Tis not my fault that I have been tumbled in the dirt far too often to maintain a lady's fair complexion."

Brogan snorted and shook his head. "Go on. Do not remind me of how you came to be in such a state, or 'twill be longer than a day before we cross into familiar land. Go on. I will find us some breakfast since we forgot about dinner."

"As you wish," Matalia taunted while bending over to pick up her crushed dress. Brogan smacked her lightly on the bottom and Matalia shrieked.

She spun around to hit him back, but he stepped nimbly out of her way and shoved one of his extra shirts at her instead. "Use this to dry off with," he said, almost laughing at her affronted face. Matalia snatched the shirt and draped it over her bare body. Brogan turned away, fighting the arousal he felt at seeing her small frame encased in his clothing. Branded from the inside out, he thought, and he breathed slowly, allowing himself to feel pleased, to think that all might be well after all.

He whistled to his wolfhound and was surprised to see the three wolves leap up to follow. He frowned slightly, wishing they would stay with their mistress to protect her, but shrugged. She had pulled her sword from the scabbard and was even now walking carefully around the river with it and her dress in her hands. It would be only a moment, he decided, and then ducked into the woods.

After only a few steps he froze. An eerie feeling swept over him, and he peered through the forest, searching for the person he knew was near. "Xanthier," he growled. "Your minions failed to kill me after your spies told of my ship's docking. Are you brave enough to try it on your own?"

"I do not need to kill you, brother. You have murdered yourself." Xanthier slid out of the shadows and faced Brogan. "Welcome home, Brogan."

Brogan snarled at him. "You welcome me home no more than I welcome seeing you again. I am sure you hoped I would perish at sea."

Xanthier shrugged. "It would certainly have made my life easier. But as I said, it is not important now.

By marrying that hellion, you have lost everything." When Brogan did not respond, Xanthier strolled closer. "Why, Brogan? Why would you risk the inheritance to marry a woman you do not even know?"

"Honor, my brother. I did it for honor, which is something you have no experience with."

"You are right. I am not burdened with those trivialities. I was raised to be strong, whereas you were raised to be weak."

Brogan shook his head. "You know nothing of the world, Xanthier. Sitting here, in Scotland, living in the shadow of our father. What have you done with your life?"

Xanthier glared at him, infuriated. "I have married. I have collected wealth. I will soon father a child. I will win Kirkcaldy!"

Brogan smiled coldly. "I, too, have married, have my own fortune, and will breed a babe. Perhaps I will win. What will you do then, Xanthier?"

"That will never happen!"

"I can feel the fear in you. Remember how we were as boys? Remember how we could sense each other's emotions? I can tell you are frightened."

"You are mistaken, Brogan. It is *your* fear you sense. *You* are terrified of *me*. What do you fear? My power? How much money I have? Perhaps you fear that your lovely bride will stray, as our mother did, and you will be cast out once again."

Brogan leaped at Xanthier, slamming his fist into his twin's face. Xanthier stumbled back, then quickly kicked Brogan in his groin, sending him crashing to the forest floor.

"Do not try it, brother," Xanthier sneered. "Remember, I will fight without honor. Until later, twin brother," he said as he walked away.

Struggling to regain his breath, Brogan glowed with hatred. "I will remember."

* * *

Matalia tiptoed through the pine needles, grimacing whenever she stepped on a buried rock. She balanced her sword in her right hand and swung it a few times in the air just to loosen her muscles. As she rounded the bend, she saw an eddy in the stream that formed a deep pool and she sighed with satisfaction. She placed her sword on the ground, then divested herself of Brogan's shirt, noting the monogram of Kirkcaldy upon its breast. She folded it carefully, making sure the embroidery was facing upwards where she could view it as she bathed. Perhaps, she thought, being married to Brogan O'Bannon would not be so terrible after all.

She slipped into the cool water and tilted her head back so her hair was immersed. She covered her exposed breasts with her hands, conscious of their state of lingering arousal. She swished her head back and forth, rinsing the dirt before lifting her hair from the water to ring it out. She then scooped some sand from the stream bed and rubbed it briskly over her skin, flinching at its roughness on her tender thighs. She shivered, cold from the water, and hurried her ablutions, rinsing her face with closed eyes. As she wiped the last of the water droplets from her face she heard a small chuckle from the creek edge. Her eyes flew open and she spun, ready to fight, when she saw Brogan standing with one foot raised on a rock. He held his shirt in one hand and was rubbing the monogram with his thumb while he stared at her with gray, ravenous eyes.

"Brogan!" Matalia gasped. "You surprised me. You found food so quickly?"

"Aye. And it looks quite tasty to me. Come have a bite," Brogan replied, his eyes narrowing with desire.

Matalia looked at him with confusion, but obediently walked out of the pool, allowing the cold water to sluice off of her skin. She walked up to him, smiling timidly, and reached for the shirt.

Brogan held it away from her and grinned. "What do I get for it?" he teased.

Matalia stopped, her hand outstretched and her head tilted. Her turquoise eyes sparkled like sunshine off the blue-green stream behind her.

"Come here," he said, seeing her hesitation, and he dropped the shirt into the mud and gripped her upper arm. Matalia sucked in her breath and placed a hand against his chest to halt him. Brogan ignored her signal and pulled her close before dropping his hands to fold them over the moons of her bottom. "That is very nice," he whispered. "Very nice indeed." Then he lifted one hand to her neck and tilted her head up. He leaned down, bending Matalia backward, and placed his lips upon hers. He pressed them against her firmly, then opened his mouth and nibbled on her full lower lip before nudging her mouth open and pushing his tongue inside her. He held the back of her head tightly and proceeded to ravish her mouth, bruising her lips in his haste.

Suddenly, Matalia felt her hair being pulled from its roots as Brogan deserted her mouth and was sent sprawling upon the ground. She gasped, involuntarily reaching for him, when she, too, was cruelly shoved to the ground and buried beneath a cloud of black velvet. She struggled for air, not understanding what was happening, frightened. She heard a sickening crunch of bone against bone and then two voices, amazingly similar, cursing each other.

As Matalia finally freed herself, she looked up and saw double, saw Brogan facing himself, grimly furious and bleeding from his mouth. She twisted and looked at the other Brogan, noting that he looked enraged, a maniacal glint deep in his eyes. He laughed evilly and held out the torn locks from Matalia's head as he backed away from the coldly stalking Brogan.

"Brother," the other said, "I thought only to demonstrate how loyal your tender bride will be."

"You bastard, Xanthier. Do not dare to touch her again or I will rip your cock off with my bare hands." Brogan swung at Xanthier, crashing his fist into his midsection in a punishing blow, causing Xanthier to double over.

Gasping, he grinned and leered over at the stunned Matalia. "It was not like she was fighting." He coughed while struggling to draw breath.

Galvanized into action, Matalia reached for her sword and raised it against Xanthier. "What is going on!" she cried. "What did you do? Why would you kiss your sister-in-law?"

Brogan snarled, stepping forward when Xanthier sprang back, out of his reach. "It was a damn fool thing to marry for honor, even for you, twin brother, although feeling her lips, I can imagine that honor was not your only motivation! Too bad she doesn't know your aversion to kissing yet, or perhaps she would have realized I was not her new husband." Xanthier grinned wickedly, climbing up on his horse, which was tethered to a tree.

Brogan cast a swift, furious glance at Matalia, who kept looking back and forth between the two men, horrified that she had not seen the differences between them instantly. "Yes, how unfortunate," Brogan murmured as he turned his back on her and glared at his brother. "If you ever touch her again, I will tear you apart."

Xanthier smiled again, sweeping his gaze over Brogan's enraged expression and Matalia's frightened one. "We will let her decide that, won't we?" He then nodded and squeezed his legs around his horse, sending it crashing through the woods until it reached the road. Both Brogan and Matalia heard it break into a canter and fade into the distance.

Startled into action, Matalia sprang up and raced over to Brogan. "I don't understand! He is your brother! Why would he do that?"

Brogan turned on her, his face a mask of seething rage. "You bitch," he snarled at her. "You whore!"

"Brogan!" Matalia gasped, falling back in the face of his attack. Brogan glared at her for a few seconds more, then swept a contemptuous glance over her wet, naked body. "Get decent," he growled, "if that is possible in your adulterous soul. We will not spend another night in the woods, nor rest until I have you safely behind the locked door of your new bedchamber."

They pushed the horses hard through the day and into the twilight. Riding still farther, they continued deep into the night, the anger leaping between them creating a wall of vibrations, making small creatures cower down into the leaves, fearing their combined wrath. The pack of wolves crowded close to the mare's heels, making her nervous. Matalia rode her with grace, her body flowing with the movements of the horse as if they were one. The red wolf, the oldest, lifted his head, smelling the air as he trotted, occasionally pausing to swing his head toward Brogan and narrow his beady eyes before continuing. The silver-tipped gray, the smallest, darted forward in small dashes, slinking down, barely visible as he blended with the moonlight. The black, the strongest, stuck next to Matalia's booted foot, his coat bristling and a silent, perpetual snarl lifting his left lip.

As a pack they were in unfamiliar territory. Not only was the terrain different, but also the demeanor of their mistress was drastically changed, and they felt compelled to modify to accommodate her. They were leaving their home behind, just as Matalia was abandoning her childhood with every clop of the horse's hooves. They twitched, they sniffed, they peered with cautious eyes into the forest, scanning for predators. They formed a protective semicircle around Matalia, shifting her horse farther from Brogan's so that both emotional and physical distance separated them.

The Irish wolfhound loped on the far side of his master, his long strides carrying him well ahead. He, too, seemed to feel the immense tension between the humans and was highly uncomfortable near them. A low whine escaped his throat whenever the horses caught up to him, and he shook his massive head, trying to dispel the gloom.

Brogan fumed, his fury at his brother spilling onto Matalia as if she were the cause of his strife. His gray eyes shimmered with the fierceness of his fury. For one moment he had let his guard down and accepted Matalia. In return, she had stepped into the arms of his worst enemy. He cursed under his breath, feeling his twin's satisfaction, and focused his anger more fully upon his new wife.

At a wide stream, Brogan's stallion balked, rearing up in fear at the churning water. Brogan leaned down, softly stroking the steed's neck, murmuring to it, until he was able to coax it, step by step, across to the far bank. Matalia watched him, hating the kindness he exhibited toward the beast, wanting him to act as uncouth and villainous to the horse as he was to her, but also appreciating his gentleness toward a creature under his control. Her black lashes swept over her eyes, hiding her expression as Brogan looked back at her impatiently when she remained halted.

"Come on, then," he snapped at her, his voice cold and furious.

Matalia glared back, despising herself for succumbing to him last eve. Her natural rebellion, now combined with the righteousness of one unjustly accused, flared hot, and she looked around consideringly. Brogan watched her, instantly aware of her flickering thoughts.

"Hurry, the water is treacherous at night," he said forcefully.

Matalia looked back at him, across the stream,

seeing his stallion prance with agitation. The water was black in the darkness, with only sparkling splashes illuminated by moonlight breaking the rushing surface. Rocks were hidden underneath, and many were slick with algae. Brogan's stallion snorted again, ringing his tail in fretfulness. On the other hand, Matalia's bay mare blew softly upon the water surface, then took a bold step forward until Matalia pulled up on the reins.

"What are you doing?" Brogan demanded, trying to soothe the stallion as he eyed her.

Matalia continued to pull on the reins, backing her horse out until all four feet stood on solid ground. With an oath, Brogan kicked his horse, asking him to recross the ford, whereupon the steed reared up, screaming in rage. Instantly employing all his skill, Brogan focused on the irate beast, trying to calm him. The stallion spun in a circle, ready to bolt from the frightening water. Brogan clamped his knees and shifted his weight while keeping a light but firm hold on the reins.

Matalia watched the display, knowing that Brogan was completely occupied with his task. She looked up and spied a small stone cottage high above the trees. It looked isolated and abandoned, but Matalia saw it as a haven, a refuge from the disastrous turn her life had recently taken. Brogan's fury was unfair. Her parents had cast her out. Her only friend was gone. She felt lonely and forsaken.

Making an impulsive decision, she turned her mare and kicked her hard, sending her into an immediate gallop through the trees. Distantly she heard Brogan shout a string of curses at her back, but she only urged her horse faster. The brisk wind lifted her hair from her neck, drying the nervous sweat from her brow, and she smiled with abandon.

Beside her the three wolves streamed in a happy, carefree cascade of color. They, too, felt the release of anxiety and welcomed the sudden burst of energy. Matalia guided her mare through the brush, bending low as branches swept over her head and leaning to the side as her horse swung by piles of granite or knots of tumbled roots. Soon she was far from the stream's edge and Brogan's voice was faint. She slowed, then stopped, peering around her to get her bearings. The darkness was only slightly alleviated by the stars, but the moon cast a glow upon the mountain up ahead. Changing her direction slightly, Matalia reset her mare into a trot as she took deep breaths, appreciating her first moments of pure freedom.

Within the hour, as her horse tired and slowed to a walk, Matalia found herself exiting the trees and entering the foothills of the mountains. On the top peak she saw an old stone building with no moat or courtyard around it. The roof was crowned with a carpet of herbs that fluttered enchantingly in the breeze, and the base was besieged by wild heather. The heady scents of oregano, purple basil, and summer savory wafted down to her, and Matalia searched hopefully for signs of human life.

As she rode up the mountainside, she came across a dirt divider. Here, the path was bare of the abundant grasses and wildflowers that covered the rest of the ground, and Matalia noticed that the path undulated in an irregular circle around the cottage, at a distance of about a five minute walk from the structure. The edges of the path were formed by a set of unusual stones, and Matalia stopped her horse, a bit uneasy to cross the border. Her hand ached, and she glanced down at the copper band encircling her finger. The Celtic symbols shimmered with reflected moonlight. She rubbed the ring absently, looking up at the stone house.

Her wolves milled around, whining and sniffing. The red one sat down and lifted his snout to the air and let out a mournful howl. As the low notes faded, all three beasts and the horse abruptly swung their heads back toward the forest, hearing movement. Matalia peered into the dark trees, trying to see what the animals could sense, but seeing and hearing nothing. Making a sudden decision, she nudged the bay over the odd path and urged her up the slope. The wolves bounded over the path, not touching the stones, and trailed after her.

As she reached the top, she saw a barn hidden behind the cottage. Fresh hay was stacked under the overhang. She smiled, pleased at the sight, and her mare lifted her head and pricked her ears forward. A whinny from inside the wooden structure completed the welcome. Matalia slipped off the mare and led her forward, looking for an empty stall.

The barn was simple, designed only to keep the majority of the precipitation off the animals' heads, and was not nearly so well designed or constructed as the stables at Roseneath. But Matalia found an empty stall, and she was thankful to lead her mare through the doorway after removing the simple bar that blocked the way.

One of the other beasts, a big-boned mule, honked at her as he caught scent of the wolves. He kicked out, striking a splinter from the side wall until Matalia reached over the divider and began to sing softly to him. She started low and peaceful, almost humming, catching the mule's attention. As his huge ears swiveled toward her, she lifted her voice into a lilting melody. She reached out, brushing her fingertips across his velvet nose, and finally slowed her song until only the last note hung in the air. The mule's eyes swung away, and he returned to his manger, feeling safe and settled.

Matalia turned back to her mare which was nudging her impatiently with her muzzle. Laughing quietly, she tugged off the bridle and, after loosening the girth, pulled off the saddle. It landed with a thump upon the dirt floor, and Matalia pushed it with her foot so it rested against the side wall. She then exited the stall, sliding the bar back in place. The mare whinnied as Matalia picked up some hay and tossed it over the bar, scattering it widely. Finally, after spying a half-filled water bucket, Matalia dragged it over as well, only spilling some during her efforts.

The wolves watched her curiously. When she appeared to settle in by ducking under the bar and sitting upon some of the hay inside the stall, they glanced at each other, their stomachs rumbling. Matalia peered out and bit her lip.

" 'Tis time we all grew up," she murmured. "Go on out and get your own dinner." She smiled as the red wolf tilted his head, whining low. The black wolf growled deep, then ended with a sound suspiciously like a bark. At the signal, the red and black wolves turned and loped down the hill, leaving the silver-tipped one to stand guard over their mistress. Matalia felt warm and blinked tears from her eyes. With a sigh of gratitude, she placed her arms around his ruff and snuggled her nose into his fur.

The wolf moved his tail, sweeping the floor, and lay down with his nose between his paws. Shifting over, Matalia closed her eyes and placed her head upon his neck, using him as a pillow. She drifted comfortably to sleep, listening to the continuous munching of the mare and the steady heartbeat of the wolf.

Chapter 9

As the night gradually shifted to morning light, an elderly woman shuffled out of the cottage and slowly made her way to the animal shelter. Her old eyes were soft and sad, and her face was lined with wrinkles. She leaned down and picked a sprig of dried brush from the path and tossed it away. Suddenly wary, she looked up at the barn and wrinkled her brow. Pulling her shoulders back, she looked down the hill, toward the stones encircling the church, and frowned further. Finally, she turned back and cautiously approached the barn. A sudden, uncompromising chorus of growls made her freeze. Terrified, she dropped her gaze and encountered a pair of glowing, wolfish eyes in the dark depths of the stall.

Matalia awoke to the vibrations of the wolf's growl under her ear. Pushing up groggily, she glanced around, sleep making her eyesight fuzzy. She turned toward the source of her wolves' warning and gasped. In the stall opening stood a woman haloed in golden light.

Matalia scrambled to her feet, bits of straw cascading down from her shoulders and curls tangling in front of her eyes. She stumbled sideways, still unsteady, until she placed a hand against the stall to brace herself. A splinter entered her palm and she flinched. "Who are you?" she asked.

The older woman raised both eyebrows and stared at Matalia without answering. Underneath her calm regard, Matalia dropped her hand and plucked the splinter out, then sucked on the sore spot. When the woman turned away and started to walk back to the cottage, Matalia hurried after her.

"Excuse me. I did not mean to be so rude. I realize I was in your stable, and I do appreciate the shelter. I was simply startled."

The older woman paused, then shrugged. She turned and stared at Matalia pensively. "Were you sent here?" she asked quietly. Matalia shook her head. "Then why are you here?"

Matalia averted her eyes and her body sagged. She lifted a hand in supplication, then opened her mouth helplessly before closing it without explanation. The woman watched her, then sighed. "Well, child, you can stay here awhile." There was thread of amusement in her voice. "And whatever ails you, a good breakfast will surely help."

Matalia looked at her gratefully while absently stroking the head of the silver wolf next to her. He still rumbled in his chest, suspicious of those he did not know. The other wolves had returned in the night and they, too, watched the woman carefully.

"I am Ansleen. Please, come into my home, and after we break the fast, you can tell me your deep troubles if you desire. Otherwise, keep your own council." The woman moved back down the path. She looked down the hillside, peering suspiciously into the trees far down the way. Faintly, almost imperceptibly, she saw movement within the forest shadows. She watched the sight defiantly, a flash of forgotten spirit sparking in her old eyes. Then the girl joined her and together they walked into the cottage.

On the other side of the dirt and stone barrier, Brogan stopped his horse and glared up the hill. A quiver ran up his spine, and he cursed under his breath. Nearby forest animals froze, frightened by the anger emanating from his angry breaths, not knowing if his fury was based upon malevolence or frustration. He stood there for long moments, not moving, not crossing the border, held back by a Celtic command stronger than his anger. Men were not allowed. He saw the old woman stare down at him, and he narrowed his eyes. When the woman and Matalia ducked under the doorway, he cursed and then rode deeper into the cover of the forest trees. He did not look back.

Matalia glanced around the cottage with surprise. The walls were richly covered with tapestries depicting pagan stories. Suspended from the high ceilings were racks of drying herbs, some withered, some fresh. The entire chamber reeked with their overpowering scents, and Matalia coughed while trying to take a full breath. Her eyes watered, but she blinked rapidly. A woman rose from a wooden table, leaving her half-eaten bread and fruit.

"Ansleen?" she questioned cautiously.

"I found her in the stable," the silver-haired woman replied while gently nudging Matalia. "She has sought our home to ease her troubles. Meet Lady Gweneath."

Matalia found herself leaning back into Ansleen's hand, nervous underneath Lady Gweneath's scrutiny. "I can be on my way . . ." she mumbled, unsure.

In answer, Gweneath stepped forward. "What is your name and how is it that you found our isolated cottage? We are not well known, for our hamlet is quite humble."

Matalia looked around in surprise, seeing the evidence of great wealth upon the walls, upon the beautifully carved table in the form of silver utensils and well-crafted plates. The two women stared at her, waiting for her answer.

"I am Matalia. I hail from Castle Roseneath from the clan McTaver. I was on route to . . . with . . ." She looked at Ansleen hopelessly, not sure what she should say. Taking a breath, she tried again. "I have made some terrible mistakes recently, and I know not what to do. I have been forcibly married to a man who is unbelievably rude and unmanageable, and I saw your home . . . I saw an opportunity . . ."

Ansleen stared at her, reading the story in Matalia's eyes much more accurately than her words revealed. She saw the passion of rebellion, the sting of its consequences, and the budding awareness of a girl who suddenly finds herself in an adult world that cares naught for the souls it crushes. She nodded slowly, glancing up as she took hold of the girl's hand.

"We have another bed, albeit a small one. What you see upon the ceiling is our trade. We grow the herbs, preserve them, and trade them in the town four times a year. Do you know aught of herbs and healing?"

"I am afraid I will be of little help to you," Matalia murmured apologetically.

Ansleen shook her head even before Matalia finished. "You are young and strong. We will find ways for you to assist."

Matalia smiled, her face transforming from beautiful to extraordinary. "I am pleased," she replied softly. "But I must warn you that my husband may find me and insist on my return."

"Who is this man?" asked Gweneath.

"Brogan O'Bannon," Matalia replied, hearing his name echo in the high chamber.

"Who? Did you say Brogan?" Ansleen replied, her voice rough and streaked with pain. Gweneath looked up in surprise, her face paling. When Matalia nodded,

Ansleen took a deep breath and touched Matalia's cheek with a weathered hand while Gweneath sat down.

"Brogan O'Bannon will not come here," Lady Gweneath said as Ansleen lifted Matalia's ring finger and staring at the wedding band.

Ansleen traced the ancient symbols with her index finger, nodded, then dropped Matalia's hand and motioned to the table. "Sit and eat, child. We welcome you."

She smiled at Matalia's disbelieving look and continued to reassure her. "Lady Gweneath speaks the truth. No O'Bannon man will come here. It is the safest place you could have taken refuge, little one. No O'Bannon will cross the stones. The only way you will leave is if you voluntarily cross them yourself."

"Then I am safe, for nothing would make me go back to that beast!" Matalia replied. The women around her looked at her sadly, each of them recalling their own painful experiences, their own avowals and ultimatums. But Matalia was oblivious to their emotions and she began eating the bread with gusto.

Later that night, Brogan returned to the far side of the stone barrier and glared up at the cottage with supreme annoyance. He saw the three wolves ranging around the hillside and knew from their presence that Matalia lingered inside. He was infuriated that she had escaped him, and he gnashed his teeth at the delay her unprecedented resistance caused him. He needed to return to Kirkcaldy immediately! Every day reduced his chances of success. He ached to stride up to the door and pull her out by her hair, but instead he clenched his fists in frustration. He debated, then turned away and formed a temporary camp. After settling his animals, he stared into the woods and cursed his ill fortune.

"You will regret this, black faerie," he growled into the darkness. "You think that you can disrupt my life and then leave? I will have you at my side whether you want to be there or not! I have not spent the last fifteen years preparing to take Kirkcaldy only to have you destroy everything!"

Inside the cottage, Matalia lay abed, insomnia warring with fatigue. Her belly felt tight and her shoulders were tense. All day long she had experienced bursts of hyperactivity followed by moments of black depression. She wallowed in the disquiet of her soul, guilt at her abrupt defection warring with her youthful arrogance. Should she have left him? Didn't she make a vow to stand by him? Despite the inauspicious beginnings, he was now her husband and she felt uneasy about abandoning him. She stared into the thatched roof, vacillating, until night penetrated and she fell into a fitful slumber.

After peeking in on her, Ansleen returned to the fire and spoke to Lady Gweneath. "She is sleeping."

"She should not be here, Ansleen. Of all people to come to our home, she is the most unwelcome."

Ansleen smiled sadly. "I would like her to stay, if only for a while. Perhaps . . ."

"Don't fool yourself. Nothing will change." Gweneath softened her voice. "I do not mean to be cruel, my friend, but our lives are over. We cannot change the past. We are old women who have been forgotten by our families. It is best if it stays that way."

Ansleen rose in agitation and walked to the window. She picked up a dried thistle and crumbled it in her hand. "It was all so senseless. Why didn't he listen to me?"

Lady Gweneath joined her and put her arm around Ansleen's shoulders. "This is why she should leave. You should not torture yourself again. It was almost thirty years ago. He cast you out. It does not matter anymore."

Ansleen smiled tremulously at Gweneath. "I know. I am sorry. But I would like her to stay for a few days. She is my only connection to those I love."

Gweneath sighed, nodding. "If it will make you happy, then she can stay. For a while."

In the morning, Matalia entered the kitchen where the two elderly women were preparing goldenseal tea. Ansleen immediately welcomed her, but Gweneath barely spared her a glance.

"Come in, Matalia. We are preparing for a journey to the village in six days. Do you know what medicinal uses this tea has?"

Matalia shook her head and slid into place at the table. "I am afraid that I did not pay attention to my mother's lessons on herbs."

Gweneath grunted and said over her shoulder, "You must have been a very spoiled child."

Matalia frowned and bit her lip, unsure how to respond.

"Tut tut, Lady Gweneath. Leave her alone. She is still young." Ansleen smiled reassuringly. "Goldenseal is made into a tea for lung illnesses. It can also be used as a poultice to stop bleeding. Many midwives use it after childbirth."

"I have no need of either use," Matalia replied.

"See," Lady Gweneath said to Ansleen. "She is so spoiled, she does not think of what she could do for others, only what could be done for her."

Ignoring her, Ansleen pointed to another plant with bright yellow flowers and a tall, hairy stem hanging from the ceiling. "That is agrimony. It helps sore throats and upset stomachs, particularly in children."

If only to prove Lady Gweneath wrong, Matalia rose and concentrated on what Ansleen was showing her. She repeated the name and the use, then pointed to another plant. Soon Ansleen and Matalia were discussing all the drying herbs, and Lady Gweneath grudgingly contributed. After several hours, they all sat down, exhausted.

"I had no idea there were so many plants with so many uses! I never thought they would be so fascinating. It is amazing how the leaves will look like a heart and will be good for the organ it resembles."

"Yes, that is often the case."

"I love this cottage. I wish I could live here forever!"

Both Ansleen and Lady Gweneath shook their heads. "Don't wish for that," Ansleen cautioned. "Believe me, you do not want that. Why don't you go outside for a while? Your animals are restless. Then you can help with dinner."

In the bright sunshine Matalia was immediately greeted by her wolves. They whined and wagged their tails at her approach. She knelt down and patted their heads, then struck out for a walk. Her youthful strides carried her quickly through the wildflowers to the stone border, where she stopped. She stared at the small stones, then turned and followed them, making a long, slow circle of the hilltop, always taking care to stay in the inner ring.

Although she did not understand how the two old women could be so certain that Brogan would not come for her, she trusted their words. So many things had changed in so short a time, she relished the sanctuary the cottage offered and chose not to question its significance. She finally completed the circle, coming back to the place where she had started. Then, after taking a large breath of fresh air, she returned to help Ansleen and Lady Gweneath with supper.

For many days Matalia helped the women prepare for market. Ansleen and Lady Gweneath taught her endlessly, and Matalia appreciated their wisdom. For the first time she found herself responding to adults respectfully, reverently, and she was quick to offer her assistance as she had never done at home. She began to understand the things her mother had tried to teach her about deference and consideration for others. Gweneath remained dubious, but Ansleen was warm and caring.

As night fell on the evening before their planned departure to the market, Ansleen and Gweneath sat in rocking chairs before the fire while Matalia sat at their feet.

"This has been the most beautiful day of my life." Matalia sighed. "This cottage is so peaceful and the smell of the flowers on the hillside is exquisite!"

"The best day of your life? Matalia, that is a very grand claim. How do you know it is the best day?" asked Gweneath.

"I am not sure. . . . I feel very content."

"Today I had a wonderful breakfast, good company, and a warm fire. I, too, am content," replied Ansleen.

"Haven't you had a favorite day? A day that was the very best day of your life?" Matalia questioned.

The women fell silent, pondering Matalia's question. "I am not sure one can always recognize the best day when it comes around," Ansleen said. "Sometimes it is later, when the day is gone, that you look back and realize it was the best one." Gweneath nodded as Ansleen continued. "I remember a very special day. It was like every other day. I woke in the morning and kissed my husband. We had breakfast and then went for a ride together. We had a picnic. He fed me tiny pieces of pie crust. . . . Then we went home and feel asleep in each other's arms."

"What made that day so special, then?" Matalia asked.

Ansleen stroked Matalia's cheek. "The next day,

nothing was ever the same. A man came to me and told me that if I did not give him gold, he would tell my beloved husband a lie. He would tell him that we had lain together."

"Your husband would not believe such an accusation!" Matalia declared angrily.

Ansleen lifted her hands helplessly. "I was not sure. I did not want to risk ruining our love. I paid the man."

Gweneath stared into the fire as Ansleen continued. "But he came back, time and again, until I had no more gold to give him. I finally had to give him a ring of mine. . . ." She paused as Matalia waited with anticipation. "I bade the man to melt the ring down, but he did not. He wore it. And my husband saw it on his finger. After that, there was no reasoning with my beloved. He believed the man's lie, even though it had never been spoken aloud. He accused me of giving the man the ring as a token of my love, and he refused to listen to my tale."

"What happened? Did not the man confess?"

"He was beheaded. The fields where my husband and I had picnicked were burned. I was banished."

"And your husband never forgave you?"

Ansleen rose in agitation. Without answering, she left the fire and went to her chamber. Gweneath watched Matalia's stunned face. "It is more truthful to say that *she* never forgave *him*."

"I do not understand."

Gweneath shook her head. "We can teach you about the herbs, about the cottage, about how to find some peace for your soul. But one thing neither of us can advise you on is how to deal with your husband. In that regard we have both failed."

Matalia dropped her face into her hands and squeezed her eyes shut. In a muffled voice, she replied, "And I, too, have failed."

*   *   *

Her thoughts faded, shifted as they followed tendrils this way and that. Her daydream swept around her, enveloping her. Connections between memories and current events crystallized, then faded and rematerialized in vague images. She felt a quickening as certain memories shifted briefly into focus, and she let the excitement of his touch wash over her as her mind replayed the new, sensual experiences. His roughness, combined with a silken thread of promised gentleness, teased her. She recalled the grasp of his hands around her arms, holding her down on the ground as his strong face loomed above her, dominating her, then his angry glance raking over her. She started, uncomfortably reminded of the other side of him, the angry, untrusting soul that was all too willing to lash out. She opened her eyes, seeing that Ansleen remained with her, and she flushed guiltily, wondering if her thoughts had been transparent.

"I drifted," Matalia stated apologetically.

Ansleen smiled. "We often do up here. One's mind has a tendency to meander. But you ought to get ready, because we will be leaving in the hour."

Spring flowers bloomed over the hill, blanketing it in a colorful collage of purple and blue, and Matalia banished her unruly thoughts to focus on hitching the mule to the old wagon. The thick smell of the herbs wafted in the breeze, and she welcomed the freshness of the morning.

Well before noon, the wagon was loaded and the women clambered aboard. Matalia saddled her mare, shifting her short sword to her left side. Then she called out to her wolves. When the three beasts were in sight, she nodded to Ansleen and they started slowly down the hill. After a brief hesitation at the stone border, the wagon rolled over the stones and finally entered the woods.

"How far is the market town?" Matalia asked. She felt a surge of excitement at the thought of seeing other people.

"If we make good time, we should be there by nightfall."

Matalia looked at the plodding mule with concern. "Do you ever make good time?" she inquired politely.

Gweneath grinned. "No." Just then the mule balked and the wagon came to a halt. Acting unconcerned, Gweneath withdrew a piece of bread from her satchel and began eating.

"Shouldn't you make the mule move?" Matalia asked, her irritation beginning to show. Her own mare pranced with high energy as eager as Matalia to keep moving.

Ansleen pulled out her own bread and shrugged. "The mule will only go when it wants to," she replied.

Annoyed by the delay, Matalia swung off her mare and gripped the mule's bridle. Yanking on the halter, she berated him for his cantankerous nature. "You beast, move on! I want to get to market!"

With a grunt, the mule relented and took two steps before planting his hooves and stopping again. "Augh!" Matalia groaned and gave up. She stared down the dirt road longingly.

Ansleen smiled. "Matalia, you can keep going if you wish. There is a beautiful loch just down the way. You follow the road for several turns. Then there is a steep path that runs beside a stream. If you follow that, you will come to the loch."

Matalia looked around with concern. "Will you be safe without me?"

Ansleen laughed. "We have made this trip many times for many years. We are old women with only herbs in our wagon and an old, ornery mule. No one will bother us. You are the one who should be careful."

Matalia patted her sword and motioned to the wolves that milled around her. "I have no fear. I will be safe. No one would dare molest me!" And then she dug her heels into the mare's sides and shot down the road.

Chapter 10

After ten minutes of vigorous galloping, Matalia noted the path that Ansleen had described. Both she and the mare were sweaty, and the wolves were panting from their exertions. Picking her way carefully along the stream, she eventually came to an open area that spread into a gleaming, crystal-blue loch.

She smiled, pleased with the discovery. Leaping off her mare, she ran to the water's edge. After a surreptitious look around her, she discarded her outer clothing and walked quickly to an overhanging rock. She wore only a loose chemise, and as she stood on the rock, a soft wind blew her linen underclothes against her body, molding her curves deliciously. There was a fullness to her breasts, a soft rounded curve to her belly. . . . Her body was the blossoming flower of childhood changing into womanhood.

"Wonderful!" she exclaimed. "How absolutely wonderful!" Matalia lifted her arms above her head and closed her eyes. Taking a deep breath, she dove off the rock, deep into the clear loch. The water sluiced around her, cooling her steaming body instantly, refreshingly. As she broke the surface, she smiled and started to hum a light, lively ballad. She swam briskly, then treaded water, looking around her at the profusion of spring growth. The trees were budding, the squirrels were chattering, and the grass was growing. Matalia luxuriated, letting the solitude wash over her.

Alternately floating or swimming, she spent long moments enjoying herself.

The man watching her scowled.

A low tremor swept through Matalia and she stopped her song midverse to glance inquiringly over at the black wolf. It was standing stiffly, hackles raised, gazing into the thick woods. Matalia glanced in the direction of his look, suddenly uncommonly frightened. She swam to the lake edge and quickly stepped out, allowing the water to wrap her chemise close to her body, forming the allure of protection while actually revealing every nuance of her form.

She grabbed her dress, desperately trying to right it, while the second of her wolves growled low in his throat. Matalia finally managed to get her dress unraveled, and she tugged it on rapidly, ignoring the dangling strings along the side. She searched for her weapon, picking up her sword and swinging it experimentally, liking the feel of it in her hands. She glared around her, daring the creature that she sensed to make itself known.

A blaze of pure desire ripped through him, just as it had the first time he had seen her. Her hair was a mass of jet-black curls wrapping riotously around her shoulders; her eyes were blazing jewels. Bits of creamy breast swelled out of her unlaced gown, taunting him, calling out to him. His grip tightened, and the hilt of his sword bit deeply into his palm while his horse pranced in the shadows. He felt the swell of his essence strain his breeches, but the pain of his arousal was welcoming, for it served to remind him of his goal. Kirkcaldy. Anything for Kirkcaldy.

Backing away, unsure of where the danger lay, Matalia moved toward the path. She pulled her wet dress up her legs, tucking it into her waist so that her long, coltish legs were completely freed. She held her sword in front of her, circling it slowly as a warning.

The wolves bounded around her, their jaws snapping, the hair raised upon their backs, making them look like furred demons in black, silver and red as they closed around her in protection. A sudden movement in the trees made the wolves snarl, and Matalia swung around to face the threat.

Brogan—or Xanthier—stepped out and saluted her with his own sword. "Are you challenging me, Matalia?"

"Who are you? Brogan or Xanthier?"

"What? You cannot tell the difference between your own husband and his twin brother?"

"I am not sure. Tell me who you are. Though I am not sure it matters in the long run. If you are Xanthier, you have probably come to kill me, and if you are Brogan, I fear the desire is the same."

"In that, my sweet, you are correct. I have very few nice feelings for you. However, I do not intend to kill you . . . yet."

"How comforting," Matalia replied sarcastically.

"I intend to prolong my vengeance." He stepped forward and smiled at her with his lips alone. His gray eyes remained flat and angry.

Matalia stepped back nervously. "Tell me who you are," she demanded once again.

"I am your enemy."

"That does not answer my question."

The man lunged at her, his sword striking hers with a clang. The wolves leaped at him as Matalia struggled to keep her balance, but he quickly disengaged from her and swung at the black wolf. His blade swept the wolve's hide, and the canine dropped back in pain. The man spun and pointed the sword at the odd-eyed silver wolf that was slinking forward. He quickly knelt down and picked up a stone from the ground. He feinted toward the silver one, then flung the rock at the red wolf, striking him in the face. The red wolf yelped, shaking his head, while the silver darted around and attempted to attack from behind.

Matalia lifted her sword and lunged, drawing blood from the man's shoulder just as the silver wolf pounced upon him. The wolf's teeth sank into the man's other arm, causing him to howl in fury. He swung his arm against a nearby tree, crashing against the wolf. At the same time he swung at Matalia, smashing his heavy sword against her light one.

Matalia had learned swordplay at a young age and had fenced often, yet the sheer power of his blows made her hand numb. In terror, she backed away, desperately trying to keep her sword raised. Seeing the black wolf's bloody injury, the red wolf's swollen eye, and the silver one lying senseless on the ground, Matalia was petrified.

"Merciful heaven!" she screamed. "Don't kill me!"

The man advanced, his eyes flashing steel daggers. "And why not! You have ruined everything! Everything I have worked for all my life!" Matalia shook her head, but he continued relentlessly. "If you are gone, I will be able to claim Kirkcaldy!"

"Please!" she cried. "If you kill me it will be murder!"

He laughed, the sound ugly. "You raised your sword against me first, m'lady."

In horror, Matalia watched as he aimed his sword at her heart. In desperation, she dropped her blade and sank to her knees. "I beg you," she pleaded. "Please . . ."

The man paused. "Pick up your weapon," he commanded harshly.

"Please . . ." she whispered again. "If you hurt me now, you will he maiming an unarmed victim."

The man growled. "There is no one to see. I could still run you through."

"Surely the next Earl of Kirkcaldy would not be so dishonorable," Matalia replied.

"You know nothing of honor, m'lady. Are you not the same woman who abandoned her own husband?

Who kissed her own brother-in-law? Who dwells with women who are known to be unfaithful?"

Matalia's eyes narrowed with anger. "Speak what you will about my actions, but do not malign the women of the cottage. They are good women, falsely accused."

"Do you know that for certain?" When Matalia said nothing, the man lowered his sword. "If I am forced to raise arms against you again, I will not be so lenient. Rise and mount your mare. We are leaving."

Matalia stood, her body trembling. "Leaving?" she replied shakily.

"Need I say it twice?" he asked angrily as he lifted his sword again, and Matalia quickly walked over to her mare and mounted.

Brogan watched her scramble aboard her horse, her damp curls riotous. He was furious. How could she not see that he was her husband!? How could she not feel the sexual pull between them? The bond they had already created? Was she truly so disinterested in him that she did not feel the same things he felt whenever he was near her? Despite her waywardness, her stubbornness, and her ability to toss his plans around with careless effort, he was inexplicably drawn to her. She was wild and fascinating. She was full of life and yet, amazingly naïve.

She turned toward him, a frown on her face. "My wolves are injured."

He shrugged. "As am I. Do you have the same concern for me? Your sword hand is quick. I have not been bloodied in many years." Matalia looked at the oozing slash on his arm with satisfaction. "Teach them to never attack me again," he stated when she did not respond to his question. He looked at the wounded black wolf, and they exchanged deep stares. When the wolf finally dropped his gaze, Brogan nodded with satisfaction.

"Will you not tell me if you are Brogan or Xanthier?"

Brogan glared at her, incensed. "When you think you know the answer, tell me. Until then, I will say nothing on the matter." He mounted his stallion and motioned toward the deep woods. "Should I tie you?"

Matalia glared at her captor and vigorously shook her head. "That is not necessary." Then, with a concerned glance toward her animal companions, she preceded him into the forest. "What do you want?" she asked. She twisted and looked back, trying to gather clues to his identity. The horse looked familiar, but she wasn't sure if it was Brogan's or Xanthier's. The man rode with fluid grace, and he treated his beast well. Although she knew that Brogan was a good horseman, she did not know about Xanthier.

Matalia felt a stirring in her nether regions as she accompanied this strange man into the dark woods. Something about how he watched her was thrilling, and she glanced away guiltily, fearing censor.

He nudged his horse to the side in order to avoid her direct gaze. He removed his shirt, feeling clammy. For some reason, her frequent glances were making him nervous, and he preferred to keep her in his view, yet stay out of hers.

She rode forward, then turned and ducked below some branches so she could better view him. However, she could only glimpse a muscled thigh before he shifted out of sight once again. Frustrated but intrigued, Matalia urged her mare into a trot, then spun her around. This time she saw his bare chest, a wide expanse that rippled with masculine power, crisscrossed with leather straps that led to his kilt. Matalia gasped, abruptly unsure of the wisdom of trying to determine who he was by his body. She backed her horse away, looking behind her to assure the safety of her retreat.

The man stopped, too, uncannily aware of her thoughts.

Matalia froze at his chuckle.

"Afraid?" he rumbled, and the sound of his voice shook her. She stayed still, debating, wondering, until he moved toward her again. She stared at him defiantly, unaware that she trembled.

Afraid? she thought to herself. *Absolutely.* The voice was more than familiar. It was the same voice that had haunted her, enraged her, tormented her these days past as she had tried to escape reality and immerse herself in the cottage life. He had come for her, she thought, a flicker of excitement threatening to emerge. She closed her eyes briefly and took a deep breath, scenting his sweat on the breeze, smelling as well the rising odor of her own arousal. He had come for her. . . . She threw her shoulders back and opened her eyes.

Brogan watched her, blood thrumming through his head, his fists clenched as he fought the desire to snatch her and throw her over his back to carry her home like some Viking barbarian stealing his bride. He swung off his stallion and moved silently toward her, motioning for her to dismount. Closer, closer still, until he could reach her in two strides, he strode forward, and still she sat, indecision on her face. He could see the thoughts running over her countenance like lightning. The desire he had created, the fear he had fostered, the boldness that was her very own.

She was not the woman he had wanted as a wife, but she was his. She was the woman he wanted to tame. She drew him, she tantalized him, she challenged him. He moved one step closer, willing to take her forcefully, when she jumped down and faced him daringly.

"If you kiss me, I will know who you are," Matalia called out.

Brogan smiled with half his mouth, the amusement not reaching his silver eyes. Bargaining was not part of the plan. He hesitated, debating quickly, as Matalia stared at him.

Brogan snarled. "Do not be a fool. I know that you now remember that Brogan will not kiss, yet Xanthier kissed you only to annoy Brogan. Neither man has the desire for pressing lips against lips with you."

Matalia flushed, suddenly hurt. She swallowed and stared at him in confusion. "Then I will never kiss you!" Hopelessness spread throughout her heart, and her throat constricted. She felt lonely, afraid, and unsure. A broken breath escaped, and she wrapped her arms around her waist in pain.

Brogan watched her collapse with alarm. She was so strong, so commanding, he was stunned by this evidence of her weakness. Without thought, he reached for her and wrapped his arms protectively around her.

"Come, little gem. 'Tis not you I mind kissing. 'Tis just not what men prefer."

"But I thought . . ." Matalia replied with a quiver in her voice. She raised her eyes to him, and he saw the tears filling them. He frowned, uneasy with his deception. He pushed a lock of hair from her face and rubbed her eyes roughly with his thumb.

"Matalia . . ."

"Don't touch me!" she snapped, highly irritated. "I do not know who you are and will not be seduced by the wrong man again."

Abruptly Brogan laughed. "Ah, Matalia, and here I thought you wounded. You were only setting yourself up to make demands, were you not? What a fine strategist you are. What if I told you I was Brogan? Would you, then, succumb to me?"

She looked at him consideringly while mumbling a tenuous assent. She searched his face, looking for something and not sure if she found it.

Brogan's smile faded as she watched him, and an ache filled him as he saw her tongue slip softly around her lips. His hand lifted involuntarily, brushing the moisture. Matalia's mouth opened, and Brogan touched her teeth. Her tongue wet his finger and his eyes darkened with desire.

He yanked his hand from her mouth and wrapped it around her throat, caressingly, smoothing his thumb over her pulse and tilting her neck with his fingers. He bent down, moving his head to bury his lips into the curve revealed. His lips stroked her there, at a safe distance from her lips but close enough to her face to make her faint with longing, giving her a small concession.

He growled appreciatively, then swept his hands down her back to her buttocks, gripping each side with powerful hands, squeezing and kneading the soft globes. Then, abruptly, he lifted her onto a fallen log so that she was sitting with her legs spread around his waist. Before she could respond to her new position Brogan had lifted both her dress and his kilt and had his cock in hand, ready to slide into her depths.

"No!" Matalia cried, although her word related more to her instant wet response than as a command to him. Ignoring her, the man wrapped an arm around her back and pulled her onto him, making her impale herself with his strength. In unison, they both gasped at the sudden, overwhelming heat generated by their friction, and Matalia gripped his shoulders in instant, fulminating pleasure, clinging to him with her nails.

Brogan plunged inside her, his pent-up desire exploding in instantaneous climax. As he came, he stroked inside her, once, twice, thrice, then gripped her tightly, shuddering while he poured into her.

Matalia was swept along with his intensity, and her rippling reply began with his first attack. She wrapped her thighs around him, clenching him inside her, letting the waves of ecstasy sweep from her toes to her eyelids. Her nightly dreams became riveting realities. She gasped in surrender, in submission, as her pleasure swept pride aside, granting her the freedom to relent. She could not keep pace with the feelings that cascaded through her, then splintered her inner core. She was overwhelmed and lost. She clung to him helplessly, vulnerable and open, her shivering endless in the wake of such a firestorm of passion.

In mere seconds they stood silent, both of them shocked. Matalia felt a final twitch from his manhood, and she gasped, her own inner muscles gripping in response. The man groaned, exquisitely sensitive to her movements, and his hands pressed against her sides, willing her to be still. He leaned his forehead against hers and closed his eyes. She leaned against him as well, relaxing her death grip on his shoulders, letting the sensations he had evoked roll over her. . . . Then she started to shake, staring at him with a mixture of horror and hope.

The man lifted his head and gave her waist a final squeeze. He slipped out of her, still half hard, and grinned at her triumphantly. "Do you know who I am now?"

"Please, God, tell me you are Brogan," she whispered.

He choked and pushed her fully away. "Come," he said, not answering her. "Mount your horse. We must reach the cabin tonight."

Chapter 11

When she continued to stare at him, he cleared his throat and motioned to the mare.

Matalia bit her lip as she slid off the log while Brogan watched her moodily. How could she still not know? When she took a step away from him, his eyes narrowed fiercely and he stepped with her.

Matalia glanced up at his still face, frightened but determined that she would decide her own fate. She took another step backward and gasped as the man followed her, his stride as menacing as a cougar's. "I have things . . . things I must attend," she whispered. "I need to tell Ansleen and Gweneath that I am safe."

"Are you?" he questioned angrily.

Ignoring him, she continued. "And I need to tend the wolves."

"The old women will know that I have taken you," he answered without pause.

"I must say good-bye. They will wonder. . . ."

"They already know." His voice was harsh and uncompromising.

A flair of rebellion awoke in her eyes, and she glared back at him. They stood, staring at each other, both daring the other silently, until Matalia suddenly dashed through the trees toward the open slope. He caught her easily, but her violent struggle forced him to let go else he hurt her. She ran down the path. He followed her, his gray eyes cold and deadly.

"You idiot," he snapped at her. "Do you fathom the danger you are in right now?"

"From you!" Matalia cried in response.

"I am not the one you should fear."

"Then you are Brogan!" she breathed.

"Aye, though you would not have known if I had not revealed it to you. What kind of wife are you that you do not recognize your husband?"

"A new one!" she replied heatedly. "We have known each other only a short while."

Brogan turned away and strode back toward the horses. "Xanthier would like nothing better than to see you fall to your death from the ledge above the loch you just bathed in. Or better yet, see you drown within its depths so your body is never recovered." His voice was so frigid, so frighteningly truthful, Matalia stared at him in dismay.

"No one would wish that upon his brother's wife," she replied uncertainly as she trailed him.

"Ha!" Brogan laughed. "You know naught of the struggle for power. In your privileged world of love and comfort you have seen nothing of what others deal with daily. I was born to fight against my kin, and murder is the least of my worries." He turned on her and raked her form with his gaze. "Are you breeding yet?"

Matalia gasped in outrage. "How would I know?" she cried. " 'Tis too soon! And pray do not call it 'breeding' as if I were a cow."

"Xanthier's wife has missed her first monthly. She is said to be carrying a babe already."

"A contest, then?" she queried in anger. "You want to know if we created a child because of a stupid rivalry between you and your brother?"

"Of course. Did you think otherwise?" His voice dripped with sarcasm. "If you are barren I will let you to wither within the cottage walls as those women have done since their husbands cast them out."

"Ohhh!" Matalia cried again. Brogan stepped back in surprise, unaware of how hurtful his words were. His life of hardship, betrayal, and intrigue had left him cold and calculating. Seeing the loathing in her beautiful eyes truly shocked him, for he understood no other way of life. He set his lips, forcing himself to push her, knowing that tenderness was unthinkable if he was to achieve his life's goal, the acquisition of Kirkcaldy.

"You promised me one year and one child, Matalia McTaver O'Bannon. When will you know if you are carrying?"

"Let me understand this. You captured me only because you want a child? Because the wife that delivers first shall gift her husband with his inheritance?"

"We are not dependent solely upon your womb. We have fought for much in the last fifteen years. I have accumulated wealth beyond the stores of my home coffers. I have proven myself a warrior of considerable repute. I have married a wife, and if you are not the docile thing I wanted, at least you are from a good family. Now you must prove me virile. It will be up to my father to make the final judgment when he assesses all that Xanthier and I have accomplished. But should all be equal, the first child born gains the inheritance."

"So I am nothing but part of your schemes."

"I was nothing but part of yours," he replied angrily, reminding her of how they had met. Matalia dropped her eyes once again, accepting the truth of his statement.

"And if I do not want to go with you?" Matalia questioned.

"Do you really want to ask?" replied Brogan, a thread of amusement in his voice. He touched the sword sheathed at his side.

Matalia looked at him askance, then kicked a stone

with her toe. She looked over at the wolves, seeing their limping forms. Changing the subject, she countered his question with another.

"What was that stone path at the cottage? Why was Ansleen so certain you would not pass through it?"

Brogan stared at her, silent.

"Can you not answer a simple question?" Matalia asked mockingly.

"The answer is more complex than you realize. I have not the words you seek."

"Than who does?"

Brogan looked pensive. "I lived there once," he murmured. "I lived there for many years." He had a sad expression on his face. "We used to get along, my brother and I. We were very close from the moment we were born, as twins often are. Even before we met, I knew he was out there. I could feel him. You see, even though we were separated at birth, our souls could not be disentangled. When we became older we would ride out and meet with each other, staying in the woods for days together, talking and playing. He was my best friend.

"But then . . . Xanthier . . . Xanthier and I began to fight over everything. We knew our friendship was doomed. We knew that brotherly love"—he spat out the final word—"was not allowed between us. We were born to be enemies." Brogan's gaze swung back to Matalia's. "But I refuse to fight over you."

She drew back, affronted.

"You must stay far from him," Brogan hissed furiously. "He will charm you like a snake, then poison you with his venom. Fear him, wife. Fear him greatly."

Matalia stared at him, terrified, feeling even more strongly that the haven of the cottage was more welcoming than returning with Brogan to his turbulent homeland. She thought wistfully of her siblings and the lackadaisical care she had bestowed upon them.

How she wished now that she had fawned over them more, relished their small accomplishments, treated them like little treasures. She acknowledged within herself how much her own parents had done for her and how lucky she was to have a caring family.

Not completely aware of her own motivations, she placed her hands upon Brogan's wide, muscular chest. She leaned up, brushing her cheek against his bristly one, and passed her lips over his face like a butterfly flitting over wild heather.

"You can trust me, husband," she murmured. Then she placed her hand in his and tugged him toward the horses. Brogan seemed frozen, his countenance betraying no response to her delicate caress. Matalia pulled harder and tilted her head when he remained still as a stone, only his eyes following her.

"There is no such word as 'trust,'" he finally answered, dredging a depth of emotion into his pronouncement.

Matalia sighed and dropped his hand, turning away from his narrowed gaze. Instantly springing to life, Brogan grabbed her hand again, holding it tightly. She turned back, and stared seriously into his troubled eyes. "You *can* trust me," she said.

"You have not proven that. You have already betrayed your vows by leaving my side," he answered.

Gently disengaging his tight fingers, Matalia shook her head sorrowfully. "You are right, Brogan, and I am sorry for my impulsiveness. I did make a promise to you. I swear that I will be trustworthy and thereby teach you to believe in the good of others."

Brogan looked at her, his innards twisted with anxiety. When she had been inside the cottage boundaries she had been completely inaccessible to him. That sense of helplessness enraged him. It reminded him of another day, fifteen years ago, when he had been torn from his mother's side, despite her whispered assurances. He still remembered his own racking sobs as she had placed him on the far side of the stone boundary, giving him over to the Earl.

"You are a young man now, Brogan," his mother had said. "I have taught you all I can. Now you must learn the skills only a man can teach you. One day you will be the master of Kirkcaldy, and I will be very proud of you."

"No!" he had shouted after her. "I will not leave without you!"

She had turned back, staring at him sorrowfully. "I cannot come to you, and you can never come back to me. See this stone barrier? Hereafter, it can never be crossed by a man of O'Bannon blood. There will be no exceptions. Do not ever return. Your life is Kirkcaldy. You will prevail. Now go claim your land." Then she had walked up the mountain, her hair blowing softly in the breeze behind her.

Xanthier had laughed at Brogan's tears, and to spite him, had picked up several rocks and flung them after their mother's retreating back. Brogan's ire had burst, and the ensuing brawl between them had been ferocious. Whatever love the brothers had shared was transformed into hatred. The caring changed into full-fledged animosity, and their lifetime of fighting began. Three of his father's knights had been required to separate them, and the warriors had gasped for air when finally they held each of the screaming twins separate from the other. Then, as Brogan wiped the blood from his nose, he had turned from the sight of the cottage and rather than submit to his father's will, he had fled into the forest and set out to seek his fortune, abandoning his mother just as she had left him.

Brogan shuddered. Walking swiftly as he relived his past, he pulled his sword from its hilt and swung it in the air. He had not only left his mother and the cottage that day, he had also left Scotland. Ignoring his mother's wish that he live at Kirkcaldy to learn warfare and leadership, he had left everything and earned his manhood abroad. Most had thought he would never return.

It had been Xanthier who had inadvertently called him home. That inexplicable bond between them had drawn him back to Scotland. As Brogan looked out over the water, he recalled his childhood fantasy of living at Kirkcaldy. Now that he was home, he had every intention of winning his inheritance. Nothing was going to stop him. Nothing and no one.

He swung the sword in the air, fighting the demons in his mind. He parried and thrust, practicing war maneuvers, releasing his fear in the only way he knew. Again and again, until he was dripping with sweat, and then he turned on branches and bushes around him, mowing them to the ground with a vengeance.

Far above him, Ansleen sat next to Gweneath in the herb-laden wagon, watching her favorite son battle the beasts of his memories. She ached for him and his obvious pain. Tears welled in her eyes at the tragedy of his life. To be cast out of his rightful home and forced to live his younger years in isolation with only two women to tend him while his father ignored his existence had hurt her enough, but now to see the deadly unrest in his soul made her faint with despair. *God bless him,* she pleaded silently. *Please let him find some happiness.*

Below Brogan, completely unaware of the women above, Matalia watched as well. She breathed quickly, thrilling at the sight of his thoroughly male form bulging with power and strength as he swung his sword, releasing his frustration and anger. The stance of his body was phenomenal, awe-inspiring, and incredibly sensual. Matalia felt weak, her body trembling with desire. She did not want to live at the cottage. Despite her misgivings, her fears, and her anxieties, she knew that she wanted to be with her husband. An emotion blossomed deep inside of her. She wanted him. She wanted his strength and his passion, for her own wild spirit ached with unfulfilled needs.

Part II

~

The Gathering

Chapter 12

With Matalia's new knowledge of herbs and healing, she had tended her wolves' injuries and now they poured around her as they all made their way rapidly through the forest. When they neared the stream that had initially separated them, Brogan roughly motioned for Matalia to take the lead, and she lowered her eyes politely as she nudged the mare through the sparkling water. Brogan's horse plunged in behind her without hesitation, and they emerged upon the other bank in unison. A hawk perched on a high branch swiveled his head sharply at the brilliant reflections of sunlight striking the wet hides of the horses. Matalia's hem emerged soaked and her waist was sprayed with a fine mist, causing a chill to race over her skin. She shivered and moved her horse forward, ahead of Brogan once again.

The unspoken truce between them was fragile, so neither felt inclined to speak. Matalia's back was rigid with tension, and Brogan could see the outline of her sweeping curves through the damp gown. His groin tightened immediately, and he cursed under his breath while casting his eyes to the side. He gripped the reins so tightly, the stallion tossed his head in agitation.

Hearing the beast's sudden motions, Matalia glanced behind her, a brow quirked in inquiry. "Is something amiss?" she questioned.

Brogan did not meet her eyes, most of his energy focused upon holding his desire in check.

"No," he replied gruffly, but his horse whinnied sharply, and Matalia was unconvinced.

"Where is your large dog?" she asked, attempting conversation.

"He awaits at the edge of the forest, where my ancestral lands begin." He closed his eyes for a moment, blocking the sight of her twisted position as she looked back at him. The cloth of her gown was held tightly against her breasts, highlighting the small pucker of her nipples, while the rest bunched around her waist, emphasizing the swell of her hips.

Matalia bit her lip, thinking she had annoyed him with her questions. She turned forward once again, hurt by his harsh behavior. Brogan sighed with relief, and transferring the reins temporarily to one hand, he lifted the other to rub his temples.

"We will reach the edge of the lands by evening, and after freshening, we will proceed to Kirkcaldy."

"Freshening?" she inquired, turning again.

The small nubs had risen to firm peaks, and a pebbling of goose bumps rippled along her arms from the cool breeze. Brogan's fierce glower shocked Matalia with its unexpectedness. She glared back, annoyed by his dour attitude, and faced forward while nudging the mare into a trot.

Brogan rolled his eyes, half amused at his body's uncontrollable twitch at the sight of her bottom bouncing gently on the saddle. When Matalia heard his muffled amusement, she flushed, thinking he was making fun of her in some unknown manner, and she spurred her horse faster. Brogan grinned, for despite the twisted tension of knowing the delights of her body yet holding himself deliberately back, he was pleased to have her with him. She belonged next to him. She belonged with him for the duration of the year—until she bore his child, he amended silently, with a returning frown.

He kicked his own steed, and the warhorse surged forward after the mare, long strides rapidly carrying him abreast of her. Matalia looked over at him, her flair of irritation changing instantly into competitiveness. She drove her heels into the mare's sides and leaned forward, and the pair swept past Brogan. His mouth crooked with something that resembled a spontaneous smile before he, too, leaned forward and sent his stallion racing.

The pair galloped madly, leaving the wolves behind, accompanied by a burst of screeches from the startled hawk. The bird rose into the air, flapping its wings until it caught a gust and then drifted downstream to calmer environs.

Brogan held his warhorse in check, allowing his lengthy strides to keep abreast of the smaller mare. They raced in tandem, allowing the wind to strip them of their accumulated anxieties, feeling the thunder of the ground accelerate their pulses. The dampness of the stream quickly changed to the sting of salty sweat, and the odor of wet horseflesh trailed after them. They galloped through an open meadow, then darted, side by side, into the tree-shadowed road that led west. The ground was hard packed under a light sponge of new grass, and the horses stretched out farther, flinging their hooves far out, gathering their legs close underneath, surging forward with fantastic speed, until the humans atop them simply melded with them, not urging or slowing, simply experiencing the thrill of the ride.

Gradually, incrementally, the horses slowed, their nostrils flared and their necks foamy. Matalia sat up and transferred the reins to one hand so she could brush her tangled hair away from her eyes. Her thighs trembled and her eyes shone as she looked over at her mate. Brogan looked back at her, noting the flush on her cheeks, the rapid rise and fall of her chest. He was at a loss for words. He opened his mouth to say something as the horses slowed to a casual canter, then shook his head and remained silent. Instead, he finally twitched the reins, permitting the stallion to change gaits, and as soon as he descended to a trot and then to an exhausted walk, the mare followed, dipping her head low and swishing her tail in pleasure.

Matalia dropped the reins entirely and stretched up, then from side to side. She took her feet out of the stirrups and pointed and flexed her toes. She grinned with delight. "Now I have galloped over unknown meadows."

Brogan chuckled, pleased that she was happy. He reached over and pulled a piece of hair out of her mouth. Watching her response to his intimate gesture, Brogan asked, "Your wolves? Will they follow?"

Matalia smiled prettily and nodded. "Of course. They always follow me."

"They seem wild."

"They are," she replied.

Glancing behind them, Brogan quirked an eyebrow in question. "Tell me about them. How did such wild beasts come to be tamed by you?"

Matalia glanced back as well. She could see their slender forms far back, still in the grassland. "Do you really want to know?" she asked uncertainly.

Brogan smiled and nodded. "I find I am curious about you. You are unlike anyone I have ever met."

Matalia cast her eyes down, unsure if he complimented her. "Do you know about my family? My mother?"

"Only a little. Remember, I have spent the greater part of my life in other countries."

"Ah. Yes, I forgot. My mother is the forest princess of Loch Nidean. She comes from a land of druids. She is very powerful and can communicate with animals as easily as she can talk to us. Do you think this odd?"

"It is unusual, but I have seen many things in my travels, and I do not disbelieve your tale."

"From her I inherited a small gift. My voice."

"You have a beautiful voice."

"No, that is not what I mean. I can . . . soothe . . . animals sometimes."

"With your voice," he repeated, watching her.

She looked up and bit her lip, nodding.

"I heard you do that the very first day I met you. You calmed my wolfhound."

"It is a slow gift, however, and not always helpful. It takes time and sometimes one does not have that luxury. That is how I came to have the wolves. I came across their mother engaged in a fight with a badger." Matalia blinked rapidly, trying to clear her eyes. "She was terribly brave! She was struggling so hard! I tried to calm the badger, but I was too late and the beast killed the mother wolf. I was devastated. I was so angry! What good was my silly gift when I could not save a mother in distress? It was awful. Then I heard the pups. They were tiny balls of fur, with wet noses and fluffy tails, and I fell in love with them at once. Because they had no one, I took them and raised them myself."

After a long pause, Brogan reached out and touched her hand. "I do not think you should feel poorly about the mother wolf. Sometimes we do not have a choice in life . . . or death. It was her time to go. Think instead that she gave you a gift of her children so that you would be protected and cared for by three beautiful friends."

Matalia stared at him, amazed by his sensitivity. He was such a tough man. He was uncompromising and hard, yet he had the ability to empathize with her feelings. Her gaze swept his face, noting the hard lines around his eyes, the strong chin, the weathered skin. She did not understand how he could have developed two such diverse aspects in his character.

Suddenly Brogan pulled away and frowned.

"What?" asked Matalia.

"He is near."

"Who?"

"My brother."

Xanthier looked up. His gray eyes scanned the forest edge and he frowned. Rising slowly from the chair, he lifted the tent flap wider and peered out. His lieutenants rose as well, looking at each other in concern.

"He in on his way," Xanthier said softly.

"Do you want us to intercept him? Ambush him?"

Xanthier glanced at Brice with distain. "You already attempted that. Need I remind you that you failed?" Brice flushed and fell silent. Xanthier stepped outside as he belted his sword across his hips. "Still, I cannot let it be known that I am hindering his progress. At least not publicly."

"Why not? Why not attack him with your army and have done with it?"

Xanthier grinned. "It would not be sporting."

The other men shook their heads, not understanding the nuances of Xanthier and Brogan's fight, but Xanthier was their captain and they would follow his orders. With an abrupt turnabout, Xanthier strode to his horse. "Come," he commanded. "Pack up the men. We will drive him to the caves. Nothing scares him more than the caves."

"Sir?"

Xanthier laughed. "The Brogan I knew fifteen years ago was a brave young man. He was bold and fearless except that he feared the dark caves."

One man grunted. "What a weakling! To be afraid of the dark!"

Xanthier rounded on him in fury. "You know nothing of him! His strength far outweighs any man's! Do you know anything about the caves or what dwells within them?"

"I know only that they travel for miles underground, and that only your family knows their twists and turns."

"Get out of my sight! I never want to hear you disparage an O'Bannon again!"

The man nodded, frightened by Xanthier's wrath. Running hastily away, he motioned to the men, and they swiftly began disassembling the camp. They brought down the tents and packed the horses, and within the hour they were ready to move out. Xanthier rode in front, his large frame dominating his warhorse. "Split the troops. Send half to Kirkcaldy in case he sends men ahead. Scatter some in town. The rest will come with me."

"Aye," the lieutenants agreed in unison as Brice shifted to ride by Xanthier's side. He waved to his contingent and, at Xanthier's signal, they galloped away from the main army.

"How do you know where to find him, Captain?" Brice questioned when they peaked the first hill.

Xanthier shrugged, unwilling to admit to the connection he felt to his twin. As far as he was concerned, the thread that bound him to Brogan was a weakness, and he detested it. For years he had felt Brogan's absence with keen intensity, and the loss had bothered him immensely. But he had always known that Brogan lived, despite everyone else's conviction that he had perished at sea. He felt Brogan. He felt his twin's heartbeat as if it were his own.

Xanthier glared at the distant hills. Such a character flaw needed to be crushed. If Brogan died, then he would be free of the connection they shared. Conflict raged within him. He wished that Brogan had never returned. Now he was obligated to destroy him or he would never win Kirkcaldy, the home where he had been born and raised. It was his home! Brogan had no right to it! Brogan had never lived within its walls, never seen its rolling fields. It was Xanthier's rightful home!

Turning, he motioned to the market village. "He will probably head for the village. We should go there and cut him off. If we drive him back, he will be forced to go through the caverns or travel over the mountain."

"Does he know the caverns as well as you do?"

"No. If he enters them he will become lost," Xanthier replied.

"So be it," Brice answered with satisfaction.

"So be it," Xanthier agreed, but his voice lacked a note of conviction.

Several hours later Xanthier, Brice and their ten men entered the market town. Wagons of all descriptions lined the roadway. Looking only for evidence of Brogan, Xanthier was oblivious to the squawking chickens, the bleating sheep and the lowing cows. Stands with sweetmeats, fresh bread and aromatic soaps did not capture his attention. His contingent rode through the streets. He passed a wagonful of herbs without a glance.

Ansleen and Gweneath watched him ride past, his tight expression striking fear into their hearts. "Was there not more I could have done to stop this?" Ansleen whispered.

"No, my dear friend. All we can do now is pray for them."

"Do you think Matalia will be good for Brogan? And what of Xanthier's bride?"

"I am not certain about Brogan's fate. Matalia might have too much spirit. She is so independent. I fear she will only escalate the situation. I just heard that Xanthier married Isadora of Dunhaven."

"She is a spiteful witch!"

"Hush," cautioned Gweneath. "She may soon be the new Countess of Kirkcaldy. It would not do well to be heard speaking poorly of her."

Xanthier was aware of the people's careful regard. He knew the people feared him as they feared his father. It was the way of things. He expected complete respect and obedience from the people because he was to be their master. Benevolence was unheard of. He was the lord of all around him, and people were expected to bow to his presence.

He pulled up and faced a brick maker. "Have you seen Brogan O'Bannon pass this way? Answer me true, or I will find much to anger me."

"No, m'lord. I have not seen him, but his caravan passed not two days ago."

"Tell me more."

"He had wagons of riches, m'lord. It was an uncommon sight! He also had an army of soldiers guarding the treasure, and they looked to be a heathen lot. Foreigners, all of them."

"What do they call you?"

"My name is Tim Wallace, m'lord."

"I will expect word if you see Brogan pass through, Wallace. Do I have reason to doubt your allegiance?" Xanthier leaned forward and raised the tip of his sword to the man's chest.

Wallace swallowed and lowered his head. "No, m'lord," he mumbled.

Nodding, Xanthier sat back up. "We will rest here for the night. Then we set up into the hills. I will find him. It is time I publicly welcomed my brother home."

Chapter 13

Above the market town, Brogan and Matalia sat on their horses and watched the bustle of the village swell with the addition of Xanthier's men.

"Is that he?" Matalia asked.

"Aye. He knew that I would be traveling through the town. He seeks to stop me before I reach Kirkcaldy. Once I enter the courtyard, he will be obligated to acknowledge my challenge. But I am one step ahead of him. I never intended to travel through the village. We will cross the mountains. I have already scouted the area and found a place I knew as a child where we can rest."

"Kirkcaldy. Is it really so beautiful that it is worth fighting for?"

Brogan shrugged. "I have heard that it is passable. I have never been there."

"Never been there! Never? But I thought it was your birthplace?"

"You know nothing about my family, do you? How sheltered you have been." He turned his horse and headed away from the village. "As a child, my brother and I explored Kirkcaldy land, but, other than the very day of my birth, I have not been inside the castle walls. Yet, I intend to win," he said forcefully. "I will win because my father believed I would not. Do you understand what awaits you there?"

Matalia looked at him quizzically, nudging her mare

to follow. "No, I suppose not. I thought to meet your clan, your father, your mother . . ."

"My mother is not there, Matalia. Surely you understand that. Ansleen is my mother."

Matalia averted her eyes briefly in shock, remembering the stories Ansleen had told of her ill-fated love. She felt great sorrow. "I have been given only innuendos, half-truths, tidbits of information. I did not realize the connection. I feel so unprepared to face your family."

Brogan stared into her eyes, the steel of his gaze somehow not as intimidating as he contemplated his answer. "You understand the . . . conflict . . . between Xanthier and me," he stated.

"You both were born to the Earl within moments of each other, but no one marked the true firstborn."

"Yes."

"There is a contest, and the winner of this ridiculous situation will inherit the title."

"I would not put it in such terms," he growled softly but with minor menace, "but you have the gist."

"Why is the title so important?" Matalia questioned.

"It is not just the title. It is Kirkcaldy. Kirkcaldy . . . my father . . . the injustice of separating us."

Matalia shook her head, attempting to interrupt. "But now you participate in the very fight that you deem wrong! I still do not understand."

"I have learned many things in the last fifteen years. I have learned that power and fortune are everything, and I will not rest until I have gained all that is rightfully mine."

"Bah! You know nothing! Even a spoiled child like me knows that the value of family love far exceeds that of power and fortune."

Brogan glanced at her, his smoky eyes unreadable. "Perhaps your experiences differ from mine."

Matalia replied just as softly. "Aye, I suppose they

do." She fell silent, deeply sorrowful that Brogan's strong-willed family was so stricken by hatred and anger. She bit her lip and thought about the tension between herself and her own mother. *Never,* she thought to herself, *never will I allow such misunderstandings to separate us as they have Brogan and his mother. As soon as I am able, I will send her my love and tell her how much she means to me.* She placed a protective hand over her abdomen and stared out over the flicking ears of her horse. *Perhaps I, too, will soon bear a child.*

"Never," she whispered softly, "never will I allow such bitterness in my family." Brogan glanced at her, hearing the soft hiss of her breath, and Matalia smiled reassuringly at him until he turned away, satisfied if not enlightened.

As their horses plodded along, their hides slowly drying and their muscles loose from their exertion, the pack of wolves slunk through the woods, closing in on them, sniffing for Matalia's scent. As they approached, the red wolf froze, lifting one paw into the air, his muzzle twitching.

Brogan shifted in the saddle and gathered his reins closer, signaling to his horse. The warhorse perked up, and his neck bunched while his steps lightened. Matalia looked at him curiously but followed suit, making sure her small mare was ready.

The shaded road curved, and Matalia could see streams of light reaching around the corner. She tilted her head, trying to see around the bend, and Brogan grinned with a return to good humor. He reined back, allowing Matalia's mare to walk ahead, and bowed gallantly from his waist while sweeping a hand forward.

"Kirkcaldy," he stated, pride filling his deep voice.

Matalia giggled at his serious expression and urged her horse around the curve, then gasped in a mixture of horror and awe. They stood at the peak of a small mountain whose gracefully sweeping sides poured down into the valley in a bubbling stream of bluebells and purple heather, dotted with wild yellow blossoms and random tufts of tall grass. The forest through which they had traveled abruptly ceased, allowing the flowered grassland uninhibited freedom to expand in undulating waves. Beyond the meadow, the valley suddenly became dotted with stony crags that tumbled and towered in profusion, forming the illusion of an ancient, ruined city. Intermixed within the stones were half-burned trees that sprouted new growth from their own rotting corpses, the fresh green contrasting brilliantly with the dull black of charred remains. Further still, the stones gathered, building strength and number, until gaping black holes dotted the countryside where caves formed in multitudes, creating a daunting wall of midnight wounds.

Matalia held her breath, not sure if the valley was beyond beautiful, or devastatingly desolate. She reached blindly for Brogan's hand, and was comforted when he responded by clasping her cold fingers in his strong grip. She swung her gaze around the valley again, searching for the castle, but locating only a small hut. She drew her brows together and bit her lip, her hand involuntarily clenching in his.

"Where is your home?" she asked hesitantly.

"All of this is my home, extending beyond the mountainside to the second and third valley before the walls of the Highlands rise upwards to the sky. Castle Kirkcaldy lies after the first rise."

"Then 'tis still a day away?"

"Aye. Two perhaps. We will have to travel over the mountain, which will be steep and treacherous. The caves . . . the caves form underground tunnels that lead much more quickly to Castle Kirkcaldy, but they present even greater risks. We will rest in the cabin for the evening, for the mists are thick at twilight and many an unwary soul has become lost within their tendrils."

"Your land is . . . gorgeous but . . . unfriendly."

Brogan smiled, nodding. "As it should be," he replied with satisfaction. "Come, let me show you what hospitality I can offer tonight."

Matalia tore her gaze from the scene and, as she looked at her husband's hard face, a surge of unfamiliar emotion swept her gut. Her heart began to race, for like the landscape, his visage held threat mixed with magnificence. She loosened her grip, swung her leg over her mare's withers, and dropped gracefully to the ground.

Brogan watched her in surprise, amazed by her spontaneous action. She flung the reins at him and hiked her skirts high. Then she flipped her hair over her shoulder and began to skip through the flowers. Brogan remained still, studying her perplexing behavior, while one by one her faithful wolves melted out of the forest and swept silently down through the grasslands to follow her path.

When one of them accidentally stepped on the hem of her skirt, she tripped and fell down, laughing, then rolled over onto her back and laughed yet more. Concerned, Brogan started after her, when she began to sing a sweet, lilting melody that curled around his ears and settled into his heart.

The wolves sat prostrate around her, and the small gray one lifted his nose and joined her with a haunting howl. Encouraged, Matalia sat up and sang louder, lifting her voice and dropping it in pure tones that vibrated softly. Her hair tossed around her shoulders, the wild curls completely unruly and innocently sensual. The red wolf placed his head in her lap and dropped his ears back, staring up at her adoringly while the black stood guard, his four legs planted far apart, ready to spring in any direction.

Down in the cottage, a large, bristly head rose from the deck, and the massive body of the wolfhound unfolded as he rose to listen to Matalia's husky voice. His rough bark joined the song, adding regular discord like the clashing of cymbals within a symphony. Brogan strolled down to where Matalia lay within the flowered meadowland and stared down at her with a half smile upon his face.

"You are a strange woman," he murmured, and Matalia smiled in response while she continued her wordless song. She reached up and gripped the edge of his kilt, urging him to sit with her, and he did, after casting an assessing glance around the meadow to be sure of their safety. The young red wolf lifted his head while the black wolf shifted over, his lips twitching slightly as Brogan lay down at a right angle to their mistress.

Matalia's song slipped lower, softer, and the silver wolf ceased his accompaniment to curl into a ball within a particularly lovely nest of yellow wildflowers. Matalia leaned up on her elbow and looked down at Brogan's tense face. She lifted his head and adjusted her position so that his head rested in her lap. Brogan's shoulders twitched as if he meant to rise until Matalia's hand started stroking his forehead and her nails eased gently through his hair to massage his scalp. With a sigh of pleasure, Brogan relaxed, letting her soothe him, letting the large black wolf guard them, letting her low voice pour over him. Bit by bit, his eyes drifted shut, and he allowed his body to simply absorb the peace that surrounded him.

The dream came to him, broken and irregular in his state of semiwakefulness, but welcome nonetheless. Gray mist swirled in his mind, and the warmth of a blanket wrapped around his cool limbs. He searched the low clouds for her presence and finally located her waiting at the edge of a lake. He walked forward, or seemed to, for his legs did not move yet he was near her. She reached out, and her hands touched his face, soothing and stroking. The sensation continued, and Brogan relaxed further, each muscle releasing its grip in tiny increments, until he felt a new peace sweep his heart. Only then could he slip into a deep, dreamless sleep, where he was infinitely calmed.

Matalia watched him slide into slumber, and she continued to brush her fingers over his face. He seemed exhausted, physically and spiritually, and she felt a touch of sorrow for him. It surprised her that he had allowed the intimacy of her fingers against his cheek, but she reveled in the chance to be so close to him, to feel the bones that formed his face. Her voice dropped to a hum, and she smiled in welcome at the Irish wolfhound as he finally reached them and lay down next to his dozing master. The wolves shifted and moved, initially agitated by the dog's presence, but then they too settled down to slumber in the warm afternoon sun.

Finally only Matalia remained awake. She breathed deeply and then exhaled with a soft whoosh, letting the tensions of the past drift away. She wove her fingers through Brogan's hair and let her mind wander, thinking of nothing and everything. She felt peaceful for the moment, her rebellious nature calm. A stirring of protectiveness woke inside her breast, and she acknowledged the difference in her feelings. No longer simply enraged at being forced to marry, she accepted her new situation.

This man, this scarred man was her husband, and the emotional burdens he had revealed concerned her. His family, his fight for his birthright . . . his estrangement from his brother and father, his unreasonable resentment toward his mother. Matalia frowned, perturbed by the information he had revealed as well as the details he had omitted. What of the father? What would the current earl be like? Why had he cast such pain upon his wife and children? She looked back down at Brogan, brushing her fingers over his brow to smooth the worry wrinkles embedded there. She knew her running away had produced more distress, and she silently apologized for her selfishness.

"I am willing to start anew," she whispered, "and I will not . . . I will *endeavor* not," she amended with a tiny grin, "to cause you more pain or strife than what you have already endured." She sighed again, and placed her hand over his beating heart, then leaned back and closed her eyes.

Brogan drifted awake, his sense of calm confusing him until he turned and found his nose buried in his wife's skirts. He blinked, and his steady gray eyes found a pair of beady black ones staring back at him. Brogan stared at the oldest wolf, the black, and raised a brow in silent challenge. The wolf opened his mouth, panting slightly, and showed his glistening canines for effect. Brogan watched him warily, but did not relinquish Matalia's lap for several more minutes.

At last, Brogan sat up, then stretched and rose to his feet. The wolves scrutinized him, while the wolfhound yawned and also rose. Brogan looked around, ensuring their continued safety, then glanced down at the woman sleeping in the grass. She was so beautiful, he thought, with her long lashes brushing against her cheek and her plump red lips. Dragging his gaze away, he studied the sun and then shrugged. He would not mind spending the night in the cabin with Matalia before they headed for Castle Kirkcaldy. It was time he got to know her anyway. Once at the castle, they would never be assured of privacy.

He bent over and gathered Matalia in his arms, causing her to wake and stare at him sleepily.

"The sun will be setting soon, and I need to collect some things for your comfort," he said by way of answering her questioning look as he strode down the hill toward the cabin. Matalia curled her arms around his shoulders, amazed that he appeared to carry her with no effort. She snuggled against him and did not demur until he deposited her near the front door and then turned away.

"Brogan?" she asked.

"I am collecting wood," he answered, pausing but not turning around. When Matalia said nothing more, he continued on his way. His limbs were loose and powerful, and a wave of pleasure rippled through her. As he disappeared around the side of the cottage, she turned to face the door. Upon the panel, the O'Bannon family crest was burned into the wood. With a shiver of disquiet she was entering her husband's home for the first time. While it was only a cottage and not the main castle, it was still a symbol of his dominance. His home, his family crest. His wife. Taking a deep breath, she opened the door and stepped across the threshold.

Chapter 14

Inside, she was surprised to see a large wooden tub in front of a stone fireplace, a rolled palate for a bed, and an open cupboard filled with stores and cooking implements. There were no other pieces of furniture. Matalia looked around again, thinking that she must have missed something in the shadows, but nothing miraculously appeared. Perplexed, she exited the cottage. Lying against the side of the building were the rotted remnants of a broken table and chairs. She bit her lip and stared at them with concern just as Brogan reappeared with an armful of wood.

He saw her gaze, then turned back with a wry look. "When the O'Bannons disagree, it is usually not safe for the furniture. The last time I was in this hut was a week before I left Scotland. Xanthier and I knew that our father was making plans to forcibly take me from the cottage. We tried to act as if nothing was happening, but we could not ignore the truth. The fight between us was inevitable." Brogan shook his head at the memory, then walked in with the wood.

Matalia looked at him incredulously as he stepped past her. She glanced back at the shattered table legs and covered her mouth with her hand. The power it must have taken to break the heavy furniture scared her. She sighed, wondering at the animosity that must have precipitated the brawl, then followed him inside.

Brogan was dumping the wood onto a leather mat, and he swiped his forehead to remove the fine bits of bark and dust. He motioned to the tub.

"I will fill it partially while you start the fire. Then we will warm some kettles and add hot water."

Matalia nodded, disconcerted at his use of the plural pronoun, but she immediately bent to start piling kindling upon some dry moss. After finding a flint in the cupboard, she soon had the fire snapping. Brogan trooped in and out time after time, hauling clear water to the tub while Matalia filled all available kettles and pots and placed them over and in the fire. Soon many were boiling and Matalia searched for other items she needed. Unrolling the palate, she found several blankets, so she shook them out and placed one near the tub to use as a towel. Next she found some soap, and despite its harsh texture, she found its scent pleasing.

As Brogan brought the final bucket inside, the sun sank over the hillside and the final orange glow of daylight changed to the richer glow of firelight. Matalia stood nervously by the cupboard, unsure of what Brogan expected. Catching her biting her lip, he chuckled. Without talking to her, he closed the door, leaving the animals outside to stand guard, then turned and stared at her, assessing.

"Tonight," he began in his deep voice, "tonight we do not argue. We do not fight. Tonight I court you. You have decided to come with me, and I am grateful. It is my intention to make you happy with your decision."

Matalia's eyes widened, and her mouth opened with surprise. Her heart started beating rapidly, and she trembled where she stood. Watching her reactions, Brogan nodded appreciatively and walked slowly over to her.

"We may be married, but I never introduced myself properly." He stopped several feet from her, a respectful distance, and bowed gallantly. "I am Brogan O'Bannon, son of the Earl of Kirkcaldy of Greater Scotland, and I would be very pleased to make your acquaintance." He smiled at her teasingly as Matalia remained in shock.

He extended his hand and without thinking she gave him her own. As he lifted it to his lips, Matalia held her breath. His voice rippled over her as he asked, "Am I to remain in suspense all eve, or will you bequeath me with the honor of your name?"

"Matalia McTaver," she answered breathlessly, "daughter of the Laird McTaver of Roseneath."

"Ah, you have delighted me, lovely Lady Matalia, for your name is as beautiful as your face."

Matalia stared at him, watching his lips move in the standard phrases, yet feeling none of her normal contempt for the words. When other men had said such flowery compliments, she had always replied sarcastically or insultingly, tossing her head. This time she simply blushed and dropped her gaze, wondering whether or not he meant the flattery.

"Tell me that such a vibrantly colored lass such as yourself is not so easily struck silent by a small warrior such as me," Brogan began, and Matalia swiftly looked up.

"Small is not how I would describe thee," she murmured, and amusement began to dance in her turquoise eyes.

Brogan grinned and motioned to a pair of overturned stumps he had brought in while Matalia had been fiddling with the pots. "Would you grace my humble home and talk with me awhile, my lady?" Matalia inclined her head regally and placed her hand upon his arm as if they were about to promenade to the grand ballroom. Instead, they walked three steps to the stumps, whereupon Brogan waited until she was seated, then sat next to her.

"I find I am consumed with curiosity about you, fair lass." With a polite demure Matalia shook her head, but Brogan continued undaunted. "Tell me something about yourself that only your husband should know."

Matalia blinked and lifted her eyes to stare at him. "Such is not a question you should ask," she reprimanded him.

"But I would have asked it, had I met you, for I would have wanted to get your attention, and thus I will ask it now."

"But you already have my attention," she replied.

He shook his head. "*Now* I have it. I would have seen the wild look in your eye from across the courtyard and known that boldness was my only hope."

"I do not favor bold men," Matalia replied, thinking of the few who had tried to kiss her in hallways.

Brogan narrowed his eyes, letting only a gleam of silver escape. "That pleases me, my lady, but it does not answer my question."

Matalia licked her lips, thinking quickly for something shocking to say. His teasing role playing was exciting her, and she was eager to contribute. Lighting upon the perfect thing, she ran her fingers through the hair at her temples and shook the heavy curls out of her face. She leaned closer as if to avoid the gossipmongers and whispered her secret to him. "I decided to try sexual intimacy before marriage."

Brogan bent his head toward hers and replied, "That is shocking only if you enjoyed it, Lady Matalia."

She gasped and sat back. "It should be shocking regardless!"

"My, how innocent we really are." Seeing how perplexed she was, he shifted closer to her again, using his bulk to block her from the supposed eyes around her. His voice dropped seductively. "I would be your servant tonight, beautiful lady, and bathe you."

"You would not say that!" Matalia stated, half-angry, half-aroused.

"I just did. What say you, young lady of Roseneath? You dared breach your maidenhood before wedding bells. Are you now afraid of my eyes and hands?"

Matalia cast her gaze down, embarrassed to admit that she was, indeed, nervous. Every joining between them had been fraught with speed or high emotion. They had never spent leisurely moments together, and the intimacy of doing so made her unaccountably shy. Correctly interpreting her hesitation, Brogan rose and began pouring hot water into the tub until it steamed in invitation.

He then turned his powerful gaze upon Matalia, who remained sitting. The aura of suppressed sexual tension emanating from him caused Matalia to quake.

"I will not take you tonight, Matalia. As I said, I want to court you."

Matalia's breath gushed out in a half laugh. " 'Tis no courtship I am familiar with, Brogan O'Bannon, unless you come from far distant shores."

"Aye, I do. 'Tis a Viking tradition, to bathe one's intended."

"Must I suspend my belief and accept this falsehood?"

" 'Tis no falsehood that I wish to make a claim, and the Vikings leave no doubt as to their intentions. Humor me, fair lass, and allow me to court you as I see fit."

Slowly Matalia rose. She shook her head, denying him, but he stalked up to her and placed his hand under her chin. He gazed at her flushed cheeks and the shorter curls that danced at her temples despite her attempts to restrain them. He noticed that her lower lashes matched the uppers in length and fullness and framed her intensely colored eyes to perfection.

"Even had your face not been so lovely, I would find you incredibly attractive, Lady Matalia."

"Oh?" she breathed.

"The fire within you . . ." Suddenly he stepped back

and hooded his eyes. "Disrobe," he commanded softly.

Matalia felt cold without his towering presence, but she rallied with several deep breaths. She asked him with a tremulous voice, "Please, advise me how, Brogan. The first time I failed so miserably. You found no interest in me."

"No interest? I have never found anything about you uninteresting."

"Yes," she rebutted, "you told me I was unattractive and that . . ."

"Matalia! Are you speaking of when you had me bound to the bed? Surely you deciphered that I was merely trying to anger you that day? My reactions to you are hardly difficult to read."

She stared at him, considering. Relenting, he sat down upon the stump she had vacated and began his instructions.

"Go over to the fire and stand between it and the steam. Now unlace . . ."

Matalia tilted her head and lifted her breasts with a deep breath so she could see the ties at her waist. Brogan's mouth went dry, and he ceased talking until she looked back up at him after releasing the air from her lungs.

"Unlace," he repeated. "Unlace slowly and let your gown fall to the floor."

"Why?"

"Because you want to see if you can hold my attention. You want to see if I have the strength to remain in control."

Matalia smiled with dawning understanding. "Like this?"

"Aye." His voice was husky.

She dropped her voice as well. "And if your actions tonight do not please me?"

"Then we both suffer," he answered gruffly.

"I find it odd that for such a ribald man, you choose to demonstrate restraint." Matalia finished unlacing, then ran a hand under the cloth at her shoulder before pausing. She blinked slowly, seductively, then repeated his name when he said nothing in reply. "Brogan?"

He shifted his eyes from her bare shoulder and met her questioning gaze. Matalia was surprised to see a fine ripple of muscular tension sweep over his arms even though he remained still. She felt an answering clench in her nether regions, but she continued to stare at him, waiting for his answer.

"Powerful women," he finally gritted out, " are particularly interested in restraint, for they are demanding lovers as well as fearsome enemies. They insist that man should have both skill and control."

Matalia lifted a brow and smiled. She then flicked her gown off her shoulder so that it hung half-on and half-off. "I have a question for you, Brogan O'Bannon of Kirkcaldy."

"I am not surprised, my lady. I am surprised only that you have delayed in taking the offensive for so long."

Matalia pursed her lips, then licked them while casting a reproachful look at Brogan's unrepentant face. "Tell me something a wife should know."

"That is too easy a question."

"Then answer it," Matalia replied as she began shifting the dress off her other shoulder. The cabin became very quiet, and only the crackling of the fire and the faint sound of water bubbling filled the cabin. Brogan debated.

Softly, so Matalia had to listen carefully to hear him, he finally answered, though his Scottish burr was thick with suppressed emotion. "I've never kissed a woman because I have never loved a woman." A veil of wariness covered his eyes, and his facial muscles tensed.

Matalia nodded, then let her dress drop completely.

She elected not to respond and instead stepped carefully into the tub. She gave him space to recover from his admission, knowing intuitively that he was entrusting her with information he had never spoken of before, but would regret immediately if she made too much of his answer.

As Matalia sank into the steamy water and let her muscles relax, Brogan's anxiety eased and he took several deep breaths to calm his knotted stomach. He watched her bare back as it rested against the tub edge and admired the strong curve of her neck that melded into a pair of supple, soft shoulders. She shifted, and her hair fell back, obscuring his vision but offering another delectable aspect of her form to his gaze.

He was pleased that she said no more of kissing, and the seed of trust between them flowered. He rose and padded up behind her, letting his gaze sweep over her. Trust was alien to him, yet like a garden, it could be built with careful tending. He shut his eyes briefly, acknowledging that one event, one storm, could destroy a planted field. Internally he wondered which would prevail within their odd marriage, the ferocious elements waging against them, or the delicate blossoms of healing herbs.

Half of her breasts peeked out from the water, and her dusky nipples were relaxed and soft from the heat. Her eyes were closed and her neck arched back slightly. He lifted the soap and noticed that his hand shook, so he clenched it tightly to obtain control of his feelings.

Without opening her eyes, Matalia posed another question, startling but pleasing Brogan. "So tell me more about this Viking tradition. I am to allow you to wash me, but we are not to engage further?"

"In the Viking ceremony, we are forbidden to do more," he answered and smiled crookedly at her purr of contentment.

"Then do not forget my toes," she commanded sweetly. Brogan chuckled and obediently picked her foot out of the water and began soaping the delicate members that wiggled under his tickling caress.

For sixty long minutes Brogan washed her, saying nothing, seeing everything. He parted her thighs and washed her nether hair. He massaged her back with soapy hands. He kneaded her breasts until they sprang tight and taunt, and he rubbed her scalp until she almost slipped under the water with lassitude. Finally, her body alternately tingling and limp, Brogan stood her up and rinsed her hair and body with clean water, then pulled her from the tub and onto the palate and wrapped her within a double cocoon of his kilt and arms.

As she snuggled with him, she blinked sleepily and asked about his travels. "Care you to tell me about your other adventures in foreign lands, Brogan? Your knowledge of the Vikings is inspiring."

Brogan's lips twitched, and he bent to rest his chin upon her head. Then he leaned back against the cabin wall and stared into the crackling fire. With Matalia half-awake, he slowly began telling her of places he had been, things he had done over the last fifteen years in his pursuit of fortune. He talked about France, England and the cold islands of the north. He talked of wars, of friends, of kingdoms.

"When I left Scotland, I joined an English navy ship. The education my mother insisted upon made me stand out, and I was obligated to defend my manhood. I learned the rudiments of sailing and the basics of swordplay."

"Was it hard?"

"No, not really. I had fought so often with Xanthier, I was well prepared. But the ship was overtaken by pirates, and that is when I truly learned how to survive."

"Pirates!"

"I'll not tell you of that time, as it was ugly and is not fit for female ears. Suffice it to say, I discovered that strength alone is not enough. One must have a will that is indomitable."

"And you, of course, have a very powerful will."

"Aye. I get what I want," he hissed. "Eventually, it became my ship, and the men would listen only to my leadership. I sailed for years, collecting riches and property, but never settling down. I never intended to return, but then, one day, I heard that Xanthier had announced that he was to be named the official heir. I immediately set sail for Scotland's shores."

"For Kirkcaldy," Matalia stated.

"For Kirkcaldy. It was as if I knew all along that I would come back and claim my inheritance. I wrote to Soothebury, offered for one of his daughters, and began my journey here."

"But Xanthier has always lived at Kirkcaldy. Why should you have it and not him?"

Brogan stared into the fire for a long moment. "Xanthier does not love Kirkcaldy any more than I. He wants it only to keep it from me. My father, the Earl, thrust me from my own home when I was only an infant. He abandoned me and decreed that I would never be able to take the reins of Kirkcaldy because I was unworthy. I intend to show him that he is wrong.

"But let me tell you of better things. France . . . France is a fascinating place. I met a count on the shores of Isigny-sur-Mer in the Bay of the Seine. . . ."

Matalia heard not just what he had experienced, but how his life had shaped him into the man he was now. She heard the pride in his accomplishments and the thin thread of loneliness he was not aware of. She noted his unrelenting ambition, his overwhelming mistrust and his unspoken need for family loyalty. She curled in his lap, imagining the scenes he so beautifully described, and felt stirrings of awe. The man she had married was complex and intriguing. She smiled softly while inhaling his scent, and drifted to sleep, feeling peaceful and protected.

Brogan glanced down, observing Matalia's slightly open mouth and lax facial muscles. He gently laid her down upon the palate and tucked his kilt over her bare toes. Despite her beauteous curves, his desire was held in check, for his mind was skipping and jumping over the myriad things he had to evaluate. He knew that Xanthier was still coming after him. He was uncertain how the Earl would receive him. The Soothebury clan would still require reparations. What would Kirkcaldy be like?

And Matalia herself: What twists, what further complications would she cause? Despite his initial impression of her as a spoiled, unappreciative child, he now felt that her previous actions were merely the effect of a young woman kept too sheltered by her parents' love. Her outrageous act of kidnapping him for sexual experimentation caused him more amusement than anger as he reminisced. In fact, he thought her wild behavior stimulating.

However, part of him remained perturbed, for he was uncertain how she would respond within the strict walls of Castle Kirkcaldy. The Earl would find her antics neither amusing nor acceptable. He had cast his own wife from the castle the day she gave birth because he would not tolerate any untoward behavior. Brogan stroked the riotous curls off Matalia's face as he thought about the upcoming months. They were bound to test Matalia's patience to the breaking point, and he was unsure how to guide or assist her. The best he could offer was to honor his spontaneous promise to let her go home after the birth of the child, but in order to release her, he would have to harden his emotions against her. He felt . . . affection for her . . . but he must remember that she was with him only temporarily. Her true home was back at Roseneath with her family. He ground his teeth together and glared at the dying embers. It would be easy to accept her completely, to expect that she would be his wife in all ways, but he must keep her distant. He must maintain an unspoken separation.

With that final, daunting thought, he closed his eyes and rested, fighting the flitting dreams that taunted his newly formed resolution.

Chapter 15

In the morning, Matalia awoke to an empty cabin. She stretched and rolled onto her stomach, propping her chin upon her fist. She whistled softly, and a black nose instantly poked through the half-open door. A second later the sleek gray body of the smallest wolf trotted in and flopped down against Matalia's warmth. She giggled and twisted slightly to run her fingers through his fur.

"And where are the others, my fine friend?" The wolf twitched his ears back and forth, then bumped Matalia with his nose. She sighed and acquiesced. With a push, she stood up and dressed, frowning ruefully at the wrinkles in her gown. "At least my hair is clean," she murmured as she braided the locks into minimal submission. She moved toward the door and had reached out to pull it when it was flung open.

"Oh!" Matalia gasped, leaping away. Her eyes widened, and she held her hand to her heart until she recovered her equilibrium. "Goodness, Brogan, you startled me."

"My apologies," he mumbled as he stared at her with granite eyes, "but 'tis time we were riding."

Matalia looked at him with some confusion, but shrugged. "I will be ready after a moment. If you would excuse me?" She exited the cabin and walked around to the far side while Brogan stared at her retreating back. He took a deep breath and reminded himself of his decision, then folded the palate and closed the cabin door.

Shortly thereafter they both were mounted and moving up the hillside, following a twisting path that circumvented the numerous cave entrances. Blackened tree stumps cast odd shadows, and Matalia peered about her, half expecting a banshee to sweep down upon them. She nudged her horse closer to Brogan and looked at him for an explanation.

"The caverns are as much a part of Kirkcaldy as the castle itself. The dark corridors are our strongest defense and our greatest advantage. Through them, the Earl can attack any intruder and escape any threat."

"Why are the trees burned?"

"The Earl decreed that the land be in mourning after the loss of the Countess."

"But the Countess Ansleen is not dead! She lives but a few days' ride away."

Brogan shook his head and stared at her with a hint of condescension. "To him, she is gone. The blackened trees also symbolize his expectation that everyone give him absolute obedience and respect."

"Because he believed that his wife did not grant those qualities to him."

"Yes. Now no one doubts his ability to keep his people in line."

"I do. I think that a man who must destroy a beautiful land in order to prove his strength is puny indeed." Matalia stared at Brogan's hard face, her vibrant eyes contrasting vividly with the bleak landscape. Returning her gaze, Brogan said nothing more until Matalia finally looked away.

The three wolves spread out, one trotting swiftly in front, the other two forming a lopsided triangle in the rear. They ran with their noses alternately in the air or on the ground, continuously monitoring for predators, both human and beast.

Brogan's large wolfhound ran next to the stallion, barking warnings whenever they approached a cave entrance. When they were near the top of the hillside, the path ran alongside a particularly large cavern. After the wolfhound gave his customary bark, a rich *wuff* echoed back from within the darkness.

Brogan reached out and grabbed Matalia's reins, halting both steeds. The wolfhound barked again, this time louder, and the hair on his back bristled to attention. The wolves froze, then crouched to the ground and began creeping forward, toward Brogan and Matalia.

"What . . . ?"

"Shhh," Brogan interrupted her as he urged the horses back, forcing them to walk backward one step at a time. Matalia stared at the cave mouth with fascination as a dark brown head emerged, followed by a massive, hairy body. It swung around to stare at the Irish wolfhound, then rose on its two hind legs to roar menacingly. The horses made to spin around and flee, but Brogan's shouted command and firm grip made them hold, although they whinnied and stamped their feet.

The wolfhound rose up as well, baring his teeth and shaking his head before dropping to the ground and lowering his head to growl, then lunging forward with a snap of his jaws. The huge beast sniffed the air, then slowly dropped his front paws and stood, rocking back and forth while trying to see the wolfhound. The big dog ceased growling and started a loud, incessant barking until the bear turned away and lumbered down the slope, choosing a peaceful retreat over an unnecessary fight.

Matalia watched him, alternately petrified and thrilled as he plodded down the hillside, trampling the flowers, and disappeared into another cave entrance.

"I have never . . . What . . . I . . ." Matalia stuttered, her heart beating so rapidly her breath was caught.

Brogan's face split with a huge grin as he watched Matalia struggle with words. He let go of her reins and whistled for his dog, which stopped barking and trotted up next to him, tongue lolling. He leaned forward and patted him, scratching his chin in affection.

"They live in the caves and are dangerous only when angered or startled. My dog makes sure we warn them of our presence so they have ample time to move out of our way."

A flash of anger rippled across Matalia's face at his continued amusement. "You had no right to hold me still," she snapped. "I would have rather taken my chances outrunning the lumbering beast."

"If you had tried, it would have chased you and torn you to shreds," Brogan answered cruelly, all amusement gone from his face. "This land is not as hospitable as your coastal birthplace. You must respect the dangers here."

"You talk as if I have lived in a sheltered courtyard. May I remind you that the coast is rugged, and the Loch Nidean forest welcomes my family but no others. And further, may you not forget that I found you bested by thieves within my own property boundaries. Think carefully before you cast aspersions on others, Brogan O'Bannon."

Brogan was infuriated that she had reminded him of their meeting and equally upset over her naïveté regarding the dangers she did not understand. He drew a calming breath and tried again. "I respect your Loch Nidean. I know of its powers and realize that I would be lost within such a land of druids. However, this land has very real dangers, with very specific consequences dealt to those who know not how to survive its malicious intentions." Brogan stared at her hard, trying to convey that he spoke not only about the various animals in the middle lands, but also about the people of Kirkcaldy. "All I ask is that you trust me to advise you."

Matalia narrowed her eyes, but said nothing about his use of the word "trust." Brogan reached out and picked up the end of her messy braid. He combed his fingers through her hair until the locks hung free, then carefully twisted his finger in one of her curls, and pulled her closer to him.

Matalia, already off balance from the sight of an unknown beast moments earlier, was totally thrown by Brogan's studied seduction. She held her breath and let him pull her near until they were nose to nose. His eyes dropped briefly to her lips, then lifted again to stare directly into her eyes. Matalia involuntarily licked her lips, then pulled her lower lip into her mouth to suck on it as she had when she was younger. Brogan slid his gaze down again, watching her actions, and lifted his other hand to stroke her throbbing mouth.

Huskily, his own voice raw, Brogan whispered to her again. "Tell me you will do as I ask, Matalia. Tell me you will take care amongst the dangers in this land."

She nodded, then dropped her forehead against his and closed her eyes. Brogan slid his hand around to the back of her neck and held her against him for several moments. A nervous prance from his stallion finally separated them, but Brogan retained his hand on the captured curl. Without explanation, he pulled a knife from his belt and cut the lock, then tied it to a loose thread on the inner surface of his kilt. Matalia instantly reached up to her hair, touching the sheared segment and opened her mouth to say something, whereupon Brogan kicked his horse to gallop up the rest of the hill without a backward glance.

Matalia stared after him in shock, not sure how to respond to his intimate thievery. Her mare fidgeted, anxious to go after the swiftly departing stallion. Relenting, and nervous to be without his and the wolf-hound's protection, Matalia galloped after him.

*   *   *

After an arduous day of travel and a sleepless night
in the valley, they set out the next morning. The final
hill shielding Kirkcaldy Castle loomed ahead, and
Matalia felt both anxious and excited. Her stomach
flopped and she felt a wave of nausea.

"Are you all right?" Brogan asked with concern
when Matalia hid behind some bushes to empty her
stomach.

"Yes . . ." she answered faintly. "I think I am worried about meeting your father."

"Come," Brogan replied. "If we get moving you
should feel better. The castle is only hours away."

Matalia nodded and rejoined him after rinsing her
mouth with water. Her face was pale and the illusion
of a faerie once again struck him. He grinned, thinking
that the week of solitude at the cottage had not made
her mild mannered, but had instead developed her
into a more fulsome woman. She stood, running her
fingers through her black curls, her turquoise eyes
flashing and her white cheeks flushed from the morning sun. A tiny fleck of sand graced the corner of one
eye. A smudge of blue underneath caused by her restless night shadowed her face. Her hair swayed around
her face, large curls tickling her nose as she absently
tried to push them aside while she swung up on her
mare. She was beautiful.

They reached the top of the hill within the next hour
and Brogan started down the other side without pause,
but Matalia reined in, attempting to absorb the sudden
sight of a grand castle nestled in the valley. She gasped,
stunned by the white walls reflecting sunlight and the
streams of banners fluttering from the turrets.

"Brogan!" she called out, and he instantly spun his
horse around, concerned for her welfare. "Brogan!"
she called again. "It is like a legend! I have never
seen white walls before. How do they make them so?"

Brogan walked his stallion back up to Matalia before answering. " 'Tis the stone. I have heard that it is actually more yellow than white, but in the sunlight it seems brighter."

" 'Tis exquisitely beautiful! It is no wonder you love the place so."

"I said I have never seen it before," Brogan corrected her.

"If you do not love it, then I ask again, why are you fighting for it?"

"Because it should be mine," he answered simply. He looked out over the valley, keeping his expression cold. He was not going to reveal the emotion that welled inside him at the sight of Kirkcaldy. This was the castle that he had been born to rule. This was the place where he should have been raised, where his mother should have lived. She had spoken of it so often that he already knew every stone, every window, every room. From the cradle he had listened to her talk about Kirkcaldy and its beauty, and he trembled internally at his first sight of its walls.

Matalia looked at him in utter exasperation, but forbore to argue further. At that moment the wolves peaked the summit, and Matalia started down the hill and into the valley with them at her heels. Several cottages dotted the open lands, growing in number until they formed a large village within the curve of a calm river. The castle itself rose high above the village, encased within shimmering bailey walls topped with iron spikes. A herd of sheep grazed in the open area around the castle, watched by a pair of young boys and a single dog. Also outside the castle walls was an encampment of Brogan's men, where over fifty tents were pitched with a makeshift fence erected to hold a herd of warhorses.

Matalia felt a tremor of excitement. Her new home, she whispered to herself. This was her new home! She set her horse to trotting, bypassing the wary Brogan, and then urged the mare into a canter as she approached the outskirts of the township. She waved gaily to a farmer in his field, but did not pause to notice that he did not return her friendly greeting. She cantered further, peripherally aware that Brogan rode directly behind her, until the houses became close. She then slowed and stood up in her stirrups to better view the main street.

Many people stepped out, their faces tight with worry. They watched Brogan and Matalia with trepidation and several shooed their children back into their houses. One child pulled out of his mother's restraining arm and dashed up to Brogan, staring up at him solemnly.

"Are you the second brother?" he asked, and his mother gasped at the rush of anger that spread over Brogan's face. Before he could respond, Matalia leaped off her horse and swept the child into her arms, placing a big kiss upon his head and ruffling his hair.

"No, silly child, you should not ask if he is the second, for surely he will insist that he is the first, just as will the other one."

The child looked up at her beautiful face. "Who are you, m'lady?"

"Why, I am the Lady Matalia, bride of Brogan O'Bannon and new member of the O'Bannon household."

"Will the other new lady make you eat turnips?"

Matalia looked at him in consternation. "I should hope not, for I detest turnips."

"So do I," the lad replied, then wriggled out of her hold.

The boy's mother joined them nervously. "Me apologies, Lady O'Bannon. The lad no understands his place."

"Do not be silly, Mistress. He is just a child." Matalia glanced at the woman in surprise, then ran her gaze over the other villagers. They, too, looked frightened and tense. Behind her, Brogan's glowering visage showed no flicker of warmth. It was harsh and distant and terribly intimidating. Matalia frowned at him but was not surprised when he showed no inclination to soften his ferocious look. Making an instant decision, Matalia smoothed her face and turned back to the people.

"I should like to come visit you all sometime, after I have settled in at the castle." She smiled, deliberately focusing on the young boy. He grinned and nodded while the others shifted in place, not sure how to respond. "Good," Matalia continued, assuming their assent. "I will look forward to it. And I will bring a picnic with me, but you may be assured that I will not pack turnips!"

The mother pressed her lips together, stifling the beginnings of a smile, and Matalia was heartened. She stepped back toward her horse and glanced sweetly up at Brogan, waiting. With a low grumble at her pretended feminine restraint, he swung down to lift her to her steed, then remounted his prancing stallion. He gruffly jerked his head and began trotting down the road toward the castle gates.

Matalia waved once again to the villagers, then demurely followed her husband until they passed the edge of the town and began the short road to the entrance of the castle.

"Why?" Matalia questioned.

Interpreting her correctly, Brogan answered, "They are commoners. I am to be the future Earl. They must fear my authority completely."

"This is how your father rules?" Matalia replied.

Brogan flicked his steel-colored eyes at her for an instant before facing forward again. "Of course," he finally stated, signaling an end to the conversation.

Matalia bit her lip but said no more. She thought longingly of her free and easy companionship with Colleen and felt a wave of longing for her friend's sunny face. The McTaver clan followed their laird out of love and respect. No intimidation was necessary. Matalia tensed, wondering what kind of man would create clan unity based on fear, but before she could think of it further, they approached the encampment and Brogan drew his sword.

Chapter 16

The light stone towered above them and the spikes cast shadowy barbs upon the grass around them as the horses walked the final few steps up to the edge of the tents. Brogan O'Bannon remained frozen in the saddle, his back straight and his eyes hooded. Many men stood at attention, their weapons held firmly in calloused hands.

"I trust that you have all made it safely," Brogan said.

"We were attacked thrice, but lost only two men. The chests are here. A cleric is still assessing the value and he, too, is under strict guard."

"And my brother?"

"He is inside the castle. He arrived yesterday with only a few men. We let him pass."

"Good. Jaimie, meet my wife, the Lady Matalia. Matalia, my first mate, Jaimie Louvre."

"M'lady," Jaimie replied with a bow.

"Jaimie," Matalia answered. She looked around for her wolves, wanting their comfort, but saw that they hovered at the edge of the field, well away from the castle. Feeling bereft, she nudged her horse closer to Brogan's. She was frightened by the fierce glowers many of the men cast her way. "Is Colleen with you?" she asked hopefully.

"I was instructed to give you the message that she

is to remain at Roseneath. 'Tis rumored that she is a poor influence and might cause mischief in your new home."

"Oh!" Matalia gasped. "She should not punished for my misdeeds! Anything I did was my fault alone! I need her friendship now more than ever!"

Jaimie shrugged. "I know little information, other than imparting the message I already gave you. She is not here."

"Then I am truly alone . . ." Matalia whispered.

"Your men are in position?" Brogan questioned Jaimie, interrupting Matalia.

"Of course, m'lord. No one will escape should anything befall you. We have ensured that all within the castle are aware of your strength. They dare not engage in open battle."

Brogan nodded. "The Lady Matalia will stay here until I have assessed my welcome."

"No, I will not!" Matalia retorted, displeased to be left alone with strangers. Her sorrow over Colleen's loss swiftly changed to stubborn strength. "This is my home now as well, and I will see it just as you do."

Ignoring her, Brogan moved his horse forward and motioned to Jaimie. "One hour."

"Aye," Jaimie answered as he gripped her mare's bridle, halting her.

Infuriated, Matalia pulled her own sword free and tapped Jaimie's wrist with the blade. "I advise you to let go, Louvre. I do not know what strange country you hail from, or how you are accustomed to treating women, but I will not be told what to do by anyone. Release my horse immediately."

Jaimie backed up, stunned at Matalia's attack, then looked to Brogan for assistance.

"Matalia," Brogan said softly. "Matalia, it may be dangerous. I do not know what Xanthier has planned. Will you do as I ask?"

She hesitated, then shook her head in denial. "I will go with you. I am eager to see your home and the people who inhabit it. Do not fear for me."

Grumbling under his breath, Brogan moved away, permitting Matalia to accompany him by a wave of his hand. "You are an obstinate woman," he said.

"I have heard that before," she replied as she straightened in the saddle and sheathed her sword. "We make a fine pair, husband."

He grunted in response, then turned his attention to the castle.

The Earl watched them approach, his gray eyes eerily similar to his son's. He noted the heated exchange between the woman he assumed to be Brogan's wife and the man he assumed to be his long lost son. Brogan had come home. After almost thirty years from the day he had cast Ansleen from his home, he was now seeing the culmination of his hasty ultimatum. His two sons were fighting for the inheritance, trying to prove which one was more worthy. The Earl carefully descended the stairs, thinking sorrowfully on his lifetime. He had made many terrible mistakes. But it was too late to change anything now. His life was closing. He could feel it in his bones. It was important that he choose wisely, for Kirkcaldy, for Scotland, and for the O'Bannon legacy.

Slowly, the gate rose. The crisscross of shadows cast by the iron gate slid over Brogan's and Matalia's faces, alternately revealing their countenances, then hiding them. Finally, accented by a clunk of chain, the gate was fully raised and the courtyard open to them. The castle doors stood symbolically closed, and the O'Bannon crest burned upon its surface glowered down at them.

Three people stood in front of the door. Xanthier,

a perfect replica of Brogan, stood at the foot of the stairs. An older man, stern and glum, was braced at the top. He appeared hard and unfeeling, and no welcoming warmth emanated from him at the sight of his son. His white hair and wrinkled skin were the only features that clearly differentiated him, for his expression and eyes were so similar to Brogan and Xanthier's that Matalia gasped. The third person was a woman standing at Xanthier's side. She was plain and dour in face, but gowned in silks of high quality. Arrayed around them were numerous men-at-arms whose angry looks made the foreign men in the encampment seem inviting in comparison. A kennel of wolfhounds on the far side of the courtyard barked at them, creating a din that made both horses prance in agitation.

Brogan swung off his warhorse, then dropped to one knee before the Earl. A kennel master yelled at the courtyard dogs, and they abruptly quieted, their bristly heads cocked in curiosity. In the sudden silence, Brogan's strong voice rang out. "I have returned to claim my birthright, the title of heir of Kirkcaldy."

A stableboy ran up and grasped the reins of Brogan's horse and led it away, leaving Matalia mounted upon her mare. Brogan's wolfhound remained at her side, his lips lifted in a silent growl.

The Earl remained impassive but replied with equal formality. "Another has also sought that title. By what right do you seek to displace him?"

"I have gathered riches in foreign countries including gold, jewels, spices and land. I have amassed allies upon several coasts and have proven my worth upon the fighting field. In addition, I have sealed my allegiance to Scotland by wedding the eldest daughter of the Laird McTaver, who claims guardianship not only of Roseneath but of the Loch Nidean forest through his princess wife, Kalial. God willing, my bride, Lady Matalia, will soon carry within her womb the continuation of the proud O'Bannon name. I have fulfilled the tasks set before me and respectfully petition to take my rightful place at your table."

"You have camped an army at my walls. How am I to take this act of aggression?" the Earl demanded.

" 'Tis only a precaution. I did not know what kind of reception I would receive. I have heard that Xanthier has men inside who are equally prepared."

"Indeed he does. But I will allow no battle at the gates of Kirkcaldy. The men may come inside as long as they remain under control."

Xanthier stepped forward, an angry glare darkening his cheeks. "If your men step out of line, I will see to it that they are punished!"

The two men stared at each other, their mutual loathing clear. "And if I hear of *your* men overstepping their bounds, *I* will see them punished as well."

"I have heard that you already created an enemy to the O'Bannon household by taking the Lady Matalia as your wife," Xanthier sneered.

The Earl stared at Brogan, demanding an explanation.

"I have made amends to Gavin Soothebury for the loss of a husband for his middle daughter." Brogan's face was hard and unrelenting, and Matalia felt a flicker of pity for the girl being discussed so callously.

"Soothebury's daughter is of good family, plain and docile. Why would you risk a feud by discarding her?" Xanthier's deep voice rolled down the courtyard and swept over Matalia, shaming her for her role in upsetting Brogan's carefully laid plans. She dropped her gaze, blinking rapidly to keep the tears from spilling over. She waited, holding her breath, wondering how Brogan would answer.

Brogan's reply surprised both her and the assembled people. "My reasons are my own, and I am pleased with my decision. I stand by it."

The Earl curled his lip in contempt and raked his

eyes over Matalia's comely form. "Bring the woman forward," he demanded.

Matalia raised her head, frightened by this harsh reception. She turned to Brogan, searching for support. He hesitated, then rose and walked with a measured stride to her side. Without speaking, he lifted her from the saddle and lowered her to the ground. He held her waist for a second longer than necessary and gave her a silent squeeze, then placed her fingers upon his forearm. Emboldened, Matalia regally inclined her head, then walked forward at Brogan's side along with the massive dog.

When she reached the foot of the stone steps, she bent down in a careful curtsy. The Earl stared at her, his face indicating he was displeased with what he saw.

"What is wrong with your eyes that they glow with such an odd color?" he demanded.

Matalia rose and, stifling a stinging retort, she dredged up the diplomacy that her mother had so valiantly tried to teach her. "If my visage appears unusual, 'tis only because I am stunned by the beauty of your home. Kirkcaldy is more spectacular than I had imagined. Thank you for welcoming me to such a marvelous abode and into such a distinguished family."

The Earl stared at her as if trying to decipher the truth of her response, then finally harrumphed in acceptance of her words. He gestured to the woman near him. "Meet your sister by marriage, the Lady Isadora. She will show you to your quarters while I confer with my sons." He then turned and opened the heavy doors of the castle and walked inside without indicating any emotional response regarding the return of a son he had seen only once before.

Following his lead, the twins also stepped into the darkened entryway, leaving Matalia and Isadora alone on the steps. Isadora stared down at Matalia, her face pinched.

"Where is your escort? Your baggage? Your servants?"

Matalia sighed, exhausted from the turmoil of the day and unable to form a likely explanation. "Please, Lady Isadora, I am tired and would like to rest."

Isadora sneered at her obvious avoidance, but nodded. "You will stay in the north tower, for although it is colder and farther from the central hall, we have already taken residence in the south."

Matalia shrugged, then added politely, "I am sure the north tower will be acceptable."

Isadora pouted, her lower lip sticking out in a gesture so like Matalia's little sisters that she smiled. Isadora lifted her skirts and entered the castle, expecting Matalia to follow. However, Matalia, irritated by the bizarre family reunion, turned away and walked back to her horse. She smiled softly at the stableboy, who appeared startled by her attention.

"Take good care of my mare, if you please. She has been a friend to me." The boy nodded fervently so Matalia continued. "I have three other companions, wolves, that left my side at the outskirts of the village. They will come forward when they feel 'tis time. Would you watch for them and let those who tend the sheep know that they are not to be hunted? They will not hurt the flocks."

The boy stared up at her in awe. "Wolves, m'lady?"

"Aye," Matalia whispered, grinning at the boy's expression. The boy flushed and nodded, running a hand over the neck of the mare to show that he would tend her carefully. Matalia patted the boy's head, then turned back to the castle door where Isadora stood impatiently.

"M'lady?" the boy called out hesitantly.

Matalia paused.

"Would you like me to take the dog to the kennels?"

Matalia looked down at the big canine fondly.

"No," she said. "My husband would prefer to have him near."

"Aye, m'lady. Although I have never known a woman to like the wolfhounds, being they are so ferocious. But I gather since you have wolves . . ."

Matalia smiled. "I expect that makes me rather different from the other women you have known."

The stableboy nodded, then flushed in embarrassment as Matalia left him to enter the castle.

Ignoring Isadora's unpleasant expression, Matalia swept up the steps. Isadora glowered, but went inside to direct Matalia to her tower rooms. Once inside the castle, Matalia was struck anew by the singular beauty of the light stone. Unlike her own home, whose great hall was brightened only by openings in the stone walls or clusters of candles in evening tide, this hall glowed as if lit from within. The walls shimmered with soft radiance, creating an impression of hospitality.

" 'Tis so beautiful!" she murmured.

"Do not get too attached to it, Lady Matalia, for you will not be staying long."

Matalia turned to look at Isadora in bemusement. "I would think that a woman who believed herself worthy of becoming a countess would be more gracious."

Isadora's color rose, but she did not retreat. "A countess does not have to be courteous to her enemies," she replied. "And she certainly does not let smelly dogs tag along at her skirts."

Matalia raised her brow. "Does she not?" she responded, deciding that she did not like Isadora at all.

Isadora said nothing but indicated a set of stairs leading to the northern chambers, then left Matalia to find her own way up to the master suite.

Matalia smiled wryly at Isadora's back, shaking her head at the woman's animosity, yet relieved to be alone. She ascended the steps with trepidation, wondering if Isadora's comments about the tower were well founded. To her delight, she found the rooms comfortable and well appointed, adorned with pleasing tapestries and well-crafted furniture.

Matalia explored, fascinated by the arrangement of rooms while the wolfhound settled in the hallway. The stairs went up to a central hub, from which four doors led to separate rooms forming unequal arcs of a circle. The master chamber faced out over the valley and made up half of the circumference of the tower. From that room a connecting door opened to another bedroom, which appeared to be designed as a potential nursery. Exiting the nursery and returning to the central landing, Matalia opened the third door and discovered a brightly lit woman's solar containing a writing desk, loom, and embroidery basket along with two pillow-filled nooks.

Smiling with pleasure, Matalia proceeded to the final door and was surprised to find a small room. Part of it was screened off for a chamber pot and basin, and the rest was a food-storage and -preparation area. Matalia blinked, confused. She entered slowly, unsure why the castle kitchen would be in an upper tower, when a petite woman emerged from a pantry and curtsied.

"M'lady."

"Hello," Matalia said, her wariness obvious. "Pardon me for intruding. I thought this tower was partitioned off for Brogan O'Bannon."

"Oh yes, m'lady. These are your rooms, and I am your servant, Peigi. Is there something you wish, m'lady? A refreshment perhaps?"

"I still do not understand. Is this the castle kitchen?"

"Heavens no, m'lady. This is just your own preparation room.'Tis designed so that whatever you wish is easily accessible to you. A luxury the previous countess created, m'lady."

"Ahh," replied Matalia, impressed by the thoughtful addition. "I can see its usefulness. I am surprised no one has thought of it before. Can you cook in here as well?"

"Yes, m'lady. Small things, that is. Are you hungry?"

"Indeed, I suppose I am."

"Then please take your leisure in the solar, and I will bring you a tray in moments."

Matalia smiled with satisfaction. "Indeed," she replied, and with a final, assessing glance around the room, she exited and retired to the solar. Not long thereafter, Brogan entered to find her happily munching upon cold meats and warm bread and sipping wine. He paused, startled by her apparent ease, struck again by her natural beauty. He slowly walked up to her and reached down to caress one of the locks of hair that rested against her chest. Matalia looked up, still chewing, and gestured for him to join her.

Brogan released the curl and sprawled upon a small couch. His gray eyes rested on her until Matalia finished her bite and looked at him expectantly.

"The Earl acknowledges my petition," Brogan said, his deep voice filling the room. Matalia nodded, not surprised. "He is, however, concerned about your reputation."

"My reputation?" repeated Matalia, shocked.

"Not your virtue, though if he knew you better he would know that he ought to be concerned about it." Brogan smiled at Matalia's affronted look, then continued. "He hears that you have been allowed free rein and suspects you do not understand the laws of marriage."

Matalia took a deep breath and stared out a window. After considering many responses, she turned back to Brogan, who waited patiently for her reply. "I did not ask for this duty," she murmured.

"I know."

"In fact," she continued, "I did everything in my power to avoid this situation."

"Yes," he affirmed.

"Yet here I am faced with your request to be a good wife. A quiet, demure, respectable wife."

Brogan's face was impassive. He waited, allowing Matalia to articulate her thoughts and decide upon her course of action.

At last, she rose from her seat and sat upon Brogan's lap. He opened his arms and enfolded her, resting his chin upon her head as she sank against his chest. "I will try, husband. I will try. I placed you in a difficult situation when I detained you. Had I known . . . I would never have deliberately caused anyone such distress as I have caused you. I know I am thoughtless at times. I have never had to be accountable for my actions until now.

"Suddenly, I feel as though I should think of you before I think of myself. You are embroiled in such an intense situation, and I am only a young, selfish woman. Because of my thoughtless actions, we are bound together by the ties of marriage. You know I was not ready for this responsibility. I did not want marriage, yet I am learning to accept life as it unfolds, and I have accepted my position beside you. But I warn you that I have little power over my own personality, and it will be hard to bite my tongue in the presence of such unpleasant people as your family."

Brogan grinned and rubbed his bristly cheek over her head. "I am fully aware of that," he answered, causing Matalia to look up at him. He touched his finger to her nose, then pulled her back to nestle in his arms. "You have done more than a man has a right to ask, Lady Matalia. I promise that I will honor my vows to you in exchange."

A cold shiver ran over her arms as she absorbed his words, recalling his promise to release her in a year's time, after the birth of their child and the fulfillment of the tasks set by the Earl. She frowned, unsure if he meant that vow, wondering if perhaps he was only tolerating her until he could safely discard her. She stiffened, then pulled away. Brogan felt her withdrawal and set his lips in a thin line, but released her despite his reluctance.

"You speak of returning me to Roseneath in one year?" Matalia questioned, hoping to hear his vehement disagreement.

Brogan's eyes turned to steel, and he opened his mouth to angrily deny her request, but then closed it and rose from his seat. "As I agreed, as long as you pretend docility when in the presence of the Earl, I care naught what you do in reality." He set his shoulders, determined to grant her what he thought she wanted.

A sob caught in Matalia's throat, but she swallowed it bravely and simply nodded. *How could I have succumbed so easily to him?* she asked herself. It took only a few days in his presence and she was longing for him to speak to her with kindness and caring. She, who never gave any thought to another's feelings, was suddenly devastated that he was so cavalier about his commitment to her. She held her breath and stared at him in pain.

Brogan looked hard into her brilliant eyes, trying to interpret the thin crescent of water lining the lower lids. When she did not reveal the source of her sudden tears, he clenched his jaw. *She must be dreading the next year,* he thought. *To her, living in this castle for four seasons must seem like a lifetime. She must want nothing better than to escape me, run home, and never see me again.* When she remained silent, he swore under his breath, exited the solar, and forcefully shut the door behind him, leaving his words unsaid.

* * *

Early the next morning, Matalia rose from her uncomfortable and lonely bed and crept down the stairs, trying to avoid any household members. The wolfhound silently watched her, but after raising his head, he lowered it again and closed his eyes. Matalia searched for the exit, desperately missing her four-legged companions and determined to spend the sunrise with them in the beautiful fields outside Kirkcaldy Castle. As she tiptoed through the great hall, she was startled by a gruff command to halt, coming from the chairs near the slumbering fire.

Matalia paused, then changed her course and approached the chair back, curious to see who was awake at this still-dark hour.

"What brings you down from the tower rooms this early, Lady Matalia?" the man grumbled, his voice weary and thin.

Matalia said nothing, but slowly circled the chair, her curiosity high. As she made her way to the front, she stared down at the old, wrinkled face of the Earl. His shoulders were covered in a woolen blanket and another covered his knees, yet still he appeared cold and uncomfortable. Matalia stared at him, still silent, wondering at the contrast of his countenance. Yesterday he had seemed cruelly powerful. This morning, he appeared frail and elderly. Matalia sank down into the adjoining chair and leaned forward to stoke the fire.

"The servants will waken soon and fix it. You need not sully your hands," he commented, but he placed little emphasis on the words. Matalia ignored him except for a quick glance and continued with her ministrations until the fire snapped, spreading warmth. She sat back and cast her gaze around the empty hall.

" 'Tis a lovely castle, m'lord."

"Aye," he answered, his eyes knowing. "Many have commented on the difference one sees and feels within its walls."

Matalia returned to scrutinize the Earl. Carefully, she replied, "Indeed. One would think that such beauty was designed with love at its core."

After a lengthy pause, the Earl acknowledged, "Before she left, the Countess did much to add warmth to Kirkcaldy."

Matalia nodded. She sat for several more moments, thinking. "You cared for her, then?" she asked hesitantly.

"Yes. And I will warn you. Love is a terrible thing. Guard yourself well from its clutches. Nothing hurts you more than love forsaken."

"Why do you give me this advice? I am no more likely to become a victim to that emotion than Brogan is."

The Earl looked up, assessing her words and the emotion behind them. "If you speak the truth, then I find favor with you. Should I find out that you have spoken falsely, I will never let you fulfill the role of countess."

"Come now!" Matalia exclaimed. "You would not deny Brogan his inheritance simply because I came to care for his well-being!"

"Indeed I would, Lady Matalia." His cold gaze swept her. "I lost my life because I loved a woman. I will never allow that to happen to one of my sons."

"You do not even care about him! He is only a piece of your flesh and blood that you can manipulate using Kirkcaldy as bait! You do not know him. You do not know anything about him. I will have no part of your schemes. My thoughts are my own and you shall never be privy to them!"

"Just the same. I am warning you."

"Very well. I have heard your warning. Until later." Then, without more than an inclination of her head to indicate her withdrawal, Matalia rose and left. The Earl watched her, seeing the youthful sway of her hips and the bright intelligence of her glance. He smiled. She was as rebellious as he had thought. Telling her to do one thing was sure to induce her to do the other. Closing his eyes, he leaned back in the chair and took a deep breath. He had made so many mistakes . . . he did not intend to make another.

Chapter 17

Outside, Matalia took a deep breath of the brisk air, then looked around to view the activity around her. Unlike inside where the castle folk slept past dawn, those in the courtyard had been awake for hours, tending the animals, starting the fires, organizing the merchants. She saw a gathering of young children with baskets, who she assumed were there to collect food for their homes from the castle stores.

All in all, she thought to herself, it was much like her own home. She smiled warmly at the children and was amused when they fidgeted, unsure how to respond to her friendliness. Spying the boy from yesterday, she strolled over to him.

"Hello, young sir, I am pleased to see you again so soon. Dare I hope that you have come to visit awhile?"

The boy looked up at her in his solemn manner, shaking his head. "No, m'lady. I have come for our weekly ration of goods."

"Ah," Matalia sighed, pretending great disappointment. "Then I shall have to be content with seeing you smile." She looked down at him so sweetly, the boy lifted his lips in return. Encouraged, she ruffled his hair. "Enjoy your day. 'Tis important that you do not work too hard, but spend time playing as well." She turned away and walked toward the open gate where milling merchants were trying to convince the gate master that they had wares of interest. As Matalia approached, the commoners suddenly quieted and pressed back out of her path.

Discomfited, Matalia smiled tentatively and offered a quiet "good morning." The people looked at her curiously, but did not reply verbally, though a few nodded or curtsied. Matalia continued on her way, passing through the bailey, wishing she could hike up her skirts and run without anyone noticing. When she finally reached the other side, she glanced back over her shoulder. The people of the courtyard all watched her, their faces a mixture of confusion and distrust. In a flash of contrary spirit, Matalia waved. She grinned happily when the people instantly turned away, embarrassed to be caught staring.

Just then, a streak of sunlight peaked over the mountain and lit the far meadow, casting an array of orange and pink shadows over the purple-tinted slope. Swiftly dropping her earthy concerns, Matalia struck off through the meadowland, heading for the sunlit area. The hem of her skirt became damp with dew, but the air was clear and Matalia did not care. As she got farther from the castle, she began to notice clusters of rock formations hiding cavern entrances similar to the ones on the mountainside. She skirted the black holes, wary of the creatures that might inhabit them, and began her wordless song.

Within moments, three sleek bodies melted out of the nearby trees and surrounded her, whining softly and covering her hands and face with wet kisses from pink tongues. Matalia climbed up upon a tall rock and folded her legs under her while hugging each wolf in turn.

"You are wonderful beasts, good and loyal. 'Tis so glad I am to see you." She laughed at their barks and frantic play, pleased to enjoy the sunrise with her familiar friends.

*   *   *

An hour later Brogan sat to the left of the Earl, across from Xanthier and Isadora. "Must we speak of the inheritance immediately?" the Earl asked.

Brogan scowled, exchanging glances with Xanthier. "It would be best if we approached the matter directly. Your cleric is finished calculating my wealth. I would like to know how it compares to Xanthier's."

"You are a fool, brother. You collected your fortune by luck whereas I made it with cunning." Xanthier gloated as he lifted Isadora's hand.

"If you mean that you achieved great funds from your marriage, I would not brag. I find such an acquisition to be . . . lacking."

Isadora rose in fury. "You should watch your words, brother-in-law!"

"Be seated!" Xanthier shouted, equally infuriated. "It is no crime to gain from a dowry. In fact, it is to be greatly admired!"

"I have no admiration for such," Brogan hissed. "I am surprised by you. I thought you had more character."

"Cease!" the Earl thundered. "I will be the one to evaluate your strengths. I will assess the numbers later. For now, I expect you to sit at the breakfast table and eat in peace. Where is your wife, Brogan?"

Brogan stiffened. "She is taking a morning walk."

"Without you? Already? How quickly your new bride strays," murmured Isadora. Brogan ignored her comments.

After several minutes of tense silence, the great door swung open. Brogan lifted his granite eyes with studied coolness when Matalia swept in, her dress grass stained and wrinkled. He said nothing as she carelessly approached, yet his breathing was tight and shallow. The Earl, noting his son's sudden preoccupation with the doorway, glanced up and glared at the woman causing the interruption.

"Have you no manners, Lady Matalia? We have already passed half the meal."

Matalia glanced at her husband, observing his obvious tension, and then looked upon the Earl. "My apologies, m'lord, but I was so awestruck by the lands of Kirkcaldy that I lost track of time. Pray forgive me." She smiled charmingly while letting her lashes shield her sparkling eyes. The Earl grunted, appeased, and Matalia made her way around the table to join Brogan. He handed her a slice of fruit, but no light of welcome lit his expression.

As she sank into her seat, she shifted close to him.

"I am shocked that you would disgrace the table wearing such soiled clothing," Lady Isadora said, pursing her lips.

Matalia froze. "Since I think it would be more inappropriate to wear nothing, I wore what I had. My clothes are yet to be unpacked."

"Forsooth! I did not mean to embarrass you by revealing your husband's lack of generosity." Isadora lifted her hands in mock concern. "One would have thought that he would provide you with new gowns."

Brogan slammed his hands upon the table and made as if to rise when Matalia deliberately knocked over a pitcher of milk, instantly redirecting his anger. "Matalia!" he broke out, jumping to his feet and pushing the bench backward. The milk splashed upon the wooden table, then sped over the sides to drench Lady Isadora's lap, causing her to shriek in horror.

Xanthier also leaped to his feet, knocking the bench out of his way and causing the wet Isadora to tumble to the ground in a heap of flying skirts and muffled yips. He ignored her and chose instead to glare at Matalia with slitted eyes. She rose from her seat, deftly avoiding the dripping white liquid, and stood calmly returning Xanthier's look.

The Earl was the only family member who remained seated, as his location at the head of the table kept him safe from a soaking. He looked back and forth between the antagonists. He reached forward and picked a roll from a platter that had escaped contamination, sank his teeth into the bread and chewed meditatively.

A servant, braving the tense atomosphere, crept forward with a rag and started to clean the table while another assisted the fallen Lady Isadora. Matalia raised an eyebrow, indicating her contempt for Xanthier's lack of courtesy to his wife. She turned and leaned into Brogan, braving a swift glance up into his face. He returned her look, his lips compressed and his face rigid.

"Perhaps you are still fatigued from our travels. Would you like to retire?" he said, his voice betraying nothing.

Unsure, Matalia turned to the Earl. The older man still chewed, but his expression was thoughtful. He nodded, granting release, whereupon Brogan placed his arm casually but firmly around Matalia's shoulders and guided her from the hall and up the stairs to their tower.

Matalia allowed him to push her gently up the stairs, but her stomach tumbled with an odd feeling. When they reached the circular landing she tentatively moved to escape his arm, but he tightened his hold and forced her to enter the door to the master chamber. Still saying nothing, he released her, then turned and shut the door.

Matalia swung around and braced her hands upon her hips. "I will not apologize for spilling the milk. That woman was odious, and I was afraid you were going to strike her for her rudeness."

"I was," Brogan whispered, leaning with studied nonchalance against the door.

Matalia paused, unnerved by his calmness. Continuing with a trace of uncertainty, she said, "I did not think hitting her would do your cause good. I did not want to see you and your brother fight on your first day home."

"Do you really think Xanthier would fight with me over striking his wife?" Brogan tilted his head.

"Of course. . . . Would he not? . . . Would *you* not?"

"Aye, I most certainly would, Matalia. However, I am not so certain of his reactions. Your consideration for me was misplaced." Matalia looked away, biting her lip until Brogan shifted away from the door and moved closer to her. " 'Twas misplaced but an admirable show of loyalty. My thanks."

"Thanks?" Matalia questioned, trembling at his abrupt, towering presence.

"Yes. My thanks. And I am the one to apologize for forcing you to endure this antagonism."

Matalia shook her head, feeling her breath shorten the longer he brushed against her.

"Might I offer you a boon?" he questioned softly.

"Boon?" she repeated.

Brogan grinned, aware of her speechlessness, and moved from her side to some trunks on the far side of the room. "Some of my men brought these in." He lifted a lid and removed a skein of blue silk. The quality was obvious, and Matalia skipped over to him, reaching to touch the cloth. "Mayhap you can have some dresses made? Some to rival the Lady Isadora's?"

Matalia drew back, irritated. "I am not competing with that woman!"

"Of course not," Brogan pacified her. "But all the same, would you like to have some new gowns?"

"I would not like you to think that I care only for fine things."

Exasperated, Brogan shoved the silk into her hands.

"I gift you with a fortune in silks and you seek to remind me that you enjoy rolling in the meadows with wild beasts. Matalia"—he paused for emphasis—"take the cloth and gown yourself. And if you need prove yourself, meet me later in your tattered gown and practice swordplay."

Matalia giggled. She shrugged her shoulders and replied loftily, "I will indeed meet with you, but I can practice gowned in silk as well as wool."

"I would not mind if you were not gowned at all," he murmured in reply, but moved away before Matalia could assess his level of interest. "I must speak with some clerks. Can I trust you to amuse yourself without causing any more 'accidents'? At least until I return?"

"When will that be?" she queried, pretending to debate.

"This eve, long past dark. You will needs sup without me."

Suddenly sober, Matalia nodded. "Aye, I will do my best."

Brogan came over, leaning toward her. His gaze dropped from hers to stare at her flushed lips. His mouth parted and he sucked in air through his teeth. For a drawn-out moment Matalia and Brogan stood frozen. Then, with a small groan, he abruptly pulled back. Looking discomfited, he picked up her hand and brushed his lips across her fingers. "Until tomorrow, then," he mumbled, then exited the room.

Matalia watched him leave, sensing that he had wanted something else, but unsure what it was. She listened to his footsteps as they descended the stairwell and raised her knuckles to her cheek. She smiled, suddenly deliriously happy. Spinning around, she turned to the chest.

Inside she found seven rolls of cloth, each a beautiful, rich color. No pastels, no docile colors, only vibrant, blazing, powerful blues, reds, purples, greens and golds. Underneath the silks were two rolls of crème sheer and rolls of lace and ribbon trim with matching threads of such tiny diameter Matalia was hard-pressed to assure herself of their strength. Replacing the materials, she grinned happily and left in search of Peigi.

She found the servant in the kitchenette, making turnovers, giving the extra dough to the wolfhound that sat begging at her side. "Peigi," Matalia asked gaily, "where would I find the best seamstress in the region?"

Peigi looked up and curtsied. "I will have her sent to you directly, m'lady. She resides in the village and will be able to assist you this afternoon."

"No, no," Matalia contradicted her. "I wish to go to her, for I would rather leave the castle for a time."

"M'lady, 'twould be more seemly for me to send for her," Peigi replied.

Matalia's eyes grew cool and aristocratic. "Then I shall seek her on my own," she stated, her chin pointed upwards.

Peigi averted her eyes and sank into a low curtsy. "I am so sorry, m'lady. I would not anger you with my thoughtlessness. I will, of course, bring you where you wish."

Contrite, Matalia touched Peigi upon the shoulder. "I was being terrible.'Tis just that I do not understand the distance between the villagers and the castle members.'Twas much different in my home."

Peigi looked surprised, but did not comment on what was to her a natural order.

Within the hour the two women made their way down the stairs and out to the stables where a wagon was being loaded with supplies. Matalia bade the dog stay behind, and he trotted over to the kennels, searching for other canine comrades. Matalia, too, found her young friend. Delighted, she gave him a brief, familiar hug.

"Would you like to go back to the village with us,

young man?" Matalia offered the boy she had met earlier in the village, seeing that he and several other boys were about to depart. Peigi gasped, shaking her head, but the boy nodded quickly and jumped into the back of the conveyance. Seeing him, the other boys looked among themselves and soon followed suit.

When the driver walked out of the stables and saw them, he drew his brows down and stormed over, yelling at them. "Get out of my wagon, you rascals! You each have a set of legs! Use them and walk on your own. I'll not have my horse burdened by your weight!"

The boys scrambled out, frowning. Matalia reached over and grasped one of their hands, saying loudly, "Sir, I would request transportation for me and my friends to the village, where I have some errands. I know it will be a bit of an inconvenience, but I can become tired and would greatly appreciate it."

The man flushed, shaking his head sternly. "No, m'lady. The Earl would not allow you to go out without an escort."

Disgusted with his deference to the Earl, Matalia cast her gaze about the yard until she located another familiar face. "Jaimie Louvre!" she called out. "Jaimie! Could you please accompany us as an escort? I have errands in town that I must attend to."

Jaimie walked over, nodding. "Of course, m'lady. As long as your husband has ordered it."

Matalia glowered, but could not answer him.

"Indeed, Mr. Louvre. I would be much more at ease if you joined us," Peigi inserted on her mistress's behalf.

Jaimie shrugged, then mounted his horse. He motioned to the wagon driver, who scratched his head and nodded in resignation.

Seeing his agreement, Matalia turned toward the shuffling boys. "Come aboard, young men!"

"Yes, m'lady," Matalia's young friend replied. The wagon driver looked at Peigi for confirmation. The house servant waved to him, then lifted her skirt and clambered aboard. Seeing that he had no choice, the man grumbled under his breath about excess weight, but tipped his hat at Lady Matalia while helping her in, then climbed into the driver's seat. The boys grinned and jumped back in, shaking the wagon in their exuberance. Matalia held on to the wagon edge until the rocking ceased, and she smiled at the boys. With a snap of the reins, the man sent the heavy wagon rumbling out of the yard, under the bailey archway, and out onto the road leading to the village proper, with Jaimie riding silently behind.

As they traveled, Matalia pulled several bits of straw from the floorboards and broke them into even sizes. Then she extracted one piece and broke it into a shorter segment. Holding them in her fist so that they appeared equal, she instructed the boys to pick one straw apiece. Grinning, they did as she asked, until a red-haired boy triumphantly revealed the short piece, indicating his winning status. Matalia laughed at the other boys' expressions and collected the pieces and started over again.

Peigi watched the antics, a strange look on her face.

The half-hour ride passed quickly with the boys getting more comfortable, until their loud voices resounded in the village main street more strongly than the grind of the wagon's wheels. Many villagers looked up, stunned to view the bride of Brogan O'Bannon, possible next Countess of Kirkcaldy, sitting in the back of a wagon practically swarmed with energetic boys and pulling bits of straw from her hand. The wagon driver glowered at the villagers, daring them to say anything as he guided the wagon down the street and off a side road, finally stopping at the door of the village seamstress.

Chapter 18

After the wagon halted, the boys poured out, flourishing their latest pieces of straw. Then they pounced good-naturedly upon the lad who held the coveted smallest one. When the winner dashed away, the boys waved to Matalia and sped down the drive after him. Matalia's friend remained and skipped up to the door, opening it and shouting inside.

"Mother! You will never guess who is here to visit you!"

When the woman stepped out and beheld Lady Matalia, she froze, clearly frightened. "I will atone for his misdeeds, m'lady, but please forgive him, for he is just a boy, as you said yourself earlier." She leaned down and gripped her son's shirt, pulling him behind her as if to shield him.

Matalia shook her head and smiled. "I greatly enjoyed the lad, mistress. He is thoughtful and clever. Far from doing anything wrong, he has made my morning bright."

The woman's mistrust was still evident. Finally relenting, Peigi stepped down and walked up to the woman. "Evie, the lady has come for your skills. Do not make her feel uncomfortable with your nervous assumptions. Instead, 'twould be better to thank her for her generosity in giving the boys a lift and bringing you fine fabrics to work with."

The woman named Evie swung her gaze to the house servant in surprise, then blushed and curtsied. "Your forgiveness, m'lady. I shall gather my things and come to the castle immediately."

Peigi stepped forward before Evie could finish. "The lady wishes to be fitted here, away from the prying eyes of the castle. I daresay you can accommodate her desires?"

Although surprised, Evie nodded and stepped back to allow Lady Matalia's entrance. Then, as Matalia moved forward, Evie jumped in her way, blocking the path. "Wait!" she interjected. "Ah . . . perhaps . . . a moment . . ."

Jaimie leaped from his horse, his face thunderous. "How dare you deny the Lady! If she wishes to enter, you shall let her pass immediately!" The driver swung down as well, his face full of concern.

Jaimie stomped up as if to physically shove Evie, but Matalia deftly interceded. "I would like to view your garden for a few moments, if you would allow, Evie? Jaimie? Driver? Please? I would like to see Evie's garden first."

Evie nodded emphatically, relieved. Peigi, spying the messy interior of Evie's cottage, suddenly understood the woman's anxiety and looked at her mistress with astonishment at her perception. "Yes, I think I would like to show the Lady your flowers." Matalia regarded Peigi with approval. Shaking his head at the ways of women, Jaimie leaned against the cottage as the driver returned to the horses and took a sliver from the wagon sideboard to pick his teeth.

Evie disappeared into her home while her son led the women around to the side of the house to see the blooms, which he motioned to with meager enthusiasm. Matalia smiled in understanding.

"What is your name?"

"Thatcher, m'lady."

"Well, Thatcher, 'tis time for you to go on about your chores." The boy grinned happily, then scampered off to stack firewood.

Peigi watched him go, then walked a step behind Matalia. "Thatcher is my nephew, m'lady," she offered.

"Oh?" Matalia replied, turning to face her. "Evie is your sister?"

"Aye."

The silence between them stretched until Peigi spoke again. "He rarely plays. I was surprised to see him joining in your game."

"All children like to play," Matalia answered.

"Not here. The Earl frowns on unnecessary activities."

"Careful, Peigi. You sound disapproving of the great lord."

Peigi kept her eyes on Lady Matalia without flinching. "I think you will be good for Kirkcaldy, m'lady."

"I see." Matalia ruminated while holding a blossom in her hand and leaning down to smell it. She stood up, glanced at Peigi, and then looked out over the valley. "Do you think the mistress Evie is ready for us now?"

Peigi nodded. "Aye, m'lady."

Matalia smiled sadly, then added, "Think you I am ready for Kirkcaldy?"

"Aye, m'lady," Peigi repeated sagely.

Matalia headed for the front door. "Well, I am certainly ready for some new clothes! Let us see what gifts my husband has given for my pleasure."

Inside the freshly swept cottage, Matalia, Peigi and Evie riffled through the trunk, quickly forgetting their class distances in the excitement of feminine discovery. Many hours later, Jaimie firmly directed Lady Matalia and Peigi back into the empty wagon, promising a return trip on the morrow. Evie waved gaily to them, still holding a set of pins in her mouth and a length of cloth in her hand.

Matalia leaned against the sideboard, exhausted. Flashes of bright colors flooded her mind, and pattern after pattern danced on the edges of her consciousness until the rocking of the wagon lulled her into a light doze.

She awoke to the *clip-clop* of hooves against the packed surface of the bailey as Peigi nudged her shoulder. A wave of nausea overwhelmed her, and she clutched her stomach with concern.

"M'lady? Are you ill?"

"No. . . . Just wait a moment and it will pass."

"We are entering the courtyard, m'lady," the driver interrupted.

Matalia sat up, rubbing her eyes and pushing her tumbled hair out of her face. She took a deep breath and smiled reassuringly. "I feel fine, Peigi. The rocking wagon just unsettled my innards." She glanced about, then yawned. "My thanks," she said to the Jaimie and the driver.

Jaimie nodded and rode off while the driver gruffly acknowledged her. "My pleasure, my lady," he answered. "You brightened the day for many, and it was a pleasant change. If you ever need anything, I am available. They call me Muldon."

Matalia nodded, descending from the wagon. "Thank you again, Muldon. I will remember your kindness." Leaving them, Matalia slowly entered the great hall, dreading meeting up with members of the O'Bannon family. Unfortunately, the Earl spotted her immediately from where they all sat in front of the great fire, and he briskly waved her to his side. Isadora glanced up, scowling with displeasure. With dragging steps, Matalia walked over to them. When she saw the man she assumed to be Brogan, her face blossomed and she smiled. "Husband," she said as she greeted him. "You returned early?"

"I am not your husband, Matalia, but I would be

pleased to offer you the same services he provides," Xanthier murmured.

Matalia flushed, both embarrassed by her mistake and affronted by his remark.

"How pathetic," Isadora muttered.

"Where have you been today, Lady Matalia?" the Earl demanded.

"I was in the village, getting fitted for some gowns."

"You should not go there. Anything you need will be brought to you."

Temper flaring, Matalia retorted, "I wished to go to the village, and furthermore, I intend to go again tomorrow."

The Earl rose to his feet, towering over the smaller woman. "I have said you should not, and I will not accept argument."

"You cannot mean that I should never leave the castle!" she snapped.

Xanthier rose from his chair as well, saying laconically, "Come now. I am sure a woman of her 'spirited' nature cannot be alone all day without seeking some adventure in the village."

"I said no argument!" the Earl repeated angrily.

Insulted, Matalia shot back, "If this is how you treated Ansleen, 'tis no wonder she lied to you!"

Xanthier's nostrils twitched, and he took a step closer, raising his hand threateningly. "You will learn that women in this household are obedient, or they live to regret it!"

The Earl trembled with rage, his face becoming mottled red. "How dare you speak her name!" he added, swaying with the force of his fury.

Matalia tossed her hair back, her turquoise eyes gleaming with defiance. "I shall say what I wish!" Xanthier swiftly struck Matalia across the face, leaving a bright handprint upon her cheek.

Matalia gasped, stumbling back.

"I am well-known for my power over women, Matalia, as you discovered for yourself on your way here," he hissed, gripping her arm. "You should not push me."

"Enough!" thundered the Earl, stepping forward. " 'Tis of my wife that she spoke. You should not have struck her, Xanthier. Release her immediately!" He turned to see Jaimie and Brogan entering the hall.

"Brogan!" Matalia cried, running across the room. The bright handprint upon her cheek was clearly visible. She tumbled into his arms, her sobs blurring her words.

Trying to calm her, Brogan turned to the Earl and Xanthier. "What has gone on here?" he inquired with deadly menace. "Who had the courage, *nay the stupidity,* to strike my wife?" He felt an overwhelming fear for her well-being, and he was infuriated that she had been harmed in his absence. He held her briefly away, scanning her face, assuring himself of her health.

Xanthier tilted his head arrogantly. "She is just a woman, brother. Why would you care?"

Brogan lunged at Xanthier, his fists raised, and punched him in the face.

"Stop!" yelled the Earl. "This is not right! You two should not be fighting. You are brothers!" Two guards raced forward and grabbed Brogan, pulling him away.

"Yes! Finish it now, Xanthier! He is the usurper. Destroy him!" cried Isadora.

Matalia spun around incredulously, glaring at the Earl. "You have brought them to this! You have pitted them against each other since the day they were born. Of course they will fight!"

"But not like this . . . not in the hall. I'd have them prove their strength in combat," he answered harshly.

Brogan easily flung off the guards' restraining grip and stood with narrowed eyes, glaring at Xanthier. "I do not care where I fight, but I will make you rue the day your hand touched my wife!"

"Do you mean when I touched her now, or when I

touched her in the forest? It is a shame that she still cannot tell which of us is her husband. I am sure that I would be able to make her remember me."

Brogan swung again, slamming his fist into Xanthier's smug face, sending him careening to the floor. "Keep your goddamned hands off of her!"

"No, Brogan!" Matalia cried, racing forward. "Don't hit him! It's not right. Don't let him goad you into—"

"Jaimie! Bring her to her room," Brogan called out over his shoulder.

"Take it outside," said the Earl. "Take it to the courtyard. I should know who is the stronger. The riches have been tabulated and they are equal. Perhaps I will be able to decide the inheritance based upon combat skills. Come, let us go outside where there is plenty of room."

"You are insane!" screamed Matalia as Jaimie tried to pull her toward the north tower. "You cannot set them against each other. They will kill each other! For God's sake, stop this madness!"

Xanthier slowly rose from the rushes and pointed to the door. "Outside," he snarled. "I will see you in the courtyard. Isadora, you, too, must leave, for you annoy me."

"Go to your room, Matalia!" Brogan stared at her, his concern obvious to everyone but her. "I want you in the chamber, where you will be safe," he added as he strode from the hall in the direction of the courtyard.

"Mistress! Please!" Peigi raced forward, gripping Matalia's other arm. "You will only distract him. Leave the men to their fight. Come. You must come. In your condition . . . you must not get so upset."

Matalia swung her gaze to Peigi, shaking her head in confusion.

"What? What are you saying?"

"Come, Lady Matalia," Jaimie said. "If you do not go willingly, I will carry you forcibly."

"Take the Lady Matalia to her rooms and guard her door well so that she does not leave," the Earl stated. "Xanthier and Brogan will fight in the courtyard, within the ring of courage. The last one standing with two feet inside the ring will be declared the winner."

"You cannot lock me in my room as if I were a child," Matalia gasped, horrified as she yanked her arm from Jaimie's grasp. "I'll not stay in the room alone!"

"The dog may accompany you." The Earl motioned behind him, and a servant ducked out in search of the wolfhound.

"That is not what I meant! Leave me be," she ended forcefully but ineffectively, for Jaimie picked her squirming body up and strode with her up the steps of the northern tower. Peigi scurried after her, trying to shush Matalia's barrage of curses directed at the Earl, Xanthier, Brogan and men in general.

Upon reaching the circular landing, Jaimie dropped a heavy trap door over the stairwell, then jammed an iron bolt in place. He carefully deposited the enraged Matalia in the master chamber and quickly withdrew before a hairbrush slammed against the closed door with considerable force.

Matalia glared at the door and stamped her foot in vexation. She spun around, pacing back and forth, fueling her anger by thinking of all the faults she had already seen in the Earl and his sons, then adding several more she suspected they had. "Is this all my fault?" she wailed. "If I had known it was Xanthier and not Brogan . . . if I had not gone to the village . . . if I had not made that foolish comment about the Countess. . . . I am such the fool! When will I grow up? When will I stop hurting those around me?" She collapsed upon the bed, feeling faint. "Peigi?" she called softly, then again when she heard no response. "Peigi! I feel ill!"

Peigi raced into the chamber, her eyes wide with concern. "Lady Matalia? Please, stop trying to rise. Rest. You should not get so upset."

"Why, Peigi? Why shouldn't I get upset? Why am I feeling so light-headed?"

"Because of your condition, m'lady."

"My condition?"

"Why, yes. Didn't you know? You are showing all the signs. Am I wrong? Are you not?"

"Pregnant," Matalia breathed, sinking back against the pillows, suddenly realizing the truth: "I'm pregnant."

Peigi nodded, confused.

"I am, aren't I? I really am pregnant. I am going to have a baby. Brogan's baby."

"Yes, m'lady. It would appear so," Peigi answered in a muffled voice as Matalia leaped from the bed and enfolded her in an embrace.

Outside, the men entered the courtyard circle. Many castle folk appeared, all drawn by the swiftly spreading tale of the imminent fight.

"Brother," Xanthier said depreciatingly, "you have already lost. Prepare yourself to call me Earl."

Brogan slowly advanced. Saying nothing, he raised his fists and swung, narrowly missing his target as Xanthier leaped out of the way.

"Your wife," Xanthier growled, "has not made a good impression."

"She grows on one," Brogan replied as he sidestepped an answering swing from Xanthier.

"She will not 'grow' upon the Earl, except to inflame his anger further. Perhaps you should retire from the contest now, so as not to feel the bitterness of defeat."

Brogan glared at his twin. "Do you not find it insulting that you would win Kirkcaldy by virtue of a woman's spiritedness?"

Xanthier turned his head and spit into the dirt. "I care not how I achieve it, for I will win." Then, narrowing his eyes, he added, "And I would not mind having a taste of your wife as I do."

"I, on the other hand, would be revolted if I had to bed your wife." Xanthier choked, but Brogan continued dispassionately. "Thus I understand your envy. Not every man is granted the gift of a beautiful, sensual and lively partner." Seeing that Xanthier was speechless, Brogan lunged forward and tackled his nemesis.

They both fell to the dirt, rolling over each other, striking out with fists and boots, until they leaped apart, their faces bloodied and filthy.

"Give up this fight, Brogan. You do not know Kirkcaldy. You have never lived here."

"I will fight for Kirkcaldy, but today I fight for Matalia's honor."

Xanthier took a step forward, shaking his head. "You are making a mistake, Brogan. This woman is not worth fighting me. Send her away."

"You must know that I cannot allow this to go unpunished," Brogan said quietly. A trickle of blood dripped from the corner of his lip, and he wiped it away carelessly.

"I do not want to fight you, brother," Xanthier whispered, a spasm of true pain crossing his face.

The men circled each other, identical faces, identical bodies mirroring each other's movements with uncanny similarity. "So you fear a fight with me, Xanthier?"

"I have no fear of you," his brother replied, his voice hardening. "You show your weakness even now by defending a mere woman against your flesh and blood."

Brogan's lip twitched, and contempt washed the air around them. "You have always been the stupid one," he said. "I am not simply defending my wife. I am pleased to strike you, for I have been wanting to for many years."

Xanthier laughed, an ugly sound echoing off the white stones. "You forget, brother, that despite our mutual hatred, we know each other well. You cannot lie to me. I am your twin. We were born of the same seed, and nothing can happen to you that I do not know about. You feel something for this black-haired girl and you hate fighting me!"

Brogan feinted, catching Xanthier off guard, then swung with his fist. Xanthier stumbled back, his nose bleeding instantly. Brogan's own nose twitched, subliminally feeling his brother's pain. "Aye," Brogan said as he stepped back to avoid Xanthier's return swing. "And I know you as well. You knew that to hit her was to draw me out. Perhaps you see something I do not. Perhaps I have found something you wish you had." Brogan ducked, but Xanthier swung again and caught him in the chest, and Brogan gasped as pain exploded from his ribs.

"You fool!" shouted Xanthier, incensed. "As soon as Kirkcaldy is mine I will see you banished forever! The girl will mean nothing in the end! She is nothing now!"

Brogan snarled back at him. "I will win Kirkcaldy! And I will be standing here with her long after you have fled into exile!" He sprang forward, grappling with Xanthier as they both fell to the dirt again, wrestling and punching each other until their faces ran with blood and the crunch of fists against flesh resounded in the courtyard.

The men fought, each unwilling to admit defeat, until their punches were weak and they could barely stand. Holding each other up, they continued to pummel the other until the Earl finally motioned to a guard to pull them apart.

"I was wrong," the Earl said sadly. "I should not have had you fight. I had hoped that one of you would win quickly and settle this matter, once and for all." He shook his head when both sons tried to reenter the circle, their ravaged faces gleaming with hatred.

Sorrow filled the Earl's face as he hung his head in despair. *What has happened?* he cried silently. *What have I created? Ansleen! Please come home and help me! I was wrong. I was so wrong that day. Please, Ansleen!*

But he remained silent as he had for many years. Ansleen would not come. He knew she would not come because he had already asked her and she had not answered his pleas.

Chapter 19

Matalia woke the following morning to an empty room. She tried to sit and weave, but the threads tangled and she gave up after a scant hour. She straightened the room, then proceeded to rearrange it, forcing Muldon and two other men to shift the massive bed closer to the fireplace and move the heavy writing desk next to the window.

Then, still feeling at a loss, she sat at the desk and started writing a letter to her mother until that, too, became a crumpled mess and she abandoned it with a huff. She was pregnant! She was going to have a baby!

She tried to think about the child it would become, tried to imagine what it would be like to be a mother, but the concept was so foreign she had a hard time contemplating it. She pushed her stomach out, pretending to be far along. Then she thought about how to arrange the nursery, but gave up when she kept trying to imagine what Brogan would want.

No one came to the tower, and Matalia stared out the window. She could not see the courtyard from her location, and for once felt envious of Isadora's southern exposure. She wondered about Brogan, biting her lip with fear. He was a strong man. He should do well in a fight, but Xanthier was his exact equal. There was no way she could predict the outcome. As the day merged into night, Matalia tried to keep her thoughts positive. Brogan was her husband, and though he and Xanthier were matched physically, Brogan was far superior mentally.

Finally, Peigi came inside and told her that Brogan was recovering.

"He is resting. The surgeon says that he should not rise for several days. He bade me to tell you that he is well and should join you soon, but felt it best to recover in solitude."

"And Xanthier?" Matalia asked.

"The same."

"A draw, then?"

"Indeed. No winner was declared. They had to drag them out of the circle because they could no longer stand."

Eating dinner alone, Matalia contemplated her status in the household of Kirkcaldy, finally surmising that she needed to help Brogan achieve his goals more actively. This idiocy must cease. Fighting among brothers was wrong. She needed to step in and solve their dilemma. She had never wanted something as much as Brogan wanted Kirkcaldy, and she felt awe for his dedication. Her small desires had been childish compared to his drive. He had more powerful convictions than anyone she had ever known.

She was his wife, and she needed to stand behind his battle for the castle. Isadora did nothing for her husband. In fact, she hindered his petition, for the servants disliked her immensely. She was ill mannered and demanding and did nothing to help the castle function.

It was time to act the part of a countess if she ever meant to take on the real role. She had been taught well. It was time to stop working against Brogan and begin to work with him. However, just because she meant to help him, she thought as she drifted off to sleep, did not mean she would help him as he expected. She would do it her own way. She would not allow hatred and anger to dictate the winner. Friendship, leadership and compassion were the qualities that should prevail, and she knew that Brogan had those properties buried in his heart. It was up to her to bring them forth. And she knew how. She had another idea.

Matalia rose the next morning with new resolutions and sweetly requested that the village seamstress be sent for so that they could finish the fittings. Peigi, surprised but thankful, happily complied, fetching Evie immediately. The trio spent the rest of the afternoon creating several dresses. As Evie cut and pinned, Peigi sewed seams and Matalia stitched lace and ribbons. In a hushed voice, Matalia also voiced her new plan, eliciting shocked but excited reactions from the two women.

"It will be our secret," Matalia whispered.

"How do you think to do it without Lord Brogan's knowing?" Evie murmured back, glancing at the closed door.

"Believe me," Matalia answered, "he will have no knowledge of it. The men in the household think that they control everything. We will show them! 'Tis time we had some fun."

Peigi nodded. "It would be fun," she said hesitantly. "As long as the Earl and his sons don't find out, it should be a wonderful event!"

Assured of their allegiance, Matalia smiled with satisfaction. They continued to plan until the light became too poor for sewing and Muldon returned to gather Evie and her things for the trip back to the village.

Evie waved good-bye and put a finger to her lips. Peigi and Matalia giggled at Muldon's curious look, but said no more. Soon even Peigi left, and Matalia put away the materials and straightened the room.

Later that evening, as Matalia finished her second lonely dinner, she was surprised by a knock on the chamber door. Rising, she opened it, expecting to see Brogan. Instead, the Earl smiled wryly and raised his eyebrows in a gesture so familiar Matalia tilted her head to view him better. "May I enter?" the Earl finally asked into the silence.

Matalia frowned, darting a look around his form, seeking to determine the presence of any other foe.

"Neither of my sons is with me," the Earl said sardonically. "They are still recovering. Do you feel remorse at your actions yet?"

"M'lord?"

"Because of you, my sons are at odds."

"Because of me?" Matalia shot back, incensed. "You are the one who set them against each other from the moment of their birth. If I must assume blame, m'lord, 'tis the blame of a catalyst, a flint, on an already smoldering fire."

The Earl stared at her, his eyes cold. Then he curled his lip. "You think that I wanted this?"

"I pray not," Matalia countered, her turquoise eyes freezing into chips of blue ice. "If you did, then you would be a truly evil man."

"Do you think I am evil?" he questioned.

"Could you make me believe otherwise?" Matalia replied. "Look at what you have created. Ansleen was banished because of your ridiculous accusations. She has remained silent, hoping that your supposed intellect would surface and see the right of it, but look where she remains, behind stone barriers. And look where your sons stand. On opposites sides of a war. No, m'lord, you have not proved your point, only convinced me of my own."

The Earl flushed, the veins on his neck rising. Then, as he stared into Matalia's strong and beauteous visage, he wilted. Casting his eyes down, he took a few steps over to the mantel and leaned heavily against it. He cleared his throat, twice, then raised his gaze back to Matalia, who watched him warily, perhaps realizing that she had said too much once again.

"You are right, of course, and I have known it for some time," he sighed. "But I cannot change anything now. Ansleen is lost to me, and my sons are enemies."

Matalia stepped back, startled by his admission.

"You remind me of her, you know. She was lovely and bold, just as you are. I came here because I would like a favor. Will you grant an old man some of your time? Will you play chess with me?"

"Chess?" Matalia repeated, confused.

"Yes." The Earl lifted his arm, showing a folded chessboard. "I came up to inquire if you would like to play chess."

Nonplussed, Matalia nodded. "I like chess," she replied. "But why?"

The Earl grimaced in what Matalia took for his version of a smile. "I would like to get to know you better. Is it wrong to spend time with my daughter-in-law?"

"Of course not," Matalia answered quietly, the force of her anger dissipating as she noticed the slight tremor in the Earl's hands as he held the board out for her viewing. He seemed so frail, so lost, and for the first time Matalia realized how tragic the situation was for him. Out of jealousy and fear, he had cast out the woman he had loved and had embroiled his own sons in a bitter, lifelong battle. No one was happy. The Earl longed for a love that was long lost, and his sons both hated and feared him. Neither cared for him, though both were inexorably determined to earn his approval. Matalia dropped her gaze, veiling her pity.

"Then let us begin," he said as he sat in one of the newly arranged chairs, leaving Matalia to sit in the one opposite. He opened the case, revealing a board with beautifully carved pieces, and proceeded to arrange them.

Many hours later, Peigi discretely entered and lit a brace of candles and stoked the fire while placing a fresh jug of wine on the table. Both the Earl and Matalia were so engrossed in their play, neither acknowledged her presence, so she left as quietly as she had entered. After the Earl had evened the score two games to two, he finally rose and bid Matalia good night.

"I expect to continue our game tomorrow eve," he told her.

" 'Tis my husband's choice," she murmured. The Earl harrumphed in disbelief. Matalia rose, a shadow of concern on her face. "He does well, does he not?" she asked.

The Earl paused as he exited and nodded. "Both fare as well as can be expected."

"And where are they resting?" she asked with studied carelessness.

"In the dungeon," he replied, and Matalia gasped, horrified, staring at his back as he descended the winding stairway.

Jaimie still guarded her door, and no amount of pleading had convinced Peigi to bring her to Brogan. Nevertheless, she was determined to see her husband and assure herself of his condition, so as darkness fell, Matalia hitched her skirt up to her waist and removed her delicate slippers. She peered out the window and assessed the irregular surface. Foot and handholds were plentiful, but Matalia was still apprehensive. The ground was a long way down. Taking a deep breath, she climbed out the window and wriggled her toes until she found a good perch. Then, step by careful step, she descended the stone wall until she reached a lower balcony.

She dropped down, landing softly, and breathed a sigh of relief. If the balcony led to an unlocked room, she would not have to scale the wall any farther. As she tried the door, she peered inside. Dust was everywhere. It cloaked the furniture and clung to the spiderwebs that hung from the ceiling. Thankfully, the door opened with ease, and Matalia entered the room. It appeared to be an old bedroom with a great, canopied bed, large trunks and massive dressers. The wall tapestries were tattered and moldy, and the mattress was moth-eaten.

She crept forward, keeping her dress up so it would not drag the floor. A mouse scurried by, startling Matalia. She watched it dart into a hole and disappear, and then Matalia saw the bassinet against the wall. Delicate lace was draped over the side and a blanket of mouse droppings filled the interior. Tears welled up in Matalia's eyes at the evidence of Brogan's birthing room. She touched the lace, crying fully when it crumbled into dust.

She stood for several minutes until her tears slowed. Then she took a deep breath and swallowed. This was the past. She did not have time to dwell here. She needed to find her husband.

Carefully opening the door, she saw a long corridor leading to a flight of stairs. She tiptoed along the hall until she was assured that no one was near; then she sped down the steps. At the base she saw a pair of wooden doors. One led to the kitchen, and she could hear the rustle of workers on the other side. The other was cracked open, and she could see another set of steps leading downward. Guessing that they must lead to the dungeons, she dashed forward and slipped inside.

Candles lit the way and Matalia paused, frightened by the cool breeze snaking up from the depths. *It feels like an entrance to a cave,* she thought. *But there are no beasts hidden here.* "Come Matalia, do not be afraid," she said, trying to brace herself.

Carefully making her way down, she trailed her fingers along the walls, noticing when the smooth stone gave way to damp rock. A set of rooms was formed by natural rock formations, and Matalia finally acknowledged that the dungeon was, indeed, a cavern underneath the castle itself. One room was lit, and Matalia walked forward, holding her breath.

Inside there were two cots. Brogan and Xanthier lay upon them, sleeping. They were both battered and bruised. Their clothing was indistinguishable, their faces identical. Matalia looked back and forth, dismayed. Which one was her husband?

She stared to hum, a soft, almost inaudible sound, then lifted her voice into a clear melody. She drifted forward, closing her eyes, and let the beauty of the song fill her. She reached out with both hands, touching both men, feeling their pain and suffering. She sang quietly, letting the melody pour out of her fingertips and spread its healing power into both men. She swayed, centering her energy on them, focusing her gift on their hearts.

For long, long moments she wrapped the unconscious Brogan and Xanthier in comfort, soothing their hurts, softening their regrets, and granting them absolution. The song slipped into their minds and calmed them, opened them, showed them how to live. It reverberated and rebounded, drenching them in peace, until they both sighed, letting their anxieties drift away.

They shared the dream, the dream of her. She stood in the mist with her arms outstretched. Brogan knew her, welcomed her, but Xanthier had never felt her before. He stood at the edge of the mist, watching, longing, but knowing that he was not part of this world. Brogan entered the mist boldly, seeking her touch. When they met, the mist began to glow as if lit from sunlight above. The golden color spread, wrapping Brogan and Matalia in its wealth. Then, as if carried on her breath, it flowed outward and touched Xanthier. The dream slowly faded, and the men slipped deeper into a dreamless slumber, once again separate but connected.

Matalia opened her eyes, feeling weak. She glanced down at the men and moved unerringly to Brogan's bed. She knelt at his side and placed her cheek against him. "Sleep well, my darling. Heal from the inside out. I will be waiting for you." Then she rose and exited the dungeons.

The next day of her enforced isolation made Matalia more anxious than ever. She twisted her hands and bit her lips so much, her fingers ached and her lips grew swollen. Evie visited her, bringing her an update on the activities Matalia had organized, but even that failed to distract Matalia from her nervous anticipation. Brogan was going to come to her tonight!

Finally, as the sun reached its zenith, Matalia could wait no longer. She leaped off the couch and raced to the mirror, staring intently at her untidy hair and drab gown. She moaned, plucking at the collar of the dress and snagging her fingers in her unbrushed curls. Pressing her lips into a mutinous line, she stomped to the chamber door and flung it open.

Jaimie looked up, surprised, and scrambled to his feet.

"I will go to the kitchen and wash," Matalia stated firmly, then flounced past the big man and yanked open the door to the wash and storage room, and slammed it shut before he could react. Peigi paused in kneading bread, and stared at Matalia curiously. "I need to be clean and presentable," Matalia explained, suddenly feeling foolish.

"Absolutely," Peigi replied, wiping her hands. "We still have time." Matalia smiled gratefully and allowed Peigi to guide her behind the screen to a basin of water. With brisk efficiency, Peigi lathered and rinsed Matalia's hair several times until the black curls shimmered in the slanting sunlight. She then helped Matalia to a cold but refreshing sponge bath, producing a small vial of scented oil for her to dab in warm places.

"Evie and I are almost finished with the dresses, but we have nothing complete yet," Peigi lamented, staring at the heap of soiled clothing Matalia had discarded before her bath. She sat now, wrapped in a blanket, in front of the kitchen fire as she diligently combed through her tangled hair.

"I will figure something out," Matalia replied airily, averting her eyes at Peigi's questioning glance. As she finally managed to tame the tresses, she rose and moved awkwardly to the door. "But if you could ask Jamie for a moment of privacy . . ."

Peigi scampered ahead of her mistress and poked her head out. "Stand back," she commanded, "and close your eyes!"

Jaimie immediately complied, turning to face the wall and covering his eyes with his hands. Peigi giggled, then motioned Matalia forward. Cautiously, she tiptoed into the circular landing, then whipped into the master chamber and shut the door firmly behind her.

Alone, freshened and enlivened, Matalia set about decorating the room, her heart fluttering with nervous excitement.

Chapter 20

Brogan groaned. Every ounce of his muscled body ached. He drew a deep breath, pleased to note that no sharp pain accompanied his actions. He stood at the bottom of the stairs, staring up at the closed trap door, dreading the coming encounter with his wife. She was undoubtedly spitting mad. His instruction to keep her in the tower had been selfish, for he was loath to let her see him bruised and battered.

He despised himself for his own violence. Brother against brother. He spit blood-tinged saliva into the rushes, casting a flickering look of steely hatred toward his father's chambers. And father against son.

It was now three days later, and although he could walk upright with no outward sign of pain, his muscles screamed at any excessive movement. The thought of ducking flying porcelain or sidestepping a series of cutting barbs was, to say the least, unwelcome.

He adjusted his clothes, making sure that the worst of his contusions were safely covered from Matalia's probing eyes, and took the first few steps. A noise from the southern stairwell made him glance over, and he saw Xanthier coming down the stairs, a twisted frown marring his face. The brothers stared at each other until Isadora descended behind her husband, the thin whine of her voice audible to Brogan even if the words were not. Breaking eye contact and casting an

irritated look at her, Xanthier continued on his way
and entered the great hall. Isadora sniffed, then followed in his wake.

Jaimie opened the door and stepped back with a
blank expression. Noting his man's lack of enthusiasm,
Brogan set his shoulders and took a steadying breath.
"Into the lair of the wolf mistress," he mumbled to
himself with a touch of dry humor. Then, he resolutely
opened the chamber door and stepped inside.

The room was dark. A few candles burned on a
table next to a chessboard and several others upon an
end table next to the bed. As he closed the door, the
faint breeze created by his entrance caused a fluttering
of ribbons around the shadowed bed. Frowning, Brogan took another step forward, then realized that ribbons were tied everywhere. Bows danced above the
mantelpiece. They trailed upon the floor, creating rippling waves of iridescent colors. They dangled mischievously from the upper canopy of the bed and winked
in the glow of the candles as they slowly twirled and
swayed.

Taking another step, Brogan beheld lace ribbons
cloaking the window, creating a latticed pattern of diffuse light upon the couch. A soft whisper of silk sliding
against silk drew his attention back to the bed, and
his senses sharpened. The aches of his body fled, leaving him ready to defend, to attack. He padded forward, his movements as lithe as the extinct Scottish
lynx, and he towered over the bed, staring down
through the ribbons at the person sprawled there.

Matalia gazed up at him, her heart beating in a
staccato rhythm, her pulse pounding in her wrists. She
lay upon an unfurled length of rich, royal purple silk,
her black tresses splayed wantonly across the pillows.
Brogan caught his breath, his whole being frozen, as
he stared at her breathtakingly displayed body.

Ribbons . . . ribbons. They draped over her in curling silk and satin. They graced her hair with flashes of filigreed gold. Around her throat, a demure bow of blue held an amulet, while a matching ribbon was tied in an endless crisscrossing array over her chest, around her bare breasts and down to her navel where it ended in another enticing knot.

Down and around her legs were countless colors, dipping deep into the shadowed areas and peeping unashamedly out the other side. Flickering textures, caught by candlelight, beckoned his senses. Her ankles, delicate, exquisite ankles, were bound by pale green, trailing tendrils that floated to the floor at his feet. Finally, drawing in a struggling breath, his eyes rose to her wrists. Swathed in broad velvet ribbon, black as midnight, sublime in seduction, her wrists were beribboned and drawn up to the posts of the bed in a posture of exquisite surrender.

Brogan took a step back, collecting himself, forcing himself to breathe slowly, carefully, in and out. He stalked around the bed, letting his fingers ripple through the dangling ribbons, stirring them into agitation just as he was stimulated. He reached the other side of the bed, near the candles, and reached out to pick one of them up and hold it over Matalia's body. He leisurely ran it over her, casting the mellow orange glow of candlelight onto her skin, making her white flesh appear honey hued. His other hand flitted over her body, following the trail of light, confirming that she was real and was bound in a fortune of female frippery.

At last he lifted his gaze to meet her fear-filled eyes. Her vulnerability tugged his heart, just as her availability pulled at his cock.

"If this is how you apologize for tying me up when we first met, I am pleased, more than pleased, at how you have returned the favor." His voice was husky, even to his own ears, but he made no attempt to clear it. Instead he smiled with seductive masculinity as the fear in Matalia's face gradually faded as she became sure that he appreciated and understood her offering.

He replaced the candle and sifted his hands through the pile of ribbons on the bed, moving them over so he could sit next to her. He picked up the silken strands, suddenly certain he would never see a bow on a woman's dress again without thinking of this moment, without wondering if it was a piece that had draped her naked limbs. He touched the strands woven around her legs, tracing his finger slowly up the satin texture, feeling the heat of her body through the ribbon.

Suddenly, abruptly, a flush of heat suffused his flesh, and his gaze raked over her form. His eyes darkened to molten mercury and an answering flash fire erupted in her belly. The inhibition she had acquired upon his entrance melted away, and she let his heated glance reassure her, comfort her, enchant her. Although frightened at the last moment, she wanted to give this to him, to relinquish her body into his care. She needed this closeness between them. She wanted this moment to bind them.

Brogan gripped one end of a ribbon wrapped around her left thigh, a scarlet satin ribbon overlaid with yellow, and gently pulled, untying it in a smooth motion. The slippery cloth slid apart easily, whispering over Matalia's skin as Brogan drew it completely off her body. A faint red mark indicated where the ribbon had lain, and Brogan leaned forward and blew on the mark, then flicked his tongue out and licked it.

Matalia sighed, the wealth of tension in her body expressing itself in the simple sound of release. Smiling, his powerful face a mixture of strength and passion, he reached for the next ribbon and untied it as well, unwrapping her slowly, steadily.

"You are so . . ." he whispered, causing Matalia

to shudder with delight as his expression finished his sentence. He shifted down and began plucking the bows with his teeth, sucking on her skin, then blowing upon the wet spot, creating a fission of cool shivers awash in a flood of fire. He paused at the blue ribbon around her chest, and instead of untying it, he shifted it, adjusting the bonds so they encircled and lifted her breasts, squeezing them slightly.

Surprised, suffused with passion, Matalia arched into the new arrangement, allowing her nipples to pucker and swell in reaction. She tossed her head, presenting her neck, and Brogan immediately complied, tonguing the exposed flesh, then removing the ribbon that graced it and dropping it and the amulet to the floor. He stood suddenly, pulling off his clothes and Matalia's mouth opened, seeing the tangled web of abrasions and contusions that marred his handsome figure.

She reached out to stroke him, but a flare of dominance in his eyes halted her hand in midair. He swung his body over hers, straddling her, and reached for the trailing velvet ribbons that encircled her wrists. Without apology, he tightened them, knotting them firmly, then lifted the loose ends to tie them to the bedposts. Matalia acquiesced, her body like limpid honey, but her eyes darkened to a near violet as each wrist was secured, tested and appraised.

With her hands drawn up, her breasts were lifted even higher, and as Brogan sat back, his cock slid between them, the velvet strength of his member rippling against the crisscrossed satin. He paused, preoccupied, and moved his hips again, then grabbed each breast and pushed their heavy fullness tight around his throbbing core.

He bucked his hips, sliding in and out of the newly discovered heaven, then adjusted his hands so that his thumbs could brush over her nipples at the same time.

A bead of moisture formed at the tip of his penis, and he held still, closing his eyes and rubbing the moisture over her, over him.

Matalia let her soul fly free. She released any thoughts from the prison of their earthly restraint and let sensation sweep her body. The bristly hardness of his thighs flanking her waist made her feel completely, utterly cocooned in his power, and the tingling of her fingers bound over her head liberated her submission. She was free to let him plunder her. She was helpless, and because of that bondage, she was emancipated.

She felt him open the gift of her beribboned body, strand by silken strand. Slowly, lingeringly, he untied the lace and silk, finding bows on every inch of her flesh, reveling in the heat of her as he released each ribbon and then let it fall unheeded into the sheets. She felt him holding his breath in awe. She felt the rush of desire swell his tumescence, until he rubbed it between her breasts, barely controlling his responses. Her head moved again, this time without conscious thought, and a subtle lift of her hips indicated her rising craving. She bent her knees, the pale green satin ribbons sliding against the purple silk and then draping over Matalia's thighs.

With a low growl, Brogan released her breasts and shifted down her body, forcing her legs back down, dragging his cock over her abdomen, across her navel and then into the pillow of her beribboned thighs.

Matalia cried out, pulling her arms as if to wrap them around his back, only to be reminded of their captured status. Instead, she opened her legs, and lifted her hips, anxious to feel the unforgettable slide of his entrance. But Brogan held back. He moved down even farther, finding yet more ribbons and untying them with methodical precision. As he reached the ribbons binding her ankles he hesitated, debating. Electing to leave them in place, he picked her foot up and ran his fingers over the shape of it, exploring every vale and hill, then rubbed his lips in the instep as if it were the palm of the queen herself.

Then, spreading her thighs apart, he rose over her. "I am going to take you now. . . . I am going to take every part of you."

Matalia nodded, her pulse frantic, a wet dewiness soaking her insides, making her inner muscles clench and quiver. She tugged at her velvet ribbons, unaware of her actions, her mind drugged with sensual fervor. The tip of him met her uplifted hips and he slid in, slowly, easily, raspily. Both of them hardly breathed as they experienced the aphrodisiac of initial penetration. Deep, deep, slow, deep, then home and still for one long, protracted moment.

Brogan bent his head, resting a suddenly sweat-soaked forehead onto hers, drawing breath after breath, holding himself back from exploding. Then, gathering his force, he pulled out of her, almost to the tip, then sank back, holding himself still once again.

Matalia squirmed, lifting her legs to wrap around his waist, arching her lower body to take more of him, to meld with him. The ribbons trailed over his hips, whispering against his flesh like invisible fingers of silken sensation. He clenched his fists around yet more of the satin strands that slipped and slid around their wet bodies, feeling them curl and enfold around both of them. She pulled against her velvet bonds, welcoming their grounding presence. Her mouth opened as she panted, and her eyelids became so heavy she let them drift closed. Warmth and lust rippled through her, capturing her, enfolding her just as his arms closed around her, holding her shoulders down and stabilizing her for his next assault.

He lifted his head, staring down at her face that rocked back and forth upon the silk-covered pillows, tossing her ribbon-bedecked hair everywhere.

"God in heaven," he murmured, then began stroking into her, deliberately pushing his cock against the inner parts of her that quivered with his touch, purposely building Matalia's erotic sensations until they spilled over, making her wild with desire.

Sounds escaped from her mouth, soft and guttural, sharp and protracted, and his voice rose to match hers, exulting in the lascivious moment, feeling nothing but the incredible ecstasy of Matalia. She wound her legs around his, pressing as close as possible, feeling tiny flecks of emotion building, building inside her. Her small sounds burst into a full-fledged scream. Brogan ducked down, gripping her nipple in his mouth, biting, then releasing, then attacking her shoulder. He felt the tide swelling, felt his cock swelling, knew the time was near.

Matalia felt the shift of pace, the new level of energy as his potency multiplied, as she rose to meet him, thrust for thrust, feeling it build even higher . . . higher. Her screams erupted, torn from her throat by the force of his domination, pushed from within by the avalanche of sensation. She came, she came. So full and so sweet she thrashed, gripping him with her thighs, bucking him with her hips. He bore her body down, down into the purple silk awash with ribbons, and surged into her once more, then let go of his control and exploded within her, deep within her, coming with mighty voltage that shook the bed and shattered his heart.

"Oh, my God," he groaned, his voice hoarse. "Oh, my God . . . Unbelievable. Oh, my God, Matalia."

Matalia could not answer, for she was still floating, her body unattached except at the heated junction of their bodies. Her eyelids flickered open, staring unseeingly at Brogan's sweaty face, her breathing as rapid as if she had raced for her life. She slowly felt her body drift back, felt the tingle of each finger, each toe, each pore. Her dilated pupils began to focus, and she blinked several times until she could see Brogan's grinning face.

"Are you back with me yet?" he whispered, softly stroking her flesh where the heat of his body had marked her with his sweat.

Matalia blinked again, her limbs completely languid. She tried to nod, but because it was unsuccessful, she licked her lips to reply verbally instead. "I—I think so," she replied, her voice jagged with sex-roughened huskiness.

He smiled in the candlelight, a warm, open, loving smile, and Matalia returned it with one of her own. He reached up and deftly untied her bonds from the bed, but left the trailing ribbons in their place of honor around her wrists. He rolled off of her and pulled the silk bolt around Matalia, wrapping her in its cool and comforting length. He then pulled the coarser blanket up from the end of the bed where it had been folded, and covered their bodies with it. Then, pulling her head to rest on his chest, they fell asleep together.

"He is terrible!" Matalia's strident voice ripped Brogan from blissful sleep to full awareness. He sprang out of bed and crouched, sweeping his hand behind him to locate his sword. Finding it, he clasped its warm handle securely and rose to face the enemy.

Matalia stood on the other side of the room, her turquoise eyes flashing dangerously. She wore a robe lined with silver fox that was belted with a matching girdle of blue tassels. The golden ribbons of last night still lingered in haphazard fashion within her wild black curls, yet Brogan's gaze brushed her face only briefly before resting warily upon the fine sword in her hand.

Matalia glared at her husband, lifting the sword tip

higher and gestured menacingly at the door. "How could he do this? This contest between you two is horrible. You were speaking in your sleep and I heard you talk to him. You were friends. You liked each other!"

Brogan relaxed his stance and lowered his heavier weapon. He lifted his eyebrows in question. "What in the world are you talking about?"

"Xanthier and you. You were friends! I heard you speaking to him in your sleep, as brothers do, with care and closeness. Why did the Earl ruin that?"

Brogan turned his back and leaned down to pick up his previously discarded breeches. A whisper of wind teased his temple as Matalia swung her sword in anger. He lifted his own weapon reflexively.

"By the saints, Matalia! What . . . ?" He jammed his feet into the clothing, hopping around in order to face her, then straightening with a snap and glaring at her in fury. Seeing her swing her sword at the chessboard, he leaped over the bed and grasped her wrist.

"He . . . he fooled me. I was beginning to like the Earl, to feel sorry for him. But when I saw your bruises in the daylight . . ." she sputtered, trying to lift her sword against the weight of his body, trying to destroy the chessboard. Brogan leaned into her, pushing her against the wall, his form dwarfing hers.

"Come now, you cannot blame him for who he is."

Matalia looked up at him bewildered. "But it is so senseless, so ridiculous!"

It was Brogan's turn to be surprised. "It is as it is, Matalia," he stated.

"Why would you do this? Look at you! Your body is black-and-blue from head to foot! How dare you! You are to be a father! How could you risk yourself like this!" She shoved against him, and Brogan stepped back in stunned surprise, his brows drawn together. Matalia instantly lifted the tip of her sword and pointed it at his shoulder. "You infuriate me, Brogan O'Bannon, and I want nothing more to do with you! I am quit of these chambers whether you will it or no. I will not bear my child in this castle. I will not allow him to be destroyed by the tragedy that fills these walls!" She stared at him defiantly, then glanced behind her and tiptoed gingerly to the door, keeping her sword raised. "I warn you!" she tossed back at him as she flung open the door and raced down the stairs.

Brogan fumbled with his clothes, alternately shocked and deliriously happy. By the time he was able to lace his breeches, Matalia had disappeared. Brogan stood silently a moment, staring at the bed. Ribbons quivered as his heart fluttered. She was going to have his baby! As his blood raced, he forgot what a child meant to his petition for Kirkcaldy. He forgot that he needed her to deliver a child in order to gain his inheritance. For a moment, his only thought was for Matalia and the beautiful spirit she would bequeath to their baby.

While Brogan recovered from the shock of her announcement, Matalia fled down the stairway, brushing past Jaimie with a threatening lunge of her sword. Her legs flashed as she wound down the steps, then raced through the great hall to stand, panting, in front of the breakfasting Earl. He looked up, his brows drawing together at her armed and disheveled appearance.

"Are you here to run me through?" he asked sarcastically, rising with both palms spread upon the table. "Do you still hold my chess moves against me?"

"You deserve to be murdered! How could you!" Matalia screamed at him, her cheeks flushed with anger.

Both Matalia and the Earl turned as Brogan leaped down the stairs and stalked swiftly toward the pair. Matalia shrank back, her eyes roving over his bare chest, touching briefly and furiously upon his bruised and abraded body.

"Look," she continued, her voice still shrill. "Look at what you have done to your son! How can you bear to see his flesh torn and broken by the hands of his own twin?"

"You are hysterical, Lady Matalia," the Earl began, but she lifted her sword to silence him.

"Do not be condescending to me, m'lord," she said, her voice dropping dangerously. "I have no tolerance for you."

The hall was suddenly, utterly, echoingly silent. The Earl's gray eyes stared into her sparkling turquoise depths, and a ray of sunlight snaked through the hall to slide lovingly upon the steel blade. A tremor floated through her arm and spread to her fingertips, making the sword tip quiver.

Quietly, without inflection, Brogan held out his hand and placed it upon the fur-clad shoulders of his distraught wife. "Lower the sword, Matalia," he commanded. "You have no wish to do the very thing you are speaking against. If you raise arms against the Earl, you are holding a weapon to your own father-in-law."

Matalia's lower lip trembled and tears filled her eyes. "But look at you . . ." she whispered. "I saw you this morning in the light . . . your bruises . . ."

Brogan smiled wryly, closing his eyes in a brief show of disbelief. Then, his glance hardening, he closed his hand over hers. "Relinquish the sword, m'lady, before the Earl decides to tie you to a stake outside for the bears."

Matalia gasped and pulled her hand out from under his, granting him the blade while turning accusing eyes upon the Earl once again. But before she could say anything, Brogan tossed the sword upon the table and swooped Matalia up into his arms, staring into her eyes with an unreadable expression.

"I'm sorry . . . I shouldn't have done that. . . ." she whispered.

"Indeed. But we have other matters to discuss," Brogan replied.

The Earl lifted his chin, disapproval radiating from his frame, but as he saw Matalia's arms creep up and around Brogan's neck, he slowly sat down and stared at them thoughtfully. When Brogan lifted his head, Matalia dropped hers into his neck and closed her eyes in submission. Son and father stared at each other over her unruly locks, gray eyes to gray.

"I would not have handled this matter as you are doing," the Earl stated.

"No," Brogan answered, "I am certain you would not have. But she is my wife, and I will see to her without your interference."

"This is my home," the Earl replied, his voice hardening.

"*But she is my wife,*" Brogan repeated, unrelenting challenge evident in his inflection and stance, "and as such, she is *my* concern." Matalia's cheek nestled deeper into Brogan's neck, and her lips brushed the hollow where his pulse throbbed.

The Earl made as if to rise again, then sank back and tipped his chair while gripping the table edge. Softly, so only those nearby could hear, the Earl spoke again. "Once Ansleen would have yelled at me if she thought I was in the wrong. I stifled that." He paused, then let the chair legs thump back to the floor. "You have the responsibility of a wife. God willing, you will do better with yours than I did with mine." He grunted at his own comment, then ripped a piece of bread from his trencher and stuffed his mouth, signaling the end of the discussion. Brogan nodded and left the hall, still carrying the docile Matalia in his arms.

Chapter 21

Brogan exited the hall and entered the courtyard. He winced at the sting of pebbles on his bare feet, but when Matalia lifted her head in concern, he shook his head. "If you say even one word," he threatened, "I will shake you. And do not tempt me," he growled as he saw an impish smile creep over her face. "Remember, you are barely clothed, and if I so wish it, I could dump you on your feet and have you face the stableboys' grinning faces."

With a suppressed cry, Matalia curled up tighter in his arms and buried her face once again as he signaled for his horse to be brought out. Within moments, the large stallion was prancing, and Brogan struggled briefly to mount and maintain Matalia's dignity. When at last it was accomplished with only a tiny flash of Matalia's bared calf, Brogan sent the warhorse thundering through the bailey and out over the meadows with Matalia seated securely in front of him.

She relaxed into his frame, letting him control the motion of the horse. Taking deep breaths, she inhaled his scent, finding it intoxicating. She twisted slightly in her sidesaddle position and pressed her lips upon his chest. A shiver traveled over his abdomen at her caress and Matalia smiled in delight at his obvious response. She nuzzled her nose through his chest hair, then rubbed her smooth cheek against his rough one.

A low growl from above her head indicated Brogan's acknowledgment of her ministrations, and she felt him urge his horse faster.

Gasping, she abandoned her playfulness and wrapped her arms around him, holding on as the horse surged up a hill. The muscles in her buttocks tightened as she felt the long, hard length of him press into her thigh and she felt her pulse quicken. Brogan transferred the reins to one hand and slid the other around her body, sliding his hand within the fox-lined robe and gripping her breast brutally.

Matalia stilled, effectively cautioned, and his hand softened, then rubbed her erotically. Then, with a pinch of her nipple, Brogan halted his horse and released her, lowering her to the ground. Matalia's robe gapped open, barely covering the light pink of her nipples and exposing the creamy swelling of her cleavage with delectable freedom.

He stared down at her, his horse breathing as hard as he, his black hair almost as tousled as the horse's mane.

"You look like a stallion," she murmured seductively, tossing her own mane over her shoulder with a flick of her head.

"And you are a mare in heat," he answered, a smile spreading over his face. His eyes dropped to her legs, which were outlined briefly as a gust of wind pressed her robe against her. "A filly with thoroughbred limbs"—his gaze drifted higher—"and taut, muscled, satin flesh." Looking into her eyes, he whispered, "And you have the heart of a champion."

Matalia's eyes widened like saucers and her mouth opened in stunned amazement. She stepped back, reflexively closing her robe as if she should hide from his stirring words. Brogan narrowed his gaze, the gray changing to glinting silver, and he leaped off his horse and began stalking her. She backed up, her body shivering in response to what he had said as it echoed in her mind.

"You amaze me." He caught her, gripping her upper arm gently but firmly.

Matalia's voice trembled. " 'Tis no need to make fun of me," she murmured.

Brogan's face became very serious, and he pulled her body close to his and leaned down so his face was even with hers. "I speak the truth, little filly. And I speak words in jest only because 'tis hard for me to say them aloud. I find your heart more pure than anyone I have ever encountered, and I wish for you to make a promise to me."

Matalia stared up at him, her heart beating wildly.

"Promise me you will instill your values in our child. Promise me that our child will know the purity of your motivations and not the blemishes of my blighted existence."

Matalia raised her shaking hands to his lips, trying to stop his words of self-hatred. "Speak not of yourself like that," she whispered.

He twisted his head away. "I am not seeking your solace for myself," he answered harshly. "I want only to hear you promise that you will give it to the babe."

Matalia dropped her fingers to his shoulders, searching his face, looking for the soul hidden beneath his hooded eyes. She licked her lips unconsciously, her mouth parted in concentration. Her soft breathing surrounded Brogan, and the gentle wind sweeping over them was like a caress from her spirit as the sky shining upon them was a blessing from her exquisite eyes.

He felt her heart beat. It rang in his ears as clear as a set of drums on the battlefield. The sound welled up and over him, cleansing him, forgiving him, granting atonement for deeds done and undone. His head reeled and flecks of black and white danced through his vision, making him feel faint, light-headed. Distantly he felt her fingers return to his mouth, brushing it, touching it, then sliding around to the back of his neck and pulling him closer to her.

His eyes clouded, turning stormy and turbulent. Flashes of dire warning spread through his body, making him stiff and unyielding, yet her sweet pressure urged him nearer and he came, inch by inch. He smelled her breath, still sweet from crushed mint. He looked at her lips, naturally red, richly curved, moistly inviting. He shuddered, feeling the demons rise around him, trying to drown him, but the beat of her heart kept them at bay. His mouth parted. His eyelids dropped.

They came together in the lightest kiss, their lips barely brushing against each other. Electricity raced through Matalia, making her sag except for the supporting arm that snaked its way around her waist and held her upright. Her eyes flickered closed, and she let the sensation of his lips overwhelm her, enfold her, possess her completely. He pressed harder, his mouth moving on its own, exploring the plump fullness of hers. She shifted, pulling back slightly, and Brogan lifted his free hand to grasp the back of her neck, imprisoning her.

He rubbed his lips over hers, tasting her, drinking her essence, nibbling her lower lip as if he would consume her. Driven by his actions, Matalia's tongue crept out and swept tentatively over his lips, seeking a taste of her own. Brogan froze, his heart stopping for one suspended moment as he processed the unprecedented feeling of her tongue touching his mouth. She licked him again, then, as he pressed his lips passionately over hers, she slipped fractionally inside his mouth before retreating nervously.

Brogan lifted his head, his eyes opening, and stared down at her captured face. With a groan, he bore her down to the grass, falling over her supine form, and threaded his fingers through her hair. He brushed a thumb over her lips and gently inserted it, opening her mouth once again. Then, as her lips swelled in anticipation, he leaned over her and kissed her again, letting his own tongue meet hers, allowing his mouth to explore this uncharted region.

Matalia felt disembodied, all her senses centered upon the possession of his lips and tongue over, within and around her own. She surrendered everything to him. She gave him her heart along with her body. She opened her soul and enfolded him within its warmth and love. She accepted him and everything that made him and enriched it with the innocent and unsullied core of her being. Brogan felt her take him in, felt her give herself to him in a way that no woman had ever done, and he gave himself back in a way he never had.

He pulled her to his side, his lips breaking from hers only to slant in a new direction, to soften and caress, to kiss the corner of her mouth, her nose, her lips once again. He kissed her, she kissed him, their entire focus upon each other's lips and mouth while the sun climbed up the hillside and bathed them in its warm glow, then slowly drifted down the other side and bade them good-bye with tendrils of warm, orange light.

He felt it happen. He felt Brogan's emotional wakening as if he were with him on the hillside with a magical woman in his own arms. Warmth swept over him, touching his cold heart with a new sensation, and he stared at the trees shielding the couple. He could not see them, but he could feel the passion blossoming between them. A tormented expression clouded his gray eyes. He shivered, Brogan's happiness causing him both pain, and strangely, pleasure. But the pleasure was tainted with envy, and he pounded his head

against a tree trunk, welcoming the sting of sap in his
new cuts.

Xanthier looked up, hearing the soft sigh of Matalia's breath against Brogan's cheek. He was jealous
that for this moment in time, Brogan was free of the
fight for Kirkcaldy. For this moment, Brogan was not
thinking about fortune and power. He, Xanthier, had
never been free of the torturous compulsion to capture the earldom. Not for one moment had he ever
found an escape from this destructive contest.

Xanthier strode away, searching for the entrance to
the cave that hid his secret belongings. Once he found
it, he pulled the brush aside and ducked into the dark.
He kneeled down and opened an old trunk. From inside he retrieved a packet of letters, all of them un-
opened. Some were addressed from Ansleen to the
Earl, and some from the Earl to Ansleen.

They had started when he was ten years old, and he
had been frightened at the possibility of his parent's
reconciliation, fearing the loss of his father's attention.
He had intercepted the letters and placed them in the
trunk. At one time there had been many letters passing back and forth, and he had been hard-pressed to
catch them all. Then, as neither Ansleen nor the Earl
received an answer to their letters, they had slowly
stopped writing to each other.

Deeper in the trunk were more letters, creased and
torn from multiple readings. These were the letters he
and Brogan had written each other. They ranged from
a tenuous, irregular childlike script to one that was
bold and powerful. Selecting an early one, he sat down
and opened it.

Dear X,
    In ten days' time Mother will be starting the gar-
den and will not notice if I am gone all day. Let's
meet at the cave entrance and hunt squirrels.

It was signed "B."

Xanthier slowly folded the letter and retrieved other, similar missives. As the writing improved, the letters changed. They spoke of happiness and freedom and then of confusion and finally of anger and resentment. It was a one-sided conversation, for Xanthier did not have the notes he had written in reply. The last letter was dated fifteen years ago. It read:

> *X, I don't know what to do. Mother insists that I must go away and learn the skills of a man. I do not want this fight between us. I do not want to lose our camaraderie. What is Kirkcaldy compared to our friendship?*

Xanthier sat back and stared at the cavern walls, remembering the interlocking caves where they had played. He also remembered his response that day. He had told Brogan that Kirkcaldy meant more to him then anything, even their brotherhood.

He dropped his head in his hands and wept.

That evening, the family sat quietly at dinner, Brogan and Matalia side by side with their legs pressed against each other. As they ate, their fingers brushed frequently and their happiness was obvious. Halfway through the meal, Matalia addressed the family.

"It is our pleasure to announce that we are expecting a child."

The Earl grinned and leaned over to congratulate Brogan. He patted him on the back in an uncharacteristic show of affection. "Well done. Then you should be having the babe near the same time Isadora is due."

"Aye, 'twoud seem so," Matalia replied.

Lady Isadora sat stiffly across from them, her lips pursed in disapproval. Her nose twitched distastefully.

"Do be careful, Matalia. You look so unsuited to childbearing. I hope you do not miscarry."

"Indeed," Matalia replied dryly. "I appreciate your concern."

"I see that your husband has finally gifted you with a new dress. Too bad he did not see fit to have it adorned with a ribbon or bow."

Brogan choked, barely restraining his own comments as he shared a look with Matalia.

Xanthier said little, his angry eyes flashing with suppressed emotion. He knew that the baby was not all that had changed today. Something else had happened on the hillside; something had been born between Brogan and Matalia. Watching the pair, Xanthier debated, wondering first what it must feel like to care for someone else, then how he could use the nascent feelings between his twin and sister-in-law to his advantage.

The Earl watched the foursome from his elevated seat at the head of the table. He needed to choose one to rule Kirkcaldy. Both had equal riches, both had large armies. Both were powerful fighters and strong leaders. Now they each had a child due within the same month. His gaze moved back and forth from son to son. Their uncanny resemblance still unnerved him. They each had the gray eyes of the O'Bannons and the dark hair of their forefathers. The angry cast to their features was similar. Lines of frowning strength echoed from visage to visage. Yet Brogan's face held something different. It was composed of the power of self-confidence and self-acceptance, while Xanthier's features were traced with bitterness. Raising a hand to his own face, the Earl wondered silently which one of his sons most resembled him.

An uneasy peace settled over the castle during the following months. Matalia acceded to the Earl's nightly request to play chess in front of the great fire, for he indicated that it gave him great pleasure to pit his mind against Matalia's. Lady Isadora spent the evenings sewing baby clothes in an obvious display of maternal regard designed to impress the men. Brogan and Xanthier avoided each other, their tension mounting as the days passed and the Earl said nothing about the inheritance.

The closeness Brogan and Matalia shared nightly was kept contained within the tower room. Matalia longed to express her feelings and tell Brogan how much he meant to her, but the Earl's warning echoed in her mind and kept her tongue silent. He had clearly informed her that he would not tolerate an excess of emotion, and she remembered his words well. She was determined not to ruin Brogan's chances because she had come to love her husband.

Matalia continued her quiet campaign to help Brogan behind the scenes. She began taking on tasks, slowly gaining the people's trust and assuming the role of lady of the house. Bit by bit, the servants relented and opened their hearts, until they welcomed her insights and came to her for suggestions.

For his part, since the moment in the woods, Brogan longed to deepen their intimacy, but Matalia appeared to hold him at a distance. He accepted her reticence, reasoning that as long as he had her passion at night, he could learn to live without it during the day, but part of him simmered with frustration. He desired her body, but even more he wanted her heart. Watching her daily as her pregnancy advanced, he sought her spontaneous smiles, wishing that she would act freely around him. Instead, he saw a veil of reserve cloak her eyes whenever they stepped out in public, and he could not determine the cause. Seeds of doubt entered his mind, and he followed her closely, making sure that no other had stolen her affections.

In time, Brogan began to be aware of a hum of excitement permeating the castle folk. He watched Matalia with wary eyes, noting that the servants now gravitated to her, seeking her advice on many matters and frequently soliciting her approval on duties they had completed. As the days progressed, more village people found their way to the great hall, and spoke quietly to Lady Matalia. When a particularly handsome mason approached her, Brogan finally left his work and strode over to see what the man needed with his wife.

"Conrad," Brogan stated, surprising the man.

Abruptly deferring to the son of the Earl, Conrad nodded and dropped his eyes to the floor. Matalia looked at her husband with exasperation.

"Do you need something, Brogan?" she queried.

He towered to his full height and a mantle of suppressed power suddenly draped over his frame, causing the mason to step back nervously.

"I am curious what the mason, the blacksmith, and the baker have to speak with you about. It seems that these last several days you are more than popular with the village."

"I was not aware of anything out of the ordinary," she said, hesitant and nervous.

Brogan looked down at her, his outward calm belied by the twitching of his cheek. "You would not be planning on deserting me again, would you?"

"Brogan!" Matalia exclaimed. "Your accusation is unfounded! Why would you think such a thing?"

"Isadora mentioned your frequent conversations with other men."

"No, Brogan! Isadora spoke out of context."

Brogan's nostrils flared and he lifted his head arrogantly. She stepped up to him, laying her hands upon his chest, but he gripped them immediately and pushed her away. Glaring at the mason, he spoke with an edge to his voice. "Be done with your business and go on your way."

"Aye, m'lord." Conrad nodded, backed away, then ducked out the door. Matalia pulled her wrists from Brogan's grasp and returned his glare with a searching look. When he did not relent, she huffed and walked away, hurt by his distrust. Brogan watched her, seeing the gentle sway of her hips and the smooth roundness of her abdomen where the baby was beginning to show. He took a step after her, aching to smooth the frown from her brow, but another servant approached her with easy familiarity, asking a multitude of questions regarding the distribution of foodstuffs to the village families, and he paused.

She easily answered the questions, radiating authority, and then moved on to some women replacing the rushes. The women stopped at her approach, smiling and nodding. Matalia spoke with them for a few moments, redirecting their efforts, then gracefully exited the hall.

Before Brogan could follow her, the Earl entered from the other direction, and strode over toward Brogan, walking with careless disregard over the clean rushes. The difference in how the Earl and Matalia treated the staff was clear. Matalia earned their complete attention by showing kindness and consideration, whereas the Earl believed a man should rule by showing strength and dispassion. The servants pressed their lips together as the Earl passed, their clear dislike of him suffusing their faces.

The Earl spoke to Brogan, who answered absently, still watching the servants. Matalia reappeared, this time carrying a pile of linens. Like magic, the dour expressions cleared and the servants rushed to gather the cloth from her arms, nodding at the list of chores she rattled at them before disappearing out the side door.

With a short nod to his father, Brogan followed the swish of Matalia's hips and ducked through the doorway of the kitchens. His gaze swept the unfamiliar environs, settling upon his surprised wife holding a spoon to her mouth while the rotund cook stood next to her, her face tense in expectation.

As the staff became aware of Brogan's presence, they all looked around at each other uncomfortably, not sure how to react to a male O'Bannon entering their domain. Matalia lowered the spoon.

"It must be important for you to follow me into the bowels of the castle. I was feared that you had not been here before and did not know the way."

Brogan blinked, then swept his gaze around the room again. "I have not been here before."

It was Matalia's turn to blink. "I was just jesting. Of course you have been in every room of the castle," she stated with a thread of uncertainty.

"No," Brogan answered while coming fully into the kitchen. "I had no reason to come here."

"Well!" exclaimed his wife. "Then 'tis time you met the people who serve you so faithfully." She introduced the kitchen staff, starting with the cook and ending with the three young girls who sat at the washbasin, cleaning utensils.

Brogan ignored the introductions, focusing instead on the nervousness he noted in Matalia's face. "You know the name of every person here?" he asked.

Matalia frowned, uncertain how to respond. Brogan took another step forward and looked down at the three girls. They pressed back against a wall, the oldest gripping the hands of the younger two. One girl burst into tears until the older girl whispered something fiercely into her ear. The sobbing instantly ceased, replaced by muffled whimpers.

"Why?" he questioned, turning back to Matalia. "Why would you bother to learn their names?"

Matalia's mouth dropped open, and she flushed with embarrassment. "They will be your people, Brogan O'Bannon. You will be responsible for their welfare. I was only trying to assist you by getting to know them."

"We can care for them without knowing their names," he responded, watching her carefully.

Placing her hands on her hips, Matalia glowered at her dunce of a husband. "Your family provides for their physical needs. Do you not think that supporting their intangible needs is also necessary?"

"What other needs?" he asked, honestly confused but curious.

"Their need for friendship, happiness, frivolity, excitement!"

"How does knowing their names help with any of that?"

Matalia hefted the spoon in her hand, disregarding the spill of soup onto her gown. She opened her mouth, then closed it again, and shook the spoon at him in mute incomprehension. Finally she flung the spoon on the table and stalked past Brogan. "I give up!" she flung over her shoulder as she marched out the doorway. Her black curls bounced angrily up and down her back, like hundreds of tiny springs.

As soon as she left, the servants swung nervously back to Brogan. He returned their gazes just as nervously, searching for the names she had rattled off so quickly. Defeated, he sank down on his haunches before the whimpering girl and gently took her free hand.

"Little miss," he said softly, "why are you frightened of me?"

"I'm sorry, sir," she whispered, ducking her head.

"For what?" he inquired.

"I am, sir! I truly am!" she gasped, then yanked her hand from the older girl's and dashed from the room.

The remaining girls looked at him with wide, terrified eyes. Brogan rose and looked about him, seeing the fear mirrored on everyone's faces.

"Are you all frightened of me?" he asked, expecting and receiving no answer. His gaze then fell back to the girls, and he smoothed the lines on his brow to smile at them pleasantly. "Do you like Lady Matalia?" he asked.

"Oh yes, m'lord," cried the oldest. "She is kind and ever so clever."

"Do you know that she is my wife?" he asked.

"Yes, m'lord."

"But you still distrust me?"

"You are one of the O'Bannons," she answered by way of explanation. Brogan stared at her, stunned by the wealth of information the simple sentence granted. He nodded slowly while reaching a hand out to pat her head. The girl bent her head forward, subtly avoiding his touch. He straightened his shoulders and turned toward the door. Just as he exited, he glanced over his shoulder. The people stared at him, tension clearly lining their faces. With a quiet oath, he left.

That evening, the dream came to him again. He was surprised, for it had slipped away in recent months, and he had come to believe that it had finally left him. But as he drifted to sleep, he felt the fog swirl around him, enfold him in its clinging arms, and beckon him back into its familiar cadence. Mist swirled and shifted, blinding him like a ship lost at sea. He reached out, trying to find something of substance to hold, but the low clouds parted around his arm, then rippled back in place as if he were dragging his limbs through water. He stumbled forward, grasping, reaching, knowing that something waited for him but unable to find it. His body tightened, ready to fight the unknown mists, and he peered into the dense fog, daring the enemy to come forward.

Then the song came to him. *Her song,* the woman of his dreams. It floated upon the mists like a friend. It dipped and swirled, achingly familiar. The soft melody penetrated his fear, his anger, his tension. It soothed his muscles and stroked his soul until he relaxed within the fog and let it embrace him.

A cool breeze whispered against his flesh, and he opened his eyes, immediately noticing the thinning of the mist. He could see his knees, then ankles, then several feet ahead of him as the mists loosened their cloying attack and drifted in thin streaks low to the ground. The song deepened, enriched, became more than a melody. He lifted his heavy lids and saw her, her silk-draped body standing at the entrance to a cave. Only the contours of her figure were visible, for the mists and shadows disguised her face, yet still he knew her. He tried to take a step forward, but as he moved, she shrank back, deeper into the cave. He stopped, truly frightened, but frightened for her. He beckoned to her, pleaded with her to come toward him. Then she was next to him, stroking him, touching his face in the timeless comfort only she knew how to give.

He let her touch him, leaned into her satiny hands, let her song wrap around him. She had always been there for him in this netherworld of mists and dreams. But this time he felt a niggling discomfort. He felt a tingling nervousness. Opening his eyes, he saw the cavern mouth gaping behind them and a shadow of a beast lumbering out.

With a jerk, Brogan awoke. His rapid breathing mirrored the frantic pace of his heart. He blinked several times, seeking truth in the darkened room. He saw the wolfhound sitting at the foot of the bed, gazing toward the window. A faint song reached his ears and he turned over, looking for Matalia, already knowing that her side of the mattress would be cold. With the tendrils of his dream still lingering, he left the bed and strode over to the window, looking out at the moon-drenched meadowlands that rose into the rocky prominences of the mountain caves. Down below he located Matalia and her wolves frolicking with innocent abandon. Her voice rose and the wolfhound joined Brogan at the window.

Matalia lifted her arms underneath her hair and held the heavy masses off her neck for a moment before letting them drop again. The black wolf leaped up, snapping his jaws near her face, snarling in playful fun. Matalia broke her song briefly, giggling, then picked up the hem of her nightgown and raced through the grass. The three canines instantly gave chase, their sleek bodies rippling with strength and health. The gray dashed in front of her, forcing her to leap over him. She successfully managed the feat, then spun around and jumped upon him, tumbling him over onto his back. The red pounced upon the gray as well, and the pair tickled him until he was squirming and yelping with delight.

Brogan breathed deeply, trying to calm himself. He cast his eyes around the meadow, convincing himself that she was safe. Almost every night now, she left his side and played with her wolves, and Brogan watched her moodily from the window. She said nothing to him of her nightly forays, and he said nothing to her, knowing that to speak of them would be to incite argument. He was uncomfortable with her out of his reach, yet understood she needed this time to connect with her animals, to escape the constant intrigue of the castle. Most strange of all, part of him yearned to join her.

Chapter 22

As breakfast finished, Brogan was astounded to see Matalia yawning. He looked at her with concern.

"Tired, m'lady?" he questioned.

"Oh," she yawned again. "I suppose a bit. Perhaps I should go lie down for the morning," she murmured, dropping her gaze guiltily.

Brogan watched her, unconvinced. He noticed that the staff was quite light this morn, for most of the servants Matalia routinely spoke with appeared to be missing. He nodded, acting nonchalant.

"Perhaps," he finally remarked. "Would you like me to attend you?"

"No! I mean, no. That will not be necessary. In fact, I would prefer to be left alone for the entire morn so I may rest peacefully. In fact, I would be pleased if you put the wolfhound in the kennels for the day." She flushed.

Brogan frowned, unconvinced. "As you wish," he murmured. "Jaimie has asked to take the men hunting today. They grow restless with inactivity. I will not return until the eve, as long as you feel no need for my presence."

"That would be perfect, ah, I mean, acceptable," Matalia stammered, then rose and fled the table. Brogan watched her go. The Earl shrugged.

"Pregnancy," he answered Brogan's unspoken question. "It makes them say and do the most unusual things."

Brogan looked at his father and grinned as a flicker of good feeling arced between them.

As soon as Matalia reached the upper tower, she dashed into the preparation room and reached an excited hand out to Peigi. "All is set," she whispered. "He thinks I am to sleep the morning away, and Jaimie has recommended a hunting expedition. They are to be gone all day."

Peigi frowned. "He questioned you not at all?" she asked, wary.

"No, why should he?"

"Because you never take to your bed. I did not think he would accept such an excuse."

"Well, then, you do not know him as I do," Matalia replied triumphantly. "Come, let us not waste any more time. I must change." Peigi shrugged, acceding to her lady's urgency, and swiftly assisted her change into sturdier garb. As soon as her dark green velvet dress was belted, Matalia placed a sheer veil over her hair and secured it with a circlet. Her turquoise eyes danced with merriment, and she spun around in golden sandals. Peigi smiled, unable to remain dour, and pronounced her beautiful. A knock on the door startled them both until Evie's face peeked around the frame. She beckoned them while placing a finger to her lips.

As they tiptoed out, Matalia flashed on another time when she and Colleen had snuck out of the castle Roseneath seeking excitement, and she shuddered as she remembered the consequences. She hung back, abruptly concerned, but Evie grabbed her hand and yanked her down the stairs before she could formally protest. A bump against her legs made her look down, and she saw the grisly head of the wolfhound staring up at her.

"Stay," she commanded in a low whisper. "Go to Brogan. You have to stay in the kennels today." The dog whined, nudging her again. "Go to Brogan," she commanded again, this time with a touch of irritation. The dog stared up at her with reproachful eyes, but he settled down and thumped his tail once to indicate he understood. She leaned over and gave him a quick kiss on the muzzle. Then the three women dashed down the stairs, along the shadows to the kitchen and out the side door into a wagon strategically placed outside. Muffling their laughter, they shoved Matalia under the straw, burying her and her fine clothes. Then they leaped onto the seat, and Evie took the reins. With a snap, they encouraged the old mare to amble out of the courtyard and down the road to the village.

Brogan stood from his bent position in the courtyard where he had been examining the foot of a horse. He brushed his hair back from his forehead and wiped away the sweat. The sun was already high and glorious, and despite the autumn breeze, it promised to be a warm day. Jaimie's horse, already saddled and mounted, stamped in anticipation, and Jaimie grinned.

A beam of sunlight fell upon the yellow straw in the back of a hay wagon and Brogan looked at it curiously. The load looked irregular. He took a step forward to warn the farmer to better balance his load when he saw Evie in the driver's seat with Peigi beside her. Brogan turned his back, and continued his examination of the horse, his brows drawn. From the corner of his eye, he watched the wagon move out of the courtyard and through the bailey. Then, as soon as it cleared the gates, he turned to the stable hand, who studiously avoided his gaze. Brogan's jaw set, and he wiped his forehead again. He stalked into the stable itself and saddled his stallion, his thoughts turning furiously.

Leading the stallion out, he motioned to Jaimie.

"Take the men without me. There is something I must check."

As they approached the village, Evie and Peigi pulled the cart to a stop and helped Matalia free herself from the clinging straw.

"Och! 'Tis extremely itchy!" she complained with good humor. She looked back up the road toward the castle. "No one noticed?" she questioned.

"Not a soul," Peigi reassured her.

"Brogan?" Matalia asked again.

"Was in the courtyard tending an injured horse and did not even notice our passing," Evie finished. "Now hurry. Let us clean you up or you'll be late for the festival."

"Come now. Forget your worries and have a bit o'fun," agreed Peigi. "Just like you said the villagers deserve."

"Very well," Matalia relented with a genuine smile. "But help get the straw out from my bodice before everyone will be believing I have lice!"

The three women laughed together as they picked loose pieces off. Then they assisted her onto the wagon seat and set off. As they traveled through the village, they joined a steady stream of people heading to the eastern glade, a meadow located a short distance from the village and surrounded by autumn-colored trees. Already a holiday atmosphere infused the crowd of people, and they grinned shyly at Lady Matalia as she jumped down from her perch.

A small platform had been raised at the edge of the glade, and Matalia ascended it while Evie and Peigi directed the distribution of logs, stones, ropes and ale casks. As everyone turned to Matalia, she flourished a bag.

"Today I have decreed a day of Scottish festival!" A wave of appreciative nods and scattered hurrahs came from the assemblage. "Winter will soon be upon us, and gatherings will be cold and dark, so today we celebrate with our neighbors, our friends and our families."

"And sweethearts!" someone shouted at the back, and many of the girls blushed and giggled while casting their gazes over the young men that strutted and primped.

Matalia smiled. "However," she said, shaking the bag, "since most festivals are between clans and we are only one, we will draw colors to choose teams. Let each man and woman come forward and pick their 'clan' for the duration of the festival!"

The people swiftly converged upon her, sticking their hands into the bag and pulling out swatches. A few groans and many cheers rose as the people sorted themselves out, locating tents that matched their selected colors. As each reached their tent, they were presented with a cup of ale or flavored cider. Men, women and children imbibed freely and jovial camaraderie abounded.

A sheep was tied to the front of the "O'Bannon" tent, but a young lad from the "Campbell" clan swiftly snuck over and untied it, then raced with it back to his own tent amid the cheers from his fellow "clan" members. As the "O'Bannon" group was still helping Matalia distribute the colors, they did not notice the sheep stealing until the feat was already accomplished, which amused several other groups. Good-natured taunts were cast, and friendly rivalries sprang up. The "McDougal" clan took advantage of the "Campbells'" preoccupation with their victory to nab one of their casks of ale, and they roared with laughter when a "Campbell" scratched his head, trying to locate the missing cask.

The contests began immediately, with tossing of the caber the first competition. A set of 120-pound logs, twenty feet in length, were placed at one end of the field. One burly member of each "clan" swaggered over to the site, each boasting that he could toss a perfect caber. As the men hefted the log onto their shoulders, then vertically balanced it, a judge raced to the front so he could mark where the caber landed. The first man, the butcher, ran forward, then heaved the caber upward, spinning it so the other, heavier end, fell over near his feet and the lighter end pointed away from him. Laughter followed the first throw, for instead of landing perfectly opposite the thrower, the caber lay twisted to the right. The butcher grumbled, insisting that the log was at fault, but relinquishing the caber to the next athlete.

Nearby, a sheaf toss was commencing. The competitors hurled a bag of hay over a crossbar while the judge determined who threw the highest. One of the "MacLachlans" grabbed Lady Matalia, pretending to mistake her for a bag of hay since several strands still clung to her hair and dress. Matalia playfully swatted the man, then bade him to toss high so her "clan" would have some challenge.

Evie gathered the children, including her usually solemn son, and organized some children's events. Sack races, tug-of-war, egg and spoon races and leaf fights abounded. Several of the older men set up their instruments on the platform, and the pipe, wail and twang of several musical renditions filled the meadow. A Celtic harp, or clarsach, was set up, and Matalia gasped with delight as the clan harper played some of the accompaniments of battle, along with a medley of festival joy.

As several women gathered to dance the *hullachan,* Matalia stepped back and smiled. Her eyes sparkled and a slight flush filled her cheeks with bright color. She placed a hand unconsciously on her abdomen, feeling the swelling that was barely noticeable to others. She rubbed it, and took a deep, soothing breath as she meandered over to her tent to procure another cup of flavored cider.

Brogan rode his mount slowly through the empty village, his wolfhound trotting alongside. He noticed the empty cottages, the lack of children, the abondoned fields. The faint wail of a Scottish reel filtered up to him from the east, and he directed his steed to follow the sounds. As he left the village proper and rode toward the eastern glade, the music became louder and the gaiety of many people joined the sound with unique harmony. He pulled his horse to a halt, then carefully dismounted and tied the animal to a tree. Bidding the horse to stay, he and the wolfhound continued onward until they could see the glade through the scattered yellow, gold, red and orange leaves.

Jealousy threatened to overtake him. Where was she and what was she doing out here? Is this how Ansleen had been? Is this how a wife strayed? He clenched his jaw, furious that his thoughts caused him such pain. He was not ready to release her. She was his wife, and he would allow no one to take her from him!

A cry claimed his attention, and he dropped to a fighting stance, gripping his sword hilt, only to see two children hitting each other playfully with bags filled with fallen leaves. One child hit the other across the chest, then followed it with another blow over his head, which caused the bag to burst open, covering the pair in crackling debris. They screamed in unison, gleefully attacking each other until they both fell into the pile of leaves, rolling over each other.

Brogan twitched, his eyes narrowing in anger as he straightened his stance. He swung his gaze away from the boys and surveyed the meadow. Many tents were strung haphazardly, and bits of colored cloth swung from their awnings, announcing the presence of other clans. When he saw the villagers of Kirkcaldy wearing scraps of cloth, pledging allegiance to other clans, a wave of fury surged through him, and he pulled his sword free. The dog beside him whined and ducked his head.

Brogan stepped forward just as a flash of green velvet caught his eye. He turned and froze at the sight of his wife standing slightly apart, absently stroking her rounded abdomen. Her black curls were demurely hidden beneath a sheer veil, but maidenly modesty could not hide her vibrant beauty. Brogan felt his heart stop as he saw the glow of happiness that filled her face. She walked to a tent marked by the O'Bannon colors and lifted a cup to her sweetly curving lips. The fury inside his soul shifted to immense pride as he watched her pick up a full O'Bannon kilt and drape it over her shoulders. Without realizing it, he walked forward, his eyes trained upon her. He stepped out into the meadow, the sword in his hand still lifted, his steely gaze piercing.

Matalia noticed a sudden cessation in the music, and an uncomfortable silence descended over the people. She looked up, confused. Then she saw him. He strode toward her, his strength and manly power spreading fear into all he passed. His gaze was pinned on her, and she was held still from its intensity. She trembled, the flush draining from her cheeks. She put a hand out to the table behind her, gripping it to keep from collapsing.

He stopped several feet from her, finally breaking eye contact and swinging his gaze around the entire meadow. He saw the games, the caber toss, the battle-ax throw, the *braemar* stone throw, the sheaf toss, the pylons for the farmers' walk. He located the clarsach, the pipes, the fiddles and the drums. He saw the children with muddied faces from losing a game of tug-of-war. His gaze drifted over the women holding haggis for the haggis hurl and standing nervously where they had been dancing moments before.

"What goes on here?" he asked quietly.

"A festival," Matalia answered after a long pause. She bit her lip, unsure of what else to say.

"Ahhh," he replied thoughtfully. He sheathed his sword. "And the various colors?"

"Teams," Matalia answered, her eyes wide.

"Which team is winning?" he asked, flicking a glance at the flags displayed on a rope above the platform. Matalia glanced at a tent across the way and gulped. Several villagers started to melt away, trying unsuccessfully to escape Brogan's sharp eyes. "Matalia," he asked again, softly, "which 'clan' is ahead?"

"The ''Campbells,' " she answered, her trembles escalating into outright shivers. Brogan walked forward and pulled her tartan closer around her shoulders, his massive form dwarfing her petite frame.

"Then I had best help out the O'Bannons," he replied evenly. " 'Twould be unseemly for my own clan to lose without a fair fight."

Matalia looked up at him, blinking frantically. When she said nothing, Brogan kissed her nose, then sauntered over to the battle-ax throw. He nodded to the other men, then gestured to the man whose turn was next. Uncertainly, the man looked at Lady Matalia. She lifted her hands in confusion, but motioned for him to continue. After the silence in the glade finally penetrated her fog, Matalia turned to the musicians, asking them to resume as well. In moments, the villagers relaxed and Matalia was stunned to see them cheering Brogan's fine throws, which far exceeded the other men's in distance and accuracy.

He looked over at her as he won the contest, lifting a brow at her shocked expression. "You seem surprised, my fine lady."

"I am indeed," she murmured as he approached her in the relative seclusion of the tent.

"You did not think I could throw a battle-ax?" he asked teasingly.

"Of course I knew you could throw the ax," she retorted. "I simply thought you would be angry with me."

He leaned down and whispered dangerously soft into her ear, "I *am* angry with you. I am displeased that you thought to mislead me. You have no idea what I thought was happening."

"I did not think you would approve of this!" she cried, twisting away and flinging her arms out, indicating the festival.

"Perhaps perhaps not. To be truthful, you are correct. I would not have encouraged it."

"Then you understand why I did not tell you!"

"No," he replied, shaking his head. "Lying because you know the answer will not be to your liking is not acceptable." His voice was gentle, reproving though not harsh, and Matalia hung her head in shame.

"Indeed, m'lord," she mumbled, a tear filling her eye.

"But," he said briskly, seeking to dispel her sadness, "since the festival is underway, I intend to enjoy it." He smiled at her sudden brightening. "And I expect to see you tossing the wellie with the other lasses."

Matalia blossomed, her face breathtakingly glorious as she smiled at him. "Then I expect to see you enter the bonnie knees contest!"

Brogan shook his head, laughing. "Come, sweetheart, let us have some fun together."

As the day wore on, the "MacLachlans," "Campbells" and "O'Bannons" fought for first position. The ale petered out, and whiskey barrels were opened instead. Young children were hustled off to bed, and exhausted grandparents sat with them so the parents could rejoin the revelry. Fierce disputes between fathers and their older daughters raged as the girls begged to be allowed to stay, and mothers admonished their older sons to be respectful of their sweethearts.

Lanterns were strung as dusk faded to dark. A storyteller sat underneath the "McDougal" tent, telling of the O'Bannons' history and heritage. Matalia cuddled against Brogan, fascinated by the rich chronicle. She was amazed at the pride mirrored in the people's faces as they heard the tales of Kirkcaldy, its founding and its strength. The first gray-eyed O'Bannon had come down from the mountains with his brave lassie and their three children and founded a family that was powerful and respected. Through wars and famine, the O'Bannons had thrived, for the valley was rich in soil and the men who tilled it were strong of heart. The caves figured in many of the stories, for they were the mysterious passages known only to the immediate O'Bannon family members. Time and again, the stories told of how the O'Bannons had used the immense caverns as a means to win a fight, hoard riches or capture a fugitive. Leading from the castle dungeons themselves, the caves stretched for miles, trapping the unwary and rescuing the talented. Matalia placed her hand within Brogan's and squeezed.

Though Brogan had heard the tales before as lessons to be memorized, never had he heard them told so colorfully. As the storyteller stood up and mimicked battles and beasts, he felt pride stir in his gut. This part of Kirkcaldy had never figured into his constant pursuit of his inheritance. He had fought to gain Kirkcaldy for its glory alone. He had wanted to win her so that Xanthier could not.

Now, looking around at the people who made up the heart of her land, he understood the true meaning of becoming the Earl of Kirkcaldy. Matalia had understood this from the start; in fact, she had tried to tell him. Now he saw the truth. These people, this heritage, this woman . . . the child. A sheen of sweat moistened his palms and forehead as he realized the depth of responsibility they all entailed.

Matalia looked up at him, noting the new cloak of leadership on his shoulders, bringing with it humility. She cradled his large hand, leaning against his side, and rubbed her cheek against his powerful arm. He glanced down at her, and she smiled at him reassuringly, without words, giving him the gift of her confidence. He looked up, seeing the people who now accepted him so trustingly. Today he had become one of them.

A drummer set a roll that expanded into a flourishing pattern of tempo and tone. A second drummer joined him, taking his drum pattern and embellishing it. The first took the drums back, making the drum sing with the speed of power in his answering rhythm. A third joined them, making the drumming into yet another competition, and the threesome traded back and forth as the villagers hopped and hollered into the night. When one man emerged victorious, he set a slow, even beat that called forth the Highland dancers.

Four men, strong warriors from the castle, came forward and flung their targes upon the ground. Brogan grinned, recognizing the emblems on the shields as his own, and nodded to the men. After solemnly returning his nod, they started the excruciatingly precise steps. Never traveling forward or back, they remained upon the small shields, their simple steps striking awe in the men and passion in the women. They held their positions perfectly, their steps in unison until they ended with a flourish and sank to one knee in front of Brogan O'Bannon.

The people clapped frantically, then shrank back as Brogan stepped forward. He pulled his sword out once again, then tipped it to the ground in front of Matalia.

Gaining her undivided attention, he placed the sword and its scabbard on the ground in an "X." Then, beginning slowly, he stepped around the sword and scabbard, taking infinite care not to brush against the weapon's razor-sharp edge. As the audience grew, the drums increased in tempo and his steps quickened. He kept his eyes lifted, the steel-gray color glinting in the lantern light, framed by the blackness of his midnight hair. His white shirt swiftly dampened and clung to his chest, highlighting his rippling musculature.

Matalia's perception narrowed to him and him alone. The sword dance was a battle dance, for 'twas said that the warrior who could dance the sword dance without touching the sword with his feet would be successful in the morrow's battle. Her heart sped as she watched his feet, then leaped as she saw one of the other warriors toss him a sword to hold in hand. Brogan slowed his steps, gripping the new sword in his right hand, waving it in the air almost leisurely. The four warriors approached him, each from a different angle, each bearing a sword of his own. Brogan eyed them warily, his feet still moving, still not touching the deadly blade. When one of them lunged, he swiftly parried.

Matalia gasped, her hands flying to cover her mouth. She gasped again as another man attacked, forcing Brogan to twist, speeding his steps. She sprang forward, enraged at the men, but Evie gripped her elbow and pulled her back.

"Do not distract him, m'lady," she admonished, and Matalia shakily nodded acceptance.

The men came at him faster, one, two, then all four, while Brogan ducked and swung, blocked and lunged, all the while keeping his feet moving with careful precision, perfect balance. His gray eyes darkened to charcoal and his hair clung to his forehead. With an abrupt upward swing he dashed the sword from one of the attacker's hands, and the man retired gracefully. Brogan began attacking more ferociously, his feet held within the marked boundaries yet his body moving in a deadly, unrehearsed ballet. He disarmed each of the men in turn, until the final sword swung in an arch to land, quivering, in the fallen leaves.

The drums slowed, then escalated until, with an echoing flourish, Brogan deliberately placed his foot underneath the hilt of his sword and tossed it up, grabbing it in the air with his left hand. The people erupted, screaming wildly at the brilliant display, stamping their feet and clapping their hands against their thighs. Matalia felt her heart start beating again, and a silly smile of adoration spread across her countenance. Brogan located her, his grin matching hers. He picked up his scabbard, sheathed the sword and tossed the extra one back at one of the warriors. The man caught it in one hand while catching a village miss in the other. The girl giggled and pulled his shirt, urging him into the shadowed tree line.

Brogan walked up to Matalia, stroked her cheek, her eyebrows . . . brushed his fingers over her long eyelashes. Without a word, he scooped her up in his arms and carried her deep into the trees.

A soft wind rippled through the branches, making a subtle sound like water tumbling over rocks. A murmur here and there signaled other lovers, but Brogan traveled away from everyone until only the faint strains of a fiddle reached them. Matalia looped her hands around Brogan's neck, staring at his strong jaw. He finally stopped, then shuffled his feet in the fallen leaves for a moment. Matalia tried to look down to see what he was doing, but the darkness disguised his actions. Then, with a suddenness that made her gasp, he dropped her into a huge pile of leaves.

She sputtered and spit, trying to swim through the leaves, but as soon as she reached a sitting position,

Brogan pushed her back again, covering her with the tinkling blanket of autumn. He laughed at her, using her struggles to slide his hand up her dress, pinching her exposed thighs and dodging her fruitless kicks.

"You beast!" she cried, laughing, then grabbed a pile of leaves and flung them at his face. Brogan froze, an affronted look upon his face, and Matalia laughed harder while scooping up more leaves to toss at him. Brogan shook his head, sending leaves scattering, then gripped the trunk of a small tree hanging over them. He shook the tree, sending a blinding torrent of yellow leaves cascading around Matalia. She shrieked, ducking her head, and grabbed his ankle and yanked. Surprised, Brogan released the quivering tree and tumbled into the leaves alongside Matalia, rolling carefully so as not to crush her. He gripped her by the waist and swung her up over him so she sat astraddle his hips, her skirts flared around them.

With deliberate actions, Brogan shifted his clothes, pushing and tugging at hers until they met flesh to flesh. She was ready; he was more so. They joined in mutual surrender, the slide of their bodies natural, familiar, exhilarating. Brogan held her waist, commanding her movements to match his urgency, and she placed delicate hands upon his chest, kneading and squeezing him with each stroke. Her modest veil enticed him, and Brogan reveled in the taking of his wife in a bed of fallen leaves within earshot of the village festival. He watched her face flush, her eyelids flutter closed, then spring open as he drove into her from a new angle. She seemed so innocent, so virginal, yet completely wanton and free. As she climaxed with soft gasps and pants, Brogan surged deep within her, feeling his fluid meld with hers. Complete, emotional satisfaction. He closed his eyes as she sank down upon him, the leaves swirling with a gust of wind to blanket them in a soft press of autumn colors.

PART III

Kirkcaldy

Chapter 23

Winter cloaked the land. The upper ramparts of Kirk-caldy Castle sparkled with crystalline icicles, and the pastures were blanketed with white fleece. Within the cold halls the inhabitants were restless and irritable from their enforced proximity. The Earl continued to withhold his decision as to who would inherit the title, stating that he now waited for the birth of the first child.

Matalia's and Brogan's only relief from the oppression came early in the morning, when sunlight blazed through the windows of the high towers and the rest of the castle slept. It was during these times that Matalia and Brogan snuggled together in the window nook, talking and touching. Brogan spent much of the time marveling at the changes in Matalia, fascinated at how her beauty only increased as her body enlarged.

He cupped her breasts, excited at the new fullness, and he kissed her nipples, now softer and larger and thus utterly captivating. Her stomach rounded day by day, smooth, silken, mysterious. He rubbed creams and oils over her, using more than was necessary because he enjoyed doing it. When the baby rippled under his hand, he paused, enchanted.

In the next tower, however, Lady Isadora ranted over her husband's lack of care. She cried and swore, complaining of back aches, stomach cramps and bloated ankles. Xanthier grew haunted as the days progressed, and he spent many evenings sleeping in a chair in front of the fire of the great hall. In contrast, Lady Isadora acted docile and sweet whenever she descended the stairs, clinging demurely to Xanthier's arm and drawing attention to her delicate condition as frequently as she was able.

Her feigned meekness irritated Matalia, causing her to be more waspish around Isadora than was her wont. The Earl watched their byplay, frowning at Matalia while soothing Lady Isadora's hurt feelings. Anticipation in the hall heightened, and servants took private bets on who would go into childbirth first. Brogan and Xanthier barely spoke, the animosity between them thicker than the snow outside. They glared at each other across the table, their few words always erupting into fierce arguments that more often than not culminated in physical violence.

The Earl tried to keep them separated, his sadness over their mutual hatred clear. He felt helpless to end the bitter feud, knowing that it was his fault, but too enmeshed in the situation to halt it. Matalia understood him, their friendship growing slowly during the evening chess games, but she was disgusted by his failure to remedy the situation.

Every now and then Matalia caught an unguarded look between the twins signifying the existence of a deeper connection. True caring existed between them, and she felt certain that had they not been pitted against each other, they would have remained very close.

One morning Brogan stood silently apart from Matalia while she bathed. Noting his quietness, she looked at him quizzically. He appeared haggard.

"What is vexing you?" she queried.

"This! This waiting! I cannot stand it! I am a man of action, and I do not like standing by helplessly while the Earl vacillates."

"The Earl is not happy either, husband," Matalia interjected.

"He has never been happy," Brogan replied harshly. Matalia dropped her eyes and resumed washing. She shrugged, and Brogan left the room.

Meanwhile, Xanthier paced in his tower, fighting the confusion that filled his soul. He finally admitted to himself that he hated Kirkcaldy. He hated the white walls and fluttering flags. He detested the villagers and the rolling farms and baaing sheep herds. He felt confined and constricted. Gritting his teeth in boiling rage, he kicked the castle wall, pouring his anger into the stones.

"I hate you!" he hissed at the wall. "You have taken over my life! You are a mistress that will not leave, a lodestone that I cannot eliminate." He glared around him, loathing everything that made up his birthplace.

"You promised me," Isadora snarled back. "You said that I would be a countess one day if I gave you my dowry. I will not allow you to give up."

"You don't understand, do you? I was forced to fight for this castle. I wanted to travel, to set sail, to explore the world like Brogan did. I wanted my freedom from the moment I was told that I had to fight my twin and rule Kirkcaldy. Yet I have done my duty. I have fought for these pale walls as if I loved them."

"Stop your sniveling. I don't care what motivates you. You must continue. If you don't win this on your own, I will assist you. I *will* be Countess of Kirkcaldy!"

"Your insinuations repulse me. I will not fail, no matter what I must do. It is my destiny to win. To do less would be to lose my reason for living."

"Nevertheless, Brogan has enemies, and we must use them to our advantage. If you do not take action, I will."

* * *

Matalia declared checkmate just as a horn sounded from the upper ramparts.

"Who comes in such weather?" questioned the Earl fiercely, his hand dropping to his side for a sword he no longer wore. Brogan and Xanthier glanced at each other, both rising. Matalia looked up from the chessboard and watched wariness wash over her husband's face. A tremor of nervousness swept over her, and she felt the babe roll in response.

"Brogan?" she queried.

" 'Tis most likely a lost traveler," he replied, but his casual words were belied by the sound of steel whispering out of its sheath. Matalia bit her lip as Xanthier drew his blade as well. The Earl struggled to his feet, his breath coming in short pants from the effort it cost him. The winter had worn heavily upon his health, and his advancing age had become obvious to all. The horn blew again, this time in a series of short sounds, and Brogan's eyes narrowed further. Brief regret flared in Xanthier's face before he lowered his sword and turned to face the Earl.

"Soothebury has come," he stated, his voice ringing across the great hall. Matalia looked around in confusion, frightened by the sudden ominous tension that filled the chamber.

"You know not why," Brogan answered angrily, but he avoided Matalia's searching gaze. Matalia rose and reached out a hand to him, which he automatically took in his own.

"I am certain I know the reason, as do you. And the Earl knows as well," Isadora sneered.

"You thought with your nether regions and not with your head. You are not fit to become the Earl of such a great land!" Xanthier shouted.

Matalia felt the clench of Brogan's fingers tighten around hers for an infinitesimal moment. Then he coldly released her hand and stepped away from her.

"Emotions do not cloud my judgment," Brogan replied, his voice low and deadly. "I made a strategic decision—"

"A decision that has cost us a war!" Xanthier interrupted, his voice bellowing with rage.

"That has not yet been determined," the Earl interjected. "We must wait to hear the messenger."

Matalia felt cold. She stood, bereft, confused by the incomprehensible words around her that were clearly of great import. She glanced at Isadora, frightened by the smug and triumphant smile on her face.

"What, pray tell, do the horns signal?" Matalia demanded. "Why are you speaking of war when the land is covered in snow and all homes are closed for the season?"

The men all swung their faces toward her, each set of features similarly closed and silent. It was Isadora who finally answered her.

"The horns signal an envoy from Soothebury. This fortnight is the traditional time to declare disputes. The clan that states a disagreement must do so now, while the snows keep armies at bay, so that there is time for an honorable resolution before fighting commences. Surely you understand?"

Matalia shook her head. "I know of no such tradition," she said, her brows drawing together in consternation.

"Perhaps you have not been taught the way of politics, the way of the ancients, because it was known that you would never need to understand complicated negotiating methods. Your family is rarely involved in such important matters." Isadora pursed her lips and stared haughtily down her nose at Matalia.

Matalia opened her mouth to refute Isadora's nasty words, but her reply died as she saw the truth on Brogan's face.

His stony eyes confirmed Lady Isadora's statement.

"Isadora understands as you do not. Soothebury comes to speak against you, to speak against me for wedding you. He comes to declare war against Kirkcaldy for breaking my marriage contract with his daughter Clarise."

"But you sent compensation. . . ."

"Is money worth a daughter's honor?" Xanthier interrupted. "Brogan shamed a woman who was already unfortunate in form, face and mind. Soothebury comes. And you have brought it upon this house. I warned you that this would happen the day you stood on Kirkcaldy's steps for the first time." His blazing eyes matched the fury in Brogan's, and Matalia shrank away from them. Her abdomen tightened, and a sudden attack of hiccups bubbled in her throat.

"We will wait for him before making a decision," stated the Earl, but he motioned to the men inside to assemble their warriors. "Both you and Isadora go to the towers."

"Most certainly not!" snapped Isadora. Matalia agreed with her for once, and she glared at the Earl while trying to stifle her unruly hiccups. The Earl had no time to respond, for the door was suddenly flung open and a burly man covered in frosty fur strode in.

"I am Lord Soothebury, and I come with a declaration for Lord Brogan, prospective heir of the Earl of Kirkcaldy. I come as well to speak against the Lady McTaver and seek to hear her defense before seeking further declaration against the McTaver clan."

Matalia stared up at the gigantic man in stunned amazement, unable to comprehend the threat against her husband's name much less against her own family. Soothebury's bushy beard was covered with sparking icicles that sprayed droplets of water down his coat as he spoke. She gaped in shock until a loud hiccup escaped her mouth and echoed throughout the great hall.

Everyone froze, then looked at Matalia in varying degrees of disbelief and disgust. She lifted her hand to her mouth, trying to stifle the unladylike noises, but the pressure of her unborn babe and her efforts only made the bursts of noise more frequent. Matalia looked up in dismay and happened to see Peigi desperately trying to gain her attention. She pantomimed holding her breath, her face turning red with the effort of her demonstration. In understanding, Matalia tried to hold hers as well. However, in her fierce concentration she was unaware of the rest of the Soothebury clan quietly entering behind their angry leader. She swallowed, hoping that the hiccups were gone, and looked up again, expecting to encounter the furious visage of Lord Soothebury. Instead, she was confronted by the mildest pair of honey-brown eyes she had ever seen.

Matalia's jaw fell, and a spontaneous smile spread to her lips and blossomed in her cheeks, making them rosy and sweet. The girl responded shyly in an answering smile, and she dropped into a dainty curtsy, which Matalia unthinkingly imitated.

"Lady Matalia," the girl said in greeting.

"Lady . . . ?" Matalia replied hesitantly, seeking the proper address. Suddenly the Earl stepped forward, and the young girl shrank back, disturbed by the anger radiating from his elderly body.

"You bring your daughter to the negotiating?" the Earl thundered, his face mottled.

"Your son is bound to see to her!" Soothebury shouted back. "He made a promise that he must keep or forever incur disfavor!"

The Earl flung a finger in Matalia's general direction. "You can see that he has obligations elsewhere! There is no possibility of your daughter's union with him. She needs find other pastures to snare a buck."

Soothebury glowered and stomped his feet, showering

snow around him like a blizzard. "He was promised to Clarise first, and *she*"—he pointed at Matalia—"is an intruder upon another woman's domain. She should be cast out as an adulterer and allow my daughter to take her rightful place."

Matalia went white, the shock of his cruel words abruptly scaring the hiccups from her. She stumbled back, feeling off balance both from her increased girth and from the unexpected verbal attack. Her hand flew out, trying to grasp something to keep from falling. Her eyes searched for her husband, who stood several feet from her side, and he leaped to help her, but was too far away. Matalia felt herself falling. Suddenly a small hand gripped her arm and steadied her, holding her carefully until her faintness passed and Brogan reached her side. Then Clarise released her and moved away, casting concerned glances at her father.

Soothebury glared at her and reached to stroke the hair back from her face where it had fallen forward in her effort to assist Matalia. "You need not touch her, nor speak to her, Clarise. She and her kind are beneath you."

Lady Isadora giggled, but the twin brothers both narrowed their gazes into steely fury at the aspersion. Brogan carefully handed Matalia back into her chair, then turned to face Soothebury formally.

"You have made your declaration clear, but I ask that you limit the words to mine own and leave the McTavers be. The circumstances of my marriage were not within their control."

A silence descended upon the hall while the laird pondered the request. Finally, he replied, "I will consider it."

"Then please accept our hospitality for the time it takes you to make this weighty decision."

"Hospitality!" shrieked Lady Isadora. "They have come to declare war, and we are to invite them into our home?"

" 'Tis still my home to grant!" the Earl thundered, rounding upon the hapless woman. "I know your feelings, and"—he held a hand up to halt the words of Xanthier—"I know your thoughts. Believe me, I am not pleased that this has come to pass, and it marks heavily against Brogan's claim. If war commences between us"—the Earl shifted his glance to include everyone—"I have no doubt that Brogan will prevail. However," he continued as Soothebury bristled, "it would drain our resources, and I am loath for it to occur. In the interest of peace, the Soothebury clan is welcome to my home during the negotiations."

"This is not right!" Isadora shouted, her eyes snapping and her hands clenched with rage. "This alone should force you to cast him out before he brings war to all of Kirkcaldy, just as he is doing to Roseneath of the McTavers."

"I said I would think upon my claim to Roseneath," Soothebury said mildly.

"You should not release them," Xanthier added. " 'Twas the McTavers that made the union that disgraced your daughter."

"I did not know that women were able to make such marriage choices," Soothebury replied sarcastically.

"Her family forced the issue," Xanthier stated.

"Why?" asked Soothebury and the Earl simultaneously. All turned to Matalia. She stared stonily back at them, recalling the promise to Brogan many months ago. She would not speak of their meeting, she vowed silently. It was Brogan's decision. She looked at him, seeing his emotional withdrawal as he stared back at her, daring her to break her promise. When she said nothing, the assemblage followed her look to Brogan for an answer.

"You must tell us," the Earl demanded. "Why did you marry the Lady Matalia and break the wedding promise to Soothebury?"

Brogan finally stepped forward, a softening in his look as his eyes briefly swept over Matalia's beautiful pale face. "I did not break a promise to you, Laird. I broke it to the Lady Clarise." He walked forward to where the plain girl stood, her eyes downcast as the drama swelled around her. "My lady," he said as he knelt before her and took her limp hand, "what I did to you was inexcusable. You deserve a better man than I. I had not met you, but instead knew of you only through letters to your father. But he spoke highly of you, and I was pleased with the arrangements. It was the misfortune of happenstance that I met the Lady Matalia only days away from your door. I was . . . captured . . . by her beauty and was literally helpless to resist. I wish you would forgive my manly weakness and know that had I but seen you first, I would have been similarly taken with you."

Matalia rose, unsure how the young lass would respond and feeling terribly guilty that her actions on that night long ago had destroyed Clarise's chance at marriage and stature, for now she would be considered abandoned and unworthy.

Clarise's honey-brown eyes filled with tears. She cleared her throat and sniffed. "I find it a sad happenstance," she said softly so only Brogan could hear, "that you would find in Lady Matalia only beauty to recommend her. If you had spoken of love, I would understand." She sniffed again, then edged away, hiding in the shadow of her father's bulk.

Brogan stared at her, his face devoid of any reaction, though he felt his insides heave. Love? What an absurd notion! She would divert a war between their families if he was in love? Such a feeling between an O'Bannon and his wife was inconceivable. He cared for her and enjoyed her company. He even felt possessive of her affections. But love destroyed a man, made him weak and helpless. It made him desperate and vulnerable. He would rather fight a war than surrender to love!

He rose to his feet, his eyes as cold as steel as he glared at the little woman who dared demand such a boon for her forgiveness. Waves of anger emanated from him, and even Lady Isadora stepped back in fear, wondering what the girl had said to incite such a reaction.

"Brogan!" chastised Matalia as she stood up and walked protectively over to Clarise. "You are frightening the child! Cease your relentless glare and leave her out of your ridiculous machinations. She is only a pawn in this display, as am I. We are more lives that you two"—she pointed at both Xanthier and Brogan—"are willing to sacrifice in the drive for your inheritance. I will have none of it. Clarise, come here. Let us leave these fools to their posturing. They can spit on each other for all I care. In fact," she said over her shoulder as she took Clarise's hand and pulled her toward the guest chambers in a rarely used section of the castle, "perhaps you could settle this all by a spitting contest. Whoever spits the farthest shall be declared the winner, and then you can all go to bed."

Clarise giggled at the image of her father and the great Earl along with his twin sons spitting into the rushes, and her eyes twinkled up at Matalia as they left the hall. The men stared after them, shared expressions of outrage upon each face.

As Matalia opened the door to the guest chamber, she wrinkled her nose at the smell of dust permeating the room. She turned to Clarise apologetically. "I do not know when last there were visitors here," she stated as she entered and wiped a finger along a dusty table. "There are many rooms in this castle that have been closed for the last thirty years. Mayhap you would prefer braving the snow and returning home?" she asked a bit hopefully.

"Indeed no," Clarise responded cheerfully. "This will be perfect."

Matalia held her tongue with a shrug. "Well, if that is to be so, then you can return to your father whilst I clean it."

"Absolutely not," Clarise repeated with a glint in her eye. "I have no wish to get in the path of their spittle. I would much rather help you make the room habitable."

"Oh, I could not ask that of a guest," Matalia replied, while assessing Clarise, trying to determine if her previous reply was meant to be humorous.

"You are not asking," answered Clarise. "But perhaps you could procure some rags and water?"

Matalia drew back, not used to having another tell her what to do. She opened her mouth to retort, but closed it when she saw the warm smile upon Clarise's plain face. She smiled back and nodded. "Very well. I can see that you will do what you want despite what I say. I should have made Brogan marry you. You would have driven him crazy within a day."

They both smiled broadly, and Clarise came forward and enfolded Matalia in a warm embrace. "I think you manage to do that on your own," she answered, and chuckled, releasing tension between them and forming a tentative bond of friendship. Matalia laughed and sat down on the dusty bed because her abdomen felt heavy, then laughed harder when a swirl of dust rose up around her. Clarise rushed forward, waving her hand, trying to get the dust away from Matalia before she choked, but the air movements caused more dirt to dance in the air. With a grin, Matalia flung herself back against the bedcovers with arms flung out, encouraging another flurry of dust to rise. Watching her, Clarise blew in the air and then twirled mischievously in the resulting dust motes. They were both coated in old dirt within seconds, and their laughter changed to coughs and happy tears.

A sudden new gust of air caused them to look toward the door in midlaugh, and they beheld Brogan and Soothebury standing bemusedly in the doorway. The women looked at each other, seeing the grime coating their clothes and faces, and they burst into another fit of laugher, crying with their mirth.

Brogan stared at his beautiful pregnant wife sprawled in a filthy bed with twin rivulets of clean streaks upon her face where her tears had cleared paths through the dust. She was clutching her lower abdomen as if in pain, but her face was wreathed in joy and she was periodically waving her arms above her head, thinking it hilarious when the dust swirled around her. Clarise stood in the center of the room, her clothes and face equally filthy and tear streaked and her left arm braced against a table to hold herself upright. The men looked at each other in befuddlement and left without a word. Women were often incomprehensible.

Chapter 24

Brogan watched Matalia undress. She was relaxed and easy, not taking note of his attention while she unlaced her girdle and pulled the dirty gown off her shoulders, dropping it into a heap on the ground. The hem of her petticoat was equally damaged, and she bent over to lift it in her hands and stare at it. She rubbed the cloth, obviously intending to brush the dust away, but the stains remained and she frowned. She shoved her black curls from her face and sighed as she finally dropped the hem in defeat. Noting Brogan, she walked over to him for assistance. She turned her back to him and glanced over her shoulder, and he complied with the silent request, taking the opportunity to brush his fingers against her silken neck.

"I trust you did not overexert yourself?" he questioned as the ties came apart in his expert hands.

"I did not," she answered, smiling. "But I am shocked that the rooms are in such disgraceful condition."

"One would think that you mean to say Kirkcaldy is in need of a permanent mistress."

Matalia pulled out of his hands, her petticoats and chemise loosened, and turned to regard him thoughtfully. "She does," she answered softly. "But I am not certain I am the woman to fill the role."

"Of course you are," Brogan replied with a trace

of anger. "Why would you think otherwise, especially now when I need your support?"

Matalia walked behind a screen to remove her linens. "I did not see it like that. I merely wondered if Clarise would not have been a better choice."

"She *was* my choice," Brogan answered harshly, still irritated at her previous remark. When silence greeted his reply, Brogan ran a hand through his hair, throwing it into complete disarray. He stared at the shadow behind the screen, seeing the image of her pregnant body. He felt an ache in the region of his heart. Through gritted teeth, he continued. "I was not your choice either," he stated, trying to take the sting from his words.

More silence answered him, and he saw the edge of the fur-lined robe disappear as she wrapped it around herself without replying. Finally she came out from behind the screen and faced him squarely. "That is not true. Not really. I did choose you, as you very well know."

"But not for a husband. You wanted me only for pleasure."

"Tell me that there is a difference?"

"Of course there is a difference," he said, his voice rising. "You wanted a ram stud, not a shepherd."

Matalia frowned, trying to figure out what Brogan wanted from her. She bit her lip, her eyes soft and concerned. Finally, because she did not know what he needed, she spoke again. "Brogan, I chose you. My mother knew that it was not a chance act, but a deed of destiny."

He spun away from her voice, the melodic sweetness in her tones matching the ambrosia of her words. He stared out the window and into the darkness lit only by moonlight glancing off powdered snow. The landscape looked blue-gray and desolate. It looked cold and stark. It felt like his heart.

"What do you feel for me?" he asked, not turning. He held his breath, afraid of her answer.

Matalia stared at the hard planes of his back, seeing the tension hum in the lines of his shoulders. She pulled the robe tighter around her, terrified of his question and of answering it incorrectly. She felt the baby flip over and give her a sharp kick, making her gasp. Brogan did not turn toward her, and Matalia was thankful that he had not heard her small outcry.

"I do not understand the question," she finally replied, her voice shaky.

" 'Tis not a hard question for a woman to answer. What do you feel for me? Now, these nine months past our forced wedding. What do you feel for me?"

"You are my husband," Matalia answered, still trying to evade answering him in a way that would anger him.

He whipped around and glared at her, the fury in his eyes reminding Matalia of his immense strength, his overwhelming dominance. "Answer me!" he shouted at her, barely restraining himself from gripping her shoulders and shaking her.

"I cannot!" Matalia shouted back, her face white with panic. "You ask for something you do not want!"

"I want an answer!"

"Then I shall tell you, and damn you for asking it! I love you and have since the day you took me from my home and made love to me in the campfire light. I cannot go a day without wanting to see you, touch you, be near you, even though you stare at me with eyes that see straight through me. I love you so much I took your people on as my own and struggled to make them see the good in you. I love you enough to bear the company of your disgraceful family, to endure the contest of hatred between you and your brother. I love you, that is what I feel for you!" She stared at him, her body trembling, waiting for his reaction.

The tension in his frame slowly eased. He took a step toward her and touched his finger to her chin to tilt it up. "And you," she whispered. "What do you feel for me?"

"You are beautiful," he whispered back, bending his head to kiss her.

Matalia drew back, avoiding his lips. "You have not answered me," she said softly, searching his face.

"I just did," he replied in confusion.

"No," Matalia said, pulling fully out of his arms, "you said I was beautiful."

"You are," he answered, stepping to take her back.

"That is not an answer!" she said sharply.

Brogan's face hardened, and he let his arms drop. "That is all I will say," he stated coldly.

"Yet you force me to reveal my feelings to you?" Matalia felt her voice rise to a wail, but was helpless to curb the sound. "How could you be so cruel?"

"What, Matalia? What did you think I would say? Did you think I would fall to my feet and proclaim a similar love for you? Did you think I would give you that power?"

Matalia stared at him, vulnerable tears that she made no attempt to curtail streaming down her face. She batted the air in front of her as if to ward off evil spirits, then took a deep breath and wiped the tears from her cheeks before replying. "You are the fool, Brogan O'Bannon. You have spent a lifetime fighting for your fortune, yet have no idea that it just slipped through your arrogant fingers." She sniffed and wiped her face once again. Then she grew calm and looked at him, wisdom clear upon her features.

Brogan stared back at her, her words washing over him like a forbidding portent over which he had no control. He felt a twist in his gut and his calf muscles tightened so painfully he felt as if he had run for four hours over rocky terrain. He tried to lift his arms in a shrug, he tried to open his mouth to retort, but in actuality he did not move. Matalia stood still for a moment, then regally turned from him to ring for Peigi.

Brogan sank back into the shadows of the room as the servant appeared with a trail of others bearing a copper tub and hot-water kettles. After they left, Matalia dropped her robe and stepped in, her rounded belly incredibly mystifying and erotic. She lowered herself completely, reveling in the warmth, and closed her eyes in apparent bliss. Brogan closed his eyes, too, feeling the pain of her absolute withdrawal.

Xanthier watched his wife lumber over to a chair and lower herself with great difficulty into it. She made a petulant face at him when he made no effort to assist her. "Why can you not be more like Brogan and help me a bit? He is always courteous to his wife."

"If I were more like my brother I would not have married you," he answered sardonically. Isadora glared at him and then grunted as she attempted yet again to get comfortable.

"Without me, you will not become Earl, so you had best treat me well." Isadora's voice was nasty, and she smiled craftily when Xanthier narrowed his eyes in anger. Knowing she had his complete attention, she continued. "Soothebury must be reminded of the terrible insult Brogan has cast upon his daughter. It has taken me months to rile him into declaring his war upon your twin, and I will not have that blue-eyed sorceress bewitching him and his daughter into withdrawing. She must be distracted."

"You have never liked her, have you?"

"Of course not. She is the enemy."

"Why do you not focus upon Brogan instead? He is the one I am fighting."

"I do not like the way you stare at her as if she

were a tasty fruit protected by thorns that you are only waiting to destroy so you can taste of her flesh."

"You speak in riddles, woman, as always."

"I only say aloud what you do not. I have never known a man so weak as you. You are pathetic, and I am glad only that I bred early so that I did not have to bear your touch for long."

Her harsh words did not affect him at all. He had said as much to her many a time, so her insults had the echo of stale food left on the table for the dogs. He shrugged and smiled slightly, his lips twisting. He stalked forward, the grace of his stance reminiscent of a wildcat pacing after a flighty rabbit in the dead of winter. Isadora shrank back and placed a hand protectively over her abdomen.

"If you hit me, I may lose the baby," she whispered.

Xanthier towered over her seated form, his hand raised. He insolently turned his hand over and stared at a healing gash on his palm. With the other hand he picked at the scab, making the wound bleed. Then, slowly, as if he did not realize what he did, he stroked Isadora's cheek, leaving a trail of blood upon her white face.

"The baby is safe, Isadora, for I would not jeopardize my inheritance simply for the pleasure of making you cry. But know that if you fail me and birth the babe after Matalia delivers hers, I shall be very, *very* angry." He noted her reaction, then let his lips spread into a larger, more chilling smile as he dropped his hand from her face. "But not to worry. I will deal with the Lady Matalia."

Matalia slowly climbed down the tower stairs and took a deep breath as she drew the wool cloak around her. She felt nervous and unsure, but she desperately needed the company of her wolves to give her a sense of stability. She was depressed, and the coldness in her heart was spreading to her fingers and toes like an insidious infection that needed the tincture of love to resolve. Brogan's refusal to declare his love had hit her hard, for she was not one to reveal vulnerability in herself easily, and once done, needed assurance that she was loved in return. She crept across the rushes, avoiding the few Soothebury men sprawled in the great hall, and entered the kitchen. The kitchen fire boy was sleeping, for he counted on the coldness to wake him if the fire petered down. Matalia felt a surge of protectiveness for him, and smiled at his young, relaxed face. Then, with a sense of purpose, she walked over to stand above him in order to stare into the flames.

She slowly braided her hair, forcing the wildly curly locks into a tight plait that fell just below her hips. Her midnight hair had always been touted as beautiful, exquisite, gorgeous. Suddenly, Matalia hated it. She did not want Brogan to see her as beautiful, but instead as she was, a loving, caring woman with much to offer. She pulled the braid, reveling in the sting it produced upon her scalp.

So Brogan thought of her beauty alone, she thought to herself. No words of love crossed his lips. Instead, he commented on how lovely he found her. While she could not change the color of her eyes, or the shape of her brow, she could remove this symbol with relative ease. She tied the braid end with a small ribbon she had brought with her for such a purpose and then pulled a dagger from the sheath at her waist.

Taking a deep breath, she sawed at the hair, cutting it just below her neck. Within seconds, a lifetime of locks were shorn, leaving only a tumbled pile of pixie curls in its place. The braid dropped heavily, and Matalia let it fall to the floor. She then replaced her dagger and looked again at the sleeping fire tender. Her head felt light, much lighter than her heart, and she sighed as she smiled sadly. Moments later she sneaked out the side door and left the safety of the castle.

From the high reaches of the southern tower, Xanthier saw Matalia leave the castle, her heavy body surprisingly graceful. A hood covered her head, and her cloak swept the snow, effectively removing the evidence of her passage. The wolves instantly materialized, a trio of gray, black and dark red, and they lifted their noses to her skirts, sniffing. The black swung his head and looked up, staring at the window where Xanthier watched. The hair on the wolf's scruff lifted in warning, and his tail bristled. Xanthier smiled in the darkness and nodded his head in shadowy acknowledgment.

Matalia felt the cold seep through her boots and she shivered. The night held a different feel. Her body felt heavy, and the weight of her unborn babe had dropped, pressing painfully against her pelvic bone. She walked a few feet to where a sled was propped against the lee of a tree. She pulled the contraption down and brushed the snow with the edge of her coat. She fiddled with the ropes, her movements more awkward than usual, until she straightened them. Then she slipped the makeshift harness over the gray wolf, feeling his body start to quiver with excitement. He leaped up, accidentally knocking her over, and then spun in circles as she lumbered to her feet. The ropes became tangled and Matalia sharply reprimanded the wolf, demanding he calm down. The wolf restrained his spinning, but his front paws lifted anxiously, right and left, and his body continued to quiver.

Matalia was finally able to attach the sled to his harness, but she held the wolf's ropes so that the upper half of his body had minimal contact with the underlying snow. She gave him another command to stay, one she doubted he would obey, and then positioned herself to drop into the leather suspended between the branches that formed the sides of the sled. She simultaneously released the wolf and dropped into the sled and the wolf leaped forward, his light body dragging hers over the firm snow crust.

They sped instantly into a gallop, the wide paws of the gray skimming the ground as Matalia held on. She shifted slightly to get a better seat, and the gray broke stride, slowing to a trot, his tongue hanging out with the pleasure of pulling. The other two wolves ranged alongside, urging their companion on.

Matalia did not try to direct her wolf. Instead she let him choose the path, and she bowed her head to avoid the crisp wind. Normally she halted their progress at the edge of the meadow, not comfortable with riding through the rocky, cave-dotted hillside that rose into inhospitable mountains behind Kirkcaldy, but today she did not care. She kept her head down, and a small trail of tears seeped from her eyes where their salty warmth soon changed to freezing paths upon her cheeks.

She did love him, and part of her was glad that she had been forced to admit it. She felt freer with the secret torn from her. But the pain of his response cut her, feeling sharper than the icicles that dangled from tree limbs and occasionally broke off to stab the snow. She felt a sharp pain in her abdomen, and she gasped, feeling the physical manifestation of her inner turmoil. She doubled over, breathing slowly, forcing her mind to relax, until the pain subsided. She smiled grimly, and silently shook her fist at the fates that had dealt her an internally tortured husband whom, despite her good judgment, she loved deeply, completely.

She could survive his lack of love, but she did not

wish to. At this moment, all she wanted was to escape
the tension and let nature soothe her body. She lifted
her head finally, feeling the gray wolf slow down as
they climbed the hillside, and she grew nervous as the
caves began emerging from the darkness. Big. Black.
Huge caverns yawned on either side of her.

Xanthier entered the kitchen only moments after
Matalia left. Snow still flurried in the freezing air in
her wake. The blast of cold woke the fire tender
and he sat up sleepily, blinking. Without hesitation,
Xanthier raised his hand and clubbed him in the
temple, sending the child into unconsciousness.

Xanthier looked at him dispassionately, only
faintly aware that he had withheld a killing blow. He
leaned down and picked up Matalia's black braid,
instantly recognizing the color and texture of her
beautiful mane. He frowned, wondering at the significance, then slid the piece into his pocket. He
walked to the kitchen door and opened it. His big
body slipped out into the cold, and he shut the door
quickly. In the moonlight he watched Matalia ride
off on her unusual transportation, and he rubbed his
hands together, weighing, thinking, trying to determine his best plan of action. He looked up into the
sky, seeing the moon, stars and clouds. Then he reentered the castle and went to Soothebury's chamber.

At Xanthier's knock the grizzled man gruffly bade
him to enter. Xanthier bowed in the chivalrous manner of Brogan and nodded with a trace of deference.
Soothebury's face cleared and he nodded in return.
"Brogan O'Bannon?" he asked.

"M'lord," Xanthier replied with a slight uplift to
his lips.

Soothebury stepped back and motioned to the
room. "Come in. What brings you at this hour?"

"I have important news, Lord Soothebury, information that is relevant to your declaration but which I hesitated to speak of in front of others." Xanthier smiled, pleased that Lord Soothebury had mistaken him for Brogan.

"Indeed?"

"Please understand that I have done only what an honorable man could do in the circumstances I relate to you, and had I a choice, I would have gladly abandoned my obligations and hastened to meet my bride, Clarise, your daughter."

"What circumstances can these be? To jilt my favorite child is no matter of light consequence."

"Perhaps the Lady Clarise should be present? For 'tis truly her choice if my explanation is relevant and soothes her injured pride."

The big man nodded thoughtfully, then bade Xanthier to remain in the chamber while he fetched his daughter from her bed. As he exited, Xanthier pulled the lock of curls from his pocket and placed them underneath Soothebury's pillow, adding a small dagger, which he sank into the mattress through the thickest part of the braid. He replaced the pillow and casually walked to his previous place and stood with his hands behind his back.

Clarise and Soothebury entered moments later. Clarise was clothed in a simple white linen nightdress covered by an equally plain robe of brown cloth. Her hair was tumbled and her honey-brown eyes were soft with sleep.

Clarise rubbed her eyes. She looked him over, and Xanthier felt a nervous shiver as if she could see through him. He held his breath, waiting for her to denounce him. Instead she curtsied briefly and moved to huddle in the shadow of her massive father. Soothebury put a protective arm around her.

"Now, what have you to say that is important enough to disturb my daughter in the middle of the night?"

Xanthier rubbed his hands through his hair and looked around as if he were embarrassed and uncomfortable. "Please," he started, "please understand that only these extreme circumstances force me to tell you of these events."

"Understood," growled Soothebury.

Xanthier looked at Clarise pleadingly. "I pray you understand why my marriage has come to pass after my tale. . . ."

"Get on with it, Brogan," Soothebury interrupted.

"The tale begins with Matalia. She is very ill."

"Ill?" gasped Clarise as Soothebury's eyes rose in surprise.

"Very ill. I met her as I was returning home and begged a night's rest at Castle Roseneath." Xanthier paused for effect and forced his features into sadness. "She has not much time to live. In fact, we are not certain she will survive the birth of her child. It was this information that she gave me that night that made me sympathetic to her plight. She begged, nay pleaded with me to gift her with a night of pleasure before she should die alone and virgin."

"For God's sake!" Soothebury exclaimed, frowning mightily at the indiscretion of mentioning such vulgar words in front of Clarise.

"I apologize for such bluntness, but I feel you both should understand the right of my actions. I was tormented by her request, bent as I was upon wedding you, Clarise, but she called it a last wish. I was honor bound to grant it. Surely a man who understands honor will understand that I could not ignore her?" He turned to Soothebury. At his slow nod, Xanthier continued spinning his false tale. "But I told her I could not take such a lady of virtue and fine family without marriage. So we wed."

"You wed . . ." echoed Soothebury, stunned.

"But, m'lord, hear this. Matalia will die soon, and I wish to promise that after she dies I will return for

Clarise." Xanthier's hot eyes swung to the demurely
dressed Clarise. She shivered and pressed closer to
her father.

"Clarise?" Soothebury questioned.

"I want to leave," she whispered. "I want this to
be over. I care naught that he wed Matalia, for if
indeed she is ill, I want only whatever pleasure she
can have before she passes. I truly had no knowledge
of her illness. She seems so . . . robust."

"Aye," pressed Xanthier. "The bloom in her cheeks
is that of fever, and the sparkle in her eyes is from
unshed tears. Have you not noticed the sheen of her
pale skin? The translucence that makes her glow? Her
illness progresses quickly. In fact, the stress of your
presence has confined her to bed."

"Oh!" cried Clarise. "Father, let us leave at once!
Let us be gone now, before the sun rises."

Soothebury looked at Xanthier thoughtfully. He
squeezed his daughter's shoulders. "Very well, I can
see you could do no less than marry her. I release the
declaration and would have peace between us."

"*I*—as the best son of the Earl, will have peace with
you," Xanthier vowed as each man touched their own
left shoulder with their right hand, and Xanthier
smiled broadly at his hidden words. He turned to with-
draw when Soothebury stopped him.

"We will have your mark to indicate our peace,"
Clarise quietly stated. Soothebury pulled a scroll from
his trunk and found a pen and ink within the chamber
desk as he nodded.

Xanthier hesitated. A tightness filled his gut at the
clear gaze of Clarise's eyes. He looked at the pen and
ink and swallowed nervously. He stared at the scroll,
unsure. With faltering steps he approached the two.
He felt the weight of what he was about to do, and
part of him hesitated. He briefly looked back, back to
the days before. Back to when he and his brother

were friends. A flash of mirror images, of two young boys with grins on their faces diving into the lake above the cottage while their beautiful mother gardened. But then the image changed, and he saw his twin as the enemy, his antithesis. And he boldly took the pen and scrawled Brogan's name.

Chapter 25

The moon had reached its zenith when the clop of hooves softly echoed upon the cobblestones and Soothebury's entourage left the mellowed walls of Kirkcaldy castle. Xanthier watched Clarise and her father close the drapes of their conveyance and saw the muted light of a lantern flicker within its peaceful boundaries. He frowned, briefly angry that the Soothebury family showed such solidarity. Such emotion, such love betwixt a father and child was irrational and only denoted weakness, he thought to himself as his jaw clenched. He would never let himself be so easily manipulated.

When the final horseman disappeared around the bend, he took a breath slowly through his nose. Now he would finish this fight. There would be only one winner. It would be himself. He opened his eyes and stared into the darkness. There was no need to repeat his vow. He knew it by heart. It would be him.

Up in the south tower his wife lay in misery, her distended body gripped in painful contractions. Xanthier ignored her panting and pulled a set of fur-lined boots out of a trunk. He pulled them on over woolen stockings and then picked up a woolen plaid to drape over his shoulders. He exited the chamber without ever once speaking to Isadora.

Before he left the castle, he returned to the guest chamber. With a dispassionate stare at the gleaming locks he had hidden there, he pulled his dagger and sliced the inside of his arm until a thin trickle of blood welled up. He held his arm over the white pillow and let a trail of blood soak the linen as well as the braid. He dribbled it along the floor and over the rushes, making the trail of blood clearly lead to the guest chamber. Then he pulled his cloak around himself and snuck out of the kitchen door, past the still-unconscious fire tender. In a rare display of kindness, he tossed a log onto the embers, ensuring the boy did not receive punishment for a job poorly done.

He stood in the moonlit snowdrift, watching his breath crystallize in front of him. He narrowed his gray eyes and stared at the path before him. A cruel smile flitted across his face. Then the sounds of wolves reached him, forming a faint melody filled with dark tones and high yips that drifted down the hillside. Xanthier nodded and set out.

Matalia stared around her, seeing the dark mouths of caverns slide silently by. Some were small, some larger, some enormous. She became aware of animal footprints in the snow that crisscrossed the moonlit landscape in myriad patterns. A chill whispered through her, and she peered into the darkness, searching for danger.

Suddenly she spotted an unusual footprint, a wide, clawed stamp that was easily as broad as two hands. She shivered, abruptly afraid, and spoke a command to her wolf.

"Gray one," she murmured, "turn back. I am afeared of the great beasts."

The wolf slowed and turned his head to view her, and his ancient eyes searched through her words and into her soul. Matalia gazed back at him, silently pleading. The wolf stopped and shook his ruff, sending a spray of snow around him. He sat down and lifted his nose to sniff the crisp air. The other wolves ranged around him and stared up as well, searching the sky.

A swift, horribly painful contraction swept through Matalia's body, and she cried out in surprise. She gripped the edges of the sled and closed her eyes tightly, willing the pain to subside. Within moments it slipped away, and she opened her eyes. A sudden urge to urinate suffused her, and she stumbled unsteadily off of the leather sled and sank quickly into the snow. Gasping anew, she pulled herself through the powder and reached a spindly tree. Gripping one of its lower branches, she breathed slowly and attempted a lopsided grin as she pressed her head against the bark. 'Twas only a late-pregnancy ache, she assured herself. She had best toughen up or the actual birth would be impossible. She looked over at her wolves, and they stared back at her, their eyes full of worry. A silent message passed among them. Then the black wolf lifted his nose and howled.

Matalia lifted her skirts awkwardly, feeling foolish although no one was nearby. She gripped the branch for support and squatted. A gush of urine escaped her and she sighed with relief, certain that the cramps that plagued her would now cease. Holding the branch, she stepped away from her spot, careful not to tread upon the discolored snow. She stared up, concerned about the sudden snowfall, and attempted to reach her sled. Another sudden, unexpected cramp caught her unawares, and she collapsed in a snowdrift. Faintly, she felt warm liquid soaking her legs, and she thought bemusedly that she was surprised she still had to pee, considering she had done so just seconds previously.

She looked up and the red wolf was standing over her, his black eyes calm and reassuring. She gripped his ruff and let him pull her up. Another pain trickled through her, but she ignored it. Rest, she thought, she only needed some rest.

The red wolf led her slowly through the snow to a cave entrance. Matalia hung back, afraid of the beasts that lived inside, but a soft melody of wolf song surrounded her, and she clumsily climbed over the cavern lip and entered its hallowed core. She instantly felt the warmth of its shelter from the wind, and she sank gratefully down to the pine-needle-strewn floor. A howl of wind joined the wolves' song, and Matalia shuffled a few feet farther into the cave. She wrapped her arms around her chest and stared out, nervous, frightened and unsure.

Another cramp slowly built, and Matalia felt it with curious detachment. It started as a flicker of warning, a subtle tightening in her lower abdomen. Then it gained momentum, spreading through her belly to encompass her thighs, her chest. Finally, with a force that made her vocalize in surprise, it chomped down and ground her insides with blunt teeth. Matalia leaned forward, bracing herself against the floor of the cave, and cried aloud.

She was distantly aware of the abrupt cessation of wolf song. She felt her companions leave, and she silently thanked them for seeking help. "Brogan," she whispered into the darkness, "please . . . please come to me Brogan. I need you. . . ."

Outside the castle, Xanthier trudged through the snow, grimly thankful for the new flakes that began dusting his footprints, obscuring them with a steady, beautiful flow. He, too, listened to the wolves, and he hefted a bow and arrow in preparation.

He pulled his plaid closer as the wind picked up. Peering into the snow, he desperately tried to locate Matalia's path before it disappeared while simultaneously listening to the dwindling howls. It was important to find her. As soon as she was dead, his inheritance was assured. There would be no child, and the Earl would be forced to acknowledge Xanthier as the heir. He forced himself to walk faster up the mountainside, bending his big frame into the wind.

Xanthier was aware of the sudden, dark silence when the wolves stopped howling. He paused, cocking his head, his steely eyes peering malevolently into the snow. He pulled an arrow through the bow and drew it partially. He slowly walked forward, feeling the strength of the predator infuse his blood. He could feel how close she was. It was only a matter of time.

Xanthier saw the sled abandoned next to a tall tree and a path of broken snow indicating Matalia's disembarkation. His nostrils flared. He glanced around, then located a cave whose entrance would encompass a person. He slowly sheathed the bow and arrow and pulled out his sword. It was time.

Matalia shivered upon the floor of the cave, her eyes unfocused and her mind drifting from cold and pain. Her short curls danced around her flushed cheeks, making her appear like a snow faerie sheathed in silken sweat. Xanthier stepped in and stared down at her. He held his sword firmly in his hand.

Matalia doubled over in pain. Her lower abdomen felt like it was going to explode and implode simultaneously. She felt muscles cramp and squeeze beyond her control, and she gripped the walls of the cave behind her desperately. Just as the contraction started to wane, she looked up and saw Brogan standing above her, an odd expression on his face. She stared up at him gratefully and opened her arms. He hesitated, his hand on his sword, but Matalia reached up for him and tugged him down so that he was forced to kneel next to her.

"Thank the heavens and gods! This is horrible! Help me. Please. Make it stop."

He nodded, and Matalia felt a tremor of unease. She cocked her head, staring closer at him. Just then another powerful contraction swept over her, and she gasped aloud and gripped his sword arm for ballast. She leaned into him, pressing her sweaty forehead against his shoulder. She wrapped her arms around him and threaded her fingers through his hair and tried to control her breathing.

Finally she could catch her breath again, and she lifted her head to stare into a set of confused gray eyes. "Take me home," Matalia whimpered, longing for the warmth of a fire and the luxury of her bed. "I am afeared that the babe will die if born out here. I should never have taken off tonight. Do you forgive me?"

Xanthier stared at her liquid eyes, and he noticed a light in them that he had never seen before. For lack of knowing how to respond, he repeated, "Forgive you?"

"Yes," she murmured, suddenly shy. "I ran off because of my foolish pride. I know you can only be who you are. I should not insist you be anyone else. I feel as I do because of who you are, and I love you."

"You love me?" he repeated again, stunned.

"Yes, Brogan." She laughed, slightly breathless. "I love you. You are everything to me. I think it was written in the stars that I find you on that night and capture you for mine own." She smiled softly, her face radiant.

Xanthier was speechless. With her body pressed against his own he felt paralyzed. Finally, when she arched a brow at him and made as if to rise, he spoke. "We cannot travel back now." He cleared his throat at her sudden frown. "It would be too dangerous. You are in active labor, and at least in this cave you are protected from the elements. You must stay. I will collect some wood and make a fire for you." He pulled her arms away from his neck and stared down at her concerned face. "Trust me," he whispered and was amazed when Matalia instantly nodded.

"Of course," she replied, then leaned back again and closed her eyes tiredly. Xanthier stared at her, his emotions tangled. He picked up his sword and stood to his full height, noting her vulnerability. He hefted the sword and stared at her neck, debating how to swing the blade against it.

Confusion swept through him, and he played Matalia's words over in his mind. Love. Trust. His brother was apparently ensnared in the emotions their father had warned him about since the day of their birth. Love meant weakness. Trust meant you would be betrayed. With grim purpose he saluted Matalia, then exited the cave.

Matalia watched him leave through slitted eyes. She was surprised by his actions, but she rationalized that she was in the midst of labor, a time well-known for women to suddenly think all sorts of strange thoughts. She folded her hands over her abdomen and sighed. He was probably correct in any case. She was safer here than on the sled.

Soon Xanthier had a fire crackling in the cave entrance. He pulled his saddlebag off his horse and dropped it next to Matalia. Contained within it were emergency supplies including an iron pan, some dried jerky, a small plaid, a bag of grain, a flask of spirits and a small sewing kit. When Matalia pulled the precious needle and thread out, Xanthier shrugged. "For injuries. I am not always near help when I need tending. I have learned to mend myself." When Matalia looked at him blankly he turned his back on her. "I am going to close the entrance so you are safe. Then I will go to the castle and inform them."

Matalia looked out nervously, not sure she wanted to be closed in the cave when she did not know how deep it extended, nor where the big beasts dwelled.

But she bit her lip and nodded, putting her faith in the man she thought was her husband. She stood unsteadily as he left and scooped a pile of snow into the cave, then filled the pan with it and placed it on the fire to melt. She was working with the contractions now, getting a sense of their rhythm so they did not sneak up on her. She paused when they flooded her and breathed slowly, bracing herself until they passed again.

He was working outside, and then she saw him dragging branches to crisscross in front of the entrance, covering all but a small gap at the top. With effort, he piled snow on the branches. Except for the area around the fire, the cave was plunged in darkness, for even the moonlight and blossoming dawn could not penetrate the barrier. Matalia stood again, pacing, worried. She pushed against the snow, shoving it aside, and peered through the branches at his face.

"I am frightened in here," she admitted, peering into his familiar gray eyes.

Xanthier frowned, displeased that she could easily move the snow. He concentrated, thinking of how to harden the snow into a solid barrier.

"Brogan!" Matalia said sharply, becoming agitated. "I do not like being closed in."

Xanthier smiled, forcing his mouth to relax the way he saw Brogan's do when his brother smiled at his wife. "You will be safe," he repeated reassuringly. "This is for the best. You must deliver the child. It will make my victory sweeter."

Matalia shivered and watched him carefully, noting his stance and the way he moved his head when he spoke. The twins were so similar . . . Carefully masking her trepidation she propped her head on a branch and curled her lips seductively. "Then come here and kiss me before you go." She crossed her fingers behind her back and waited.

Xanthier stared back at her, thinking rapidly. Then he smiled victoriously and sauntered over to her, meeting her eyes through the tangle of brush that resembled the bars of a prison. He lifted a finger and brushed her nose in a patronizing stroke. "Matalia, you know I do not kiss. Why would you even ask?"

She felt her face crack, but she steadfastly maintained a smile. While shivering in fear, she pretended to blink demurely. "I was simply hoping . . . that perhaps today you would make an exception."

Xanthier twisted his lips and stared down at her. "I have told you, I will never kiss. If you truly knew me, you would know that."

"Aye," Matalia replied, a thread of strength infusing her words as she pulled away from the tangled branches. "I know you."

Xanthier nodded appreciatively, missing her true meaning. Matalia listened as he piled on more snow, then built a second fire outside to melt the snow into what would soon form a crust of solid ice. She was trapped.

Chapter 26

Brogan was jerked awake by the haunting sound of Matalia crying in the wind. He leaned over, searching for her in the bed, but her warmth was missing. He fell back into his pillow and tried to close his eyes, but the howling refrain drifted through the windows and made him stare sightlessly into the canopy above. He cursed the sound, still angry from his last conversation with Matalia, and turned over to bury his face beneath the pillow.

A shaft of pain ripped through Brogan, and he flung the pillow aside and paced rapidly to the window. He stared down to the meadow as he had many a night, searching for evidence of Matalia, but found none. A storm was brewing and its early snow flurries obscured his vision. The wolfhound whined and joined him at the window. Brogan absently stroked his head, listening to the agitated sounds of the wolves in the far distance. With sudden decision, he spun around and pulled on his clothes.

Brogan raced down the stairs, urgency pumping in his blood. He stopped at the base of the tower, seeing a trickle of red upon the rushes leading to the guest chambers. Dread welled inside of him and he walked forward, his breath held tightly within his chest.

He pulled his sword and swiftly walked toward the guest chamber, following the thin trail of blood. The wolfhound barked at the kitchen door, but Brogan ignored him. His entire attention was focused on the droplets of red that led to Soothebury's room. Using his sword to open the door, Brogan beheld a rivulet of blood upon the bedding. His heart froze as he lifted his eyes to the hank of exquisitely curled and sumptuously displayed black hair upon the pillow. His mouth opened and his entire soul trembled with horror.

Brogan howled. His anger and pain ripped through the castle like a hurricane destroying a glade of butterflies. He fell to his knees, his hands gripping the shorn locks, and screamed louder than the banshees. The wolfhound abandoned his stance at the kitchen door and cowered in terror. The fire tender woke from his forced slumber and retreated into the dark recesses of the cabinets, petrified of the beast that moaned in pain within Kirkcaldy's walls.

The Earl rose from his lonely bed and looked for the specter of death, certain his Maker had finally come to call for his miserable soul. Isadora stared into the darkness of her own room, thankful that another suffered as she felt more contractions ripple through her misshapen body. She joined the unearthly howl with a scream of her own.

Within moments, the castle was ablaze. All men-at-arms rushed to the great hall, and servants assembled behind them. The Earl recovered, and he pulled on a robe and joined the crowd, searching for the source of the screams. Within moments, he and several others located Brogan in the guest chambers, clutching Matalia's bloodied locks.

Brogan spun around, his eyes haunted. He located the shocked face of the Earl. "They killed her! They murdered her! Not a Soothebury soul will survive," he promised. "I will destroy them all!" He stood for a moment, daring the Earl to contradict him, but his father said nothing. With an imperceptible nod, Brogan strode past him and raced to the tower to collect his implements of war. As he strapped on his sword and donned his thick leather vest, he carefully placed Matalia's lock of hair through his belt and secured it with a turquoise ribbon he located still dangling from the canopy. He rubbed the ribbon for a moment, recalling how the room had looked that one afternoon, and a shiver of emotion rushed through him. His nose flared as he lifted the ribbon to his face and found her scent.

Jaimie soon joined him, and they rapidly descended the stairs and collected the men. Within the hour, they rode out of the bailey and thundered through the dark snow ready to wage revenge upon the unsuspecting Soothebury clan that ambled slowly toward their home. Vaguely Brogan was aware of his wolfhound's agitated barks, but in his fury, Brogan ignored him. When the canine tried to jump at his horse, Brogan kicked out, sending the large dog sprawling in the snow with an outraged yip. Even the uncharacteristically cruel behavior toward his dog did not burn off Brogan's fog of rage. An overwhelming sense of urgency drove him, and he urged his horse faster, pushing his strong legs to plow through the snowdrifts as another shaft of misery whispered through his consciousness.

The nightglow shifted, became gray in the wintry predawn. Brogan pushed on, aware that his horse trembled with fatigue but nevertheless urging him on. The company fell behind as Jaimie kept the men at a slower, more reasonable pace. Brogan dismissed Jaimie's advice to proceed with caution. Soon he was far ahead of the army.

Within the hour, he topped an isolated mountaintop. The morning twilight made shapes into ephemeral shadows and caused distances to loom inconsistently. It was as gray as fog and just as confusing, although the only true mist came from the nostrils of the heaving steed.

Brogan's vision filled with a strange water, and his

throat constricted. He blinked and rubbed the back of his hand across his eyes while squeezing them tight. When he opened them again he glimpsed a series of wagons down the hillside for a moment before they disappeared into the mist.

Oddly, he pulled up, pausing. He rubbed his eyes again, trying to remove the film of tears that kept returning. He dropped his head and shuddered. Matalia . . . Matalia. He searched for her in his soul, yet found nothing of her essence coming from the wagons ahead. No returning connection from his desperate and silent search. He lifted his gaze and looked around, recognizing the gray desolation that followed him in his dreams, yet not hearing the soft sound of her melody soothing him. No woman materialized and walked toward him. No Matalia joined him and touched his face to brush away the tears.

Instead, a cold wind swept around him and tossed snow into his face. Brogan instantly hardened his heart, his face closing and his eyes narrowing. Unconsciously echoing his brother's words, he spoke aloud, "It is time."

He kicked his warhorse, and the brave steed set out again, picking its way down the hill, using the wagon ruts as much as possible. As Brogan forced the horse closer and no echo of Matalia's spirit reached him, Brogan felt his insides get colder until he was just as frozen inside as the world outside. He pulled his sword and lifted its shimmery blade in front of his face, looking at his distorted reflection. The blade glimmered with frost, but Brogan welcomed its warmth in comparison to the frigid iciness of life without Matalia. He lowered it and pulled it slowly, shallowly over his arm. A flow of blood swelled, then spilled over and dripped onto his thigh where Matalia's hair rested. His bright blood mingled with the tresses and unbeknownst to him, mingled as well with the blood of his brother.

Then he slid off the exhausted horse and crept forward.

Brogan saw the flair of a lantern in the second conveyance and saw the silhouette of a woman through the canvas. He angled his approach and noted the location of Soothebury in the first wagon as well as the tired and cold outriders that rode with fur hoods covering their faces. He smiled grimly and, hugging the gray shadow of the vehicle, he snuck up to Clarise's wagon. Carefully gripping the wooden edge, he swung up and under the canvas flap with sword drawn.

Clarise started and looked at the infuriated face of one of the Earl's sons. Seeing the foul twist in his lips and chin, Clarise held her hand out in fear as if her fragile fingers could ward off his evil intentions.

As Brogan lifted the sword to the side, Clarise saw the drying blood upon his arm. She shook her head frantically, suddenly realizing his murderous goal. "Lord Xanthier!" she gasped, incorrectly guessing his identity, for such putrid hate she associated with Xanthier and not with Brogan. "We have peace!" she gasped, pointing to a scroll lying in a silk basket at her feet as she scrambled backward. But Brogan was in midswing and the sword grazed Clarise's delicate throat, cutting deeply.

Through his maddened haze, Brogan heard her choked gasp and blood well up as she desperately attempted to stanch the flow with her hands.

"Your family murdered Matalia! I will have your blood in return!" He raised his sword again.

Clarise stared up at him, her mouth open in shock, as she frantically shook her head. "No," she gasped. "We would never hurt her!"

Spying the document Clarise had pointed to, he drove the tip of his sword into the floorboards and lifted it. His gaze swept down the page to the signature at the bottom. Then he read it again in horror. He started to shake, and he looked at the Clarise in despair.

She lay upon the furs where she had fainted, the steady flow of blood swiftly draining her. Leaning down, he ripped part of her nightgown into a strip and wrapped it tightly around her neck in an attempt to slow the blood loss. He clutched the scroll and felt himself breathing, panting, hyperventilating in the gloom. He stared down at Clarise's pale cheeks and felt sick for what he had done.

"Stop!" he shouted. "Stop the wagons!" As his cries attracted attention, he knelt beside Clarise and rubbed her wrists. "Lady Clarise, I have wronged you terribly. Please . . ."

Distantly he heard Soothebury call out to his daughter, inquiring, then sounding more urgent. Brogan leaped up and spared one agonized glance at Soothebury as the man entered the wagon. Soothebury glanced at him in surprise, and they stared at each other for a millisecond that seemed to last for eons before Soothebury's gaze fell to his daughter's white face.

"Clarise!" he cried. "My baby? My baby! What have you done to her?"

Clarise's eyes fluttered open and she stared up, locating her father's visage. "Father," she whispered. " 'Twas a mistake. Please do not harm him. He acted only out of love."

"I will kill you!" Soothebury raged as he drew his own sword, facing Brogan.

Brogan felt detached, sickened, ill with remorse. He faced Soothebury without defense, willing to accept his punishment for attacking an innocent woman.

"Father," Clarise said again, her voice stronger. "Do not make this worse. Leave him be. He thought we had taken Matalia. She must be in danger. Let him go to her and help her. They love each other. Please, Father. I will survive. Let him go."

"Xanthier . . ." Brogan whispered, facing Soothebury. "This was arranged by Xanthier. He knew I would come after you and seek revenge. He manipulated us. . . . He forced me to act the worst kind of man." Brogan shook his head in disbelief. "No longer, Xanthier. No longer will this be between us."

Then, from inside his head he heard her soft melody. He felt her warmth sweep over his face and touch his forehead, caressing him, calming him. She loved him, forgave him, understood him. Brogan trembled with self-revulsion, but the sickness was soothed by the song, and he became light-headed as if a huge weight had been lifted from his chest. It was not important anymore. Kirkcaldy was not important.

And meanwhile, his Matalia was now vulnerable. She was unprotected, and the blood of vengeance that had swept unthinkingly through Brogan was the same blood that sludged through the fetid heart of Xanthier. Brogan reached out into the air just as he often did in his dream, but unlike in the midnight visions, this time his fingers connected with something. His sword.

His fingers curled around the warm hilt without thought, and he pulled it free from the wood with a fierce tug. Xanthier's bold stroke at the bottom of the scroll mocked him. The black curls at his waist had tricked him. He had almost killed an innocent woman because of the manipulating hands of his twin, because of their quest to inherit Kirkcaldy. It was time to end the fight.

Chapter 27

Isadora screamed, flinging anything within her reach at Xanthier's head. Her face was mottled and flushed, and her hair hung in greasy strings across her forehead. He did not attempt to hide his revulsion. He strode over to her and gripped her flailing arm and shoved it hard against the mattress. "All you have to do is bear me a son. Other than that, I care naught if you die in labor. In fact, I would welcome it, so do not tempt me to hasten your return to your Maker." His snarled comments drew gasps of distress from the attending midwife and her assistant. Isadora's eyes were wide and spitting with hate.

"You fool! Do you think I would leave myself so vulnerable to you? If I do die, or am banished like the last countess, I have left instructions for a letter to be read publicly. And can you guess what the letter contains?" She jerked her hand out of Xanthier's hold and propped herself up on an elbow to glare triumphantly at him. "It states that the child is not of your seed. So it appears that you should pray for my safe delivery."

Xanthier's left nostril lifted and wrinkled as if the stink of decay had reached him. With an oath he leaned over her again, but forbore to touch her sweaty skin. "You know the child is mine."

"It will not matter. Once doubt has been cast, the Earl will choose Brogan. He already favors him."

"He favors me!" Xanthier shouted and raised a fist, slamming it into the pillow a hairbreadth from her face. The women in the room screamed and fled from the room, but Isadora hardly flinched. She stared up at him smugly and shook her straggly hair out of her face. Calming, Xanthier composed his expression and spoke again in a controlled voice. "I wish only that I had found Matalia first. She is a wife worthy of an Earl."

Isadora gasped and struggled to rise, but the midwife rushed forward and pushed her back, admonishing her about the baby's safety. "What qualities do you think that witch possesses that makes her so valuable? She is nothing more than an enchantress with a cold heart!"

Xanthier shook his head. "I think not. But it does not matter anymore. Matalia is gone."

Isadora was silent, noting Xanthier's wet clothing and tousled hair. Softly, pushing the attendants away, she asked him, "What have you done? Where is Soothebury?"

"You need not know the details. Suffice it to say, Brogan is starting a feud that is completely unprovoked while his wife and child perish in the elements. I will be left with everything."

"We."

"Indeed, my mistake. *We,* we will be left with Kirkcaldy, and Brogan will be banished, or better yet, imprisoned for his foul deeds on this night. There is a signed peace agreement that he just broke. No one will ever believe his word again. He will be considered the lowest of all men. A man without honor."

" 'Tis amusing, is it not," Isadora murmured, "that the truly dishonorable brother will be rewarded?"

Xanthier glared at her, her comment unexpectedly blistering. Then another contraction contorted her face, and he left the room without responding.

The hours dragged on, and the screams from the

upstairs tower filtered over every activity, drifted through everyone's peace like a spirit haunting the Highlands. The Earl stood at the front door, letting the deep cold swirl into the castle as he watched the road for Brogan's return. The image of Matalia's bloodied hair was etched in his memory, and he felt her possible loss more acutely than he would have imagined. His old brain pondered the events of his life, leading to the confrontation last night. He was stunned that things had changed so quickly, that Soothebury would kidnap and possibly harm Matalia after promising to sleep on the matter. But a lifetime of mistrust made him calloused, and he did not doubt the events that had enfolded.

Xanthier watched him from a chair near the fire, and his brooding eyes monitored the increasing concern on his father's face for Brogan and Matalia's absence. Brogan's wolfhound sat next to the Earl, staring down the snow-covered hill from whence he knew his master would return. Just beyond the gates, their shadows backlit against the snow, three wolves ranged, their movements agitated. They alternately sat and howled, calling in wolf song for something the Earl could not decipher.

An old servant handed the Earl a fur wrap. The Earl looked at him with a certain fondness. He had been a boy when the Earl had been a child, decades earlier. Now they stood as two old men together, and the Earl sighed.

"What do you think makes the wolves act so oddly? Are they ill?" the Earl asked.

"They are the wolves of Lady Matalia," the old servant replied.

"Ahhh. The wolves of the Lady Matalia. I did not know she had such fine wild animals under her care."

"Perhaps she is under theirs."

The Earl was silent, staring out over the snow. The

old servant rubbed his chin and stared with the Earl, but could find no answer to his simple question. The daylight shifted, changed, lengthened, became afternoon. Soon one wolf left, then another, until only the black remained, his black fur stark against the white snow. The old servant drifted away, finished a chore, collected hot cider and brought it back to the Earl.

Isadora's screams were softer now, hoarser and coming at regular intervals. One of the assistants raced down the stairs, announced the crowning of the infant, and then ran back up.

The Earl glanced back at Xanthier, who rose slowly. In a low voice, he addressed his father. "I have won. My child is coming forth, your first grandchild. I should be named as the heir."

"We know not the fate of Matalia. You will wait for me to decide to name you or not."

"You can delay only so long. It has been close to thirty years. It is time to decide the matter."

"I will not be pushed!" the Earl thundered. "We wait until Brogan arrives."

"I see him, my lord. Lord Brogan on his steed comes over the hill," the older servant interjected just as a scream shattered the air and a midwife's cry of encouragement filled the rafters. Xanthier looked over the Earl's shoulder and peered out, straining to pick up the black smudge that moved slowly forward. Suddenly the black wolf spun around and spied it as well. The canine set off like a black streak, his neck and tail low to the ground.

Brogan glanced up, seeing the white walls of Kirkcaldy rise above the snowy expanse. A wolf raced toward him. Brogan recognized it as Matalia's darkest companion and quickened his horse's pace. The worry in his heart swirled, overwhelmed him, and he desperately tried to swim through the thickness of emotions that drove him.

Brogan's horse shifted in fear and snorted when the wolf reached them. The black canine twisted and growled, showing his teeth. He spun in circles and yipped. Brogan watched his unusual antics with high anxiety. Then, with fear racing through his soul, he kicked his horse into a dangerously fast gallop toward Kirkcaldy Castle.

As Brogan thundered through the icy bailey, the wolf was joined by the wolfhound and the pair flanked the horse's sides. He drew the warhorse to an abrupt halt and leaped off him. The huge gray wolfhound and the black wolf mirrored Brogan's steely eyes and midnight hair, and the tense fury in his face was echoed in the silent snarls of the beasts. Xanthier stood in the doorway, his bulk blocking the entrance. Beside him, suddenly seeming small and insignificant, leaned the Earl.

"You are not allowed here, brother," sneered Xanthier as he took a threatening step forward.

"Where is she?" Brogan replied, ignoring the threat. Then he froze, hearing the cry of a woman in labor.

Xanthier smiled cruelly. "Isadora labors. My child will be born first."

Brogan's face hardened, and he stared intently at Xanthier. He repeated as if he were speaking to a child, "Keep Kirkcaldy. Just tell me where she is. Where is Matalia?"

"What does it matter, brother? I have won. Matalia is gone. You should thank me, for now you are free."

"Gone?" Brogan replied, dumbfounded. "What do you mean?"

"Exactly what I said. You lost. The inheritance is mine. Forget about the woman and leave here."

Brogan stared at Xanthier, feeling a wealth of emotions spin and stir within him. He did not want to be free of her. He did not want to leave without her. But a certain lightness did sweep over him. He was free. He was free of the ambition that had driven his life. He was free of the yolk of Kirkcaldy. Peripherally he saw the black wolf sit back, place his ears flat against his skull and start a low, mournful howl. Brogan felt dizzy. He swayed upon the step. He felt her. He needed to get to her.

Xanthier stepped forward again, pushing his chest against Brogan's. Brogan fell back, still light-headed. "I won. Leave," Xanthier repeated. Gray eyes clashed with gray. Then there was a whisper of steel, and blade met blade.

"I will leave after I find her," Brogan said in measured tones. His mind cleared and he felt his love for Matalia warm his soul. He wanted, needed to be by her side. He wanted to feel her rounded body flush against his own. He needed her exquisite eyes staring truthfully into his heart. He needed her brilliance, her fire, her passion . . . her love. He had been blind. Blind and thoughtless. He should have told her that the beating of her heart drove his own, for without her, he would cease to live. The inheritance did not matter. The competition with Xanthier did not matter. Only Matalia did.

"You will never find her," Xanthier answered as he raised his sword and touched Brogan's blade with a soft ting of metal against metal.

Brogan's answer was swift and hard. He twisted his wrist and lunged, slamming the flat of his blade against Xanthier's hand. Xanthier gasped and fell back, his hand trembling as it barely retained its grip on his sword. Brogan pushed forward, slicing a neat mark upon Xanthier's face, just at his jawline. Instant blood welled from the mark and dribbled down his neck. Brogan pulled back, glaring. "Just tell me what I want to know, brother, and I will leave you to this pile of rocks."

Slowly at first, then more quickly, servants and men-at-arms were drawn to the courtyard steps where Xanthier and Brogan stood facing each other. Ripples of unease swept through the crowd as the faint cries of Lady Isadora reached them, and the people watched helplessly as fate unwound its plan in front of them. Xanthier would succeed. His wife would bear fruit first.

"Why should I tell you anything?" Xanthier hissed. He lunged back, his hand recovering strength with the flush of hatred in his veins. "She suffers even now from your uselessness! She is as abandoned as was I when you left Scotland."

Brogan parried, stalled, tried to sort through the tangled thoughts of his opponent. "You speak in circles," he responded, stepping to the side, reaching, then blocking as Xanthier suddenly attacked. "I left because I did not want to fight you."

"You were always the favorite, but now I have beaten you!" Xanthier's face contorted with rage and his free fist came up. "You spent your childhood with our mother while I was cast aside!"

Brogan's brows crashed down and a wave of inner anger infused him. "*You* were the favorite!" he shouted back. "I was held back while you were brought up in the castle as if you were already declared the eldest." He lunged at Xanthier, but his brother struck back and their swords vibrated against each other, hilt to hilt as the brothers crouched face-to-face. Except for the thin streak of blood upon Xanthier's jaw, their images were identical. Rage, hopelessness, confusion, fury . . . two men whose childhood wounds had festered into purulent abscesses of the soul.

Brogan pushed Xanthier back with a mighty heave and swung his sword, slicing through the meat of Xanthier's sword arm. The howl of the black wolf abruptly stopped, and far in the distance an answering pair of voices drifted on, filling the void. Brogan's inner wounds suddenly opened and drained, flushed clean with the clear disinfectant of Matalia's memory. He felt his anger wash away. Felt sorrow fill its place. He stepped forward, raising his sword and pressing it against Xanthier's bare throat. His twin stood against the mellow stones of Kirkcaldy, his head raised defiantly, blood pouring from his injured arm, his sword hanging uselessly in weakening fingers.

In the recess of his mind, Brogan understood that if he killed Xanthier now, he would win the Scottish fortune, the inheritance of Kirkcaldy. But more important, he would lose Matalia. He would lose himself. He would even lose that part of him that throbbed within Xanthier. He pulled back fractionally and stared at his twin with calm eyes. "Tell me where she is," he demanded softly.

Xanthier shivered with the force of his fury. He twitched but felt Brogan's blade touch his chest again. He glared like a cornered dog and gnashed his teeth until bits of spittle formed at the corners of his lips. Finally he leaned forward, into the steel and smiled furiously. "Remember when we were young, Brogan? Remember the caves that you feared? Remember the beasts that slumbered within them? I remember your fear. I remember the nightmares you had after I left you in one of those caverns."

Brogan felt icy dread infuse his spine and flashes of the dark caves whisked across his consciousness. He banished the fear, trampling it ruthlessly, yet a thin streak crept back up as Xanthier continued. "I put her there, Brogan. I put her in the dark. I put her in the dark and locked her in. She thought I was you, Brogan. She thinks that you left her to give birth alone. To die alone with her frozen infant in her arms."

"She would never believe that," Brogan countered, his voice confident.

"Why would she not? You have always made it clear that the inheritance comes first. She is clever. She will decipher that you lost and now wish to eliminate her. You never meant to marry her anyway, did you, brother?"

"No," Brogan answered truthfully.

"She knows that. You can see it in her eyes when she watches you. She knows you do not want her."

"I do want her." Brogan looked around at the assembled people, scanning until he found the Earl. His father looked at him sadly. When he slowly shook his head, Brogan repeated the phrase again, louder. "I do want her, and in her heart she knows that. She knows I would never leave her to harm."

"Just like you would never harm an innocent woman?" Xanthier taunted, and Brogan felt a wave of nausea as he recalled Clarise Soothebury.

"You deliberately turned me to them, knowing I would retaliate for the kidnapping of my wife." Brogan stared at his twin accusingly, swamped by remorse and anger equally. "You tried to get me to commit murder. But you did not succeed. Clarise lives, and everyone will know of your treachery."

Xanthier came down a final step and leaned closer, whispering, "You are so easy to manipulate. Your feelings for the woman make you weak."

Brogan took a step back as if singed. His face curled in disgust. "You are the fool, Xanthier. Now tell me where in the caves you left her, and my family will leave you to your personal misery."

Xanthier glowered and shook his head. He pointed behind him to the sounds of Isadora's labor. "I will tell you when she is done."

The Earl stepped forward, aghast. "She could be hours yet! Tell Brogan where the lady is. Matalia should not die for your greed! Too many people have been destroyed in this family. I was wrong about love. The power of it flows between Brogan and Matalia. I would not have him live in loneliness as I have done, as you will do if you do not change your ways. Tell him where he can find her."

Xanthier stared down at his father, his face impassive. Then he turned and walked up the stairs.

Brogan raced after him. "Brother," he said. "Why are you certain she mistook you for me?"

Xanthier stared at the great doors, not turning. Over his shoulder he finally replied, "She told me she loved me. She told me she trusted me. . . ." He paused, then added into the sudden silence, "And then she asked for a kiss." Xanthier turned slowly and smiled.

Brogan stared at him, his heart beating fast. "Did you kiss her?" he asked.

Xanthier smiled broader and shook his head. "I made that mistake once, brother. This time I refused her."

Brogan felt his head spin. He blinked slowly, recalling the mountaintop where he and Matalia had connected, lips to lips. He remembered the sweet surrender of her strong spirit and the sparkle in her brilliant eyes. He could even taste the beauty of her mouth. Xanthier was wrong. Matalia would know instantly. He loved to kiss her. More than anything, he loved to kiss her.

The black wolf stepped closer, brushing against his sword arm. Brogan looked down into the beast's wise eyes. Then, with a small salute to the Earl, he turned and left the castle grounds.

Chapter 28

Matalia doubled over as pain racked her body. She gripped the cavern rock until her knuckles were white. She panted as she sweated and shivered. The fire gave only meager warmth, so her skin was cold, but the cramps turned the inside of her body into a furnace. Beads of sweat rolled down her forehead, and she shook her head, then wiped her face with one hand and the contraction eased away. She was desperately afraid and overwhelmed with pain.

The early light made the icy wall glow, but the structure was strong and solid. No amount of pushing, chipping or shaking had budged it. Except for the small hole at the top, it was impenetrable.

She was beyond fearing Xanthier anymore. Earlier she had worried about Xanthier pretending to be Brogan, wondered what he intended to do to her. But her anxiety now centered on her abdomen, and she concentrated solely upon bringing her child safely into the world. She heard the wolves alternately howling on the other side of the barrier, and she leaned upon their nearness for spiritual strength. She blinked, hearing another sound in the depths of the cave, and she peered into the recesses, fearing the wild beasts that inhabited the caverns.

She stood laboriously and stumbled closer to the fire. She threw a few more pieces of wood upon it and let the flare of bright light briefly illuminate the stone chamber. A flash of red eyes deep within the cave stared back at her for an instant, then disappeared. Matalia fought a moan from coming forth, and she positioned herself between the weakening fire and the icy wall.

Then another contraction built, and her fear slipped away, replaced by pain. This time she moaned aloud, not caring what heard her. She glared into the darkness and threw her desperation into rage. She screamed at the cavern beast, daring it to come forward. Her short black curls danced around her face and reflected madly against the cave walls as she shook her fists and cried out for help.

Brogan pushed his weary horse through the snow, up the hill and into the mountains where the caves dotted the landscape. His wolfhound paced alongside, barely standing upon the crust. Occasionally his large frame broke through, and he would scramble while he tried to climb back onto the surface of the snow. The black wolf whispered ahead of them both, his light body skimming along easily. He ran with his nose low to the ground, then stopped and lifted his muzzle while pricking his ears forward. As they ascended the hillside, his tail began to lift and brush from side to side in sway with his stride. Far ahead, the wolf song of his pack mates led them forward.

Soon the horse faltered, then shivered to a slow halt. Brogan leaned down, encouraging him, but the steed hung his head and refused to plow through the snow any farther. Brogan looked ahead, noting the sun peeking through the clouds. The sense of urgency that had driven him climbed with each inch of the sun's path. He shifted his sword and twisted around to grasp the buckle of his saddlebag. From its depths he pulled a pair of greased leather guards, which he tied around his lower calves, making the snow less likely to fill his boots as soon as he took a step. He then wrapped a fur skin around one shoulder and underneath the alternate arm, leaving his fighting arm free for rapid movement. Finally he pulled forth a small bag of provisions and looped it over his neck. The black wolf whined at the delay, but Brogan carefully checked his supplies again. It would do no good if he found her but could not help her. At last, he swung off the horse's back and dropped deep into the snow.

As he trudged forward, he tried to remember his childhood rambles in the dark caves without succumbing to fear. He did not want to let his fear of the dark hinder his search. Today, he vowed, today his past was behind him, for now he needed to find the woman of his future.

An hour of walking seemed like an eternity, but finally he reached the larger caves and the sound of the other wolves came to him clearly. His heart thudding, he pushed through a snow-laden set of pines and found a set of sled tracks, several human footprints, and numerous wolf tracks. Fighting to keep his voice calm, he called out.

"Matalia? Matalia!" he shouted as he followed the tracks. Hearing no answer, he focused on the snow, seeing the path lead up and to the right. Almost immediately, a series of yips and barks answered his call, and the black wolf darted forward. The Irish wolfhound growled deep in his throat and hugged up against Brogan.

"Matalia?" he called again, hurrying onward. Just as he rounded the right-hand curve, he saw a dark brown shape lumber forward. Glancing up, he had only a second to perceive the rearing form of a brown bear before a sudden strike to his head resulted in splintering pain and sudden blackness.

The wolfhound darted forward, snapping his jaws

at the enraged beast. The bear turned from Brogan's prostrate form and swung again, this time at the wiry canine. The wolfhound leaped out of its way, but then collapsed through the snow crust and floundered.

As the bear crashed down on all fours and lumbered toward the wolfhound, the three wolves circled him, sneaking forward and taunting him. Distracted once again, the bear turned and swatted the snow. A pile of white coldness whistled through the air, then crashed against the branches of the nearby pine trees. More snow cascaded down, sprinkling Brogan's face with its wetness.

He stirred, feeling dizzy but gaining alertness. Opening his eyes slowly, he felt an enormous pounding in his temples, and he breathed slowly through his mouth to diffuse the pain. He tried to sit up, but fell back as the shadow of the infuriated bear brushed over him. The bear turned, seeing his movement, and plodded the few steps it took to confront him.

Brogan pulled his sword, waving it carefully as the bear fixated upon its glinting surface. Then, without warning, the bear lunged forward. Brogan braced his blade, waiting for the impact. The wolfhound turned and sprang at the same time. The wolves converged, their teeth snapping as they ducked underneath the beast and bit its legs, trying to rip its tendons.

The bear rotated, checked its momentum, and swung out at the wolfhound. Its massive paw connected and sent the large dog flying, but one of the wolves bit deep, tearing and ripping, and maimed the bear. The beast dropped down on its forefeet, forgetting the man and sword that stood beneath his chest, and plunged down upon the blade.

The bear roared, reared back up, but Brogan scrambled forward, shoving the blade deep into the bear's heart. The beast roared louder, sudden pain making it oblivious to anything around it. Its eyes rolled and it shuddered, trying to dislodge the sword, spraying the snow with blood.

Brogan abruptly released the sword, leaving it embedded in the bear's chest cavity. He stumbled back, ducking the bear's swing. One of the wolves leaped between man and beast, flashing his red tail, snarling at the dying bear as it fell forward again, embedding the sword deeper.

The beast screamed with rage. Blood filled its mouth and nose, and it shook its head, showering more droplets. A softer growl came from its throat, a *wuff,* and it leaned to the side to avoid pressing its weight on the steel. It rocked its head again, confused, and its beady eyes peered out at the animals ranged against it. Then, slowly, majestically, it fell to its side and took several brief, wet, agonizing breaths.

Brogan carefully approached, keeping well clear of the bear's reach. He watched the beast's eyes roll and glaze. Then, gripping the blade firmly, Brogan yanked it free and stepped back quickly. The bear tried to heave itself upright, but a whistle of air cut its efforts short as its lungs caved in. Almost immediately, Brogan raised his sword again and plunged it in, right behind the bear's elbow and deep into its bleeding heart.

Matalia braced herself and stood up. She cocked her head, listening intently. Her wolves were barking, but her tired and frightened mind also conjured up Brogan's voice, and she strained to see if it was her imagination. When she heard a second call, she shouted in relief, but just as the sound left her lips she heard the ghastly roar of a bear on the other side of the ice wall. She screamed again, terrified, ripping at the branches that formed her prison, pounding at the solid ice that cemented them together until her nails broke and bled and her fingers swelled.

Matalia doubled over, clinging to the her side of the barrier. Tears streamed down her face as she listened to the fight between Brogan and the bear. She fought against the contractions ripping at her insides, and plaintively begged them to stop so she could focus on Brogan's plight. She tried to call out to her husband, but her weak cries could not penetrate the raucous sounds of fighting. Leaning against the frozen blockage, she heard the furious roars of the cave beast, and they filled her with terror. In addition to the beast outside, she feared the animals within, for deep within her cave she saw the red glowing eyes become more agitated as the roars outside became louder.

She felt an overwhelming urge to push the baby forth, and she crouched, panting, her mouth and eyes wide open. Nature would not stop. The birth would not wait. Desperately trying to survive, she struggled to find a burning stick and she grasped it, digging her fingers into its singed bark, not feeling the heat of it reddening her frozen hands. The eyes in the back of the cave turned and another, smaller pair joined them. Matalia gasped, unable to slow the labor, and she squeezed her lids together as she gave in to pushing. For her, the world collapsed into a tiny pinpoint centered entirely upon the infant inside her. She pushed, feeling the beat of its heart take on its own pattern. She pushed, feelings its soul making demands she was destined to fulfill.

Outside, panting from his own exertions, Brogan shuddered at the sight of the great beast dying on the snow. He felt immense sorrow at the loss of such a creature, and as he pulled his sword free once again he bowed his head with respect. Then, gaining strength, he approached the man-made barrier of wood and ice.

"Matalia?" he called out again, slightly out of breath. "Are you all right?"

Matalia felt the contraction subside, and she heard Brogan's voice next to her head. She smiled and nodded, forgetting he could not see her until he called out again. With effort she raised her voice to reply. "Brogan? I am . . . I need you now. . . ."

"I am coming, my love. I am coming. Hold on." He grinned weakly with relief and set about hacking at the ice. Matalia felt the prison wall shake, and she crawled away from it, circling the dwindling fire. Just as a few pieces of ice began to fall, she heard a *wuff* from the cave depths, and she looked up in horror.

In front of her a great black shape materialized. Its fur was long and bristly and the tips glowed faintly in the firelight, casting a halo around its immense shape. A rich, pungent odor wafted from the beast, and Matalia gagged. The shape took form and she crouched on all fours in front of an enormous female brown bear. The bear opened her jaws, scrunched her nose, and tilted her head sideways as she rumbled a warning roar.

Brogan froze, hearing the sound from inside the cave. He turned swiftly, noting the still, prostrate bear he had killed, and then turned back and stared at the wall. Frenzied now, he hacked at the ice, afraid to call out and terrified he would be too late.

Matalia lay on her side, unable to escape. Her distended abdomen clenched, and she closed her eyes, not moving. She felt a rush of warm air wash over her face as the bear leaned over her, smelling her. The scent of blood and fluids, birth and sweat, filled the nostrils of the female bear, and she rocked back and forth on her front paws. Matalia lay between her feet. As she opened her eyes in resignation, she looked at the wicked claws in front of her and sighed. The contractions did not hurt as much now. She stopped fighting them, and they suddenly flowed through her, firmly but lovingly. She gave in and welcomed them. It was time to give birth.

The bear *wuffed* again and looked at the crumbling wall. The smell of smoke was strong, for the fire had just flickered out, but her ability to smell was even more powerful than her eyesight. She smelled the rancid blood of death, and the alarming scent of man and wolfhound. She sensed the familiar scents of the three wolves, but noted their anxiety. A sudden movement from the woman at her feet drew her attention again and she growled softly, warningly.

Matalia let herself float. She heard Brogan swing franticly against the ice. . . . She heard the perturbed sounds of her wolves as they dug alongside her husband. She heard the low growl of the bear above her and the answering noise of a second, smaller bear hidden deeper within the cave. Without conscious thought, she began to sing.

The bear jerked her head straight. She stopped rocking and strained to listen to the new sound. Matalia lifted her husky voice into pure tones of melody. She let the sounds find their own way through her chest and into her throat to fill the cave with musical echoes.

She emptied her mind and sang to her new baby. She sang for the sorrow between the Earl and Ansleen and for the joy in her parents' home. She sang of the ecstasy of human touch and the peace of omnipotent love. She lifted her voice to include the beasts of the caves, the wild wolves of the mountains, the powerful beasts of burden that faithfully lived to serve. She sang for Brogan and all that he had given her . . . her freedom, her maturity, her faith in healing, her child.

Then suddenly the bear was gone and Brogan was beside her as sunlight flooded the cave. He gripped her tightly and his body's warmth seeped into her cold limbs. She pushed, because her body demanded it, and squeezed his arm for support. Beside her she felt rather than heard his whispered words of encouragement, and she let herself relax once more before she gave it her focused effort.

A warm fur was wrapped around her, and the fire blazed to life. Then the contraction rippled through her and she screamed. Brogan held her, and she screamed again, not in pain, although it hurt, not in fear, although she was frightened, but in joy, because she was flooded with beautiful emotion.

Brogan clutched the baby as it came forth, his hands shaking with awe as he pulled the slippery infant into his arms. Stunned, not sure what to do, he felt the wolves surround him and lick the baby as they crooned softly to the infant in wolf song.

"Oh my love . . . Oh my love . . ." he repeated, and Matalia smiled into the cavern's dim interior, for she could not decipher if he spoke to the baby or to her. She held out her hands, and Brogan gave her the child. Under her direction, he helped her cut the cord, clean the child, wrap it and cuddle it. "A boy?" he asked as if she could answer the question better than he when he turned to rebuild the fire.

She grinned and nodded. "A boy," she repeated softly. He suddenly looked fierce, and he glared around the cave, searching. Matalia laid a hand on his shoulder and pulled him back. "It is all right now." She lifted her fingers to stroke his face. "You are hurt," she murmured, but Brogan shook his head.

"It is nothing. Are you? What do you need? Can I wash you?"

Matalia sighed, and the last of the fluids drained out of her as she leaned back against the furs. She grimaced, embarrassed, but Brogan used the pan to melt snow and tore a piece of cloth off his shirt and gently wiped her inner thighs. Matalia relaxed and unlaced her bodice. She stared down at her new baby, mesmerized by his blue-green eyes. "I do not think babies are supposed to be so quiet," she finally stated, making Brogan look up with concern.

He dropped the cloth and peered at the baby. The infant was staring back at Matalia, his red face wrinkled and covered with a fine, white fuzz. His lips were pursed, and he opened his mouth like a bird asking for a worm. He had a brush of fine black curls on his head. Both parents watched his steady, even breaths. The baby watched Matalia's clear turquoise eyes. He lifted a tiny fist and batted her cheek. A brilliant smile spread over Matalia's face, and she shifted him carefully to her bared breast.

Brogan flushed, nervous, and turned back to his ministrations. "He seems to be doing the normal things," Brogan murmured.

Matalia gasped as his small mouth found her nipple and latched on.

Brogan looked up, frowning. "Are you sure?"

"Sure about what?"

"About . . ." He waved at the baby and her, keeping his head lowered.

"Come here," she whispered.

"I should leave you," he replied, rising.

"Come here!" Matalia insisted. Brogan paused, flicking a glance at her and biting the inside of his cheek. He knelt down and studiously avoided looking at the nursing babe. "Are you shy? Have you never seen a baby feeding before?" she asked.

"No," Brogan answered honestly.

"You can watch," she said soothingly. "It is fine. I used to watch my mother with my sisters."

Brogan looked up nervously. The infant's eyes were still open, and his gaze remained trained upon Matalia. Brogan stared at the sight, transfixed. He slowly lifted a strong hand and gently caressed the babe's face, then let his fingers drift to stroke the upper swell of Matalia's breast. He raised his eyes and met hers while gradually lifting his free hand to her temple, where he stroked her shorn curls. He threaded his fingers through her hair at the back of her head and pulled her slowly to him.

"Your hair . . ." he whispered.

"Are you angry?"

"No, my love. I don't care about your hair or your face. It is you whom I love."

Matalia leaned forward, her eyes half closing, and surrendered to his lips.

He took her firmly but leisurely, as if he would kiss her forever. His body carefully protected the nursing infant while his lips devoured her mouth. He pressed a lifetime of love into his actions, trying to tell her how he felt, trying to show her how much she meant to him. He pulled back for a moment and kissed her closed eyelids, then drifted down to kiss her nose, her throat. As Matalia's eyes opened, he bent his head and kissed her swelling breast and then the black curls of their son.

The baby's mouth was slightly open, but his eyes were shut and he breathed deeply in slumber. Matalia smiled and carefully pulled away from Brogan's hold to shift the baby, laying him on the fur. After seeing him peacefully placed, she turned back toward her husband and opened her arms. Brogan gratefully settled next to her and the child. He turned his back to the coldness outside and bent his large frame around them both, letting Matalia use his arm as a pillow.

"I thought you had been murdered. I attacked Soothebury and almost killed Clarise. Perhaps my soul is as black as Xanthier's."

"Does she live?"

"Aye."

"Do you have any more misunderstandings between you?"

"No. Soothebury is a generous man. I would not have forgiven so easily."

"Then, shush. You are a good man, and I love you."

She turned on her side with a sigh and quickly joined the babe in relaxed sleep as her breaths slowed and a small snore escaped her nose. Brogan smiled, nuzzling her neck. He felt the warm bodies of the wolves curl up behind him and saw the huge shadow of the wolfhound sitting guard outside. His eyes remained open, but his thoughts meandered lazily. He felt safe. He felt happy.

Chapter 29

An hour later, Matalia shivered despite the sense of feeling overwhelmingly hot. She opened her eyes and located the outline of her child. She pulled him closer, placing him to her breast, and then let the lassitude sweep over her again, and she slept on. As the day changed to night, Brogan left for minutes at a time only to collect wood and skin the massive bear lying in the snow.

He cut the meat, unwilling to waste such a precious commodity. Using his sword and a strong branch, he dug a hole and buried most of the meat, setting aside a small portion in anticipation of Matalia's hunger. He spent some time scraping the hide, feeling that the bearskin symbolized his conquering of the beasts that raged inside him. He rolled the unfinished skin and returned to the cave. As Matalia continued to sleep, he noticed the baby's eyes watching him as he roasted the meat and he smiled shyly in return. The baby lifted his arms and waved them, then scrunched his face and started to cry.

"Well, it seems you have a voice after all," Brogan replied, and looked over to the sleeping woman. When she did not respond to the infant's cries, he frowned and peered down at her. He looked around as if expecting someone to be watching, then squatted next to the child with concern. "Your mother is still sleeping. What do you want?"

The baby quieted and stared up at Brogan. In awe, Brogan reached out and picked him up, being very careful to support his head and neck. The infant blinked several times and stared. Brogan stared back. Deep within his soul, too deep to verbalize, Brogan knew that as of this moment, he was forever changed. His life was now dedicated to another. He was bound to protect and cherish a small, living creature. The conflict between him and Xanthier seemed incredibly trivial. His anger at his mother seemed inconsequential. Here, in his arms, was the truth. Here, beside him, was his wife. This was what life was about, not seeking riches or power or fortune. Sitting next to Matalia and holding their son was all he wanted.

When morning came, Matalia still slumbered. Her forehead was hot and she shifted restlessly. Brogan had clumsily learned to clean the baby and had positioned him for feeding several times, but now Brogan stared down at his wife with growing concern. Despite her flushed face, she seemed pale. He nudged her shoulder, but she simply flung out an arm to ward him away and slept on. When the wolves bumped her with their noses and whined, Brogan became seriously worried.

"Matalia," he murmured, quietly at first, then louder.

She flicked her eyes open for a moment and stared at him with confusion. "Thirsty . . ." she whispered. "My baby?"

"Here," Brogan replied, giving her some water. "The baby is fine, but I am worried about you. Is this normal?" Her eyes drifted shut, but Brogan spoke to her harshly and she grudgingly opened them again. "Is this normal?" he repeated. "You seem ill. You are feverish, and you have been sleeping for a long time."

Matalia drew her brows together and peered up hazily. She shook her head and then gave up the struggle to communicate. She slipped back into sleep, simply clutching Brogan's hand in response.

Brogan felt his heart stop, and for several seconds he found it hard to breathe. He looked at the infant nestled trustingly in his arms and at the beautiful woman sleeping fitfully at his feet.

"God, no," he breathed. "God, please no!" Suddenly, he was galvanized into action. The wolves leaped out of his way as he swiftly gathered his things and fashioned a sling to carry the baby. He tied the rolled bearskin onto the saddle and tucked the other fur around Matalia's limp form, then carried her in his arms out to the horse that he had found and tended earlier. He swung up on the rested stallion and carefully arranged his helpless family. Without thought, he headed the assemblage down the hillside, past the caverns, toward Kirkcaldy.

One of the guards spotted the odd group and called a warning down to the gate. By the time Brogan and the canines reached the bailey, Xanthier stood with sword drawn, blocking his path.

"You are not welcome here, brother," Xanthier said harshly.

Brogan ignored him, casting his eyes past Xanthier and locating the Earl. "You are still master here, Father. I come seeking assistance for my wife. She ails after the birth of our son."

"Your son?" the Earl questioned incredulously. "Does he live? When was he born?"

Brogan narrowed his eyes, but nodded nevertheless. "He thrives, but his mother sickens, and I need only a few days to tend her with warmth and nutrition." As Matalia moaned, Brogan looked down at her with fear. "I need a midwife immediately!"

All of a sudden, a stunned Xanthier was shoved back as several servants and men-at-arms swarmed toward the Earl and crowded around Brogan's horse. Jaimie pushed his way through the throng and held his arms up, taking Matalia's limp form from Brogan's arms. A low growl from one of the wolves made him step back nervously, clutching Matalia carefully. As Brogan stepped down, he confronted the Earl.

"Can we stay, Father? Will you help us?"

The Earl nodded quickly and motioned to the tower.

Brogan dismounted. He turned, expecting the wolves to slink back to the forest, but they remained, forming a protective shield around their mistress. Jaimie watched them carefully, but the wild beasts did not act upon their threatening sounds. The wolfhound stayed at Brogan's side, his lips twitching as his massive head turned to stare at Xanthier, who hovered in the background.

A stableboy came forward for the horse, and Brogan gave quick instructions regarding him and the bearskin strapped to the back. The boy looked at the massive head of the bear and gasped in awe. He led the horse away while motioning to several others, showing them the great beast.

Brogan shifted the sling on his back amid the gathered people's curious stares, then took Matalia back from Jaimie, who relinquished her gratefully. The wolves quieted, but they made no move to leave. Shrugging, Brogan strode through the crowd and entered Kirkcaldy. A shriek from inside signaled the wolves' appearance in the great hall. Almost immediately, the servants scurried inside after Brogan, leaving Xanthier and the Earl alone.

"Kirkcaldy will go to him, Xanthier. He has proven himself a capable leader and a powerful fighter. He has the strength of character Kirkcaldy needs."

Xanthier looked at him in silence. Then he turned on his heel and left. Above them, unnoticed by all, stood Isadora at the window of the southern tower. Her face turned purple with rage, and she pounded her fists against the stones.

"It is not over!" she hissed to the empty courtyard. "It is far from over!"

Inside, Brogan rushed up the stairs, followed closely by the wolves and the gray wolfhound. Peigi met him at the top of the tower, her smile of welcome quickly changing to concern when she beheld his dual burden. She reached for the babe, but was startled by the snarl of canines confronting her. Brogan ignored the ruckus and deposited Matalia gently upon the covers.

"She sleeps deeply ever since the birth," he told her as he rapidly undressed Matalia and tucked her naked form into the bed.

"Did she rouse at all?" asked Peigi. "Did she bleed too much?"

"She spoke and tended the babe, and I am not certain if it was too much blood. It seemed like a lot, but I do not know about such matters."

Peigi flushed. "Of course not, m'lord. May I?" she asked, pulling the cover back.

Brogan frowned but stepped back. "She shivers," he offered, motioning that Peigi should re-cover her quickly.

Peigi nodded and tried to smile reassuringly, but she worried deep in her heart for Matalia's recovery. "Perhaps you should leave," Peigi suggested, but was startled by Brogan's fierce refusal.

"I will not leave her side. Do what you must, but I shall never leave her side again." His stance was threatening, and Peigi cowered for a moment, certain he would strike her. When he turned away and pulled the blankets back over Matalia, Peigi slipped from the room in search of assistance.

"Jaimie, please fetch Evie and Mistress Meghan, the old midwife. Tell them to bring their supplies. Kirkcaldy's mistress lies abed with childbirth fever."

"Aye," the big man replied, and set out at a run to do her bidding.

Peigi returned with a bassinet and small chest including swaddling clothes and soft blankets. Brogan was sitting on the side of the bed, running his fingers through Matalia's short locks and cradling the babe in his lap. Peigi was anxious about the calm attitude of the infant, for he seemed more peaceful and content than many a baby she had ever witnessed. Brogan looked up, and the misery in his face took Peigi's breath away.

"We will take care of her, m'lord. Fear not. She will be walking around in no time," Peigi promised even though she doubted her own words. She unfolded some of the baby clothes and laid them on the bed. As long as she stayed a few feet from the baby, the wolves remained quiet.

Brogan nodded wearily, then lay full length against his wife's body. "Please," he whispered. "Please don't let her die." Then he glanced up. "I want her to be cleaned up, and I want her to have some broth."

"It is already being prepared," Peigi replied, glad to give him some good news. Searching for more, she said, "Lady Isadora birthed a fine girl. She is a lusty soul, and long for her weight. She will be a tall lass. She has no hair yet, not like the fine curls your son has, but she carries the gray eyes of your ancestors."

Brogan smiled. "Good," he murmured. "I am pleased to have a niece. Perhaps one day I will have a daughter, too."

"Absolutely. You will have many children, m'lord. Many, many children."

The two adults were looking at each other, each trying to soothe the other, when Evie and Mistress Meghan walked in. The old midwife carried a large bag of powders, which she set upon a table. She started to shoo Brogan from the room, but his cold look changed her mind immediately.

Again the covers were removed from Matalia's burning body, and this time Brogan saw the thin trickle of blood coming from between her thighs. It had stained the mattress, creating a steadily spreading red circle. The midwife clucked and motioned to Brogan to remove the infant, and he stepped up quickly to take his son into the safety of his own arms. Mistress Meghan spread Matalia's thighs and cleaned her carefully. She directed Evie to make a wash of warm water and goldenseal to act as a hemostatic poultice.

She and Evie pulled Matalia until she was at the end of the bed, then placed a basin beneath her. Very gently, and quite aware of the man and wolves watching, the midwife washed Matalia again, pressing the thin paste she had made inside the birth canal. Next she motioned to Evie, who came forward with needle and thread. She diligently stitched the small tear that was visible. Brogan blanched and sat down. He cradled the baby and made certain to stay well out of the women's way.

When those tasks had been completed, the women covered Matalia and let Jaimie inside with the tub, whereupon he rapidly filled it with warm water. As he left, Mistress Meghan pulled some dried nettles from her bag and dropped them gingerly into the warm water. Immediately, the rich smell of nettles filled the room, and the baby stirred, interested in the new scent.

"What will that do?" Brogan finally questioned, unable to keep quiet any longer.

"The semiwarmth will cool her slowly, and the nettles will bathe her inside and out, fighting the evils that are invading her blood."

"Will you place leeches upon her?"

"No," answered Meghan, "not today. If she survives 'til the morrow, I will bleed her of the bad blood so she will have room for the good."

Brogan watched as they struggled to lift Matalia's flaccid body. Relenting, he placed the baby in the bassinet and lifted Matalia with ease. As he placed her in the water, he felt the stinging touch his hands. He jerked back, swearing.

"They still sting!" he accused the midwife, holding Matalia protectively out of the bath.

"Aye, they are supposed to. Put her in, and we will see if she wakes."

"I will not hurt her," he replied angrily.

"Fine," replied the old woman, "then let her die." Meghan turned around and started to pack her things. Brogan frowned fiercely at her back.

"Who are you, anyway?" he asked. "I know not your name or face."

The old midwife turned and smiled sadly. "I am the oldest midwife of these lands. I have tended the births of hundreds of babies, including the birth of your very own father."

"My father's midwife was the same who tended the birthing of the Countess when Xanthier and I were brought into the world."

"Aye, I was here when your mother gave birth to you and your brother."

"You were banished."

"Aye."

"Then how is it you are here now?"

The woman shrugged. "I knew as well as anyone what decree was made upon your heads that terrible day. I knew your wives were near childbirth. I wanted to see the end to this tragedy before my time was done." Mistress Meghan lifted her hands in supplication. "I am sorry, Lord Brogan. Please forgive me. I loved your mother. She was the kindest woman, so gentle, so faithful. I was more concerned about her at that moment than about you, and for that, I ruined not only her life, but the lives of all the O'Bannons. I truly beg your forgiveness for the wrong I committed. Let me save this woman. Let me show you that

I am sorry by helping her as I could not help the Countess."

Brogan nodded, stunned. He searched the woman's eyes, the set of her lips, looking for some familiar sign. But of course he could not remember her. He pulled his gaze away from her pleading look, not sure how to respond. But for this woman's carelessness, his life would have been settled, arranged, predestined. He would not have wandered the seas looking for gold and treasure. He would not be embroiled in a battle with his own brother. But also, he thought, he would not have become ensnared by a long-haired, turquoise-eyed siren of the woods. Nor would he be holding her soft body in his arms and listening to the sweet gurgles of their son lying nearby.

He lowered Matalia into the bath of nettles, ignoring their feather-soft prickles that immediately inflamed his hands. Matalia gasped, her eyes springing open, and she floundered, trying to rise. Mistress Meghan rushed over and held her shoulders, forcing her to remain in the bath. She and Brogan held Matalia partially submerged while the stimulus propelled Matalia from unawareness to blistering reaction.

She flung her arms around Brogan and tried to pull herself from the bath, whereupon Mistress Meghan relented and released her. Brogan pulled her body from the water, letting the fragrant leaves sluice off her flesh and drench his own. He winced from the sting, but carried her to the bed, where Meghan waited with soft linens.

Matalia looked up at him with confused eyes, and Brogan lowered her gently to explain. "You are ill. You have a fever and you are still bleeding. We are trying to help you."

"The baby?" Matalia asked, suddenly searching the room.

"He is well."

"Xanthier!" Matalia cried. "Beware of Xanthier!"

"No fears, my love. I will stay with you and watch over you and the child. Your wolves stay nearby as well. You will be safe here until you recover."

"I do not want to be here," Matalia whispered. "I want to leave this place, go somewhere new. Can you leave? Can you abandon Kirkcaldy?"

"Yes, my sweetling. We will leave. I will leave Kirkcaldy to Xanthier. You are the most important thing in the world to me. As soon as you are able, we will depart."

Chapter 30

Two days later, Brogan rubbed a hand over his haggard eyes and scratched his jaw. He sat in the window seat with the baby on his chest. A movement from the bed drew his attention. Matalia watched him sleepily. She reached her arms out, and Brogan instantly rose, bringing the babe to her. He watched him nurse with adoration.

"You seem to have gotten over your shyness, husband," Matalia said, her voice husky from disuse.

"Aye. I have learned a good many things about babies in the last few days. You will be impressed."

Matalia smiled softly, and a small laugh escaped her lips. "We need to name him," she said.

"Indeed," he answered. "I am looking forward to calling him something other than 'baby.'"

"I would like to name him Mangan, my little bear."

"As you wish."

Matalia grinned. "Will you always be this agreeable?"

"I doubt it. If I were you, I would make the most of it. Let me call Mistress Meghan in. . . ."

"No! No more beastly baths! I have had ten too many," Matalia interjected hurriedly.

"Hardly ten. Three," he replied with a laugh. "But I do not think you will get another. Stay put, and let me fetch her."

Matalia sighed and turned her attention back to Mangan while Brogan walked to the door and called out to the midwife. After examining her thoroughly, Meghan left for some food and returned with a large platter and her two friends, Peigi and Evie. The pair was delighted to see Matalia doing well, and they swarmed over her with pleased exclamations.

"You are feeling better?"

"Yes, although still a bit weary. But, please, help me rise. I want to leave as soon as possible."

"Do not be ridiculous. You are going nowhere at this moment. Stay abed for a few days. Recover," admonished Evie.

But Matalia was shaking her head even before Evie finished speaking. "I want to leave now, before anything more dreadful happens. I do not want my child embroiled in the sadness here."

Brogan entered as she spoke and strode over to her. "We will depart in two days. I sent word to Roseneath."

"We travel to my home?" Matalia asked with delight. Her short curls danced about her pale face, making her look like a young child. Brogan smiled and leaned over her, running his fingers through her hair.

"I promised that I would return you after one year. I am honoring my word." He stared at her seriously.

Matalia smiled and leaned her cheek against his hand. "We will visit my family. Then we will build our own home."

In the next tower, the domestic scene was drastically different. Xanthier paced the tower room, his brows drawn thunderously. The infant lay in her cradle, her loud wailing ignored. Isadora sat in her bed as she screamed at her husband.

"You will not let them take this from me! My child was born first! I should be the next countess!"

Xanthier rounded on her, enraged. "Do you think I am any less disappointed than you are? In case you have forgotten, this is my inheritance, my home, *my title!*"

"They are mine as well," Isadora shouted back. "You promised them to me in exchange for my dowry. You would never have made a fortune large enough to impress your father without my assistance. I did my part. Now you do yours!"

"And what would you have me do?"

"Get rid of them." Isadora's voice dropped and she stared at Xanthier coldly. "Your pathetic attempt failed. Why you did not just slit the woman's throat, I do not comprehend. Why did you leave her there? And with provisions no less!"

Xanthier moved away from the bed with distaste. "I could not murder her."

Isadora laughed harshly. "You think to protect your fool conscience by simply allowing her to die? What about sending your brother to Soothebury where you hoped he would be killed? Do you think your soul will be less sullied by your indirect evil? Are you less of a murderer if you let a thousand people starve or kill them with your bare hands? You are more stupid than I thought. You are already corrupted down into the recesses of your cold heart. Accept that and do not try to draw lines of morality that do not exist."

Xanthier stared at her, his heart beating rapidly. Finally the screaming infant caught his attention, and he gestured toward it with irritation. "Quiet the child," he muttered. "You are her mother. Act like it."

Isadora raised her eyebrows. "She will be tended by the wet nurse."

"Then I will move to another room. I care naught to abide in the same chambers as a screaming harpy and a wailing infant." Xanthier strode out of the room, but just before he left he turned for a final comment. "Let it go. Kirkcaldy will go to Brogan."

Isadora narrowed her eyes. "I will not give up!"

Xanthier glared at her without replying, then strode down the stairs and out of the castle.

In the fresh air, he took a deep breath and looked up at the sky. He rubbed his neck and chin in agitation, unconsciously imitating his brother. He stared sightlessly over the snowy courtyard and let his shoulders sag.

Suddenly, Brogan was beside him, staring up at the stars as well. "I should hate you for what you did," Brogan said quietly.

"Aye," Xanthier replied in a similar tone. "You should."

After a long silence, Brogan asked, "Remember when we counted the stars?"

Xanthier smiled. "There were thousands that summer night. We fell asleep still counting them."

"Yes. The stars are like pathways in life. . . . There are thousands of them, and if you lose count, you can always start over again."

Xanthier nodded, digesting the words of his twin brother. When he turned to reply, Brogan was gone.

The next day the Earl started to ail. He had no fever, his mind was clear, yet he began retching uncontrollably until soon he began to vomit blood. Xanthier stood at his bedside, having no idea why his father was suddenly dying. He held the Earl's frail hand, fearful of losing him. His father had always been a powerful ballast in his world, and it was impossible to conceive of life without his influence. Xanthier alternated between confusion and fury, not knowing how to react to this unexpected turn of events. The house servants sank away, fearful of his wrath, although the old servant who had been the Earl's personal assistant remained to hold the basin whenever the Earl required it.

"You must get Brogan," the Earl whispered to Xanthier. "He must know that I have chosen him."

"We should not talk of this now," Xanthier replied earnestly. "It will tire you."

"It needs to be settled. Brogan will have Kirkcaldy, and I need to have him write a letter for you to open next year."

"If there is something you need to say to me, tell me now," he demanded.

But the Earl shook his head. "Call Brogan."

When the Earl's summons came to them, Brogan ignored it.

"Lord Brogan," the servant repeated. "The Earl does not request your presence. He commands it. Tonight he will state who will inherit Kirkcaldy."

"Can you not see that my wife has barely recovered? Kirkcaldy goes to Xanthier. Let him have it. I must stay with my wife and child."

The servant cleared his throat and looked at the floor. "With respect m'lord, the inheritance has not yet been decided. You must come." He looked back up with sympathy. " 'Tis only for a moment. Surely you can grant your father that?"

Matalia lay against Brogan's chest, weak but cool. She tugged on Brogan's sleeve to get his attention. "Go, Brogan. Get it done with. Then it will be officially over. Meghan will stay with me." When Brogan frowned she added, "And Jaimie as well. For safety."

The servant smiled gratefully and bowed before leaving.

"I do not want to leave your side," Brogan whispered.

"It is for only a moment, as the man says. Please, I want this finished." Matalia's reply was soft, and it was clear she made an extreme effort to speak clearly.

Brogan nodded to assure her, but then decided that she was correct. It would be good to have this done. When she slipped into sleep, he carefully laid her back and stood to stare out the window.

In a few moments it would be over. He lovingly stroked the white bricks that formed the window. His Kirkcaldy. He had always thought of it as his. He had never considered losing it. He had always assumed that these beloved walls would one day be his own. Accepting the loss was monumental. In his mind, he walked the halls for a final time, touching, looking, experiencing. The elegant towers, the clever designs, the beautiful stones. He felt the wrench of his failure deep in his gut and had the urge to vomit. He gripped the stone with white-knuckled hands and pressed his forehead against the wall, relishing the rough texture. His eyes burned, and he pressed his lids together tightly.

Suddenly he felt a soft touch on his shoulder, and he spun around. Matalia stood behind him, one hand braced against an end table. Her beauty was dulled, her eyes cloudy, but she lifted her other arm to embrace him, and he silently stepped into her circle of comfort.

She held him for several long moments, trying to tell him that she understood his sacrifice. She ached for the pain in his soul. She understood what Kirkcaldy meant to him. She understood that not once in his life had he gone a day without thinking about this moment. He had battled and fought and plotted to be the one named heir, but now he was about to hear another named in his stead. Tears slipped from her eyes, and she let them fall freely, knowing that he would not be able to shed his own.

Then, finally, he picked her up and placed her in bed. With a small smile of gratitude, he stepped away from her and headed down to the great hall.

Isadora sat at the foot of the long table, her hair

perfectly arranged and her cheeks flushed with good health. Xanthier stood behind and to the right of her, and he looked up at Brogan as he approached the table.

"Brother," greeted Xanthier.

"Brother," Brogan replied with a level look. He pulled the sword from his side and lifted it into the candlelight. Xanthier tensed and pulled his own sword. The hall was silent as the men faced each other with drawn steel. Brogan flicked a glance over Xanthier, his eyes sweeping down, then up again. He nodded infinitesimally, then placed the gleaming sword on the table. Xanthier relaxed slightly and did the same.

"Our father lies dying."

"Dying?" Brogan asked with surprise. "How could he be dying?"

Isadora smiled brightly. "The old often do, you know," she said with feigned compassion.

Brogan tightened his lips. "I should go to him."

"Yes, yes, of course. But first you two should sit and talk. I will check on the Earl myself," she replied as she lifted a goblet to her grinning lips.

Brogan did not reply. He faced Xanthier instead. "I prefer to finish this now."

"Talk, then see him," Isadora insisted. Brogan tightened his jaw but said nothing. She gave a brittle smile. "Indeed, have peace between father and sons alike. Sit by the fire and drink together for a moment." She rose and headed for her tower. "I will personally bring the Earl some of my family wine."

Xanthier and Brogan looked at each other warily. Then, as the servants filled their cups with ale, they sat down together.

"Why is he ill?"

"I do not know. He suddenly took to a severe stomach ailment. I do not think he will recover. I have wanted to give him something for a long time, but I have never done it. Now I fear it is too late." Xanthier pulled two packets of letters out as he spoke and handed them to Brogan. "Perhaps you should give them to Ansleen. They will explain much."

Brogan looked at the writing in one set, recognizing his mother's script. The other packet was clearly from the Earl. "These are letters, dated almost twenty years ago. . . ." Brogan murmured.

"Aye. I intercepted them."

"Why?" Brogan asked, shaking his head in bemusement.

"I was afraid of losing our father's attention. He was all I had. I was only a child and I was lonely. I did not realize how much pain my actions would cause."

"Oh, God." Brogan rose. "You must tell him." In mutual accord, they nodded. Brogan understood and forgave. The bond between the twins was stronger than years of mistrust and misunderstandings. They were brothers.

They made their way to his chambers, walking side by side. When they opened his door, they saw Isadora holding a cup of wine to the Earl's lips and forcing him to drink. The Earl was weakly pushing against her, trying to avoid the bitter fluid, while pointing to a scroll lying on the nearby table.

Isadora stood up and wiped her hands on her dress. "He has worsened," she said. "He can no longer talk. Thankfully, I was able to get his final words on paper." She lifted the scroll and held it out to them triumphantly.

The Earl convulsed, bloody vomit bubbling in his throat. He moaned in agony, tossing his head back and forth. Xanthier picked up the wine goblet and walked over to Isadora, his face devoid of emotion. He smelled the wine. Then he placed the goblet carefully upon a table as Brogan scanned the document.

"The scroll states that Kirkcaldy goes to you, Xanthier, as I expected. At least his final words have settled the matter."

Xanthier looked at Isadora as she stared back at him. She smiled evilly. "Indeed, he was clear about his intentions. There can be no doubt. I wrote it as he dictated, but he signed it himself."

The Earl moaned again, his mouth unable to form words. Spittle ran down his face and he rolled over in agony.

"You have murdered our father," Xanthier whispered into the cold room. "How could you? How could you poison him?"

"What are you talking about, Xanthier?" Brogan asked.

"She poisoned him. He was leaving Kirkcaldy to you and she knew it. She poisoned him and wrote a false testament."

Brogan leaped forward, slamming her against the wall. "Why? Why would you kill him? I was leaving! What did you use? What witches' brew have you concocted?"

Isadora tossed her head and grinned. "It does not matter. He is too far gone. Accept defeat, Brogan. You have lost Kirkcaldy!"

"Kirkcaldy? Are you still concerned about these stones? I do not care about the title. I had already planned on leaving regardless of the Earl's decision. You poisoned him for no reason!"

"Ansssss . . ." the Earl muttered, fiercely concentrating between seizures. "Ansssleeeen . . ."

"Bring him to her," Xanthier commanded. "I will take care of my wife. Bring him to our mother."

"He will not make the trip over the mountains," Brogan replied even as he lifted the man over his shoulder.

"You will have to take the caverns," Xanthier answered. "It is the only way to get to the cottage quickly."

Brogan paused, then turned and stared at his brother. "You are right. There is no other way."

"Good-bye," Xanthier said as his gaze softened. "Perhaps someday I will find my star. I am glad you found yours. Protect her and love her, for she greatly loves you."

Brogan smiled, remembering their conversation about the heavens just a few nights ago. Then he strode from the room, carrying the dying Earl.

Chapter 31

Brogan burst into the north tower, startling Matalia. She gasped, seeing the Earl's body in Brogan's arms, seeing the blood- and vomit-stained shirt.

"What happened?" she cried as she leaped out of bed.

"He has been poisoned. We must get him to Ansleen and Gweneath immediately. If I travel over the mountain, he will die before I reach them, so I must go through the caves."

"I am coming with you."

"No! It is too dangerous. There is no light, and there are winds that douse any lantern. The paths are treacherous and freezing. And there are bears."

"I am coming with you. I will not stay here alone. We can stay here arguing or we can get going."

Brogan stared at her, debating quickly, but in the end he agreed, knowing that he had no choice. He struggled to place the baby in the sling he had fashioned earlier, then strapped the Earl to his back and slung his sword across his hips. Blood trickled from the Earl's lips, and he paused to wretch again before falling unconscious.

Matalia looked at Brogan as he packed, and nodded mutely at his agonized expression. She dressed in silence. Then they raced down the stairs and into the harsh snow-swept courtyard, accompanied by the wolfhound and three wolves. The freezing wind whirled around them, and Matalia clung to Brogan, who in turn leaned heavily upon the wolfhound as the wolves dashed out, eager to leave the castle behind.

Brogan lifted Matalia onto her mare and wrapped the large bearskin that now hung, scraped and dried, around her shoulders. Removing it from the rack this soon would ruin the skin for a rug, but the warmth of the fur was more important. He tied it around Matalia, then gripped her hand with reassuring pressure. She was still weak from her fever, but she nodded reassuringly. When he was satisfied that she would not fall off, he mounted his stallion and settled the Earl behind him, balancing him carefully. He positioned the baby against his chest, then nudged his horse forward. In single file, they left Kirkcaldy and headed for the caves.

Xanthier watched their stumbling progress from the castle ramparts. He breathed deeply as the wolves led the horses up the hillside where caves dotted the snowy expanse like yawning pits of bleakness. His eyes did not waver as the animals brought Brogan and Matalia to a large cavern, and he saw them approach the entrance.

Gripping the window ledge, he pressed his head against the white stones, but unlike Brogan, he did not lament her loss. He trembled with relief, overwhelmed with joy that he was finally free to abandon her halls and leave the responsibilities to Brogan. He had never been given a choice; he had been expected to fight for the inheritance, even at the expense of his soul.

Yet, despite the resentment he felt toward his father, he could no longer be angry. The sadness that had driven the Earl had been of his own making, and he could have improved his circumstances at any moment. The intercepted letters should not have stopped a man in love from going to his wife and begging her forgiveness. The day of their birth, the Earl had challenged Ansleen to "raise the stronger man." By teaching Brogan independence, humility, love and self-worth, she had taught him values far more important than the Earl's ideas of power, strength and dictatorship.

Xanthier pulled a dagger from his belt and lifted it to the moonlight, forming a wordless apology to Brogan, to Matalia, to the people of Kirkcaldy. Then, with the tip of his dagger, he carved a pledge into the white walls of Kirkcaldy and signed it with his name.

A sudden noise behind him made him spin around. Isadora stood there, smiling triumphantly. "The Earl will die, and we will inherit. With Brogan gone, there is no other obstacle."

"Brogan will return and take his rightful place, Isadora."

"No, he won't. Look." She gestured to a shadowed figure trailing Brogan's party. "I hired a man to follow them and kill them. You could not do it, so I took matters into my own hands."

Xanthier took an angry step forward. "You are evil! How can you smugly admit to murder? You will be punished!"

Isadora stepped back hastily, and Xanthier saw that she cradled their newborn child. "Stay away from me, Xanthier. I did what needed to be done." She shifted over to the edge of the rampart and looked over. Glancing at Xanthier, she motioned him back. "You don't understand what needs to be done. I have to finish this. . . ."

Xanthier took another threatening step forward. "What are you talking about? What else needs to be completed? What are you planning?"

Isadora lifted the baby and held her in the air. "We

need a boy child. A girl is not good enough. When my man kills Brogan and Matalia, he will steal their child and bring it to us. We will say it is ours."

"Isadora!" Xanthier cried, aghast. "You cannot mean that!" He stepped closer. Then, seeing her climb up onto the low ledge and hold the baby farther out, he sprinted forward. "No!" he shouted as the child suddenly burst into tears from the blast of freezing wind.

Isadora stumbled back, knocked flush against the sill as Xanthier grabbed her from behind. "Let me go!" she screamed.

"Put the child down! Put her down!"

"It is for the best!" she shouted back as they struggled. She twisted her arms, trying to free them from his restraint. Finally, desperate to complete her mission, she opened her hands and pushed, flinging the infant.

With the instant reflexes drilled into him from decades of warrior training, Xanthier shoved Isadora aside and grabbed the baby. He caught the swaddling blanket edge, and as it unraveled, he desperately sought to hold on to the child buried within.

Isadora tripped, off balance, and she tottered on the ledge. "Xanthier! Help!" she cried as her hands flailed in the air.

Xanthier clutched the infant, his big hands rescuing her from death. For a split second, he stared into his baby's eyes, transfixed by their beauty. Huge, blue-gray, frightened eyes stared at him, and he was paralyzed at the thought that he had almost lost her. Then Isadora's shouts claimed his attention, and he reached out, trying to catch her hand.

"Help!" she screamed again, as her own momentum carried her over the edge and she tumbled downward. In horror, Xanthier watched her descent, helpless to stop the inevitable. The final crunch of her body landing on the snowy courtyard reverberated in his ears, resoundingly loud against the wail of the wind.

Xanthier stared down, unable to move. He stared at her body lying still, her bones broken, her evil silenced. Then the infant began to cry, and Xanthier shifted his attention to her. Slowly shaking his head back and forth, he stared into her eyes and felt completely helpless.

The wolfhound entered first, his coat bristly with anticipation. The wolves were next, and they lifted their noses. Brogan paused, and Matalia inched her horse next to his to lend a supporting hand, even though she wavered in place. They smiled at each other.

A sound behind them caused Matalia to start. "I hear something," she said, catching Brogan's attention. "It is another horse."

"Another horse? Who would be out here other than us?" As Matalia shook her head in confusion, an arrow whistled through the air and thudded into Brogan's chest, narrowly missing the infant.

"No!" Matalia screamed. Mangan instantly started to cry, and the Earl groaned in agony. Brogan's horse bolted into the cavern, and Matalia was left alone. She turned her mare, seeking the attacker among the forest trees. "You coward!" she screamed. "Come forth and fight!" She pulled her sword free, relishing the hiss of the steel.

A man rode out into the open. He laughed. "You are only a woman. You cannot fight me. Lay down your weapon, close your eyes and prepare to feel my sword pierce your flesh."

Matalia nudged her mare closer. "Who are you, and what are you about?" she challenged as she bore down on him.

"I am from the Lady Isadora, and I have come to kill you and your husband and then steal your babe."

"And for what purpose?"

"When I place the infant in Lady Isadora's hands, she will call him her own and raise him to be the next heir."

Infuriated, Matalia spurred her mare and swung her blade at the man. He barely had time to lift his own sword in defense. "I will die before I allow you to touch my family!" she screamed, swinging again.

The man parried, trying to keep balanced on his horse as she attacked him. He cried out as her sword found an opening and her blade bit deeply into his side. "You witch!" he shouted, horrified that she had broken through his defense. Using his strength, he lunged, trying to kill her in a single blow.

Suddenly, the wolves erupted from the cave and swarmed the fighters. Snapping and growling, they leaped upon him, tearing his flesh and ripping his muscles until he toppled from his horse and landed in the snow.

The black wolf bit his neck, tearing him apart while the red one attacked his sword arm. The silver wolf shredded his abdomen with his nails, digging at him until he could bite down and disembowel him.

Matalia turned her mare and raced to where Brogan rested, trying desperately to catch his breath. "Brogan!" she cried. "Oh no!"

"I will be all right," he gasped. "As long as we get there soon . . ."

"Yes! Yes, we will hurry. For both of you," she replied quickly, seeing the Earl's ghastly face.

"The bears . . . the wolfhound needs to go first to watch for bears."

"Yes, I understand," Matalia whispered as she wrapped a bandage around his wound. The arrow was out, pulled free moments earlier by Brogan himself. "I can take Mangan."

"No, you are still weak yourself. I will take the load

as long as you keep us safe." He smiled at her weakly.
"I love you. You fought magnificently."

"I love you," she whispered in return.

"I fear the dark," Brogan admitted as they walked
the first few steps into the cave. "We have no
lantern."

"I did not think you were afraid of anything," Matalia answered. As they went deeper, darkness
descended.

Brogan shrugged. "Everyone has a fear. Mine is
the dark."

"Why?"

"Xanthier and I used to play in these caverns. Once
Xanthier deliberately confused the way, and I became
lost." Brogan recalled the boyhood moment as the
horses clopped into the dark cavern. Matalia was
grateful for his voice, for his form disappeared into
the blackness. "I tried to find my way out, but I could
not. After hours, I was exhausted and frightened. I
could smell the bears, I could hear the bears, but I
could not see them. I was terrified that I would run
straight into one. I finally fell asleep." He paused,
reaching out to touch her. "That is when I started
having these dreams, these dreams about a woman
finding me in the darkness and rescuing me. She had
such a voice and such wonderfully soft hands. She
saved me that night and on many others in the years
to come."

"How beautiful," Matalia murmured.

"She came to me on the night I met you. And now
she has a name and a face. She is my wife." His voice
dropped, and he expressed his love clearly through
the nuances of his tone. Matalia was silent, overwhelmed. Then she took a heartening breath and
began to sing, wanting to soothe his fears. She sang
the wordless song he was familiar with, and it kept
the dark at bay. Her soft voice echoed off the dank
walls, making it into their own personal cathedral of

love, filled with stained-glass melodies and streaming sunlight harmonies.

As the minutes passed into hours, she hummed and sang, gathering strength and giving courage as they traveled through the caves. And when they were too exhausted to travel any farther, she built a small fire with the supplies Brogan had assembled and he sang with her, letting his deep voice join with hers. The baby wriggled upon the bearskin, his wrinkled face showing pleasure in the harmony around him, and the wolves occasionally lifted their own snouts to add a mournful howl. The Earl rested, knowing that every moment brought him closer to Ansleen.

The cave bears heard them pass. Matalia's song reached them in their dens, infiltrated their minds and soothed their concerns. They instinctively knew that the humans posed no risk, and, other than lifting their muzzles and letting out a warning *wuff*, they left the party alone.

By the following morning, the small entourage emerged on the other side of the mountain. Matalia felt immense relief, for Brogan was in great pain, and the Earl had lapsed into unconsciousness. But now, as Brogan indicated the last turn, a stream of light pierced the darkness and beckoned them forward. Small dust motes rippled through the sunlight, and Mangan stared at them in fascination. When they finally exited, Matalia looked down at the small house where they had spent one memorable night long ago. She turned toward Brogan happily.

But, when she saw his face in the light she felt faint. His voice had seemed so confident, so soothing in the darkness, but now she saw that his injury was severe. He was ghostly white, and pools of blood stained his shirt. He was slumped forward and swayed precariously in the saddle. She gripped the stallion's bridle to prod it forward. They were going to Ansleen's cottage.

The going was very slow, but as Brogan's strength

failed, Matalia's gained. She took Mangan from Brogan and held and nursed him. Mangan's constant gurgling kept Matalia's spirits elevated. The wolfhound pressed close to Brogan, his small eyes periodically glancing up. The wolves kept the party safe, ensuring the wild animals kept wide berth.

At long last they crossed the frozen river. When Brogan's stallion balked again, Matalia scolded him furiously and tugged his bridle while the wolves nipped at his hind legs. Defeated, the stallion leaped across, nearly unseating Brogan, which elicited another string of angry words from Matalia. Brogan glanced up, his eyes cloudy, and he tried to shush her to no avail.

At last they reached the smooth hillside leading to the cottage. Matalia looked up, nervous. She remembered what Ansleen had said about no O'Bannon ever coming to the cottage. She glanced at the two O'Bannon men and licked her lips. Then, nodding to herself, she determinedly started the horses up the hill.

She was halfway up when suddenly Brogan's stallion balked again. She tugged on him, then scolded him, but the horse would not move. Matalia jumped down, intending to lead him, but her ankle twisted on a rock buried beneath the snow. She yelped and hopped, then braced herself against her mare. The stone barrier. Brogan could not pass across the stone's boundaries. She tried again, pulling and tugging. The wolves ranged around, yipping, but the stallion would absolutely not proceed. He partially reared and stomped his hooves in reaction. The wolfhound growled and finally Brogan opened his eyes and stared up the hill to behold his childhood home.

He blinked, confused, then comprehension dawned. "You brought me here. . . ." he murmured weakly. "I cannot enter. . . ."

Matalia cried out with frustration. "I see that, but

you must. The women have herbs and healing skills. Surely the stones are just symbolic. We must get up to the cottage."

Brogan shook his head and faded again. Trying to rouse, he said, "Bring Ansleen down here. . . ."

Mangan began to fuss. His mewling cries reflected her anxiety, and she calmed down so as not to frighten the baby. Abruptly she remounted and kicked the mare, who bounded over the stone barrier as if it did not exist and surged up the hill. Matalia rode her back like a Viking princess, the bearskin flapping around her wild midnight curls. She pushed the mare up the hill, then pulled her to a shuddering stop in front of the cottage.

"Ansleen! Gweneath! We need your help," she yelled. "Come out here and help your husband and son! They both will die without immediate healing."

The door was flung open and Ansleen stood in her night rail, her face tense with shock.

"I do not have the power to lift the curse alone," Ansleen replied. She looked up at Matalia, but sadness filled her old face. "Those that are separated by the barrier must come together to remove it."

"The Earl is below. He is dying. It is time you both lifted the curse of your thwarted love and let no boundaries separate you!"

Gweneath stepped forward, murmuring quietly in the Countess's ear. She trembled, and silent tears slid down her wrinkled face. She nodded. Gweneath turned toward Matalia. "Come, child. You are right. It is time to break the barrier."

Stunned, but unbelievably grateful, Matalia nodded. She stepped aside as the elderly women walked down the hillside through the cold snow to confront the restless stallion. The Countess stepped forward, staring at the hunched form of her son. Sensing her, Brogan pushed himself upright. "Mother," he murmured.

The Earl roused, lifted his head and beheld his wife. He shook, his mouth working, trying to say the things he had wanted to say for thirty years. Thousands of thoughts whirled in his mind, millions of declarations he wanted to make, but he could not form a coherent sentence. He clenched his hands in despair and finally managed to say the one word he had been trying to say for three decades.

"Sorry," he whispered.

Ansleen walked up to the barrier and reached over it. The Earl stared at her hands, his expression cracking. He looked up at Matalia, seeking her help. She walked calmly forward, stepped over the stones and lifted him down from his saddle. She whispered soothing words in his ear, words of love and forgiveness. Words about family and trust. He slumped against her, fixing his gray gaze on the Countess. Despite his weakened state, his eyes flashed with strength, and Ansleen smiled.

Matalia urged him forward as Gweneath encouraged the Countess, and bit by bit, the two came closer. The Earl slowly lifted his hands and touched hers. Their fingers brushed against each other, then gently held, then clasped. From one side of the barrier to the other, the warm press of hands opened the stones and the barrier drifted away with the snow flurries.

Epilogue

Kirkcaldy rose to tower over the melting spring landscape, its white walls looking like sunshine draped with crystal. Ronin and Kalial carried their grandson, Mangan, with pride while Brogan and Matalia rode ahead, hands clasped in mutual comfort and support. The Countess rode last in a covered vehicle whose wheels dug deep ruts in the wet ground. She stared up at the walls of her home and regretted the years lost while appreciating the promise of those ahead.

The Earl was dead. The poison had overwhelmed his system, and after a few days of struggle, he had passed away in the arms of his wife, Ansleen. Those final days had been filled with bliss, for despite the physical pain of his illness, his heart had finally mended. The misunderstandings, the lost letters, the wealth of pride that had separated them had, in the end, meant nothing compared to their emotions, and they had spent their precious time confirming their love and devotion. Now his body was traveling back to Kirkcaldy in a closed casket.

The villagers swarmed out to greet them as the procession passed, their friendliness a stark contrast to the first time Matalia had ridden up their main road. Banners flickered over every inch of the meadows around the castle, and bagpipes wailed in the distance where maidens danced to the delight of the gentlemen.

A shout rose from another group of men tossing the caber in friendly competition until their caravan was spotted.

Suddenly more people rushed to greet them, and Matalia gently nudged Brogan forward. He was the new Earl of Kirkcaldy. Xanthier had left the country and bequeathed his infant daughter to Brogan and Matalia, trusting that their love would serve the child well in her formative years. Isadora was buried in an unmarked grave, her crime unmentioned.

Brogan looked at Matalia, the love in his eyes clear for all to see. Then he pushed his stallion into a wild gallop and raced up the twisting road to Kirkcaldy's bailey. Spinning the steed, he turned to face the lairds of the clans that had come to pay their respects to the old and to the new. He bowed, honored by their respectful acknowledgments, then entered the castle yard.

He sprang off his steed and strode toward the ramparts, climbing the steps rapidly to the walk overlooking the valley. Gazing out, he saw the hundreds of people that had already gathered, and saw more groups still arriving. He saw the McTaver flag and knew his wife and child rode with them. With deep satisfaction, he stepped into the shadows to see the message he knew awaited him. He felt his brother's essence and knew that his twin was far across the seas, searching for what would make him whole. And he knew that Xanthier could sense his own return to Kirkcaldy.

Taking a fortifying breath he read what Xanthier had carved into the stones.

I, Xanthier O'Bannon, self-proclaimed second son of the fifth Earl of Kirkcaldy, pledge my allegiance to the sixth Earl, my beloved brother, Brogan O'Bannon. May this home grow and prosper

*under his wisdom and this family strengthen with
the blessings of love.*

A moment later Matalia joined him. Her black curls
were growing back, and they danced around her face
like the woodland faeries he had once mistaken her
to be. Her incredible eyes shone with love, and Brogan held his hand out to her. She entered his embrace,
curling her arms around his powerful shoulders. As a
breeze swept over the white walls of Kirkcaldy's highest tower, Brogan leaned down and pressed his lips
against her neck. Then, as she sighed with satisfaction,
he nibbled her throat and captured her lips, devouring
them passionately.

Don't miss the first book
in the
Wild Series by Sasha Lord
UNDER A WILD SKY
Available now
from Signet

And read on for an excerpt
from the next book in the series,
ACROSS A WILD SEA
Coming in February 2005
From Signet Eclipse

By morning the squall had died, leaving the ocean a seething mess of seaweed and debris. Planks of wood were scattered along the beach, and bits of wreckage dotted the coast. Alannah used a stick to walk along the sand, checking her path before stepping forward. Her bare toes curled in the wet gravel, and she could feel the soft silt of newly tossed ocean floor cast upon the isle's seaside. With a quick intake of breath she paused before stepping on a jellyfish. Carefully avoiding it, she knelt down and let her hands hover over it.

Using a piece of bark, she scooped up the jellyfish along with some sand and carefully returned it to the sea. The cry of seagulls caught her attention as she straightened up and she turned her head, listening to their warning signals. Cautiously exiting the gently rippling waves, she followed the sounds of the birds. Her stick bumped against a log that had not been on the beach before, and Alannah smelled it. It was freshly burnt, probably struck by lightning. Touching the fallen tree, she felt the remaining heat that simmered deep in the tree's core. The seagulls cried again, and Alannah frowned. She stepped over the log and walked slowly forward, seeking the cause of the animal's distress.

*   *   *

Xanthier crawled up onto the beach, his body trembling with fatigue and cold, his face blazing with pain. His fingertips were blue where they were wound around the barrel's bindings, but the feel of earth beneath his knees was incredible. He stared angrily at the sky, silently reveling in his success against the storm. No man, or beast, or act of God would beat him!

He uncurled his fingers and flexed them, making the blood rush through his hand once more. Then he touched his face, feeling the ravaged flesh where the burns blistered. The action was excruciatingly painful, but Xanthier did not flinch.

Taking slow, deliberate steps he walked up the beach, searching for shelter. He knew he needed to tend his wounds, and find food to eat. It did not occur to him to feel sorrow for his shipmates. His heart was cold. He stumbled, but rose again. Weakness would not subdue him! He raged internally. Xanthier clenched his teeth and frowned. The storm had taken the lives of many. Only the strong survived. Only the strong *deserved* to survive. It was the way of the world.

Stumbling a few steps further, he rounded a peninsula that formed one arm of a sheltered cove. Above the cove was a high cliff with a sheer face. Xanthier frowned, searching for somewhere to rest. A movement up the beach made him spin around. A woman walking toward him, her auburn hair blowing in the gentle breeze. Her face was turned up to the sky and she waved a stick in front of her like a woman swinging a parasol in a manicured garden. He blinked, not certain if what he saw was real. She was like a goddess . . . so tall and slender . . . so ethereal and composed. His legs gave way and he fell to his knees. His head screamed in pain and his muscles quivered with fatigue. Black spots danced around his vision, and he tried to clear them by shaking his head. He did not want to lose sight of her. But, despite his powerful force of will, the black spots spread out, and he collapsed, unconscious.

Alannah heard a groan and she froze, her stick in mid-swing. A sense of foreboding overwhelmed her and she hesitated, not sure what to do. Tilting her head, she listened. Slow, raspy breaths came to her on the wind, breaths that did not sound like any animal she knew. They were deeper, huskier. She shook, suddenly frightened.

She heard another groan, and abruptly realized that the creature she sensed was nearby and hurt. "Oh!" she cried, "How could I be so selfish?" As she chastised herself, she walked forward, not allowing fear to halt her steps. "I am only being silly. It is probably a poor animal hurt in the storm."

As she got closer, the sense of strength emanating from the creature made her steps falter yet again. She wrinkled her brow, confused. Then, with a deep breath, she kneeled down and stretched out her fingers. They contacted warm, supple, hairless flesh. She jerked back, stunned. She smelled the air. No scent of wet fur came to her. She trembled but was inexorably drawn back to touching the creature again.

Smooth yet hard. Muscled. She stroked down, feeling the contours of a human arm—yet an arm that was three times the size of her own, and easily five times as strong. As her fingers swept along the arm, she encountered hands that confirmed that the hurt creature was human. Both excited and alarmed, she reached out with both hands and gripped the human's shoulders, ran down its slightly furred chest to the waistband of clothing that covered the legs. She brushed against a bulge and paused, intrigued, letting her fingers feel what her eyes could not see.

Xanthier woke groggily, to the sensation of light touches sweeping over him. He was immediately aroused, and without thinking, he grabbed the woman and rolled his body over hers, tucking her easily beneath him. He leaned down, intent on kissing her, when a blast of pain erupted in his head.

"What!?" he gasped. The woman punched him again as she struggled to get out from under him. "Stop that!" he commanded, trying to get his bearings. The ache in his groin warred with the pounding in his temples.

"Get off!" she screamed, pummeling him with her fists. With a hard kick, she shoved his weight off hers and scrambled to her feet. "What are you? Who are you?" she shouted.

Xanthier blinked and shook his head, then looked up at the woman towering over him. Her hair was disheveled and her eyes were darting around. "I am Commodore Xanthier O'Bannon, and may I point out that you were touching me. I only accepted your blatant invitation."

"Who are you?" Alannah repeated, stunned to hear a human voice other than her own and Grandmother's. Except for the few visits from Grandmother's old friend, who came every five years to deliver supplies and see to their welfare, she had no interaction with other people. "What are you doing here?"

Raising his eyebrows in disbelief, he motioned to the ship's debris that littered the coastline. "Is the reason not clear?"

"Why are you here?" Alannah repeated sharply. She took a step back and leaned down, trying to locate her pole.

Xanthier watched her hands sweeping the sand. He frowned again, wondering at her strange behavior. "Are you simple? Can you not see that my ship lies in broken bits all around me? It sank in the storm, and the crew was lost. By the grace of my own fortitude, I am on this isle in one piece."

"You can not stay here. Go away!" Alannah commanded.

Xanthier laughed. "Are you blind? I have nowhere to go. I have no ship. I have been shipwrecked and stranded. I might have expected a touch of courtesy. At the very least, a warm bowl of soup."

Alannah flushed. She turned away, hiding her eyes from the stranger. For the first time in her life, she felt uncomfortable with her lack of sight. She had always known that other people roamed the seas. Grandmother had described their white sails and sloping hulls as they silently passed the island, skirting its hazardous coral reef. Alannah knew that she herself had come from far across the water, born to a family that had cast her out, presumably because of her blindness. Grandmother had told her how cruel people could be, how they would reject people because of their defects.

Alannah had no desire to interact with the outside world. The Isle of Wild Horses was her life. She knew every inch of its beautiful hills and every beast that grazed in its meadows. But this man was here. A man from across the sea. A man named Xanthier, who was wounded and in need of care. If he had been a colt, she would not have hesitated to offer tender concern. It was not right of her to deny him simply because he was of a suspect species.

"Xanthier O'Bannon," she finally said. "You appear to be injured."

"I think that is obvious," he retorted. "Blood covers my face, and most people who survive a night in a storm with only a piece of wood to help keep them afloat would be injured."

"There is no need to be rude," Alannah responded as she turned back to him. "I am sorry that I reacted as I did. I will offer you assistance until your people come for you. They *will* come for you, won't they?" she asked with sudden trepidation.

"They will come," Xanthier said grimly as he glanced out over the calm water. "They will come or I will go after them and make them regret having left me behind."

Alannah nodded, satisfied. "Then follow me." She immediately walked away, leaving him to scramble to his feet unassisted. The stick she carried swung in front of her in a graceful, smooth arc, occasionally brushing against rocks or debris. She walked with confidence, never breaking stride.

Xanthier glared at her back, irritated by her cavalier attitude. "If you think you can dismiss me so easily," he grumbled under his breath, "think again." He followed her slowly, unable to force his tired legs to keep up with hers. When she rounded a curve and was lost to sight, he shouted after her. "Miss! Miss! Is this what you call consideration? Have care that I am just a tad tired!" He leaned against a fallen tree, exhausted. "You probably will give me a pile of bitter leaves to eat and some milk to drink," he complained to himself, anticipating her lack of hospitality.

The thunder of hooves interrupted his thoughts. Glancing up in alarm, he beheld a herd of horses racing across the upper cliff. In the lead was a dark brown mare, and following closely at the rear was a pristine white stallion. Trumpeting, the stallion skidded to a stop, then wheeled and reared in the air. The other horses slowed, then turned in unison, heading in the other direction. The stallion came down on all fours and stood staring down the cliff.

Suddenly, the stallion leaped. He galloped down the cliff on a narrow path that zigzagged until ending at the beach. Without stopping, the stallion raced forward and flew out of sight behind some rocks. Xanthier, amazed at the animal's agility and strength, moved to where he could see the horse. "Incredible," he whispered. "It is wilder than any beast I have seen in Scotland. Clearly he has never been tamed by a human hand." Xanthier looked the stallion over, noting his heavy musculature and intelligent eyes. "You would be worth a fortune . . ."

Alannah appeared from behind an outcropping, and the stallion wheeled to face her. He swished his tail, then lifted it high in the air as he arched his neck. She had dropped her stick, and approached the wild horse. Xanthier watched in surprise as she gripped his rippling mane, and swung onto him with lithe grace.

Xanthier stumbled back, blinking. His mouth dropped open and he held his breath. She was so beautiful . . . they were so beautiful together. Her long legs were wrapped around the beast's broad girth and her proud chin was tilted at the same angle as his equine jaw. Xanthier had never seen such a perfect union. He felt his soul shudder, incapable of comprehending anything so clearly beyond his experience.

Swaying, he widened his eyes, trying to focus. Suddenly the horse seemed to be moving and the girl riding him was talking, but he could not understand her. Her voice echoed oddly, as if it were coming from underwater. He fell to his knees, fighting the loss of control. The horse brushed against him, providing ballast. Xanthier looked up, trying to see into the sea-green eyes of the woman as she tilted her head down toward him. Her eyes saw through him, not looking at him but *into him*. He tried to pull away, but overwhelming weakness made it impossible to escape her penetrating gaze.

As black spots flickered in his vision, her voice came to him again. She seemed to frown, then reach her hand down to him. Xanthier clasped it with his own, eager to feel her palms. They were calloused, yet soft like a woman's. She was dragging him up on the magnificent stallion's back. Then he lost all sensation and his world went black. . . .